# G R JORDAN'S
## Unravel Your Destiny

## Framed

"To go wrong in one's own way is better than to go right in someone else's"

Fyodor Dostoyevsky

Framed

# Acknowledgement



To Louise and James, my play testers and supporters, thank you for all your help.

To Simon, I deeply appreciate your kindness in spreading the word.

And to all my kickstarting backers, I may have built this tome, but you brought it to life. Thank you all.

Framed

# TABLE OF CONTENTS

# Map of the Island



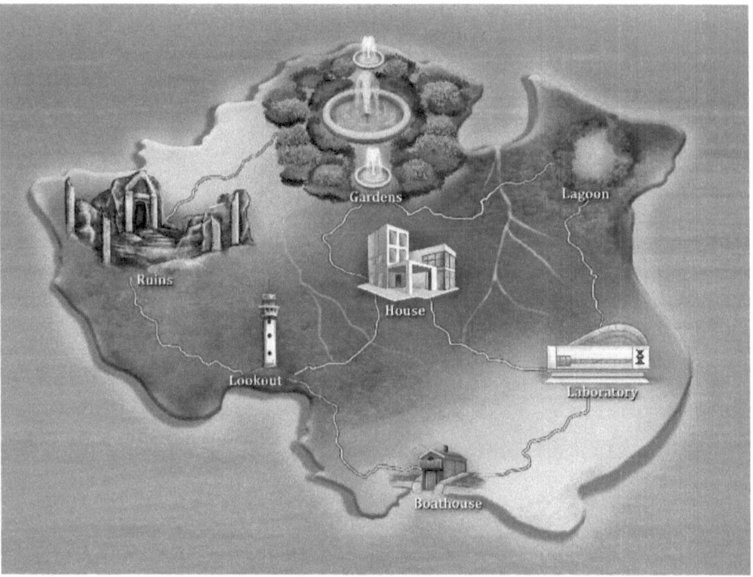



This is the island where your adventure will take place and will use the map to navigate your route around it. Pay close attention to details about your options. There is a large version of this at the rear of the book.

# How to Play

Hi and welcome to the second *Unravel Your Destiny* adventure, *Framed,* where you play as a gofer accused of killing your own boss. You will explore an island trying to gather evidence to prove to the police that you did not kill Dr Munroe and show them the real killer.

If you haven't experienced a gamebook where you make the decisions before, don't worry, it's easy to play but not so simple to win. You'll start at the paragraph numbered

# 001

and from there you move to other numbered paragraphs depending on your decisions. Make sure you hold your finger on the section you are moving from until you have reached the one you are moving to, in case you forget the number. Remember, your journey and the success of it depends on you. Your choices, your consequences and yours the glory if you can pull it off.

During the adventure you may collect items or outfits. Be sure to write these down in your **Fugitive Sheet** section at the rear of the book. Also, these pages are good to write down any clues, codes, or important information you acquire. Better to rely on your pencil rather than your memory, in the heat of being pursued. There is a codewords checklist at the back of the book for your use. The Fugitive sheet and the codewords list may be reproduced for use with the book.

During some sections you may be required to work out codes that take you to a numbered paragraph. If that paragraph doesn't make sense then you are at the wrong one. Go back to the paragraph you came from and follow the instructions.

Framed

The island where you work is displayed on the previous page to this one and is also available at the rear of the book. You will have to make choices about how to navigate the island and the map will help you decide how best to do this. Note that because of certain problems you face you will be restricted at times to what route you take, so use the map to help you follow where you are, and where you are going.

Please note there are no dice required for this book. Occasionally your decisions may be a matter of luck. If so, simply choose one of the numbers given to you. Not everything in life can be predicted or calculated, sometimes we just have to go on chance.

Certain choices mean you will cease to exist and at this point you have a few options. You can return to the previous paragraph and choose another option. You can return to the main start point for that particular location, but you will need to make a note of the location starting number when you arrive to do this. Or you can do as the book suggests and go back to **001** and start all over again. Whatever you do, have fun!

When you start again, erase all evidence and clues gathered as each time you play the killer may be different and any retained notes or keywords will confuse the game's internal system, and lead to an inaccurate reading at best, and a shambles at worst.

Now prepare for the scramble of a lifetime, outrunning a killer and the police, and see if you can walk free again in the light of the sun.

# Let the adventure commence!

Framed

# UNRAVEL YOUR DESTINY #2: FRAMED

Framed

# Introduction

Your head pounds as you open your eyes, blinking at the strong electric light in the room. Is this the worst hangover ever, or something else? You try to recall just what happened before you blacked out. Or did you collapse? It's time to take a moment and think. Rest your eyes while it comes back to you.

Peter O'Malley, that's you. Only halfway through your twenties and struggling for work. It was time to stop slumming around and get a proper job. That's why you were at the interview those weeks ago. How many? Three, maybe four. Gofer, they had said, a driver of sorts for a Dr Flavius Munro. Little did you know he would own an island where he carried out top secret research. Not that you get to see any of it. For you, it's take the boat to the mainland, fetch this and that, bring it back, see to the Doctor's and the house's needs and supplies. You've fetched groceries, mended the toilet, maintained the boat, and taken a few lectures from Grandma Munro about muddy footprints in the house.

Grandma Munro, the strange grey-haired old lady who seems to be in a world of her own. Dr Munro rarely speaks to her, but she makes his meals and gets to potter about wherever she wants. At only five feet two she is a diminutive figure, but when she speaks the voice sounds like a god from the Greek myths. But there was something about her. She never seemed happy with her son, if that's who he is. The Doctor almost seems too old to be the woman's son.

But the job's been going well, keeping you on good terms with your bank manager and paying for the small flat you live in on the other side of the bay. And the doctor seemed to be pleased with you, not that he ever smiled. But you knew he was excited about a recent development in the laboratory on the island. In fact, he had gathered a group of his staff and backers to celebrate something. Not that you were one of this elite group, but as the island boatman, you had to stay on to bring the guests across and then ferry them back that night.

Yes, you remember now, glad to have done it too. There were four guests, but one of them you knew already. Kyla Mertens works in the lab, and you have to bring her across on the ferry every morning. She's a shy woman, probably in her late thirties, but a key part of the Doctor's research team as he is always keen to know when she arrives. Although she tends to hide behind her glasses, she's always struck you as a pleasant person, kindness in her eyes.

There was a lithe blond-haired man around your own age but in much better shape. Daniel Lyle was clearly an athlete of some sort, although not being heavily into sports, you're not sure exactly what sport he played.

One thing was for sure, he seemed rather nervous on the boat. Maybe that was because the lake was beginning to get choppy, a portent of the stronger winds and wilder weather expected that night. In fact, you had said to the doctor that maybe he should go across to the town for the event, given that passage across the bay may be impossible later on. But he insisted, saying that Grandma could prepare rooms if she had to.

The thick set businessman was certainly having no issues with the motion of the water and stood, calm as you like, enjoying the wind across his face. He had a confident smile, and you recognised Patrick Davidson from the financial paper that Doctor Munro occasionally left in the boat on his travels. But you had also heard the man's name on the Doctor's lips occasionally and curse words that came along with the name gave you the impression the Doctor was no fan.

But as much as you had noticed these three guests, the one you cannot forget is the Spanish-looking newspaper reporter who made the journey across the lake worthwhile. Elsie Gonzales had curly, thick, black hair that framed a tanned face and a smile which you found hard to turn away from. Confident and feisty, she noticed you staring a few times as you crossed the bay, but she only ever gave a gentle smile back. You remember thinking that maybe you could take her back alone on the return journey, and who knew what might happen. Nothing probably, and you laugh inside, but who knew...

On coming alongside at the boathouse, you escorted the guests to the house where the Doctor had a small reception for them before allowing them to wander around the grounds of the island. That evening the Doctor would be announcing something important, something they would all want to take note of, but you did not know what. Maybe it had to do with the laboratory, with his work, but then that was no clever deduction. His work was based here, so it was the perfect place to announce something new, maybe secretive.

You remember that the Doctor asked you to go to the cellar to pick up a selection of wines, some special ones that Grandma had forgotten to collect. The light at the top of the stairs had not worked, and you had used your small pocket torch to descend the stairs and begun to look for the wines. But as you did so you, you remember hearing footsteps and then feeling a blow on the back of your head. And then nothing. Something happened and you cannot for the life of you remember what.

As you slowly begin to sit up, you feel disorientated and are still in darkness. Are you still in the cellar? It certainly feels damp and smells musty, like the storage basement, but you have an uneasy feeling. There's something touching your right hand. Something metallic. Before you can think further on this, a blinding light comes on and you squint at it as you hear voices descending from above.

Your eyes adjust slowly to the illumination, and you realise you are at the bottom of the cellar steps and looking up, you see the guests you brought over making their way down the steps towards you. Elsie, the newspaper reporter, is at the front and she looks as lovely as she did on the boat, but you see concern in her eyes. And then she screams.

"He's got a gun! He's killed him."

Wondering what the excitement is all about and still feeling somewhat woozy, you see the guests run up the steps, fighting to get past each other as quick as they can. You look at your right hand and the metallic object just beyond it. It's a gun, one you have never seen before, but it has a silencer on the end. Your heart jumps and you begin to search the cellar frantically, scanning quickly before your eyes find a body slumped amongst a selection of smashed bottles.

Before you is the Doctor, his face in a fixed grin but his forehead has a bloody wound that leaves you in no doubt he is dead – and he has been shot! Glancing at the gun beside you, your brain makes a terrifying connection. Did you do that? No! You couldn't do that. You were out cold; you can't remember anything. Surely you would remember killing someone. Someone has framed you. Someone has killed the Doctor and wants you to take the rap for it. And everyone has seen you with the gun.

You need to prove your innocence, need to find out who set you up. Otherwise, it's going to be a life in prison for you.

Now go to **001** and get ready to scramble for your freedom!

# 001

You are in the cellar, sitting on your bottom with a gun by your side. Opposite you is the body of Doctor Flavius Munro, with an ominous grin on his face. There is smashed glass around him as well as many intact bottles on the racks that dominate the cellar.

The gun is evidence against you and leaving it here may be a bad idea. Or being innocent maybe it's best not to touch it. But you could also need it, as it could help persuade others to talk. Or you could carry it to somewhere else and get rid of it. Remember, you're now THE suspect in the Doctor's murder. You'll need to convince any investigation of your innocence. Then again maybe finding the guilty party would do that for you. But can you do it before the authorities arrive?


Do you:

Pick up the gun – if so, **note the gun in your inventory** – then continue below

Leave the gun – continue below

Now you wonder should you run and hide, or do you investigate and find out who the killer is? Maybe there's a clue on the Doctor, or maybe even in the cellar. Whatever you do, you believe you cannot retrace your steps as you go along lest someone catches you, or worse, the real killer comes for you. You decide you shall only go to an area once.

Do you:

Examine the Doctor's body – 733

Examine the cellar – 263

Leave the cellar – 675

# 002

You try the key, and it does not fit. If you have another key to try, then go to 929 again. If not go to 096 and make a different decision.

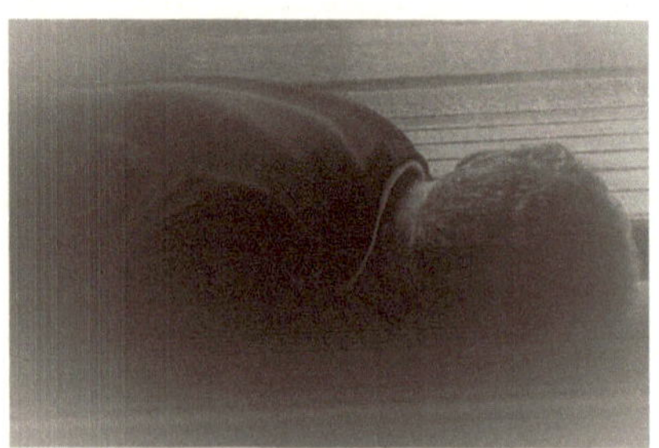

# 003

You look at the simple switch and flick it. You see the water of the lagoon suddenly light up. There must be some sort of lighting underneath. Enter the code **Beam** in your code list. Now that's better, but what next?

Do you

Swipe the card reader with the Doctor's access card, if you have it - 963

Enter a code on the pad (only if you have found one) - 320

Or leave the item alone and

Check out the tin - 250

Or if none of this inspires you, go back to the lagoon entrance and make another choice - 423

# 004

You take a look at the ivy and then the ladder above it. You can do this! So, you jump up and grab the ivy, hauling yourself up to the ladder. From there the climb is easier but you are still in the drizzle. You shiver with cold, but you are determined and continue your climb. At the top of the Lookout, you reach a balcony that circles the top floor of the tower. Above, you see a half broken weathervane on the round roof.

There is but one door on the balcony and you try the handle finding it locked. There is a lock you could try a key in. Or maybe you could smash a window allowing you to access the room.

Do you

Have a key for the lock – <u>868</u>

Want to smash a window – <u>406</u>

Or if this all seems too much you could climb down and try one of the options at <u>151</u>

# 005

The Doctor's office is full of filing cabinets, and you quickly open up many of the drawers, but you are simply overwhelmed by the amount before you. Most of the papers are talking about a new drug that is being commissioned and how it helps humans achieve a peak level of performance for an elongated period of time. The word revolutionary is used many times. Much of the paperwork is however beyond you using technical terms about how the drug works and you find yourself panicking for time and not able to comprehend the science.

As you turn to his desk, you see a set of personal correspondence between the Doctor and Elsie the newspaper reporter. The letters are deeply romantic and there are even some photographs of Elsie waving on beaches in various items of swimwear. What interests you most is one particular letter where Elsie seems to be vehemently attacking the use of performance drugs.

"... I must implore you to stop your work on the drug for it can only bring trouble. My brother was forever affected by a performance enhancing drug that went wrong, causing him to be in a wheelchair for life. You know we are close, and I ask that you do this for me and not betray the feelings that I have for you. It would break my heart to be at opposition to you, but I will if you do not desist from your research. I would kill to stop such experimentation as this..."

The attitude of Elsie is quite shocking, but it could be something to be aware of. In your code list write the word **wheel**.

You search but there is nothing else of interest in the office. Leaving the office and closing the door, where will you go now

Enter the canteen – 083

Try to get into the cleaners' cupboard – 592

Try to enter the office of Kyla Mertens – 840

Or

Return to the hall – 805

# 006

This time the pad flashes red in a crazy fashion and you can hear an alarm going off. You look around you in a panic wondering if anyone is close and coming for you. Best not to wait around and besides you can't get into the Lookout anyway. You run to the coastal path to choose your next location at <u>988</u>

# 007

You watch in silence as Daniel sprints away from you and out of the building. He's an athlete and you'll never catch him. You search the rest of the building but there's nothing of note.

Do you

Check out the fountains area – <u>156</u>

Take a look in the walled garden – <u>926</u>

Wander over to the gardening equipment sheds – <u>262</u>

Or if you doubt the gardens will be of any use then take the coastal path at <u>211</u> but note that you have visited the gardens

## 008

You see the door close and huddle up tight under your large leafy plant. After an hour nothing else has happened and you wonder how long before the police get here. You decide you need to keep moving on to other locations in search of evidence to clear your name. Go to 983

## 009

*"Thanks for taking the rap, Peter. You're a nice lad if somewhat stupid. Still, you'll get out again after some twenty years or so!"* The words still haunt you and you remember how hard you had to run to escape. Could this be the killer's handwriting? You can't say who, but

this is an important piece of evidence which may help
save you.

# 010

There are simply masses of clothes in the drawers and
wardrobes, and you wonder how a man could need so
much. But in one of the jackets, you find a bank
statement. Looking at it closer you realise it is not the
Doctor's bank account but Elsie Gonzales. The
account is heavily in the red and there's a handwritten
annotation which reads, "so you see I need this story,
so make sure you make it public."

Elise is a newspaper reporter so what does it all mean?
There's nothing else in the clothing so best get on.

Do you

Examine the bed – 269

Return to the landing – 119

# 011

As you look at the path ahead you can hear cries close
by. From the words being uttered you realise it is a
search party and they are looking for you. You knew it
was only a matter of time until the police came but are
you ready to give them the evidence they need to
acquit you? Do you have enough to make them

investigate further? Or do you have nothing and reckon you are bang to rights?

Maybe you think you can escape and make a life for yourself elsewhere. The island has some dense vegetation which would give you some great cover. Maybe you have seen something on your travels that would give you optimism about escaping. Did you actually kill someone on this escapade? Then maybe you should run, or will they believe it was an accident?

Weigh up your options carefully and then decide what to do. Do you,

Call out and offer yourself up to the authorities – <u>519</u>

Make a run for it – <u>1000</u>

# 012

"Hey, it's okay, I'm innocent. I was knocked out and then the gun planted on me. Maybe you could help find out who killed the Doctor. See who framed me. Please, I really need some assistance."

Patrick steps forward a little nervous, but with an outstretched hand. You take it and he pulls you close before driving his knee up into your groin. You fall to the floor and hear him running off.

When you recover, albeit a little sore, he is long gone. So much for friendship!

Do you

Try to get into the cleaners' cupboard - <u>571</u>

Examine the door belonging to Doctor Munro - <u>439</u>

Try to enter the office of Kyla Mertens - <u>237</u>

Or

Return to the hall - <u>212</u>

## 013

As you descend below the upper deck, everything becomes dark. You feel your way to the bottom of the circular stairs and can just about make the outline of a corridor out in the dark. Reaching out with your hands, you can feel a door behind you, there's open space before you and the walls also move away to one side.

As you stand there wondering what to do, you can hear scratching from the area ahead of you. You're not sure but it may be someone. If you have a gun you realise that you can't see anywhere, and you'll need both hands to move about, so you keep it tucked away.

Do you

Try the door behind you – <u>844</u>

Walk directly ahead to investigate – <u>478</u>

Follow the wall to the side and trace your way along there – <u>882</u>

Or

Check out the wheelhouse – <u>096</u>

Look at the lockers at the aft of the upper deck – <u>601</u>

Or

Go back onto the pontoons and jump onto the speedboat – <u>624</u>

Or, if you haven't already

Make for the main building – <u>370</u>

Or if you want to continue elsewhere take the coastal path at <u>981</u>

# 014

The vegetable garden has an array of crops growing from cauliflowers to lettuces and some have shrouds over them to protect them from the seasons. In the corner is a series of compost bins and there's a wheelbarrow against a far wall.

Do you

Examine the shrouds – <u>620</u>

Open the compost bins – <u>872</u>

Have a look at the wheelbarrow – <u>606</u>

Or leave and

Enter the orchard – <u>560</u>

Wander to the ornamental garden – <u>420</u>

Or

Check out the fountains area – <u>526</u>

Make your way to the greenhouse – <u>722</u>

Wander over to the gardening equipment sheds – <u>121</u>

Or if you doubt the gardens will be of any use then take the coastal path at <u>770</u> but note that you have visited the gardens

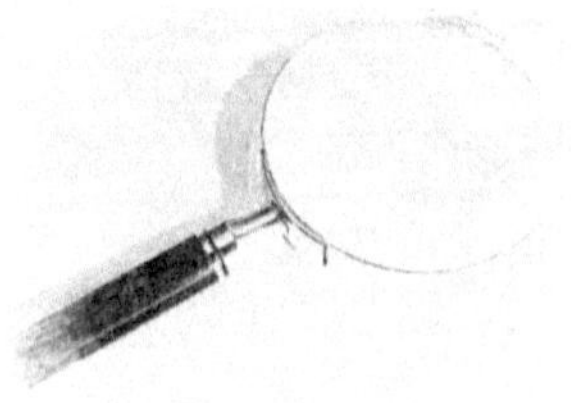

# 015

You draw the gun that was in your hand when you regained consciousness and begin to spin around, pointing it at the hedgerows. At first you see nothing and then you hear someone make a move, catching a shadow running behind a piece of thin hedge. By the time you get through the hedge whoever it was is gone.

Returning to your search you find a capsule on the ground. It's small and looks like it would be swallowed but you're not going to be so daft as to swallow something you cannot identify. **If you decide to pocket it, make a note now in your inventory.**

Well, there's not much else to see in the private garden so what next?

Examine the vegetable patch – <u>104</u>

Take a look at the patio – <u>662</u>

Or

Decide to head off on one of the main paths – <u>297</u>

# 016

You hold up your offering and approach Elsie who looks at them and nervously licks her lips. You sit down on a recliner, and she cautiously joins you on the one beside, and you let her tuck into the food.

"I'm starving, "she says, "but no funny business. You hear me. Keep your hands where I can see them. There's a story going on here. Something tells me you were set up. I have no proof, but I know Patrick Davidson was meeting up with the Doctor. You see I had to spend some time here with the Doctor after I arrived, to interview him and so he could enjoy my company. But he made off to speak to Patrick Davidson. Was the last I saw of him, until gathering at the house. And then of course we found you with the gun."

You stare at the woman wondering if she's genuine, but she seems fully convinced of what she's saying. Have you missed something? You try to ask more pertinent questions but she's now just eating. Has Elsie become an ally?

Do you

Ask how she got here – 342

Draw your gun (if you have one) and tell her to start talking – 969

Or

Leave Elsie in peace and retreat from the cave

If you entered by torch light – 441

Otherwise – 408

# 017

You tell the detective about the note Grandma Munro wrote explaining that aliens were coming and probing her. He has to pick himself up off the floor from laughing. "Seriously, Peter, you expect me to believe that. Where's the note?"

"I accidently burnt it," you tell him.

Oh dear, that didn't go down well. Have you anything else?

If you have any of the following codewords go to that section. Follow the list downwards and only go to the first section that you have a codeword in.

**Taunt** - 027

**Grumble** - 446

**Pads, Paddy, Silent Papers, Cold Blood, Murder, Hitman, Merto** - 415

**Gutted** - 048

Otherwise - 995

# 018

Padlock opened. Congratulations. You open the door and find a long wetsuit inside. The doctor was a larger man than yourself so that will be quite useless for you. There is a set of keys on the little shelf at the top of the locker. Looking at them, you see the keyring has a tag saying speedboat. Take the keys if you wish by noting **speedboat keys** in your inventory.

You search the rest of the locker but there's nothing else of note. What next?

Examine the dinghy - 060

Look at the lifejackets - 436

Take the stairs to the upper floor - 581

Or

Head over to the marina - 465

Or if you want to continue elsewhere take the coastal path at 980

# 019

There's a horrible buzzer that tells you that the code is wrong. Blimey, one more chance or you'll be locked out. What do you do? Try a different code if you have found one

9746 - 713

3267 - 934

2758 - 512

Another code - 303

Or do you decide this is too risky and decide instead to

Hide in the undergrowth surrounding the facility and see what happens - 971

Walk around the facility and see what you can find - 739

Call this a bust and find the coastal path - 986

# 020

You show Daniel the surfer key and she recognises it as the Doctor's speedboat key. Together you run in the rain and let the speedboat slip its moorings and power off out into the sea. As you get clear of the island, Daniel suggests you make for the mainland. However, you could make for the open sea and another country although the sea is very rough.

Do you

Make for the mainland – 726

Route towards the open seas and another country – 830

# 021

Go to 337

## 022

You climb into the dinghy and push away with the oars. It's a struggle just to get out of the dock but you continue. As you start to make way you reach where the waves are breaking, and the dinghy is flung this way and that.

Do you have a lifejacket?

If so – 339

If not – 193

# 023

You sit in the dark hearing the footsteps come right past you and you feel the sweat on your brow. You shake a little but control your nerves, remaining quiet as the footsteps pass by and go to the exit of the tomb. You wait several minutes until all is quiet again and you are sure the unknown intruder is clear of the tomb. It's too dark in here and you can't see anything. Who knows who is lurking in here? You decide to retreat to another part of the ruins and

Enter the temple – 273

Check out the sacrificial slab – 742

Look at the gaming board – 165

Or

Decide this area is no longer useful or too risky and continue along the coastal path at 996

# 024

You enter the room and struggle to see anything. There's a smell of something in the air and you wonder what it is until a hand closes over your mouth. You pass out almost immediately.

You wake up and your eyes are stunned by bright light. The lights are on in Kyla Mertens' office, and something is in your hand. It's a gun. If you carried the one you had in your hand when you awoke in the house cellar, you recognise it as the same one.

You shake your head and look around. Beside you, Patrick Davidson lies dead, blood on his shirt. Apparently, he has been shot. There's an alarm going off in the building as well and you suddenly panic. It's time to get away quick.

**First make an entry in your codes list of Paddy. If you want to take the gun with you, note it in your inventory**, otherwise you simply drop it. Either way you run as fast as you can down the stairs to the hall and out to the path that leads to the coastal circuit and your next choice at 983

# 025

You draw your gun and point it at Kyla. "That's a load of nonsense, tell me the real truth."

"Now, now," says Kyla, stepping towards you and swinging her hair out behind. "I like a young man with spirit but there's no need for that." Kyla is walking directly to you, a smile on her lips. She'll be on you in a moment but what is her intention. Do you trust her?

Do you

Fire your gun – 240

Put your weapon down and let her approach – 842

Run away – 694

# 026

You pull out the charts you found in the main building and motor off into the night, reaching the coast of a foreign country by dawn. At first you hide out but soon find a local farmer who lets you tend his sheep for some pay and food and lodgings. Over the next two years you earn enough to start again and have a comfortable life.

One day in a café you see a newspaper article which states that you are the killer of a prominent researcher back in your home country. Whoever was responsible has got away but at least you have been able to start again, albeit away from any loved ones or friends you know.

This may not be a win but it's not a loss either. Maybe it's a draw. If you want to do better, head back to 001 and start again. At the moment you certainly cannot call yourself a super sleuth!

# 027

You tell the detective about the note you received at the fountains when someone tried to kill you. You say it's from Grandma Munro and the detective disappears for a few hours before returning.

"Well, Peter, it seems that your story checks out, that someone did try to kill you. Unfortunately, it's Elsie

Gonzales' handwriting. We are looking to charge her with your attempted murder."

If you have any of the following codewords go to that section. Follow the list downwards and only go to the first section that you have a codeword in.

**Grumble** – 446

**Pads, Paddy, Silent Papers, Cold Blood, Murder, Hitman, Merto** – 415

**Gutted** – 048

Otherwise – 939

# 028

Drawing your gun, you fire several shots into the desk, splintering the wood. Standing to admire your work, you hear a quiet, *psst!* and something hits you in the shoulder. Suddenly everything goes dark.

You wake up and the room looks the same, but you feel that your hands have been tied. Someone has tied you up and your weapon is gone. You rage in frustration, but you can do nothing until the police eventually arrive and take you into custody. Did you get all the evidence you needed to exonerate yourself? Now go to the <u>519</u> section to discover your destiny

# 029

You tell the detective about your threatening note from when someone tried to kill you at the fountains. The detective takes it away and returns an hour later with a smile on his face.

"We checked out your story about nearly being killed and the handwriting on the note. I believe you son, and the writing is that of Patrick Davidson. I have just arrested him for your attempted murder. However, you are still the prime suspect for the Doctor's death. Do you have any other evidence?"

If you have any of the following codewords go to that section. Follow the list downwards and only go to the first section that you have a codeword in.

**Grumble** – <u>583</u>

**Pads, Paddy, Silent Papers, Cold Blood, Murder, Hitman, Merto** – <u>636</u>

**Gutted** – <u>048</u>

Otherwise read on:

The detective still says you have enough evidence against you that you must go to trial. It seems that the jury sees enough uncertainty for you are found not guilty. However, the papers do not see it that way, a man with a gun in his hand at a body. Your life becomes a hell, followed by the press, until you leave the country. It might seem unfair but at least you are not in jail. As for who actually killed the Doctor, you still don't know. Maybe try again at <u>001</u>.

# 030

You cannot believe your luck. It seems Elsie really likes you, and you can overlook her misdeeds in return for a life with her. You travel together in the car to an airfield on the far side of the mainland. There Elsie pilots a plane, taking you over the water to another country. As she passes over land she announces that you will both parachute out, letting the plane crash and giving the investigators the impression you both have died. You must be some five thousand feet up and she hands you a parachute, while donning one herself.

Elsie opens the door and tells you to follow, jumping out. You see her chute open out quickly and you follow her out the door. Quickly, you grab the parachute chord and pull. There's nothing. As you pass Elsie in your descent you swear you can hear her laugh. Still, it's a nice view on the way down before..., well let's say it's not pretty.

That's a big leap of faith that went wrong for you. Still, try again at <u>001</u>, and this time, trust no one!

# 031

You approach the alcove door, and it opens easily. Inside, you see a toilet in what is a rather cramped space. You guess the Doctor has functions like everyone else. On the floor is a magazine but there is little else here other than the toilet and a roll of toilet paper.

Do you

Read the magazine – 305

Examine the toilet (yes, it really does say that!) – 994

Or

Examine the bed – 046

Check the silk dressing gowns – 505

Descend the stairs – 991

Or leave the Lookout completely and head for the coastal path – 990

# 032

There is a whirring sound from the lock, and you gently push the door open. Step inside at 821

# 033

The tomb entrance may be in darkness but there is an even darker shade through the hole that leads to the interior. You trip over a stone as you run down to the entrance, highlighting just how dark it is. Reaching the entrance, you step inside the tomb and stop almost immediately once you are clear of the wind and rain. You can see nothing. Reaching out with your hands, you find a wall and realise it goes on into the darkness.

This is precarious to say the least. But maybe there's something inside the tomb.


Do you

Have a torch – 221

Shout into the darkness to see if anyone is there – 274

Proceed into the darkness anyway – 374

Decide this is a bad idea and instead

Enter the temple – 280

Check out the sacrificial slab – 246

Look at the gaming board – 426

Or

Decide this area is no longer useful or too risky and continue along the coastal path at 998

# 034

Go to 337

# 035

You punch in the numbers and the pad flashes red and a claxon sounds, deafening all around you. Someone might be on their way with all that noise, so you decide you need to run. Make your way to the coastal path at 503 and escape to another location.

# 036

Well, this is enterprising! You fire up the blowtorch and then climb onto the lawnmower, reaching up to the higher shelves and try to read the bottles. As you stretch you see the words petrol, kerosene, and diesel on the bottles. But you also feel yourself tipping and grab the shelf in your hand. It comes away and you fall to the ground, the bottles coming down with you.

Are you a lucky person? Try your luck

Here – 197

Or here – 422

# 037

You take hold of the rubber cover, and it flips up easily, revealing a number keypad and a swipe card reader. Looking about you, you cannot see anything the pad could activate but it's obviously important. It also warns that a double failure of a code entry will result in an alarm going off and authorities being advised. Sounds serious. Should you activate it? Do you know how? What will it do?

Do you

Swipe the card reader with the Doctor's access card, if you have it – 963

Enter a code on the pad (only if you have found one) (only if you have found one) – 320

Or leave the item alone and

Check out the tin – 250

Investigate the switch – 003

Or if none of this inspires you, go back to the lagoon entrance and make another choice – 423

# 038

The lock on the door makes a whirring sound and you open it - go to 629

# 039

Oh dear, that hasn't worked. You have one try left. Do you wish to try again? If so

4837 - 243

9746 - 371

2758 - 255

Another code - 132

Or if you have the Doctor's access card you could try that - 557

If none of this excites you then do you

Enter the canteen - 083

Try to get into the cleaners' cupboard - 592

Try to enter the office of Kyla Mertens - 840

Or

Return to the hall - 805

## 040

Inside the cabinet are several pills but most look like vitamins. There's also a number written on the rear of the cabinet door, 9746. It might be of use, who knows, write it down if you think so. There's nothing of note so return to the landing and decide your next move – 119

## 041

You take the candle and bend down to the table with it bringing it close to the paper. Suddenly flames erupt and you drop the candle from the shock causing the chair to catch fire as well. You dive out of the door as the whole folly becomes ablaze.

Standing safely on the outside of the fire, you realise, others may come, and you feel you need to get clear of the gardens and search elsewhere. Note the codeword **Blaze** in your codeword list. You run to the coastal path, there to make your next choice at 770.

## 042

The ornamental garden has a bewildering array of plants, and you struggle to identify even a quarter of them. But that's not your purpose here and you look around the ground for anything unusual. There appears to be a small aperture in the ground beside a hazel tree. Just beyond it is a lever on a pipe running just above the ground. Maye this could be something.

Do you

Turn the lever – <u>507</u>

Or leave and

Enter the orchard – <u>447</u>

Walk to the vegetable garden – <u>398</u>

Or

Check out the fountains area – <u>156</u>

Make your way to the greenhouse – <u>745</u>

Wander over to the gardening equipment sheds – <u>262</u>

Or if you doubt the gardens will be of any use then take the coastal path at <u>211</u> but note that you have visited the gardens

# 043

You are thrown about here and there but the lifejacket keeps you afloat. The water is freezing but fortunately you are not that far from land, and you manage to reach a gravelly bay. Staggering up through the trees at the shores edge you find yourself at the perimeter path's junction for the boathouse. Well, you've had enough of that so decide where you go next at <u>980</u>. But lose every item in your inventory other than the lifejacket, for they are now in the sea.

# 044

The dinghy is a small two-person wooden construction and has a set of oars inside. It looks seaworthy and has two flat planks inside for sitting on. There is a sou'wester inside, but it looks too small for you. Otherwise, the dinghy is empty.

Do you

Decide to escape in the dinghy out into the sea – 093

Or

Look at the lifejackets – 496

Take the stairs to the upper floor – 315

Check out the locker at the rear of the room – 584

Or

Head over to the marina – 909

Or if you want to continue elsewhere take the coastal path at 981

# 045

The hatch functions exactly as it does from the kitchen room side. There's nothing different looking in from this side.

What now?

Do you want to examine the other side of the table – <u>140</u>

Take the door to the kitchen – <u>183</u>

Check out what is causing the curtains to move – <u>251</u>

# 046

The bed has not been slept in, but you find some reading material under it. There is a newspaper, showing a story from what you think may be the financial section, judging by the suits in every photo, and a rather distressed picture of Patrick Davidson. The story is in Spanish, and you have no idea what it means. Otherwise, there is nothing of interest.

Do you

Check the silk dressing gowns – <u>505</u>

Check the alcove door – <u>952</u>

Descend the stairs – <u>991</u>

Or leave the Lookout completely and head for the coastal path – <u>990</u>

# 047

The door opens easily, and you step inside at <u>506</u>

# 048

Suddenly you grasp your stomach. Your vision starts to blur. Something is wrong with you. You hear the Police staff run to you and shout for medics, but it is too late as you slip away. As you depart, you remember the fall you had from the lookout, maybe it was more than you thought. An autopsy will record that internal injuries caused death. You'll never know just how the Inspector's case ended. But you can try again at <u>001</u>, and this time tread more carefully.

# 049

You show Elsie the surfer key and she recognises it as the Doctor's speedboat key. Together you run in the rain and let the speedboat slip its moorings and power off out into the sea. As you get clear of the island, Elsie suggests you make for the mainland. However, you could make for the open sea and another country although the sea is very rough.

Do you

Make for the mainland – <u>230</u>

Route towards the open seas and another country – <u>894</u>

## 050

The hallway has a few plants in copper vases, long leafy arrangements by the kitchen door. There is a standard telephone sitting above the table with the diary on it. You'll need to be quick as anyone roaming about the house will surely come through here soon. There's only time to look at one item, but which one.

Do you want to examine,

The telephone – <u>533</u>

The diary – <u>265</u>

The plants – <u>388</u>

## 051

The tumble mechanism makes a click, and you are able to open the safe. Inside there's a card with the Doctor's image and name on it. It has a magnetic strip down the side, and you wonder if it will be useful for accessing certain locations.

There appears to be nowhere in this room for the card to be used so you pocket it (Note you have the **Doctor's access card** in your inventory) and decide your next move.

Do you

Examine the desk with the computer – 220

Look at the small pile of books and the chair – 634

Examine the coat stand – 428

# 052

Go to 417

# 053

You launch an almighty kick at the desk which shakes it. But as you stand to admire your efforts, you hear a quiet, *psst!* and something hits you in the shoulder. Suddenly everything goes dark.

You wake up and the room looks the same, but you feel that time has passed. Suddenly you get nervous that you may have been here too long, and you need to get a move on. Without a thought you run out of the Lookout and make your way to the coastal path, keen to try and find clues in another location. Go to 988

# 054

Inside the refrigerator you see a left-over chicken sandwich and two small phials marked rat deterrent. Otherwise, the appliance is empty and smells a little of stale cheese. You can take any of these items with you, and if you wish to do so, mark them in your **inventory**. There's nothing further in the refrigerator and you ponder what to do next.

Do you, if you haven't already,

Examine the file – <u>600</u>

Check out the lab coats – <u>652</u>

Wander over to the stools – <u>233</u>

Or

If this is all too much you could return to the entrance hall – <u>805</u>

# 055

You draw your gun and shot at the pieces causing pieces to fly off them. None of them seem to fall over and now when you try to lift them, they seem stuck fast. More than that, the noise from firing the gun caused a loud retort and echo and will surely bring people this way. You decide you need to move on quick and high tail it to the coastal path at <u>996</u>

# 056

You examine the canister and note that it says lamp oil on the side. However, it is almost completely empty.

Do you

Pick up the paper to read – 480

Grab the candle to examine everything a lot closer – 782

Or leave the folly and choose to look elsewhere – 156

# 057

The lock on the door makes a whirring sound and you open it – go to 629

# 058

The letter between Elsie and the Doctor about her wheelchair-bound brother is brought from your belongings and the detective peruses it. "Wow, this is great. Says she would kill. That should help your defence. She's certainly a possibility. But have you anything else?"

Do you have the codeword **Taunt** – 935

If not, and you have any of the following codewords go to that section. Follow the list downwards and only go to the first section that you have a codeword in.

**Grumble** - 583

**Pads, Paddy, Silent Papers, Cold Blood, Murder, Hitman, Merto** - 636

**Gutted** - 048

Otherwise read on:

The detective arrests you for the Doctor's murder saying that you were still seen with the gun over the body. All you have is a potential heated comment. At the trial you cut a lonely figure as it only takes the jury an hour to convict you. From your jail cell you wonder if you were right in your choice of killer. You'll never know. Maybe try again at 001.

# 059

"Don't do it, Peter, whatever it is you want don't do it. Lower the gun and we'll talk."

You see the fear in her eyes, and you may have her on the rack. On the other hand, maybe some trust might gain some rewards.

Do you

Lower the gun - 162

Keep the gun pointing at Kyla - 645

# 060

The dinghy is a small two-person wooden construction and has a set of oars inside. It looks seaworthy and has two flat planks inside for sitting on. There is a sou'wester inside, but it looks too small for you. Otherwise, the dinghy is empty.

Do you

Decide to escape in the dinghy out into the sea – 479

Or

Look at the lifejackets – 436

Take the stairs to the upper floor – 581

Check out the locker at the rear of the room – 957

Or

Head over to the marina – 465

Or if you want to continue elsewhere take the coastal path at 980

# 061

You tell the detective of your conversation with Kyla in the ruins and of how she admitted to feeling the drug was her work stolen by the Doctor.

"Now that is interesting, but it is also not proof. You still have a lot to answer for. Do you have anything to back up this evidence?"

If you have any of the following codewords go to that section. Follow the list downwards and only go to the first section that you have a codeword in.

**Scrap** – 079

**Taunt** – 864

**Grumble** – 446

**Pads, Paddy, Silent Papers, Cold Blood, Murder, Hitman, Merto** – 415

**Gutted** – 048

Otherwise, read on:

The detective arrests you for the Doctor's murder saying that you were still seen with the gun over the body. All you have is a potential heated comment. At the trial you cut a lonely figure as it only takes the jury an hour to convict you. From your jail cell you wonder if you were right in your choice of killer. You'll never know. Maybe try again at 001.

# 062

You tell the detective about the note you found in the ruins that is in your backpack. He retrieves it and take a while studying it before returning to you.

"Now that is interesting, but it is also not proof. You still have a lot to answer for. Do you have anything to back up this solid piece of evidence?"

If you have any of the following codewords go to that section. Follow the list downwards and only go to the first section that you have a codeword in.

**Confess** – 196

**Scrap** – 079

**Taunt** – 864

**Grumble** – 446

**Pads, Paddy, Silent Papers, Cold Blood, Murder, Hitman, Merto** – 415

**Gutted** – 048

Otherwise, read on:

The detective arrests you for the Doctor's murder saying that you were still seen with the gun over the body. All you have is a potential heated comment. At the trial you cut a lonely figure as it only takes the jury an hour to convict you. From your jail cell you wonder if you were right in your choice of killer. You'll never know. Maybe try again at 001.

# 063

You examine the canister and note that it says lamp oil on the side. However, it is almost completely empty.

Do you

Pick up the paper to read – 286

Grab the candle to examine everything a lot closer – 041

Or leave the folly and choose to look elsewhere – 526

# 064

The buzzer howls even louder this time and the number pad flashes before the numbers change from bright green to red. Looks like it's locked the door. More than that it will have set off an alarm. Time to get out of here. You run hard around the laboratory to the coastal path at 983

# 065

The detective reads the letter from Elsie Gonzales editor saying that all of the staff could be laid off due to low newspaper sales and that he needs a story. As he strokes his chin thoughtfully you think he is coming around to your point of view. However, he shakes his head saying, I doubt this will be enough. Do you have anything else?

If you have any of the following codewords go to that section. Follow the list downwards and only go to the first section that you have a codeword in.

**Wheel** - 718

**Taunt** - 462

If not, and you have any of the following codewords go to that section. Follow the list downwards and only go to the first section that you have a codeword in.

**Grumble** - 583

**Pads, Paddy, Silent Papers, Cold Blood, Murder, Hitman, Merto, Merto** - 636

**Gutted** - 048

Otherwise - 995

# 066

The door behind you swings open easily and you quietly sneak inside. There is almost complete darkness inside and you gently feel around before your hand finds a note on the floor. You open it and try to read it but cannot. You'll need to get out to some light to read it. The next time you are above this deck, read the note at 450 before returning to the section you had reached.

You can still hear movement in the passage you came from.

Do you

Stay here and wait – 741

Run back upstairs – 609

Walk directly ahead in the passage to investigate – 911

Follow the wall to the side and trace your way along there – 319

# 067

You look at the photographs on the wall and note that most of them are of the Doctor's mother and him. Clearly, he loves the old woman and possibly dotes on her.

What next? Do you

Examine the radio handset – 989

Have a rifle through the drawers – 229

Look at the writing desk – 361

Or

Climb up the spiral staircase – 824

Descend the spiral staircase – 845

Decide to leave the Lookout and make your way to the coastal path – 988

# 068

Locker opened. Congratulations. You open the door and find a long wetsuit inside. The doctor was a larger man than yourself so that will be quite useless for you. There is a set of keys on the little shelf at the top of the locker. Looking at them, you see the keyring has a tag saying speedboat. Take the keys if you wish by noting **speedboat keys** in your inventory.

You search the rest of the locker but there's nothing else of note. What next?

Examine the dinghy – 044

Look at the lifejackets – 496

Take the stairs to the upper floor – 315

Or

Head over to the marina – 909

Or if you want to continue elsewhere take the coastal path at 981

# 069

Go to 337


# 070

The number pad goes red, and you hear a horrible buzzer indicate you are wrong.

Do you try another number?

4837 - 279

2758 - 856

9746 - 032

Another code - 294


Or do you

Use the Doctor's swipe card on the reader if you have it - 134

Try to climb the Ivy - 004

 Or if this all seems to hard or unwise, you could simply keep on walking the coastal path to your next location at 990 but note that you have visited the Lookout

# 071

Do you have the code word **Murder**, if so go to 987.  If not, read on.

You open the door of the canteen and see Kyla Mertens, the scientist, holding a cup of coffee. She turns around, sees you and drops the coffee. You can see the look of fear on her face, and she goes white.

"Don't kill me, please don't kill me."

Do you

Hold up your hands and try to reassure her that you are no threat - 162

Take out the gun and threaten her with it for information - 059

Try to knock her out - 860

Ask her to join you in clearing your name - 823

# 072

The wardrobe has a jacket hanging inside and you search it thoroughly before finding an envelope inside. Opening it, you find correspondence to Doctor Munro from Patrick Davidson stating that Mr Davidson is aware of the Doctor's intention to make the drug patent free so that everyone can have it at a sensible price. Mr Davidson threatens the Doctor, saying that his company has invested too much money in the drug to simply allow it to be given away for nothing. He recommends the Doctor comes to his senses and says he will speak to him privately at the gathering on the island.

The wardrobe contains nothing else so what now?

Examine the bed – 804

Rifle through the kitchenette – 768

Try out the chairs – 630

Or

Investigate "The Hollow" – 819

Dive into the lagoon and see if you can find the Doctor's secret stash – 924

Decide you have had enough of the lagoon and make your move to the coastal path and your next destination – 549

# 073

You lower your gun and walk from the temple. Getting a short distance away, you turn back and look at Kyla who is standing against the wind in her long coat. She shakes her head and then turns back, walking into the temple.

You decide to stay clear of the temple, but you can still search other parts of the ruins of you haven't already. Do you

Make for the tomb and shelter from the rain – <u>877</u>

Check out the sacrificial slab – <u>742</u>

Look at the gaming board – <u>165</u>

Or

Decide this area is no longer useful or too risky and continue along the coastal path at <u>996</u>

# 074

Stepping back inside the hut, you feel safer away from the wind and rain and that lunatic on the other side. Congratulating yourself as you see the bridge you would have been running across fall to the sea, you then watch the figure head to the other bridge. They are going to cut that one too.

Do you

Try to run across the last remaining bridge – <u>826</u>

Stay where you are – <u>084</u>

# 075

The waft of cold air hits you as you open the fridge and look at the wide range of beer inside. Maybe you could take some time and sup a cold one. After all you have been under pressure.

Do you

Put your feet up and have a beer - <u>137</u>

Or continue your search

Examine the pool table - <u>110</u>

Look at the darts board - <u>248</u>

Read the magazines - <u>424</u>

Take hold of the scrap of paper - <u>270</u>

Or

Enter the toilet - <u>655</u>

Check out the chart room - <u>618</u>

Investigate the room with no name - <u>521</u>

Return to the lower floor - <u>795</u>

# 076

The keypad goes red, and a claxon begins to sound, deafening you. This is likely to bring lots of people and you decide to get as far away as possible from the building. You run out of the front door and make your way to the coastal path. Go there now at <u>983</u>

# 077

"Hello there," you say climbing out of the water.

"Get back, get back. Have you come from them? Did you arrive in the ship? I have seen the lights and I think you took my Flavius."

You are somewhat bemused but wonder if the old woman is bluffing you with this bizarre act. How should you play this?

Do you

Pull your gun (if you have one) and tell her to start talking sense – 627

Offer the woman some food if you have any in your inventory – 474

Ask her if she knows who framed you – 327

Ask if she knows anything about why everyone was here – 403

# 078

You punch in the numbers and the pad flashes red and a claxon sounds, deafening all around you. Someone might be on their way with all that noise, so you decide you need to run. Make your way to the coastal path at 549 and escape to another location.

# 079

You tell the detective about the note from Kyla Mertens to her father, saying how Doctor Munro must be stopped and that she is entering a dark place.

"Now that is interesting, but it is also not proof. You still have a lot to answer for. Do you have anything to back up this evidence?"

If you have any of the following codewords go to that section. Follow the list downwards and only go to the first section that you have a codeword in.

**Taunt** – 357

**Grumble** – 446

**Pads, Paddy, Silent Papers, Cold Blood, Murder, Hitman, Merto** – 415

**Gutted** – 048

Otherwise, read on:

The detective still says you have enough evidence against you that you have to go to trial. It seems that the jury sees enough uncertainty for you are found not guilty. However, the papers do not see it that way, a man with a gun in his hand at a body. Your life becomes a hell, followed by the press, until you leave the country. It might seem unfair but at least you are not in jail. As for who actually killed the Doctor, you still don't know. Maybe try again at 001.

# 080

You open the top of the nearest compost bin and recoil. It stinks! Regardless, you tip it out and start poking through it. You find some paperwork form Elsie Gonzales. It appears to be a letter from her boss stating that the paper is not selling well. It's not directed to Elsie but rather a general employee message.

After further searching you find nothing else and decide to continue elsewhere.

Do you

Examine the shrouds – 271

Have a look at the wheelbarrow – 487

Or leave and

Enter the orchard – 447

Wander to the ornamental garden – 042

Or

Check out the fountains area – 156

Make your way to the greenhouse – 745

Wander over to the gardening equipment sheds – 262

Or if you doubt the gardens will be of any use then take the coastal path at 211 but note that you have visited the gardens

# 081

You quietly sneak over to the greenhouse and there seems to be no one outside. You open the greenhouse door and march in. Then you see the crowd of police officers standing over a dead body. Did you forget? You panic and turn to run as you are instructed to halt. You killed the man lying there so you don't heed what they say and try to run away. As you hear a shot ring out you feel it hit your chest and you stumble before your breathing becomes difficult. You briefly hear the police come towards you but then everything goes dark.

Alas you failed to achieve to clear your name or even escape. You can try again at 001.

# 082

You move the woman to your chosen location and then step back to watch. With horror, you see the woman crumbles before you. Quickly you try to grab one of the other pieces, but they are stuck fast to the ground. How does this all work? You shake your head in the pouring rain and decide to get away from this game as quick as possible

Do you

Make for the tomb and shelter from the rain – <u>033</u>

Enter the temple – <u>280</u>

Check out the sacrificial slab – <u>246</u>

Or

Decide this area is no longer useful or too risky and continue along the coastal path at <u>998</u>

# 083

You open the door of the canteen and see Patrick Davidson, the businessman holding a cup of coffee. He turns around, sees you and drops the coffee. You can see the look of fear on his face, and he goes white.

"Don't kill me, please don't kill me."

Do you

Hold up your hands and try to reassure him that you are no threat – <u>310</u>

Take out the gun and threaten him with it for information – <u>867</u>

Try to knock him out – <u>105</u>

Ask him to join you in clearing your name – <u>012</u>

## 084

You hold your position as the figure runs to the other bridge and then begins their work with the axe. Soon that bridge falls to the sea. But you are safe, if a little trapped. You have a fretful night until the morning comes, and you see police officers by the fountain. It takes most of the day for a specialist team to rescue you and you are then placed under arrest. Do you have much evidence? Will you be able to defend yourself because they clearly think you committed the murder of Doctor Munro? Go to 519

## 085

There is no way you are going to trust this woman and she's now coming very close. You believe there's no point in engaging any further and simply turn and run away to the coastal path. She seems to be staying at the ruins and you catch your breath before walking to your next destination at 996

## 086

The Detective Inspector brushes his moustache as he enters the room and takes a seat opposite you. A recording machine is started, and the man stares at you before giving a cough. His eyes are old and have seen everything, or so it seems to you. Can you bluff this man? Or will you tell the truth?

He says that everyone saw you beside the Doctor's body. He says, currently, you are the prime suspect. However, he wants you to admit to it as things will be a lot quicker that way. Of course, they will be, but you are innocent!

The detective now sits back in the chair and asks you to explain what happened. Do you know? Who will you blame?

"I didn't murder the Doctor. In fact, it was..."

Who will you say killed the Doctor? Remember you'll need some evidence to help your cause.

Was it

Kyla Mertens – 392

Patrick Davidson – 296

Elsie Gonzales – 884

Daniel Lyle – 443

Grandma Munro – 527

# 087

You turn to run away, and someone throws something at you. It hits the wall, but you don't stop until you reach the coastal path at 980. Go there and choose your next destination quickly.

# 088

Glug, glug, glug. Oh dear, you don't make it, drowning in the bay. Tough luck but then you were basically on the run and life was not going to be great. Try for a better life by returning to 001.

# 089

Oh dear, that hasn't worked. You have one try left. Do you wish to try again? If so

4837 - 243

9746 - 371

3267 - 880

2758 - 255

Another code - 132


Or

If you have the Doctor's access card you could try that - 557

If none of this excites you then do you

Enter the canteen – 083

Try to get into the cleaners' cupboard – 592

Try to enter the office of Kyla Mertens – 840

Or

Return to the hall – 805

# 090

When you were in the Lookout, you saw a boat in the water on the far side of the island. It's a bit further north than the boathouse where people arrive on the island so it might offer a discreet way of escape. Getting out there will be difficult but it's worth a shot.

You fight your way back into the vegetation and go off-path as you make your way to the Lookout. It seems that there is a minimal presence around the Lookout. Maybe the police cannot get in to search it. You pass by it through the undergrowth and make your way down to the shore.

The storm is quieter than it was, but those waves look choppy. It'll be a crazy swim but maybe you can do it.

Do you have a **lifejacket** – 542

If not, time to swim for it. You're not convinced, and it will require some luck to get out to the boat.

Do you

Take the risk – 485

Decide against it and look for another option

Make a run for the boathouse – <u>568</u>

Hide out in the gardens – <u>499</u>

Go to the ruins to try and hide – <u>838</u>

Or

If you checked the following codeword while making your initial decision then you may follow this option

Codeword **Quiet Place** – <u>224</u>

Or give yourself up - <u>519</u>

# 091

The curtain twitches as you get close and then a hand shoots out from between the curtains. The arm is bony but the grip on your shoulder is incredibly strong. The curtains fly back, and you see the wild face of Grandma Munro.

'They're here, boy. Run to the hills. Run for your life, boy, before the silent one comes. He's everywhere.'

With that, the old woman pushes you backwards, causing you to stumble and fall to the floor. She races past you and you can hear the front door closing hard behind her.

Brushing yourself down, you take a quick look behind the curtains but there's nothing to see except the rain and wind terrorising the island's plant-life.

You feel it's only safe to check out two items in this room before moving on.

Do you:

Check out the China hutch – <u>792</u>

Examine the drinks cabinet – <u>635</u>

Look at the bookcase – <u>541</u>

Or if you have already examined two items, or want to leave this room (and have not already visited these places),

Enter the dining room – <u>576</u>

Enter the kitchen – <u>298</u>

Go upstairs – <u>119</u>

Leave by the front door – <u>384</u>

# 092

From the window, you look out onto a rough sea which is a mass of dark shades, constantly changing. But then you see a boat out there, a motor cruiser of some sort from the shapes you can make out, the vessel being lit up by its own lights.

But that's it, except for the rain. Note the code **Boat** in your code list

So, what next? Do you

Examine the books around the wall – <u>757</u>

Check out the table with its cup and cake – <u>707</u>

Proceed up the spiral staircase – <u>811</u>

Decide to leave the Lookout and make your way to the coastal path – <u>988</u>

# 093

You think it's all getting too much, and you can't just wait for the police to arrive. If you can get away, maybe you can escape to the mainland and beyond to start a new life in another country.

You open up the gate doors of the dock and see the wild sea outside. The waves are crashing in and now the door is open, the water really starts to splash inside the dock. The dinghy bounces about but you are an experienced sailor, albeit on larger vessels.

Do you want to take the boat out - 022

Or is this a bad idea. If so do you,

Look at the lifejackets - 496

Take the stairs to the upper floor - 315

Check out the locker at the rear of the room - 584

Or

Head over to the marina - 909

Or if you want to continue elsewhere take the coastal path at 981

# 094

You draw your gun and point it at Kyla. "That's a load of nonsense, tell me the real truth."

"Now, now," says Kyla, stepping towards you and swinging her hair out behind. "I like a young man with spirit but there's no need for that." Kyla is walking directly to you, a smile on her lips. She'll be on you in a moment but what is her intention. Do you trust her?

Do you

Fire your gun – 610

Put your weapon down and let her approach – 517

Run away – 470

# 095

You switch on the beam and see a pair of legs. They are slender in their trousers, and you struggle to remember what the women were wearing when you were found with the gun in your hand, the same one you are holding now. Whoever it is runs.

Do you

Shout at them to stop – 834

Run after them – 139

# 096

The wheelhouse contains charts of the local area and is looking quite messy. Maybe someone has been planning a trip, but you also notice that a few coffee cups lie about unwashed. You find several paper clippings on the floor. One talks about dementia in elderly people while another is commentary from a national paper written by Elsie Gonzales, lambasting today's overreliance on drugs.

There is a radio onboard, but you cannot start it as it seems to require the power to be switched on, and you don't have a key that seems to fit the ignition.

If you have a key with which to start the boat then - 929

That appears to be it in the wheelhouse, so

Do you

Go to the lower deck via the stairs - 013

Look at the lockers at the aft of the upper deck - 601

Or

Jump onto the speedboat - 624

Or, if you haven't already,

Make for the main building - 370

Or

if you want to continue elsewhere take the coastal path at 981

# 097

Go to 199

# 098

The picture shows a gathering of people, but you cannot for the life of you recognise anyone in it. No one looks like anyone who came to dinner. You are wondering why the Doctor has this picture but then you notice it is not level either but has a slight slant to the left. Quickly you grab the picture and finds it comes off its hook easily. Behind the picture is a tumble lock showing 12 digits, each to be entered separately. That's a pretty big selection of numbers. Are aware of the code?

If you want to enter this code – 330

Otherwise

Examine the desk with the computer – 220

Look at the small pile of books and the chair – 634

Examine the coat stand – 428

# 099

The door opens easily enough and there is a flight of stairs leading you up to a small corridor where you can see four doors. The first you come to has a small viewing window and shows a canteen. The door is open slightly and you can see someone inside. Stepping quietly past you find three more doors. One entitled cleaners' cupboard, another "Doctor Munro" and the last "Kyla Mertens".

Do you

Enter the canteen – <u>071</u>

Try to get into the cleaners' cupboard – <u>571</u>

Examine the door belonging to Doctor Munro – <u>439</u>

Try to enter the office of Kyla Mertens – <u>237</u>

Or

Return to the hall – <u>212</u>

## 100

Your heart sinks as the keypad flashes and then the numbers turn red. A claxon begins sounding in the building. You feel the panic rising and glance up and down the hall. You need to get out of here quickly. It's time to move on to the coastal path. You flee the building and reach the path at <u>986</u>

## 101

Do you have the **foreign charts**?

If so – <u>026</u>

If not – <u>720</u>

# 102

You grab the phials and throw them at the creature. At first it rears up and then sniffs the broken phials. But it soon ignores it and begins to charge at you.

Do you have a gun? If so, use it – 412

Otherwise – 781

# 103

**Yippee!** You spin the code in and tug at the cupboard. The door springs open, and you find neatly arranged charts for the waters beyond the local area. You know that many of the areas are treacherous to travel through and these charts would be handy. If you want to take them then enter **National charts** in your inventory.

With those safely tucked away what will you do next?

Take a local chart off the wall – 596

Shoot the cupboard open – 402

Or

Go to the Rec Room – 234

Investigate the room with no name – 521

Return to the lower floor – 795

# 104

The vegetable patch is a three feet square piece of ground with small sticks half planted into the soil. It really is quite dainty, and you notice that a part of it seems to have been recently turned over. The soil is sticky and wet, but this small part does look to be somewhat different.

Do you

Unearth what's underneath – 927

Or leave the vegetable patch and

Pay a visit to the private garden where you saw the glint of light – 914

Take a look at the patio – 662

Or

Decide to head off on one of the paths – 297

# 105

You decide to silence Patrick by knocking him out and rush forward to the frightened man and grab him by the throat. Surprisingly, he's quick and steps to one side before kneeing you right where it hurts, and you double over.

When you manage to get back up to your feet, Patrick is long gone. So much for that.

Do you

Try to get into the cleaners' cupboard – 571

Examine the door belonging to Doctor Munro – 439

Try to enter the office of Kyla Mertens – 237

Or

Return to the hall – 212

# 106

You run as hard as you can, but the figure is mighty quick with the axe. Go 931

# 107

The door clicks open, and you pull the handle, allowing yourself to step inside. Time to find some evidence. Go to 805

# 108

The keypad goes red and a claxon begins to sound, deafening you. This is likely to bring lots of people and you decide to get as far away as possible from the building. You run out of the front door and make your way to the coastal path. Go there now at 986

# 109

"I didn't kill him, someone else did and framed me. I'm the victim here." You stare at Kyla, hoping she can read your sincere face. You have so little evidence to offer.

Kyla smiles at you. "Poor thing. Someone has played us both. And you are so young. Come to me. You must be cold. We can hide away in the tomb over there. It's sheltered."

Kyla steps towards you and you wonder just what this woman is to you.

Do you

Step into her embrace, after all you need a friend – 815

Run away from the ruins, she's a threat – 085

Draw your gun for a better answer – 094

# 110

You check the balls on the pool table and find them to be normal game balls. A check of the pockets finds nothing and when you grab a cue, you find yourself shooting the two ball into the corner pocket. You need to snap out of this, you're trying to clear your name, not looking to become a hustler.

Do something else quickly.

Look at the darts board – 248

Open the fridge – 075

Read the magazines – 424

Take hold of the scrap of paper – 270

Or

Enter the toilet – 655

Check out the chart room – 618

Investigate the room with no name – 521

Return to the lower floor – 795

# 111

You move the woman to your chosen location and then step back to watch. With horror, you see the woman crumbles before you. Quickly you try to grab one of the other pieces, but they are stuck fast to the ground. How does this all work? You shake your head in the pouring rain and decide to get away from this game as quick as possible

Do you

Make for the tomb and shelter from the rain – 877

Enter the temple – 273

Check out the sacrificial slab – 742

Or

Decide this area is no longer useful or too risky and continue along the coastal path at 996

# 112

You tell the detective about your threatening note from when someone tried to kill you at the fountains. The detective takes it away and returns an hour later with a smile on his face.

"We checked out your story about nearly being killed and the handwriting on the note. I believe you son, and the writing is that of Elsie Gonzales. I have just arrested her for your attempted murder."

If you have any of the following codewords go to that section. Follow the list downwards and only go to the first section that you have a codeword in.

**Grumble – 446**

**Pads, Paddy, Silent Papers, Cold Blood, Murder, Hitman, Merto – 415**

**Gutted – 048**

Otherwise, read on:

The detective still says you have enough evidence against you that you have to go to trial. It seems that the jury sees enough for you are to be found guilty. As you sit in your jail cell, you wonder if Kyla really did kill the Doctor, or was it Elsie. You'll never know. Maybe try again at 001.

# 113

**By golly!** You spin the code in and tug at the cupboard. The door springs open, and you find neatly arranged charts for the waters beyond the local area. You know that many of the areas are treacherous to travel through and these charts would be handy. If you want to take them then enter **National charts** in your inventory.

With those safely tucked away what will you do next?

Take a local chart off the wall – 153

Shoot the cupboard open – 453

Or

Go to the Rec Room – <u>528</u>

Investigate the room with no name – <u>685</u>

Return to the lower floor – <u>370</u>

# 114

You see the caves in the ruins and quickly see there is no one outside them. Without hesitating you run inside and are suddenly surprised that there are several lights in the dark, all focused on a body. It's Kyla Mertens, who died at your hands. This was a bad idea. Someone cries, "Halt! Police!" You turn and run for all you are worth. There is a shot and then nothing.

Alas you failed to achieve to clear your name or even escape. You can try again at <u>001</u>.

# 115

Oh dear, that hasn't worked. You have one try left. Do you wish to try again? If so

4837 – <u>614</u>

9746 – <u>038</u>

3267 – <u>643</u>

2758 – <u>100</u>

Another code – <u>626</u>

Or

If you have the Doctor's access card you could try that – <u>057</u>

If none of this excites you then do you

Enter the canteen – <u>071</u>

Try to get into the cleaners' cupboard – <u>571</u>

Try to enter the office of Kyla Mertens – <u>237</u>

Or

Return to the hall – <u>212</u>

# 116

You tell the detective about your threatening note from when someone tried to kill you at the fountains. The detective takes it away and returns an hour later with a smile on his face.

"We checked out your story about nearly being killed and the handwriting on the note. I believe you son, and the writing is that of Kyla Mertens. I have just arrested her for your attempted murder. However, you are still the prime suspect for the Doctor's death. Do you have any other evidence?"

If you have any of the following codewords go to that section. Follow the list downwards and only go to the first section that you have a codeword in.

**Grumble** - <u>583</u>

**Pads, Paddy, Silent Papers, Cold Blood, Murder, Hitman, Merto** - <u>636</u>

**Gutted** - <u>048</u>

Otherwise read on:

The detective arrests you for the Doctor's murder saying that you were still seen with the gun over the body. All you have is a potential heated comment. At the trial you cut a lonely figure as it only takes the jury an hour to convict you. From your jail cell you wonder if you were right in your choice of killer. You'll never know. Maybe try again at <u>001</u>.

# 117

You lean back and fire your gun again. The bullet ricochets again and bounces off something before hitting you in the neck. You fall to the ground, unable to breathe properly with your punctured neck. Ironically as you slip away to the blackness, the cupboard door swings open, but you don't see what's inside as you sink into oblivion.

Gunplay never ends well. But learn that lesson by returning to <u>001</u> and having another go.

# 118

You swipe the reader with the Doctor's access card.
You look around but cannot see anything different. Do
you want to swipe it again?

If so – <u>379</u>

If not – <u>475</u>

# 119

You take the stairs up past some portraits of the
Doctor and his mother. It seems weird knowing the
man is dead and you note that his mother looks no
less crazy in the pictures than she does in real life. As
you reach the landing on the first floor you can see
three doors. One is open and you can see a bedroom.
Another is closed but has the legend "Office" on it. A
third is half open and you can see a sink.

Do you

Enter the office – <u>817</u>

Enter the bedroom – <u>791</u>

Enter the third room – <u>387</u>

Return to the hall – <u>675</u>

# 120

Well, it seems he hates you as the boat capsizes and you find yourself out in the maelstrom of the sea.

Do you have a lifejacket?

Yes – <u>344</u>

No – <u>088</u>

# 121

You approach the gardening sheds and see four different sheds in front of you. Three of them are locked and any keys you have are not the correct size for the padlocks. One is open with the door slightly ajar.

Do you

Step inside – <u>204</u>

Or

Check out the fountains area – <u>526</u>

Take a look in the walled garden – <u>625</u>

Make your way to the greenhouse – <u>722</u>

Or if you doubt the gardens will be of any use then take the coastal path at <u>770</u> but note that you have visited the gardens

# 122

Yes, best to leave well alone. You walk out of the room backwards and close the door. Just what was in there. Someone, surely there was someone. You take the table the telephone sits on and block the dining room door with it. You cannot hang about, but you still want to see if the house holds any more clues. Maybe you should go upstairs where you will have some distance between you and whoever was in the dining room. Or should you simply leave the house? After all, that could have been a murderer behind the curtains. Whatever you choose, you decide it's best to leave the ground floor alone.

Do you

Go upstairs – 119

Go outside – 384

# 123

You turn the key and the radio springs to life. The boat's engines also fire up briefly before sputtering to a halt. You have several options now.

Do you

Put a call out on the radio – 738

Have the code word **Fuel** – 300

# 124

There's a sudden fizz and then nothing. You blink your eyes which are spotting because of the sudden light. So that didn't work. Which will you try now?

Attach the wire to JJ7 – <u>399</u>

Attach the wire to 526 – <u>377</u>

Or decide this is a bad plan and instead surrender – <u>648</u>

# 125

You make your way down to the third fountain which has a dolphin in a mid-air pose with gushing water coming from it. The rain pouring down makes you feel less impressed than you maybe should be but the thought of getting clear of the downpour for a moment in the tunnel is certainly appealing.

As you approach the fountain and see the entrance to the underground section, you think you see a shadow moving into the tunnel. Could this be one of the other guests? If there is someone in there, should you go in? Maybe you have the gun and could question them under duress? Or maybe it's a trap?

Do you

Enter the tunnel – <u>705</u>

Hold off in the rain and wait – <u>806</u>

Or

Take a look in the walled garden – <u>625</u>

Make your way to the greenhouse – <u>722</u>

Wander over to the gardening equipment sheds – <u>121</u>

Or if you doubt the gardens will be of any use then take the coastal path at <u>770</u> but note that you have visited the gardens

# 126

You gently approach Elsie, careful not to scare her. Slowly you wrap your hands around her as she cries onto your shoulder. She sniffs and then holds you close to her as she stands up. You seem to have been quite a boon to her and you feel pleased.

"Thank you, Peter," she whispers in your ear. "You are as gullible as the Doctor!"

Your heart jumps but it's too late as she drives a knife up and into your gut. Slowly you sink to the floor and see her smiling face, intoxicating but very deadly. Well, at least you know who did it. Or was she simply so scared of you that she killed you? You'll never know. Trusting folk can sometimes be the death of you. Try again at <u>001</u>

# 127

You draw your gun. "I want to know everything." You see the panic in Patrick's eyes. He turns and begins to run. You can't hope to catch him.

Do you

Fire a warning shot – 383

Shoot at Patrick – 809

Let him go – 920

# 128

You tell the detective about the note you received at the fountains when someone tried to kill you. You say it's from Patrick Davidson and the detective disappears for a few hours before returning.

"Well, Peter, it seems that your story checks out, that someone did try to kill you. Unfortunately, it's Elsie Gonzales' handwriting. We are looking to charge her with your attempted murder.

If you have any of the following codewords go to that section. Follow the list downwards and only go to the first section that you have a codeword in.

**Grumble** – 446

**Pads, Paddy, Silent Papers, Cold Blood, Murder, Hitman, Merto** – 415

**Gutted** – 048

Otherwise – 939

## 129

Getting desperate? Okay then, there's some cauliflower in one pot, gravy in another and a type of bean in a third you are struggling to recognise. Unless you are hungry let's get on!

Do you

Check out the fridge freezer – 822

Have a look through the cupboards – 887

Examine the hatch – 347

Look at the knife block – 353

Return to the hall – 675

## 130

You tell the detective of your conversation with Kyla in the ruins and of how she admitted to feeling the drug was her work stolen by the Doctor.

"That's enough," says the detective. "I'm going to investigate Miss Mertens rather more closely."

It takes the rest of the day, but the detective returns in the evening letting you know that Kyla Mertens has buckled under questioning and that you are a free man. He congratulates you and you step out into the fresh air once more. It feels good to be free and you wonder what else life has in store for you. Well done, super sleuth!

# 131

You have documents indicating that Daniel Lyle has been dropped from certain tests he was to take part in. You don't understand the detail, but you know he had experienced increased performance in earlier tests he had done. Is this enough for murder? It is at the very least evidence for motive.

# 132

Your heart sinks as the keypad flashes and then the numbers turn red. A claxon begins sounding in the building. You feel the panic rising and glance up and down the hall. You need to get out of here quickly. It's time to move on to the coastal path. You flee the building and reach the path at 983

# 133

You suddenly feel a tremble in your body and then your breathing becomes difficult. The Police staff run to your aid, but it becomes strangely dark. You hear the Inspector shout, "he's been poisoned."

But then you suddenly rally and can sit upright. You are taken to a paramedic and then a doctor who advises the police you have been poisoned but that an antidote in your system kicked in and prevented your death.

"This changes nothing," says the detective. "Just because you had some concocted plan about being poisoned doesn't mean I won't need more evidence. After all they saw you over his body."

Return to 519. They might not believe you are innocent but at least you'll have a chance to show them you are.

# 134

You swipe the Doctor's access card, and the lock makes a whirring sound. Pushing the door, it opens freely. Enter at 821

# 135

Oh dear, that hasn't worked. You have one try left. Do you wish to try again? If so

4837 - <u>614</u>

9746 - <u>038</u>

2758 - <u>100</u>

Another code - <u>626</u>

Or if you have the Doctor's access card you could try that - <u>057</u>

If none of this excites you then do you

Enter the canteen - <u>071</u>

Try to get into the cleaners' cupboard - <u>571</u>

Try to enter the office of Kyla Mertens - <u>237</u>

Or

Return to the hall - <u>212</u>

# 136

You walk the path to the Lookout and see it before you, long before you reach it. A three story tower, it has a beacon on top which is shining out to the world, almost like a lighthouse for that side of the island.

Although you have been to the Lookout, you have never entered as it is the private hideaway of the Doctor. He has disappeared here for days sometimes but that may mean it holds clues for you. Enter the codeword **Tower**.


You reach the bottom of the Lookout, the rain still hammering down, and you see with dismay that it has a number pad and swipe card access. A warning is located under the number pad stating that an incorrect code entered twice will activate an alarm and authorities will come. There is some ivy growing up the side of the Lookout which may be another option. It leads up to a ladder on the side of the building that stops short of the ground floor. Maybe you can get access at the top.

Do you

Try to enter a code on the number pad (only if you have found one) – 672

Use the Doctor's swipe card on the reader if you have it – 520

Try to climb the Ivy – 277

Or

if this all seems to hard or unwise, you could simply keep on walking the coastal path to your next location at 988 but note that you have visited the Lookout

# 137

You grab a beer and crash onto the sofa with your feet up, supping gently on the beer. You get to thinking about what's been happening, wondering if you'll ever clear your name. After getting to the bottom of the beer you think about another one. As you get up for the fridge it dawns on you someone is at the door. You turn to see who it is but there's a gunshot.

Who was the murderer? Why did they do it? Well, you won't know because you are dead. Imagine letting your guard down like that. Let's grow up a little and try again at <u>001</u>

# 138

You grab a beer and crash onto the sofa with your feet up, supping gently on the beer. You get to thinking about what's been happening, wondering if you'll ever clear your name. After getting to the bottom of the beer you think about another one. As you get up for the fridge it dawns on you someone is at the door. You turn to see who it is but there's a gunshot.

Who was the murderer? Why did they do it? Well, you won't know because you are dead. Imagine letting your guard down like that. Let's grow up a little and try again at <u>001</u>

# 139

You run after the woman, but you slip on the wet floor and when you pick yourself up, she's away. By the time you reach the entrance, she is gone into the night. You return to the tomb and sweep the torch around finding a letter on the ground. Read it at 352

# 140

As you slide round the table you see the curtains billow again. You're not sure there's a draught or open window but maybe they did air the room. Suddenly the lights go off.

Do you

Search for the light switch – 900

Flee the room – 157

# 141

You tell the detective to check your belongings for the notelet from the Doctor to Elsie Gonzales that you found at the boathouse. When the notelet is brought to the detective from your belongings, he gives it some careful attention before turning back to you.

"So, the Doctor had some concerns about her. However, that's a stretch to then make out she's a killer. I think he was referring to what she could do to herself."

You're still in trouble. What else do you have?

If you have any of the following codewords go to that section. Follow the list downwards and only go to the first section that you have a codeword in.

**Space letter** – 656

**Granferno** – 017

**Taunt** – 027

**Grumble** – 446

**Pads, Paddy, Silent Papers, Cold Blood, Murder, Hitman, Merto** – 415

**Gutted** – 048

Otherwise – 995

# 142

Go to 965

# 143

You yell at the woman to stop but she's away and by the time you reach the entrance she is gone into the night. You return to the tomb and sweep the torch around finding a letter on the ground. Read it at 252

# 144

You punch in the numbers and the pad flashes red and a claxon sounds, deafening all around you. Someone might be on their way with all that noise, so you decide you need to run. Make your way to the coastal path at 549 and escape to another location.

# 145

You pummel the glass with your fists, but it doesn't want to budge. Time and again but to no avail you try, only giving yourselves sore hands in the process. You'll need to try something different back at 356

# 146

The door opens easily enough and there is a flight of stairs leading you up to a small corridor where you can see four doors. The first you come to has a small viewing window and shows a canteen. The door is open slightly and you can see someone inside. Stepping quietly past, you find three more doors, one entitled cleaners' cupboard, another "Doctor Munro" and the last "Kyla Mertens".

Do you

Enter the canteen - 083

Try to get into the cleaners' cupboard - 592

Examine the door belonging to Doctor Munro - 775

Try to enter the office of Kyla Mertens - 840

Or

Return to the hall - 805

## 147

You switch on the beam and see a pair of legs. They are slender in their trousers, and you struggle to remember what the women were wearing when you were found with the gun in your hand, the same one you are holding now. Whoever it is runs.

Do you

Shout at them to stop - 834

Run after them - 139

Shoot at them - 429

## 148

You turn and dive out the open window before running off in the dark as far away as possible. At first you hear something behind you but then it must have given up for there is nothing you can hear. Shaking and wet you arrive at the coastal path - 983

# 149

No one knows about this place except maybe the Doctor and Granma Munro, but then again, you took care of her. It is a rough two weeks, and you are barely getting by on water and the little food there is in the cave. You carefully come out at night after the fortnight and find the island mainly deserted except for the laboratory. The police must have come and gone, and you are able to sneak away from the island in the Doctor's cruiser.

You make for a foreign land and once ashore you manage to find some basic work and hide out in the country for a few years. One day on the television you see your face, described as the island murderer. Of course, you have no hair now and wear glasses. It seems you need to live in exile for the rest of your life.

Maybe this is a win, but you still don't know who set you up. Try to solve the mystery again at <u>001</u>.

# 150

You remember the letter from the folly from Kyla Mertens to a friend.

"he must be stopped. And if I cannot get the appropriate credit then I shall make sure he sees no reward from the work."

It was certainly a threat, but it is now gone, burnt in the folly fire. Should you mention it? Will it mean anything coming from you or will the police see it as a desperate attempt to avoid blame for the Doctor's murder? You will certainly need to use this knowledge wisely, if at all.

# 151

You walk the path to the Lookout and see it before you, long before you reach it. A three story tower, it has a beacon on top which is shining out to the world, almost like a lighthouse for that side of the island. Although you have been to the Lookout, you have never entered as it is the private hideaway of the Doctor. He has disappeared here for days sometimes but that may mean it holds clues for you.

You reach the bottom of the Lookout, the rain still drizzling now, and you see with dismay that it has a number pad and swipe card access. A warning is located under the number pad stating that an incorrect code entered twice will activate an alarm and authorities will come. There is some ivy growing up the side of the Lookout which may be another option. It leads up to a ladder on the side of the building that stops short of the ground floor. Maybe you can get access at the top.

Do you

Try to enter a code on the number pad (only if you have found one)- 482

Use the Doctor's swipe card on the reader if you have it - 134

Try to climb the Ivy - 004

 Or if this all seems to hard or unwise, you could simply keep on walking the coastal path to your next location at 990 but note that you have visited the Lookout

# 152

"It wasn't me," you say holding your hands up to Elsie. "Someone has framed me."

Elsie looks at you quizzically but then smiles. "I didn't think you had it in you. I'm so scared, I just ran out here in my heels. My feet are so sore. I think we should just get off the island. That's why I'm here. But I can't start these boats. But you are the pilot of the ferry, aren't you? You could help me escape. We could both run away. I have contacts. I could clear your name once we get away."

Do you

Wish to run away with Elsie on a boat - 677

Tell her no, you want to stay and clear your name - 906

## 153

You take a chart off the wall you recognise well, removing the drawing pins and fold it up. Place it in your inventory as a **local chart**. What will you do next?

Try to enter a code for the cupboard (only if you have found one)- 972

Shoot the cupboard open – 453

Or

Go to the Rec Room – 528

Investigate the room with no name – 685

Return to the lower floor – 370

## 154

What the heck, you go for it and speed the boat out into the waters. At first it all goes swimmingly, but then you feel something hit the underside of the vessel and you are suddenly pitched overboard out into the cold sea.

Do you have a lifejacket?

Yes – 344

No – 088

# 155

As you hit the ground you realise the blowtorch is still working. It ignites the fuel that has spilled from the bottles and the shed goes up in an inferno. You never find out if they find you innocent or guilty, as your curiosity has brought about your own end. You can try again at <u>001</u> and this time stick to the investigation and not idle whimsy.

# 156

The fountains area has got four descending fountains, leading down to the final water feature where the water is sent shooting through the air into the sea. The Doctor once told you that sea water was taken up to the top fountain by pump to then find its way through the various features back into the sea. But, as wonderful as the features are, there is not much to search.

Looking closely, you see a few potential areas to examine. There is a small folly beside the largest fountain, nearest to you. The second fountain has an area where you are able to throw coins into the fountain. There is a tunnel at the third fountain which you have never been in. And the last fountain has the walkway that the fountain shoots over before the water falls to the sea.

Do you

Make your way to the folly - <u>444</u>

Check out the coin throwing area - <u>704</u>

Head for the tunnel - <u>605</u>

Walk down to the final fountain and its walkway - <u>524</u>

Or

Take a look in the walled garden - <u>926</u>

Make your way to the greenhouse - <u>745</u>

Wander over to the gardening equipment sheds - <u>262</u>

Or decide to leave the Gardens by going to the coastal path - <u>211</u>

# 157

You run quickly back out into the hall, closing the door behind you. Just what was in there. Someone, surely there was someone, after all the hall lights are on. You take the table the telephone sits on and block the dining room door with it. You cannot hang about, but you still want to see if the house holds any more clues. Maybe you should go upstairs where you will have some distance between you and whoever was in the dining room. Or should you simply leave the house? After all, that could have been a murderer messing with the lights. Whatever you choose, you decide it's best to leave the ground floor alone.

Do you

Go upstairs – <u>119</u>

Go outside – <u>384</u>

# 158

"No, I need to stay here and clear my name."

"Okay," says Daniel "but be careful. I was their pride and joy and then they ditched me. Cleared me right out of the program. There are plenty of people here who will hang you to save their own skin."

With that, he steps forward and slips past you. He never looks back and you hear the outside door close abruptly.

You feel a little unsettled but look around the room. There are several canisters on the shelving, which must have looked like boxes in the dark. You open one and smell diesel. They are quite heavy, and you decide you can't simply carry them around. But you know where to come of you need them. Note the codeword **Fuel** in your code list.

That was eventful but what do you do next?

Check out the chart room – <u>848</u>

Go to the Rec Room – <u>528</u>

Investigate the room with no name – <u>685</u>

Return to the lower floor – <u>370</u>

# 159

The kitchenette has all the best of equipment including a coffee maker and a small grill. It also has a fridge and inside you find some sandwiches in a plastic tub. You open it and try one – salmon, your favourite. But here's no time to eat now. You can take the sandwiches with you by entering **Sandwiches** in your inventory. But time to get on.

Do you

Look inside the wardrobe – 896

Examine the bed – 789

Try out the chairs – 650

Or

Investigate "The Hollow" – 509

Dive into the lagoon and see if you can find the Doctor's secret stash – 810

Decide you have had enough of the lagoon and make your move to the coastal path and your next destination – 503

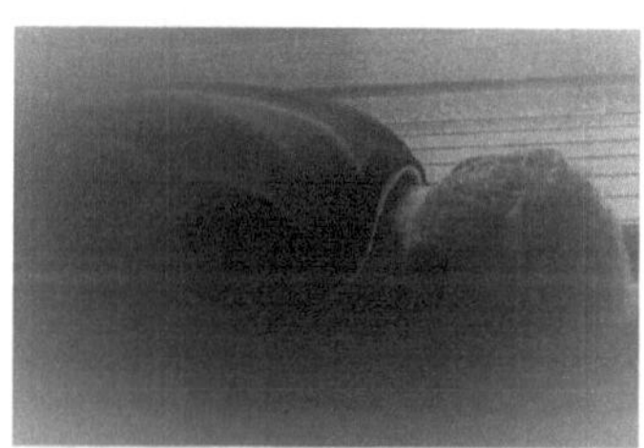

# 160

You turn around confident that the curtains are just being blown by the wind. After all, there is a storm outside. As you switch on the light, there is a pain between your shoulder blades, followed by another, ever sharper stabbing. You desperately try to support yourself on the wall, but you sink down and everything slowly becomes dim. The lights go off and you see a foot beside you, but you are too far gone to even recognise your killer before you slip off to the great adventure beyond this life.

Oh dear, you didn't last long. I suggest you start over, and this time take a bit more care when you see possible danger, after all, there is a murderer afoot.

**Return to 001 and start again. And this time, please be more careful.**

# 161

You pick up the paper and in the light, you try to make out the writing. It is in cursive and difficult to understand but you soon get the flow of it. As best you can make out, it says

*Thanks for taking the rap, Peter. You're a nice lad if somewhat stupid. Still, you'll get out again after some twenty years or so!*

Your heart skips a beat, and you hear a crash. One of the bridges has collapsed and you see a figure with an axe running for the other one. You have a bit of a head start but not much. You pocket the note and make a run for it. Enter the word **Taunt** in your code list and go <u>680</u>

# 162

You hold up your hands. "Look Kyla, I'm no threat. I was framed, trust me. You understand. I just want to clear my name."

"I don't trust you, Peter. You were holding the gun."

"But why would I kill my employer? I have it good here, Kyla," you tell her. "Somebody else must have wanted the Doctor dead. Do you know of anyone who would?"

"Certainly not me. I worked with the Doctor; we were onto something good here. The work on the performance enhancing drug would have put us up there, if we made it safe enough. He just needed to see that it was too powerful in its present form. Sometimes the Doctor had a very blinkered view of things."

You can see the woman is sweating and not happy with your presence. "So, who else would have a reason to kill our employer?" you ask.

"I shouldn't say this because it's confidential information, but Daniel Lyle was rejected from the tests this time around. He was the poster boy, but the drug was not working smoothly with him. Without it, he would be as good as you and me in his sport. Well, maybe not that bad but he certainly would be nowhere near the top."

"So, he'd be furious then. That's a good reason to carry out the murder as revenge. But would he know how to plant a gun on me?"

"Look, Peter, he could carry on with the drug if he stole supplies with the Doctor dead? What better story than to frame you and carry on with his career with no one knowing he was still using." The woman comes closer, seemingly more at home with you. "Let's go get a seat and talk properly, Peter. I'll help you."

You nod and as you turn to walk out the door, Kyla shoves you against the wall and the woman runs.

"Sorry, Peter, I just can't afford to trust anyone."

As you get to your feet, she is long gone. You take a quick look around the canteen but there's no evidence here. Time to get going again.

Do you

Try to get into the cleaners' cupboard – 571

Examine the door belonging to Doctor Munro – 439

Try to enter the office of Kyla Mertens – 237

Or

Return to the hall – 212

# 163

The darts board seems normal with the twenty segments and inner rings. At the side is a scoreboard starting at five hundred and one which is painted and then has scores in chalk descending. One of the totals has reached zero. Just like Patrick's company is written in a scrawl. Otherwise, there's nothing else here.

Do you

Examine the pool table - 340

Open the fridge - 559

Read the magazines - 531

Take hold of the scrap of paper - 790

Or

Enter the toilet - 828

Check out the chart room - 848

Investigate the room with no name - 685

Return to the lower floor - 370

# 164

You return to the main building and haul a load of fuel back to the cruiser before filling the tanks. It should be enough for a day or so. Starting the engine, you gracefully take the cruiser out into the rough waters by the island.

So, what is your plan?

Do you

Want to meet the authorities and surrender – <u>322</u>

Decide to try and outrun the authorities – <u>833</u>

# 165

You approach a fascinating marble board with four characters on it. It sits on the ground, slightly pronounced with a lip on all four edges of the board. The board has chess type squares but has only three squares per side giving a total of nine squares. You can see four different figurines on the board.

In the middle of the board is a carving of a woman with a laurel wreath on her head. She wears a long flowing garment and is cast in white. She has a sad look on her face with tears falling from one eye.

Two of the other figures are in the middle of a side, one to the left of the woman as you look and one beyond her. The last figure is on a corner square.

The three figures are a snake with three heads, an eagle with its wings outstretched, and a man with a large broadsword holding it high above his head. He is wearing chainmail and is facing the woman. The snake has one head extended out to the woman and the eagle has a wing reaching for her.

Walking around the board you can see no crevices, or openings. Giving the eagle a gentle push, you find it can be easily lifted, as can the other pieces when you try them.

Do you

Try to figure out this mystery – <u>820</u>

Shoot the pieces and board with your gun (if you have one) – <u>055</u>

Decide this is a waste of time and

Make for the tomb and shelter from the rain – <u>877</u>

Enter the temple – <u>273</u>

Check out the sacrificial slab – <u>742</u>

Or

Decide this area is no longer useful or too risky and continue along the coastal path at <u>996</u>

# 166

Breathing a sigh of relief, you work your way along the tunnel until you find a tiny alcove. On the ground is a small briefcase, something you identify by touch rather than sight. Taking it back to the tunnel entrance, you find it contains some documents indicating that Daniel Lyle has been dropped from certain tests he was to take part in. The actual detail around the tests is complex but it seems he had experienced increased performance in earlier tests he had done. Note the word **Tests** in your code list.

Now where do you want to go?

Make your way to the folly – <u>444</u>

Check out the coin throwing area – <u>704</u>

Walk down to the final fountain and its walkway – <u>524</u>

Or

Take a look in the walled garden – <u>926</u>

Make your way to the greenhouse – <u>745</u>

Wander over to the gardening equipment sheds – <u>262</u>

Or

Decide to leave the Gardens by going to the coastal path – <u>211</u>

# 167

You pour one of the phials on the cheese and throw it at the creature. At first it rears up and then sniffs the cheese. But it soon ignores it and begins to charge at you.

Do you have a gun? If so, use it – <u>261</u>

Otherwise – <u>960</u>

# 168

You try the key in the lock but that's not working. Do you have another key? If not then you'll need to go elsewhere.

If you have another key, is it

A key with green tape – 679

An ornate key – 700


If not then do you, if you haven't already

Enter the canteen – 071

Examine the door belonging to Doctor Munro – 439

Try to enter the office of Kyla Mertens – 237

Or

Return to the hall – 212


# 169

Go to 812


# 170

The Detective Inspector brushes his moustache as he enters the room and takes a seat opposite you. A recording machine is started and the man stares at you before giving a cough. His eyes are old and have seen everything, or so it seems to you. Can you bluff this man? Or will you tell the truth?

He says that everyone saw you beside the Doctor's body. He says at this time you are the prime suspect. However, he wants you to admit to it as things will be a lot quicker that way. Of course they will be, but you are innocent!

The detective now sits back in the chair and asks you to explain what happened. Do you know? Who will you blame?

"I didn't murder the Doctor. In fact, it was..."

Who will you say killed the Doctor? Remember you'll need some evidence to help your cause.

Was it

*Kyla Mertens* – <u>910</u>

*Patrick Davidson* – <u>495</u>

*Elsie Gonzales* – <u>746</u>

*Daniel Lyle* – <u>442</u>

*Grandma Munro* – <u>175</u>

# 171

You make your way over to the tree hut and climb a wooden ladder up to the small balcony at the front of the house. Stepping inside, you see a single room but one with a small kitchenette, a double bed, and a small wardrobe. There is a television on the wall and a small wine collection on a table. There are also two relaxing chairs in the middle of the room.

Well, the doctor certainly knows how to live but is there anything worth looking at in here?

Do you

Look inside the wardrobe - <u>896</u>

Examine the bed - <u>789</u>

Rifle through the kitchenette - <u>159</u>

Try out the chairs - <u>650</u>

Or

Investigate "The Hollow" - <u>509</u>

Dive into the lagoon and see if you can find the Doctor's secret stash - <u>810</u>

Decide you have had enough of the lagoon and make your move to the coastal path and your next destination - <u>503</u>

# 172

You swim closer to the rocky side of the lagoon and see the passageway in front of you.

Do you have any of the following codes in your code list?

Code **Sesame** - <u>513</u>

Code **Baba** - <u>808</u>

Neither - <u>611</u>

# 173

You tell the detective about the note you found in the gardens when you crossed the rope bridge to the hut. He listens to your story of how you were attacked with interest before disappearing to retrieve the note you spoke of from your confiscated belongings. He returns over two hours later.

"Mr O'Malley, you have been inaccurate in your accusations. The handwriting on the note is that of Elsie Gonzales. Having put pressure on Miss Gonzales she says she did this because she knew you killed the Doctor and were not set up. We have arrested her with attempted murder of yourself, but we checked out some other factors."

If you have any of the following codewords go to that section. Follow the list downwards and only go to the first section that you have a codeword in.

**Grumble** – 272

**Pads, Paddy, Silent Papers, Cold Blood, Murder, Hitman, Merto** – 282

**Gutted** – 048

Otherwise – 995

# 174

You throw caution to the wind and run as fast as you can to the front door, catching it by your fingertips and they become caught between the door and its frame. You suppress the scream that wants to come and using your other hand you open the door. Carefully you step inside before hearing the door click closed behind you. Well, you are inside and there's no sign of Patrick Davidson who must be in here somewhere. It's time to be careful as you search. Go to 805

# 175

"Grandma Munro," says the detective stroking his moustache. "You're going to have to show me some evidence sunshine, she's just an old woman. How on earth do you believe it's her? What can you tell me?"

You think over your evidence, but you don't have anything that would incriminate Daniel Lyle, specifically.

If you have the codeword **Taunt** and wish to use that evidence – 932

If not and,

You have the codeword **Gutted** – 048

If you have neither – 048

# 176

The keypad goes red, and a claxon begins to sound, deafening you. This is likely to bring lots of people and you decide to get as far away as possible from the building. You run out of the front door and make your way to the coastal path. Go there now at 986

# 177

What code will you try? Add the single digits of the code up, then add 50, and then go to the numbered section that corresponds with the total. If it starts with **Locker opened**, continue with that section. If not, then return here.

If you cannot open the padlock and want to give up, then choose another option.

Examine the dinghy – 044

Look at the lifejackets – 496

Take the stairs to the upper floor – 315

Or

Head over to the marina – 909

Or if you want to continue elsewhere take the coastal path at 981

# 178

"Daniel, just stop, I know who the real killer is."
Daniel holds up but keeps a distance from you.

"Maybe you do, maybe you don't but just keep away from me, alright. When they come from the mainland, you can tell them, and they can sort it all out. Until then I am staying clear of everyone. You understand. It's the safest way. I'm just a pawn."

With that Daniel looks to run away.

Do you

Tell him you are scared too – 921

If you have one, pull out your gun and threaten him with it for information – 646

Let him go – 007

# 179

You sit in the dark hearing the footsteps come right past you and you feel the sweat on your brow. You shake a little but control your nerves, remaining quiet as the footsteps pass by and go to the exit of the tomb. You wait several minutes until all is quiet again and you are sure the unknown intruder is clear of the tomb. Then you switch your torch back on and sweep the passageway again. You find a document on the floor of the tomb, which looks like a letter. Read it at 252

# 180

You hold up your hands, telling the old woman you have no gun. She shakes her head and looks beyond you.

"The portal is opening. I need to go. Tell the Sergeant that the alpha ray is not available, but I'll gut these reptiles yet."

Grandma Munro gives you a smile and wishes you "Good luck" as she brushes past you and runs down the stairs. Before you can react, she is gone, out the front door and off into the night, leaving you with a toilet before you. On the floor you see a magazine. Well, this should be great fun!


Do you

Read the magazine – 305

Examine the toilet (it still says that!) – 994

Or are you done with all this toilet shenanigans and instead

Examine the bed – 046

Check the silk dressing gowns – 505

Descend the stairs – 991

Or leave the Lookout completely and head for the coastal path – 990

# 181

You tell the detective to check your belongings for the note from the Doctor to Patrick Davidson that you found in the toilet bowl. When the note is brought to the detective from your belongings, he gives it some careful attention before turning back to you.

"So, there was a change of plans and Mr Davidson didn't like it. But if he killed the Doctor then who would make the decision not to go ahead. Kyla Mertens told us she wanted the drug stopped from going on commercial sale so simply killing the Doctor may not have been enough Do you have anything else you can tell or show me."

You're still in trouble. What else do you have?

If you have any of the following codewords go to that section. Follow the list downwards and only go to the first section that you have a codeword in.

**Taunt** - 321

**Grumble** - 446

**Pads, Paddy, Silent Papers, Cold Blood, Murder, Hitman, Merto** - 415

**Gutted** - 048

Otherwise read on:

The detective still says you have enough evidence against you that you have to go to trial. It seems that the jury sees enough uncertainty for you are found not guilty. However, the papers do not see it that way, a man with a gun in his hand at a body. Your life becomes a hell, followed by the press, until you leave the country. It might seem unfair but at least you are not in jail. As for who actually killed the Doctor, you still don't know. Maybe try again at 001.

# 182

You reach up to the box on the shelf and pull it down. It appears to be an old wooden box, quite long and slender. There is a lock at the front of it and the box is shut tight. Do you have a key to try on the box? If so – 734

If not there's two choices

You could try and smash the box by throwing it onto the ground – 207

Or you could leave it alone and instead

Take a look at the lawnmower – 558

Examine the blanket on the floor – 267

Or leave the shed and

Check out the fountains area – 526

Take a look in the walled garden – 625

Make your way to the greenhouse – 722

Wander over to the gardening equipment sheds – 121

Or

If you doubt the gardens will be of any use then take the coastal path at <u>770</u> but note that you have visited the gardens

# 183

You stride up to the door at the kitchen and find it is locked. No matter how you twist the handle there is no purchase from the door. But you are in luck, for there is a key in the lock. You try to turn it and find it doesn't move. Taking the key out of the lock you notice it is quite ornate and totally the wrong key for this simple lock. Take the key if you want and note it as an **ornate key** in your inventory.

What do you do now?

Do you want to examine the other side of the table – <u>140</u>

Check out what is causing the curtains to move – <u>251</u>

Examine the hatch – <u>401</u>

Return to the hall – <u>675</u>

# 184

You look at the photographs on the wall and note that most of them are of the Doctor's mother and him. Clearly, he loves the old woman and possibly dotes on her.

What next?

Do you

Examine the radio handset – <u>668</u>

Have a rifle through the drawers – <u>865</u>

Look at the writing desk – <u>897</u>

Or

Climb up the spiral staircase – <u>506</u>

Descend the spiral staircase - <u>821</u>

Decide to leave the Lookout and make your way to the coastal path – <u>990</u>

# 185

The Detective Inspector brushes his moustache as he enters the room and takes a seat opposite you. A recording machine is started and the man stares at you before giving a cough. His eyes are old and have seen everything, or so it seems to you. Can you bluff this man? Or will you tell the truth?

He says that everyone saw you beside the Doctor's body. He says at this time you are the prime suspect. However, he wants you to admit to it as things will be a lot quicker that way. Of course they will be, but you are innocent!

The detective now sits back in the chair and asks you to explain what happened. Do you know? Who will you blame?

"I didn't murder the Doctor. In fact, it was..."

Who will you say killed the Doctor? Remember you'll need some evidence to help your cause.

Was it

Kyla Mertens – 392

Patrick Davidson – 702

Elsie Gonzales – 717

Daniel Lyle – 443

Grandma Munro – 527

# 186

You fire your gun and Daniel tumbles to the ground. For a few moments, he struggles but then she is suddenly motionless. Your ears are ringing from the noise of the gun, and you reckon it must have carried for miles. Kneeling, you realise Daniel is dead. Note the codeword **Last Sprint** in your code list. This really isn't the game, is it? You're trying to solve a murder, not commit more. Panicking, you decide to flee before anyone else arrives.

Sprint to the costal path at 981 to get to your next destination

# 187

You tell the detective of your conversation with Kyla in the ruins and of how she admitted to feeling the drug was her work stolen by the Doctor.

"Now that is interesting, but it is also not proof. You still have a lot to answer for. Do you have anything to back up this evidence?"

If you have any of the following codewords go to that section. Follow the list downwards and only go to the first section that you have a codeword in.

**Taunt** – 357

**Scrap** – 239

**Grumble** – 446

**Pads, Paddy, Silent Papers, Cold Blood, Murder, Hitman, Merto** – 415

**Gutted** – 048

Otherwise, read on:

The detective still says you have enough evidence against you that you have to go to trial. It seems that the jury sees enough uncertainty for you are found not guilty. However, the papers do not see it that way, a man with a gun in his hand at a body. Your life becomes a hell, followed by the press, until you leave the country. It might seem unfair but at least you are not in jail. As for who actually killed the Doctor, you still don't know. Maybe try again at 001.

## 188

You hold your ground unable to see but the noise in the passage seems to be coming closer. There is some heavy breathing. Suddenly it all seems so close, and you feel your heart thumping.

Do you

Run back upstairs – 468

Stay and face whatever's coming – 202

## 189

You switch off the beam of light and hunch down in the passageway. As you wait, holding your breath, you hear footsteps coming closer, making their way towards you. They are so very close.

Do you

Switch on the light – 095

Stay in the dark – 594

## 190

You switch off the beam of light and hunch down in the passageway. As you wait, holding your breath, you hear footsteps coming closer, making their way towards you. They are so very close.

Do you

Switch on the light – <u>578</u>

Stay in the dark – <u>179</u>

# 191

The boathouse lies ahead of you at the end of the coastal path. Beyond it you see the path going on into the trees. The rain is beating down and the wind howls showing you a rough sea before you. The white of the wave tops come and go and despite the rain, the sound of crashing waves can be heard.

The boathouse has a small marina attached to it, with a large cruiser and a speedboat docked there. The main building is in darkness, much as you left it earlier that day, but you note that the ferry boat you usually pilot is gone, having made a return to the other side earlier that day for workers to get home. Enter the code word **Ferry Gone** in your code list.

The building has two levels, the lower level a covered dock and the upper level containing rooms for charting and refreshment. It all looks a lot less friendly than usual, given the darkness and the situation.

Do you

Make for the main building – <u>795</u>

Head over to the marina – <u>465</u>

Or

If you want to continue elsewhere take the coastal path at 980


## 192

You punch in the code and the pad turns red and a coarse noise like a bad input on a computer sounds. Nothing happens and you are left with the pad again.

Do you enter another code? Which one?


2758 - 774

3267 - 144

9746 - 343

4837 - 616

Another code - 078

Or do you leave the pad alone? If so, make your next choice at 037


## 193

The boat tips up and you are thrown out into the surf. You get caught by the undertow and you are dragged out. You have no extra buoyancy and cannot get to the surface. Despite your best efforts you don't find the surface of the water again.

It's three weeks before your body surfaces at an inlet on the mainland. The police had thought you escaped because the dinghy was never found but now, they know their killer has suffered natural justice. Who actually killed the Doctor? Well, you'll never know.

Next time, listen to the maritime authorities and take a lifejacket. You can try again at <u>001</u>

# 194

You wander over to the hedgerow, looking carefully into the darkness. You definitely heard and saw something and now push back a piece of hedge. A fist hits you in the face and you spin around falling into the garden.

Do you

Run - <u>728</u>

Turn to fight back – <u>825</u>

# 195

The wind takes the feet from under you, but you fall heavily onto the roof before sliding off and landing clumsily on the balcony. It takes you several minutes to recover but you are in one piece, a little bruised but nothing broken. When you rise, you manage to smash the window with the piece of metal from the weathervane and gratefully step into the room beyond, delighted you are still in one piece. Go 824

# 196

You tell the detective of your conversation with Kyla in the ruins and of how she admitted to feeling the drug was her work stolen by the Doctor.

"That's good but it's not clinching it for me, have you anything more?"

If you have any of the following codewords go to that section. Follow the list downwards and only go to the first section that you have a codeword in.

**Scrap** – 239

**Taunt** – 357

**Grumble** – 446

**Pads, Paddy, Silent Papers, Cold Blood, Murder, Hitman, Merto** – 415

**Gutted** – 048

Otherwise, read on:

The detective still says you have enough evidence against you that you have to go to trial. It seems that the jury sees enough uncertainty for you are found not guilty. However, the papers do not see it that way, a man with a gun in his hand at a body. Your life becomes a hell, followed by the press, until you leave the country. It might seem unfair but at least you are not in jail. As for who actually killed the Doctor, you still don't know. Maybe try again at <u>001</u>.

# 197

As you hit the ground you realise the blowtorch is still working. It ignites the fuel that has spilled from the bottles and the shed goes up in an inferno. You never find out if they find you innocent or guilty, as your curiosity has brought about your own end. You can try again at <u>001</u> and this time stick to the investigation and not idle whimsy.

# 198

You remember the letter you found in the folly and ask the detective to fetch it from your bag. Now in the full light he reads it to you. It is a letter stating that

Doctor Munro has been taking the credit for Kyla's work.

"He must be stopped. And if I cannot get the appropriate credit then I shall make sure he sees no reward from the work."

"Wow," says the detective, "that helps you a lot, but do you have anything more.

If you have any of the following codewords go to that section. Follow the list downwards and only go to the first section that you have a codeword in.


**Theft** - 617

**Confess** - 187

**Scrap** - 079

**Taunt** - 864

**Grumble** - 583

**Pads, Paddy, Silent Papers, Cold Blood, Murder, Hitman, Merto** - 636

**Gutted** - 048


Otherwise read on:

The detective still says you have enough evidence against you that you have to go to trial. It seems that the jury sees enough uncertainty for you are found not guilty. However, the papers do not see it that way, a man with a gun in his hand at a body. Your life becomes a hell, followed by the press, until you leave the country. It might seem unfair but at least you are not in jail. As for who actually killed the Doctor, you still don't know. Maybe try again at <u>001</u>.

# 199

You move the figure and place it in your desired spot. At first nothing happens but then you notice that the woman is crumbling. In a few seconds the entire figure has collapsed. You try to put your figure back but realise that the remaining three are all now stuck fast to the ground. How does this crazy game work? Frustrated you decide to move on.

Do you

Make for the tomb and shelter from the rain – <u>033</u>

Enter the temple – <u>280</u>

Check out the sacrificial slab – <u>246</u>

Or

Decide this area is no longer useful or too risky and continue along the coastal path at <u>998</u>

# 200

There is a doubt in your mind about this plan. Elsie and the Doctor know this place. He's dead but she isn't. You hide out, fearing every sound in the cave and one day, a police officer walks through a secret passage in the cave, arresting you. Enter the codeword **Caught** in your list and try to defend yourself at <u>519</u>

# 201

You tell the detective about your threatening note from when someone tried to kill you at the fountains. The detective takes it away and returns an hour later with a smile on his face.

"We checked out your story about nearly being killed and the handwriting on the note. I believe you son, and the writing is that of Patrick Davidson. I have just arrested him for your attempted murder. However, you are still a suspect for the Doctor's death. Do you have any other evidence?"

You shake your head nervously.

If you have any of the following codewords go to that section. Follow the list downwards and only go to the first section that you have a codeword in.

**Grumble** - 583

**Pads, Paddy, Silent Papers, Cold Blood, Murder, Hitman, Merto** - 636

**Gutted** - 048


Otherwise read on:

The detective still says you have enough evidence against you that you have to go to trial. It seems that the jury sees enough uncertainty for you are found not guilty. However, the papers do not see it that way, a man with a gun in his hand at a body. Your life becomes a hell, followed by the press, until you leave the country. It might seem unfair but at least you are not in jail. As for who actually killed the Doctor, you still don't know. Maybe try again at <u>001</u>.

# 202

You peer into the darkness but you can only hear someone coming. You hold your breath, eyes straining but as you finally catch the faint outline of a figure, you realise it is on top of you. Something hits you on top of the head.

In the following days, the police blame you for the murder and the person who attacked you walks away scot-free from there dastardly deed with the Doctor. Of course it's..., no you'll need to play again at <u>001</u>, but this time beware the dark

# 203

The buzzer howls even louder this time and the number pad flashes before the numbers change from bright green to red. Looks like it's locked the door. More than that it will have set off an alarm. Time to get out of here. You run hard around the laboratory to the coastal path at <u>983</u>

# 204

Inside the shed you see a lawnmower, a box on a shelf, and a blanket on the floor of the shed. There are several other bottles higher up on shelves, but you can't reach them. The shed is dark but small and it seems warmer than it should.

Do you

Take a look at the lawnmower – <u>558</u>

Get the box on the shelf – <u>182</u>

Examine the blanket on the floor – <u>267</u>

# 205

You grab the desk with both hands and begin to shake it violently, trying to open the drawers. As you shake them, you hear a quiet, *psst!* and something hits you in the shoulder. Suddenly everything goes dark.

You wake up and the room looks the same, but you feel that time has passed. Suddenly you get nervous that you may have been here too long, and you need to get a move on. Without a thought you run out of the Lookout and make your way to the coastal path, keen to try and find clues in another location. Go to <u>990</u>

## 206

You enter the numbers, and you hear a click and some whirring. You try the handle, and the door opens easily. Go 854

## 207

You pick up the box and hurl it at the ground in front of you. There's an almighty crack of gunfire and a shot ricochets briefly around the shed. Fortunately, it doesn't hit you, but that noise was so loud, you panic and decide to get out of the gardens quickly. You flee to the coastal path at 770

## 208

As you pull out the cleaver, a note comes away with it from inside the block. You place the cleaver on the table and open the note seeing a handwritten message that reads:

"I knew you'd go looking for help. Well, this won't help you as the handles been poisoned. But I am nothing if not sporting. There's an antidote somewhere on the island, so you'd better find it. Good luck. By the way, if you don't find it, the police will have a corpse not a suspect on their hands. You might last until morning. The formulas called Capernaum, just so you know."

Oh heck, you're in trouble now. You'd better find that antidote. Mark the word **Capernaum** on your code list. Looks like you need to hurry up.

What are you going to do next?

Check out the fridge freezer - <u>822</u>

Have a look through the cupboards - <u>887</u>

Examine the pots on the cooker - <u>129</u>

Examine the hatch - <u>347</u>

Return to the hall - <u>675</u>

# 209

You tell the detective about the magazine article you read, that Patrick Davidson's company is a start-up in need of money.

"That's not evidence. It's a big jump to go from a magazine article to a conviction. You have nothing."

If you have any of the following codewords go to that section. Follow the list downwards and only go to the first section that you have a codeword in.

**Bowl** - <u>181</u>

**Taunt** - <u>321</u>

**Grumble** - <u>446</u>

**Pads, Paddy, Silent Papers, Cold Blood, Murder, Hitman, Merto** - <u>415</u>

**Gutted** - <u>048</u>

Otherwise read on:

The detective arrests you for the Doctor's murder saying that you were still seen with the gun over the body. All you have is a potential heated comment. At the trial you cut a lonely figure as it only takes the jury an hour to convict you. From your jail cell you wonder if you were right in your choice of killer. You'll never know. Maybe try again at 001.

# 210

This time the pad flashes red in a crazy fashion and you can hear an alarm going off. You look around you in a panic wondering if anyone is close and coming for you. Best not to wait around and besides you can't get into the Lookout anyway. You run to the coastal path to choose your next location at 988

# 211

You find the coastal path at the end of the gardens and realise you can walk one of two ways; take the right-hand path to the lagoon or take the left to the ruins. Choose wisely for you won't be coming back this way.

Do you

Go right to the lagoon – 879

Go left to the ruins – 759

## 212

The entrance hall of the laboratory is clean and efficient with some chairs and a table with magazines. But there is no reception desk, and you wonder if they get many visitors. From the hall there are three doors indicating the following: Offices, laboratory, special projects.

Do you

Try the door labelled "Offices" – 099

See if you can enter the laboratory – 678

Head off to the special projects – 425

Or maybe you could check out the magazines – 985

Or

Leave the building and head to the coastal path to try another location – 986

## 213

Do you have codeword **Silent papers** – 497

If not – 200

# 214

Breathing a sigh of relief, you work your way along the tunnel until you find a tiny alcove. On the ground is a small briefcase, something you identify by touch rather than sight. Taking it back to the tunnel entrance, you find it contains some documents indicating that that Doctor Flavius' mother is struggling with reality. But despite the fact she is at risk, the Doctor has insisted on keeping her close and not sending her away to a medical facility.

Now where do you want to go?

Make your way to the folly – 766

Check out the coin throwing area – 579

Walk down to the final fountain and its walkway – 676

Or

Take a look in the walled garden – 625

Make your way to the greenhouse – 722

Wander over to the gardening equipment sheds – 121

Or

Decide to leave the Gardens by going to the coastal path – 770

# 215

You pick up the man and move him to the other side of the woman like you would jump a piece in checkers. As you let the female figurine, rest on her new space, you see a small drawer pop out from the edge of the board. Inside you find a key with a large dolphin on a key chain. You try to close the drawer, but it won't budge and when you now try to move the pieces, they seem to be stuck fast. How unusual. Still, you have a new key so note it in your inventory as **Dolphin key**. There seems to be nothing else you can do here so

Do you

Make for the tomb and shelter from the rain – 033

Enter the temple – 280

Check out the sacrificial slab – 246

Or

Decide this area is no longer useful or too risky and continue along the coastal path at 998

# 216

Inside the shed you see a lawnmower, a box on a shelf, and a blanket on the floor of the shed. There are several other bottles higher up on shelves, but you can't reach them. The shed is dark but small and it seems warmer than it should.

Do you

Take a look at the lawnmower – 311

Get the box on the shelf – 535

Examine the blanket on the floor – 699

# 217

You stand up and look all around you. With the rain, it's hard to hear but something suddenly moves to your right, directly towards you. You jump but then suddenly realise it's a rat, which sees you and panics, heading off into the darkness. You search the BBQ again and find a piece of burnt paper.

You take the paper up to the house and by a dim light you read a piece of paper which indicates that Dr Munro had borrowed significant amounts of money from Patrick Davidson. How was he going to pay that back?

You note that evidence and ponder your next move

Check out the lounger and table – 518

Or

Pay a visit to the private garden where you saw the glint of light – 914

Take a look at the patio – 662

Or

Decide to head off on one of the paths – 297

# 218

You step onto the slab and then lie prostrate on it to try and read the engraving in the middle. It is difficult and instead you trace it with your fingers. It takes a moment, but you manage it.

*Neptune says thanks for his lunch*

Well, that's a bit of a laugh from whoever restored this, after all that's not from anyone from the past. You chortle to yourself and then you hear ropes moving and the slab begins to tilt to the sea. You look across and someone is at the mechanism. You can't tell who and have little time to think about it as you descend off the slab and onto the rocks below.

They find your body over a week later when the sea gives you back. They say guilt drove you to it, but it was a murder. Problem is, you'll never know who. Next time let's not climb on board ancient killing devices! Try again at <u>001</u>

# 219

There are three drawers along one side of the desk, but all are locked. There's nowhere to pull them open but instead one has a lock for a key. What will you do?

Do you

Try a key you have – 756

Try to jimmy the drawer if you have a crowbar – 307

Or instead

Try to put a code into the computer – (only if you have found one) 283

Read the papers – 500

Or just leave the desk alone and

Look at the small pile of books and the chair – 634

Check out the picture on the wall – 098

Examine the coat stand – 428

# 220

The computer looks fairly standard, but it is locked out and you don't know the password to gain access. There are a large number of papers scattered about and it will take a bit of reading to get through them all. That's if you can make sense of them, after all, most seem to be random numbers, their meaning hidden to you. There are also three drawers on the desk which you could examine.

Do you

Try to put a code into the computer (only if you have found one) – <u>283</u>

Read the papers – <u>500</u>

Try to open the drawers – <u>219</u>

# 221

You take your torch out and switch it on. The beam of light penetrates the darkness but there are still plenty of dark areas either side of the beam. Yet you can see a passageway heading down into the ground and you feel a chill from the walls. The air is certainly colder down here. As you walk deeper into the tomb, you hear a sound up ahead, like footsteps. You freeze instantly.

Do you have a gun and wish to draw it – <u>889</u>

Do you wish to switch off the torch and wait in the dark for the owner of the footsteps – <u>189</u>

Do you want to keep on searching – <u>999</u>

Or

Decide this is a bad idea and instead

Enter the temple – <u>280</u>

Check out the sacrificial slab – <u>246</u>

Look at the gaming board – <u>426</u>

Or

Decide this area is no longer useful or too risky and continue along the coastal path at <u>998</u>

# 222

You remember the cave under the lagoon. That could be a good place to hide out. There was a little food, some drinks. It's a possibility.

If you want to use this option – 224

If not, or you want to consider other options then return to 1000. You can return here if needed to follow this option.

# 223

You remember the note from Kyla Mertens to her father that you found in the boathouse.

"I told him as his research assistant that the drug is too powerful and not suitable for public distribution, but he will not listen. I need to take decisive action, father. I shall mail this note to you and pray for me as I enter a dark place."

This certainly shows motive and may help you. But is it enough to show she murdered the Doctor?

# 224

You go off-path through the vegetation back to the lagoon. It's slow work but as you break the greenery at the lagoon, you are relieved to find that no one has reached here yet. You dive into the lagoon and find your way back to the cave underneath.

Which of the following codewords do you have?

**Granocide** or **Iberian** – 843

**Swim** – 776

If none of these – 213

## 225

You begin to sweat, even through your already soaked clothes as something approaches. As it nears you struggle to see it but it's an animal of some sort with padded feet and it is quick. Seeing you, it tears past, about the height of your knees. Go 214

## 226

You punch in the code and the pad flashes green but nothing else happens and you are left with the pad again. You decide to leave the pad alone but enter the word **Baba** in your code list. Make your next choice at 816

# 227

You spend half an hour swimming around, diving up and down but to no avail. The rumours of the Doctor's treasure are ill-founded. You climb out of the lagoon and decide you won't go back in unless you find better lighting. So, what next?

Do you

Investigate "The Hollow" – 819

Climb up to the tree hut – 410

Decide you have had enough of the lagoon and make your move to the coastal path and your next destination – 549

# 228

You think there is a door in the rock but as much as you push at the rock within the outline you can see, nothing moves. You dive down several times, but nothing changes. Maybe it's nothing. You climb out of the lagoon and decide you won't go back in unless you find better lighting.

Do you

Investigate "The Hollow" – 509

Climb up to the tree hut – 171

Decide you have had enough of the lagoon and make your move to the coastal path and your next destination – 503

## 229

You examine the set of drawers beginning at the top, finding a selection of socks and pants. There is also a set of keys hidden away and you wonder what they could be for. They are silver, modern and have a surfer logo attached to them. You may enter **surfer logo keys** in your inventory if you wish to. They do seem very familiar.

The remaining drawers have sweaters and trousers and other daywear but there is little else of note.

Let's move on. Do you

Do you

Examine the radio handset – 989

Check out the photographs – 067

Look at the writing desk – 361

Or

Climb up the spiral staircase – 824

Descend the spiral staircase - 845

Decide to leave the Lookout and make your way to the coastal path – 988

## 230

You make for the mainland, your hand on the wheel and Elsie hanging onto you. She seems scared but you fight through the waves before arriving at a small beach alcove which Elsie seems to conveniently know about. There is a car with keys in the ignition up on the cliff top above where Elsie stops you and tells you she has something to confess. With the beach behind you, some fifty feet below, Elsie confesses to killing the Doctor, saying she hated his drugs that he was designing to enhance human performance as her brother had suffered before.

As your eyes open, she bows her head asking if you can forgive her and run with her, away to a new life abroad. She has it all arranged, and you can come to, but she wants you to promise her.

Do you

Promise her and run with her - 030

Promise her but intend to betray her later – 898

Tell her no way and that she should hand herself in – 604

## 231

The boat tips up but somehow it manages to come back down without tipping. That was close but you soon find calmer water as you reach the open sea and make for a foreign country. Go to 871.

## 232

You throw caution to the wind and run as fast as you can to the front door, catching it by your fingertips and they become caught between the door and its frame. You suppress the scream that wants to come and using your other hand you open the door. Carefully you step inside before hearing the door click closed behind you. Well, you are inside and there's no sign of Kyla Mertens who must be in here somewhere. It's time to be careful as you search. Go to 212

## 233

As you get close to the stools, you notice that one of them is smashed. It appears that there was a heated debate, or maybe even a fight. There are several pieces of paper on the floor, and you try to pick them up and place them on the nearby bench. You don't have all the pieces, but you can make out the words, "rejected for further trials". The letters DL are also recognisable.

Mean anything to you? Where now?

Do you

Examine the file – 600

Look in the refrigerator – 054

Check out the lab coats – 652

Or

If this is all too much you could return to the entrance hall – 805

# 234

You step inside the rec room and see a pool table in the middle with a darts board on the far wall. There's a fridge holding beers along the nearest wall as well as a sofa and some magazines scattered around. There's also a scrap of paper on the floor, under the pool table.

The room is decorated with a sports theme, and you know it as the Doctor's hangout when down at the boats, but you have never been in this room. After all, you are only staff! Or at least you were.

Do you

Examine the pool table – 110

Look at the darts board – 248

Open the fridge – 075

Read the magazines – 424

Take hold of the scrap of paper – 270

Or

Enter the toilet – 655

Check out the chart room – 618

Investigate the room with no name – 521

Return to the lower floor – 795

# 235

You cautiously step out onto the rope bridge nearest to you which is swinging in the wind. You don't trust it and place two hands on the ropes at either side and slowly make your way over to the hut. When you reach it you step inside but find the platform it is standing on to be moving in the wind as well and you stomach goes queasy.

The hut is very basic with a bench and a table but also with lots of room for a crowd to stand. The wind howls outside and you shiver as you bend down to the table. There is a sheet of paper on the table with some rather swirly handwriting.

Do you

Decide there's nothing here and return via the rope bridge – 857

Examine the paper closely - 318

Look out to sea and check if there is anyone coming to the island, maybe the authorities – 419

# 236

So, you have a code. As you go to type in the numbers you realise that there is a sign underneath stating that only 2 attempts are allowed before a lockout ensues for an hour and an alert is sent. Crikey, you'd better get this right.

What code do you enter?

4837 - <u>019</u>

9746 - <u>890</u>

3267 - <u>335</u>

2758 - <u>853</u>

Another code - <u>760</u>

Or do you decide this is too risky and decide instead to

Hide in the undergrowth surrounding the facility and see what happens - <u>971</u>

Walk around the facility and see what you can find - <u>739</u>

Call this a bust and find the coastal path - <u>986</u>

## 237

The door to Kyla Mertens' office appears to be open but there are no lights on in the office. You hesitate at the door and think you can hear someone inside the office. Maybe this is not such a good idea.

Do you

Continue inside - 786

Stand and wait - 948

 Or if you haven't already

Enter the canteen - 071

Try to get into the cleaners' cupboard - 571

Examine the door belonging to Doctor Munro - 439

Or

Return to the hall - 212

## 238

Go to 111

## 239

You tell the detective about the note from Kyla Mertens to her father, saying how Doctor Munro must be stopped and that she is entering a dark place.

"That's enough," says the detective. "I'm going to investigate Miss Mertens rather more closely."

It takes the rest of the day, but the detective returns in the evening letting you know that Kyla Mertens has buckled under questioning and that you are a free man. He congratulates you and you step out into the fresh air once more. It feels good to be free and you wonder what else life has in store for you. Well done, super sleuth!

## 240

Kyla gets close to you and reaches out a hand. You don't trust her and fire your gun. You're not the best at handling a firearm and you watch her tumble to the ground. After a few moments, she doesn't move. You get close and realise you have killed her.

Enter the codeword **Murder** in your code list. You do realise that you are meant to be investigating a murder, not committing one. The gunshot was loud, and you think others may now come so you decide to get out of here by running to the coastal path at <u>998</u>

## 241

You put the key in the lock and twist it, opening the box. Inside you find a gun and realise it is fully loaded. You can pocket it if you want by **noting the gun in your inventory.** What now?

Do you

Take a look at the lawnmower – <u>558</u>

Examine the blanket on the floor – <u>267</u>

Or leave the shed and

Check out the fountains area – <u>526</u>

Take a look in the walled garden – <u>625</u>

Make your way to the greenhouse – <u>722</u>

Wander over to the gardening equipment sheds – <u>121</u>

Or if you doubt the gardens will be of any use then take the coastal path at <u>770</u> but note that you have visited the gardens.

## 242

From the letter you found in the garden from Granma Munro to the Doctor, you know she is insane. She states that she has been probed for her DNA by aliens. Or is that a code? Surely, there isn't an alien invasion happening! If she's this mad, could she be a killer too? Who is to say?

## 243

Your heart sinks as the keypad flashes and then the numbers turn red. A claxon begins sounding in the building. You feel the panic rising and glance up and down the hall. You need to get out of here quickly. It's time to move on to the coastal path. You flee the building and reach the path at 983

## 244

There is a whirring sound from the lock, and you gently push the door open. Step inside at 845

## 245

Daniel bolts past you and you lift your arms up letting him go. He soon exits the main door, and the boathouse becomes silent again.

You feel a little unsettled but look around the room. There are several canisters on the shelving, which must have looked like boxes in the dark. You open one and smell diesel. They are quite heavy, and you decide you can't simply carry them around. But you know where to come if you need them. Note the codeword **Fuel** in your code list.

That was eventful but what do you do next?

Check out the chart room – 848

Go to the Rec Room – 528

Investigate the room with no name – 685

Return to the lower floor – 370

# 246

The sacrificial slab is a large wooden block with a slab inset, and appears to have been restored. The slab, a square piece of marble, framed by wood, has several ropes running from it to a lever several metres away. Half of the slab hangs out over the sea, and you think you might understand how this works. In the old days, the poor victim would be sacrificed by the slab being tipped and the person would be deposited into the sea below. It seems somewhat brutal but surely a replica.

From your position beside the slab, you can see writing in the middle of it, but it is very finely engraved, probably from wear. The mechanism across from you looks fascinating.

Do you

Examine the mechanism – 664

Climb onto the slab and read the engraving – 348

Leave the slab alone and

Make for the tomb and shelter from the rain – 033

Enter the temple – 280

Look at the gaming board – 426

Or

Decide this area is no longer useful or too risky and continue along the coastal path at 998

## 247

You take a shot at Daniel and watch him fall to the ground. Hopefully you've tagged him so he can't escape. You approach and there seems to be quite a bit of blood. Getting nearer, you check his breathing and realise he isn't. Well, if you weren't a murderer before, you are now. You'd better get moving and also start thinking how to explain this away. Note the codeword **Killer** in your code list. Run hard to the coastal path at 211 and try to live with your guilt.

## 248

The darts board seems normal with the twenty segments and inner rings. At the side is a scoreboard starting at five hundred and one which is painted and with scores in chalk descending below it. One of the totals has reached zero. 'Just like Patrick's company' is written in a scrawl. Otherwise, there's nothing else here.

Do you

Examine the pool table - 110

Open the fridge - 075

Read the magazines - 424

Take hold of the scrap of paper - 270

Or

Enter the toilet - 655

Check out the chart room - 618

Investigate the room with no name - 521

Return to the lower floor - 795

# 249

Oh dear, that hasn't worked. You have one try left. Do you wish to try again? If so

4837 - 243

9746 - 371

3267 - 880

Another code - 132

Or if you have the Doctor's access card you could try that - 557

If none of this excites you then do you

Enter the canteen – <u>083</u>

Try to get into the cleaners' cupboard – <u>592</u>

Try to enter the office of Kyla Mertens – <u>840</u>

Or

Return to the hall – <u>805</u>

# 250

You look at the tin and find it to be ornate and have a relief of cupcakes on the lid. Opening it, you find several cupcakes inside. Hungrily you eat, finding them to be delicious. However, that's enough stuffing your face. If you wish you can take them with you by entering **tin of cupcakes** in your inventory. But what next?

Do you

Swipe the card reader with the Doctor's access card, if you have it – <u>963</u>

Enter a code on the pad (only if you have found one) (only if you have found one) – <u>320</u>

Or leave the item alone and

Investigate the switch – <u>003</u>

Or if none of this inspires you, go back to the lagoon entrance and make another choice – <u>423</u>

# 251

As you near the curtains, you note that they bulge, and you could swear you see the shape of a person in them. As you step closer that shape seems to retreat. You look for feet at the bottom of the curtains but there are none. Of course, you don't know how deep the window is set back so someone could still be there. You feel nervous but know that it would be unwise to simply carry on in this room. Instead, you must either leave or see who is behind the curtains. You gulp realising the next choice you make could be crucial.

Do you

Pull the curtains open – <u>794</u>

Leave the room for the hall – <u>122</u>

# 252

The letter is from Kyla Mertens to Doctor Munro and accuses him in no uncertain detail of stealing her work with regard to a performance enhancing drug. She alludes to his papers which detail her work but with his name on it. The last paragraph indicates that the pair should meet, and it has today's date on it.

This is quite a development, and you pocket the letter. Make a note in your code list of the code **Theft**.

There's nothing else in here so it's time to route back out of the tomb and instead

Enter the temple – 273

Check out the sacrificial slab – 742

Look at the gaming board – 165

Or

Decide this area is no longer useful or too risky and continue along the coastal path at 996

## 253

What code do you have? Is it

9746 – 764

4837 – 313

A different code – 740

## 254

"Daniel I really want to help but I haven't got a key for the boat."

"Okay, But I'm not staying with you," says Daniel "Be careful. I was their pride and joy and then they ditched me. Cleared me right out of the program. There are plenty of people here who will hang you to save their own skin."

With that, he steps forward and slips past you. He never looks back and you hear the outside door close abruptly.

You feel a little unsettled but look around the room. There are several canisters on the shelving, which must have looked like boxes in the dark. You open one and smell diesel. They are quite heavy, and you decide you can't simply carry them around. But you know where to come of you need them. Note the codeword **Fuel** in your code list.

That was eventful but what do you do next?

Check out the chart room – 848

Go to the Rec Room – 528

Investigate the room with no name – 685

Return to the lower floor – 370

# 255

Your heart sinks as the keypad flashes and then the numbers turn red. A claxon begins sounding in the building. You feel the panic rising and glance up and down the hall. You need to get out of here quickly. It's time to move on to the coastal path. You flee the building and reach the path at 983

# 256

Where do you move the woman?

Beside the Snake – 111

Beside the man – 238

Beside the Eagle – 772

# 257

You lower your gun and walk from the temple. Getting a short distance away, you turn back and look at Kyla who is standing against the wind in her long coat. She shakes her head and then turns back, walking into the temple.

You decide to stay clear of the temple, but you can still search other parts of the ruins of you haven't already.

Do you

Make for the tomb and shelter from the rain – 033

Check out the sacrificial slab – 246

Look at the gaming board – 426

Or

Decide this area is no longer useful or too risky and continue along the coastal path at 998

## 258

You fire your gun and Elsie tumbles to the ground. For a few moments, she struggles but then she is suddenly motionless. Your ears are ringing from the noise of the gun, and you reckon it must have carried for miles. Kneeling, you realise Elsie is dead. Note the codeword **Silent papers** in your code list. This really isn't the game, is it? You're trying to solve a murder, not commit more. Panicking, you decide to flee before anyone else arrives.

Sprint to the costal path at <u>980</u> to get to your next destination

## 259

The hatch has a sliding lock, and you pull it back allowing the hatch to open. However, you see a complimentary door on the other side, which is locked, possibly from the other side. After all that's how these food hatches work. You are about to close the hatch up again when you notice a small key at the side of the opening. It has no markings except for a small piece of green tape on it.

Pocket it if you want and make a note of it in your inventory as **green tape key**.

What do you do now?

Do you want to examine the other side of the table – 140

Take the door to the kitchen – 183

Check out what is causing the curtains to move – 251

Return to the hall - 675

# 260

How fast can you run?

This fast – 471

Maybe this quick – 565

Surely not this quick – 106

# 261

You take out the gun and fire it quickly four times. Something in front of you is knocked back several feet but the noise of the gun reverberates around the room and probably the building. You are able to escape by the way you entered the building, leaving the creature for dead, but decide to strike out on foot for the coastal path before anyone arrives to find out the reason for the gunshots. Join the coastal path at 986

# 262

You approach the gardening sheds and see four different sheds in front of you. Three of them are locked and any keys you have are not the correct size for the padlocks. One is open with the door slightly ajar.

Do you

Step inside - 216

Or

Check out the fountains area - 156

Take a look in the walled garden - 926

Make your way to the greenhouse - 745

Or if you doubt the gardens will be of any use then take the coastal path at 211 but note that you have visited the gardens

# 263

The cellar is not overly large, and you are able to look around it quickly. There are a number of bottles of wine, and you recognise some as the bottles the Doctor asked you to fetch. Carefully you try not to touch any and look behind them. Apart from a few mouse droppings, you see nothing of interest.

Do you (if you have not already):

Examine the Doctor's body - 733

Leave the cellar - 675

# 264

The number pad goes red, and you hear a horrible buzzer indicate you are wrong.

Do you try another number?

4837 – 279

3267 – 309

9746 – 032

Another code – 294

Or do you

Use the Doctor's swipe card on the reader if you have it – 134

Try to climb the Ivy – 004

Or

if this all seems to hard or unwise, you could simply keep on walking the coastal path to your next location at 990 but note that you have visited the Lookout

# 265

Quickly, you make your way over to the diary on the table and begin to flick through the pages. There's a lot of dates that show meetings with Kyla Mertens, Daniel Lyle, and the occasional one with Patrick Davidson.

The Patrick Davidson meetings all seem to have taken place off the island while the others are in the laboratory. There is no mention of Elsie Gonzales and Grandma Munro is only mentioned on her birthday. There are a few meetings pencilled in after today's date, but none are with the suspects in this matter. You close the diary unsure if you are any wiser.

Do you (if you have not already done so):

Enter the sitting room – 763

Enter the dining room – 576

Enter the kitchen – 298

Go upstairs – 119

Leave by the front door – 384

# 266

Do you have the codeword **Cure** – 133

If not,

You suddenly feel a tremble in your body and then your breathing becomes difficult. The Police staff run to your aid, but it becomes strangely dark. You hear the Inspector shout, "he's been poisoned," and then there's nothing more. You never did find that cure for the poison you took on in the house. You were warned. Who knows how the case ended up for the Inspector? You can try again at 001, but next time find a cure. Better still, don't get poisoned.

# 267

You kneel down and look at the blanket on the floor. There is the smell of a woman's perfume on it, and you think it may be that worn by Elsie Gonzales. Turning the blanket over, you find a note underneath which simply says

*The shed, four o'clock. We'll get a half hour. The Doctor*

Well, I think we can see what's going on there. There's nothing else unusual about the blanket or the ground around it so what now?

Do you

Take a look at the lawnmower – 558

Get the box on the shelf – 182

Or leave the shed and

Check out the fountains area – 526

Take a look in the walled garden – 625

Make your way to the greenhouse – 722

Wander over to the gardening equipment sheds – 121

Or if you doubt the gardens will be of any use then take the coastal path at 770 but note that you have visited the gardens

# 268

There is a whirring sound from the lock, and you gently push the door open. Step inside at <u>845</u>

# 269

You pull back the satin sheets but find only a clean smooth bed underneath. As you remove the pillows you see an envelope addressed to the Doctor. On opening the envelope, you find the following note inside.

"I trust our great venture is near completion and that is the reason for my invite. I greatly look forward to seeing the progress you mentioned and if it makes a man that much improved then it will certainly impress the investors. I knew you would make me a killing. Will see you soon.

Your good friend,

Patrick"

So, the Doctor was involved in research that would be profitable to Patrick Davidson. Still, there's nothing else around the bed so let's get on.

Do you

Check out the drawers and wardrobes – <u>010</u>

Return to the landing – <u>119</u>

# 270

The scrap of paper is heavily crumpled but unravelling it you see a message.

*E, meet me at the lookout, love F*

You are beginning to think that the Doctor may not be so good at secret messages. Maybe that was important information. But it's time to move on.

Do you

Examine the pool table – <u>110</u>

Look at the darts board – <u>248</u>

Open the fridge – <u>075</u>

Read the magazines – <u>424</u>

Or

Enter the toilet – <u>655</u>

Check out the chart room – <u>618</u>

Investigate the room with no name – <u>521</u>

Return to the lower floor – <u>795</u>

# 271

The shrouds look like cheap versions and a number of them are falling apart. You wonder just how invested in his vegetable garden the Doctor is. In the soil you discover a bottle labelled *Capernaum antidote*. If you have the codeword **Capernaum**, you drink the contents quickly. Enter the codeword **Cure** in your list. If you don't have this codeword you may pocket the bottle if you wish.

Do you

Open the compost bins – 080

Have a look at the wheelbarrow – 487

Or leave and

Enter the orchard – 447

Wander to the ornamental garden – 042

Or

Check out the fountains area – 156

Make your way to the greenhouse – 745

Wander over to the gardening equipment sheds – 262

Or if you doubt the gardens will be of any use then take the coastal path at 211 but note that you have visited the gardens

## 272

"It seems we have your DNA on the Doctor's body, Mr O'Malley. Peter, they saw you there, a gun in your hand, your DNA's on the body and you have no other evidence implicating anyone else in the Doctor's death. Miss Gonzales will be tried for attempting to kill you, but you'll pay for your own crimes. Take him away, officer!"

It seems your lot is sealed. Not enough evidence gathered to protect yourself. Try again at <u>001</u> and see if you can get more evidence next time.

## 273

The ruined temple has two great pillars at the front of it where a large roof used to run away from them supported by other now gone pillars. The floor is a marble slab, and you wonder how on earth this structure ever came to be here. But it is a shadow of its former self with just a few stumps the last remainders of those vanished supports. As you step past the large pillars at the front of the temple you see someone at the stumps. It's a serious looking woman in a long coat and she stands as you come closer.

Now in the poor light you can tell its Kyla Mertens and she begins to smile as you come close.

"Some people would say you did me a favour. You know he was stealing my work. Trumped up little

Doctor. He was the face to the world, but it was my work. Do you understand? And then you killed him."

You hold your hands out and edge closer. Note the code **Confess** in your code list.

Do you

Say you didn't kill the Doctor – <u>109</u>

Draw your gun (if you have one) and ask for the truth – <u>094</u>

Ask Kyla why the drug was so important – <u>295</u>

# 274

You shout into the darkness, and you hear your voice reverberate around the tomb. If someone is in there they will certainly know you are coming. You decide that without a torch it would be foolish to proceed.

If you have a torch and wish to try it – <u>221</u>

If not,

Enter the temple – <u>280</u>

Check out the sacrificial slab – <u>246</u>

Look at the gaming board – <u>426</u>

Or decide this area is no longer useful or too risky and continue along the coastal path at <u>998</u>

## 275

You look at the simple switch and flick it. You see the water of the lagoon suddenly light up. There must be some sort of lighting underneath. Enter the code **Beam** in your code list. Now that's better, but what next?

Do you

Swipe the card reader with the Doctor's access card, if you have it - 118

Enter a code on the pad (only if you have found one) (only if you have found one) - 491

Or leave the item alone and

Check out the tin - 400

Or if none of this inspires you, go back to the lagoon entrance and make another choice - 879

## 276

You wait, holding your breath, your ear cocked to the office. But now there's nothing, no sound and no observed movement.

Do you

Enter - 304

Decide against it and if you haven't already

Enter the canteen - 083

Try to get into the cleaners' cupboard - 592

Examine the door belonging to Doctor Munro - 775

Or return to the hall - 805

## 277

You take a look at the ivy and then the ladder above it. You can do this! So, you jump up and grab the ivy, hauling yourself up to the ladder. From there the climb is easier but you are getting pelted by the rain. You shiver with cold, but you are determined and continue your climb. At the top of the Lookout, you reach a balcony that circles the top floor of the tower. Above, you see a half broken weathervane on the round roof. There is but one door on the balcony and you try the handle finding it locked. There is a lock you could try a key in. Or maybe you could smash a window allowing you to access the room.

Do you

Have a key for the lock – 433

Want to smash a window – 356

Or if this all seems too much you could climb down and try one of the options at 136

## 278

"Kyla Mertens," laughs the detective. "What on earth makes you think that? I know she was working with the Doctor on a performing enhancing drug, and they were to start production with it. Everything we have says she was happy with the arrangements. Do you have any evidence to the contrary?"

If you have any of the following codewords go to that section. Follow the list downwards and only go to the first section that you have a codeword in.

**Water** - 198

**Theft** - 062

**Confess** - 061

**Scrap** - 874

**Taunt** - 435

**Inferno** - 281

**Blaze** - 463

**Grumble** - 583

**Pads, Paddy, Silent Papers, Cold Blood, Murder, Hitman, Merto** - 636

**Gutted** - 048

Otherwise - 995

# 279

This time the pad flashes red in a crazy fashion and you can hear an alarm going off. You look around you in a panic wondering if anyone is close and coming for you. Best not to wait around and besides you can't get into the Lookout anyway. You run to the coastal path to choose your next location at 990

# 280

The ruined temple has two great pillars at the front of it where a large roof used to run away from them supported by other now gone pillars. The floor is a marble slab, and you wonder how on earth this structure ever came to be here. But it is a shadow of its former self with just a few stumps the last remainders of those vanished supports. As you step past the large pillars at the front of the temple you see someone at the stumps. It's a serious looking woman in a long coat and she stands as you come closer.

Now in the poor light you can tell its Kyla Mertens and she begins to smile as you come close.

"Some people would say you did me a favour. You know he was stealing my work. Trumped up little Doctor. He was the face to the world, but it was my work. Do you understand? And then you killed him."

You hold your hands out and edge closer. Note the code **Confess** in your code list.

Do you

Say you didn't kill the Doctor – <u>832</u>

Draw your gun (if you have one) and ask for the truth – <u>025</u>

Ask Kyla why the drug was so important – <u>511</u>

# 281

You tell the detective about the threatening note that Kyla wrote to a friend, saying that her work was being stolen and that she said that Doctor Munro had to be stopped. When the detective asks where this note is you look sheepish explaining you burnt it by accident.

"Well, then you have nothing he says."

If you have any of the following codewords go to that section. Follow the list downwards and only go to the first section that you have a codeword in.

**Grumble - 446**

**Pads, Paddy, Silent Papers, Cold Blood, Murder, Hitman, Merto - 415**

**Gutted - 048**


Otherwise, read on:


The detective arrests you for the Doctor's murder saying that you were still seen with the gun over the body. All you have is a potential heated comment. At the trial you cut a lonely figure as it only takes the jury an hour to convict you. From your jail cell you wonder if you were right in your choice of killer. You'll never know. Maybe try again at 001.

## 282

"We've found other bodies, Mr O'Malley. You've been busy!" You remember the blood you spilt. That's what they will see. "Miss Gonzales will be tried for attempting to kill you, but you'll pay for your own crimes. Take him away, officer!"

It seems your lot is sealed. Not enough evidence gathered to protect yourself. Try again at 001 and see if you can get more evidence next time. Oh, and don't kill anyone!

## 283

Have you discovered a code for the computer? It looks like a four digit one but what is it?

Have you discovered a code from elsewhere? Then go 253

Will you take a random shot at it? Then go 899

Or is this a bad idea? Is so do you

Read the papers – 500

Try to open the drawers – 219

Or

Look at the small pile of books and the chair – 634

Check out the picture on the wall – 098

Examine the coat stand – 428

## 284

You quickly don your lifejacket and just in time, as the boat tips up and you are thrown out into the surf. You get caught by the undertow and you are dragged out before your lifejacket pulls you up to the surface. You fight hard and manage to swim to the boathouse. As you struggle back through the open doors of the boathouse, you gasp for breath. Hauling yourself back onto the side of the interior dock, you collapse and take a moment. You really should have been dead but for the lifejacket. Taking it off you believe you may be missing some things.

**Look at your inventory. From the top down, items 1, 2, 4 and 6 are missing if you have that many. The only exception is if the item is a lifejacket as you have it on.**

Well at least you are alive. What now?

 Look at the lifejackets – 436

Take the stairs to the upper floor – 581

Check out the locker at the rear of the room – 957

Or

Head over to the marina – 465

Or if you want to continue elsewhere take the coastal path at 980


# 285

There's a horrible buzzer that tells you that the code is wrong. Blimey, one more chance or you'll be locked out. What do you do? Try a different code

9746 – 064

3267 – 203

2758 – 107

Another code – 787


Or do you decide this is too risky and decide instead to

Hide in the undergrowth surrounding the facility and see what happens – 440

Walk around the facility and see what you can find – 608

Call this a bust and find the coastal path – 983

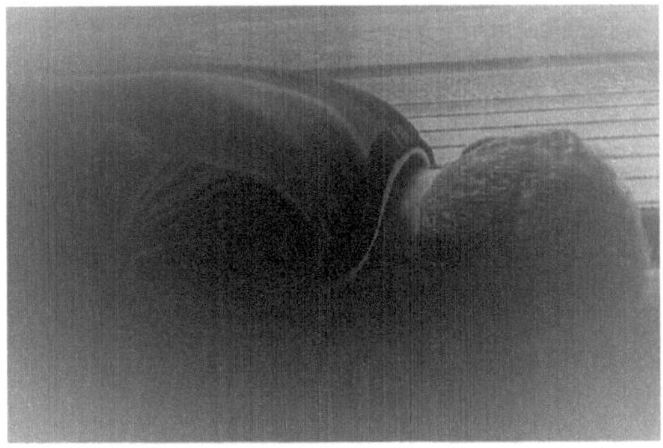

# 286

You pick up the papers on the table and find them to be a letter, dated today but the writing, made in pen, is slightly blurred due to the leaking liquid on the table which has contaminated the page. The writing is hard to make out and may be better in daylight.

Do you

Try to read it with the help of the candle – 590

Read it anyway without any increased light – 968

Or simply leave it and decide on a different option – 766

## 287

Oh dear, that hasn't worked. You have one try left. Do you wish to try again? If so

4837 – <u>614</u>

9746 – <u>038</u>

3267 – <u>643</u>

2758 – <u>100</u>

Another code – <u>626</u>

Or if you have the Doctor's access card you could try that – <u>057</u>

If none of this excites you then do you

Enter the canteen – <u>071</u>

Try to get into the cleaners' cupboard – <u>571</u>

Try to enter the office of Kyla Mertens – <u>237</u>

Or

Return to the hall – <u>212</u>

## 288

You tell the detective about the note from Kyla Mertens to her father, saying how Doctor Munro must be stopped and that she is entering a dark place.

"Now that is interesting, but it is also not proof. You still have a lot to answer for. Do you have anything to back up this evidence?"

If you have any of the following codewords go to that section. Follow the list downwards and only go to the first section that you have a codeword in.

**Taunt** - <u>201</u>

**Grumble** - <u>446</u>

**Pads, Paddy, Silent Papers, Cold Blood, Murder, Hitman, Merto** - <u>415</u>

**Gutted** - <u>048</u>

Otherwise, read on:

The detective still says you have enough evidence against you that you have to go to trial. It seems that the jury sees enough uncertainty for you are found not guilty. However, the papers do not see it that way, a man with a gun in his hand at a body. Your life becomes a hell, followed by the press, until you leave the country. It might seem unfair but at least you are not in jail. As for who actually killed the Doctor, you still don't know. Maybe try again at <u>001</u>.

# 289

Where do you move the snake?

Beside the eagle - <u>337</u>

Beside the man - <u>021</u>

On the other side of the woman - <u>069</u>

# 290

You quickly scout round the rest of the laboratory, but it is locked up tight. Looks like your options are limited and that rain is getting heavier if anything.

Do you

Go back to the window and try and break it – 936

Go back to the front and hide in the undergrowth to await developments – 440

Forget all this and find the coastal path to somewhere else – 983

# 291

Go to 199

# 292

You punch in the code and the pad turns red and a coarse noise like a bad input on a computer sounds. Nothing happens and you are left with the pad again.

Do you enter another code? Which one?

2758 - 883

3267 - 966

9746 - 226

4837 - 035

Another code - 836

Or do you leave the pad alone? If so, make your next choice at 816

## 293

Oh dear, that hasn't worked. You have one try left. Do you wish to try again? If so

4837 – 614

9746 – 038

3267 – 643

Another code – 626

Or if you have the Doctor's access card you could try that – 057

If none of this excites you then do you

Enter the canteen – 071

Try to get into the cleaners' cupboard – 571

Try to enter the office of Kyla Mertens – 237

Or

Return to the hall – 212

## 294

This time the pad flashes red in a crazy fashion and you can hear an alarm going off. You look around you in a panic wondering if anyone is close and coming for you. Best not to wait around and besides you can't get into the Lookout anyway. You run to the coastal path to choose your next location at 990

## 295

"What's the deal with the drug? Why is it so important?"

Kyla comes closer and smiles at you. "It is a work of genius. It makes a human being maintain their top performance for longer; physically, mentally and, dare I say it, spiritually."

You have no idea what *spiritually* having a top performance means but you are aware she is getting very close now.

Do you

Step into her embrace, after all you need a friend – 815

Walk away from the ruins, she's a threat – 073

Draw your gun for a better answer – 094

## 296

"Patrick Davidson," says the detective stroking his moustache. "You're going to have to show me some evidence sunshine, as he's a respected businessman. I know he was backing the Doctor's new drug. What can you tell me?"

If you have any of the following codewords go to that section. Follow the list downwards and only go to the first section that you have a codeword in.

**Bowl** - <u>386</u>

**Taunt** - <u>128</u>

**Gutted** - <u>048</u>

Otherwise - <u>995</u>

# 297

From the house you have three options along paths that are sodden with rain. Where you go will be determined by what you have found out so far. Or maybe you'll just guess. Check the map at the front of the book to see what lies beyond your three choices. Remember, you have decided to not go backwards so once you leave a destination on the edge of the island you cannot retrace your steps but rather continue around the coast.

Choose well for this may decide your fate, if you have enough evidence to hand before the police arrive. Which path will you take?

Head for the Laboratory – <u>753</u>

Seek out the gardens – <u>570</u>

Run to the Lookout – <u>136</u>

## 298

The kitchen whilst being small is a busy affair. There is a myriad of cupboards around the room as well as a gas cooker on which sits several pots. The smell of vegetables fills the room, and you see a fridge freezer in the corner. There is also a knife block with a single handle sticking out of the wood. A hatch is on the wall that backs onto the dining room. You're not sure what you will find here of help but maybe it's worth a look.

Do you

Check out the fridge freezer – 822

Have a look through the cupboards – 887

Examine the pots on the cooker – 129

Examine the hatch – 347

Look at the knife block – 353

Return to the hall – 675

## 299

You tell the detective to check your belongings for the note from the Doctor to Patrick Davidson that you found in the toilet bowl. When the note is brought to the detective from your belongings, he gives it some careful attention before turning back to you.

"So, there was a change of plans and Mr Davidson didn't like it. But if he killed the Doctor then who would make the decision not to go ahead. Kyla Mertens told us she wanted the drug stopped from going on commercial sale so simply killing the Doctor may not have been enough Do you have anything else you can tell or show me."

You're still in trouble. What else do you have?

If you have any of the following codewords go to that section. Follow the list downwards and only go to the first section that you have a codeword in.

**Taunt** – 912

**Grumble** – 446

**Pads, Paddy, Silent Papers, Cold Blood, Murder, Hitman, Merto** – 415

**Gutted** – 048


Otherwise read on:

The detective arrests you for the Doctor's murder saying that you were still seen with the gun over the body. All you have is a potential heated comment. At the trial you cut a lonely figure as it only takes the jury an hour to convict you. From your jail cell you wonder if you were right in your choice of killer. You'll never know. Maybe try again at 001.


# 300

You remember the fuel you found in the main building and if you go and fetch it, you could maybe make a break for somewhere off island. It's a bigger boat than you are used to, but it will ride the storm better than the speedboat.

If you want to make a break for it on the cruiser - <u>164</u>

If not return to <u>738</u> and choose another option

# 301

"Kyla Mertens," laughs the detective. "What on earth makes you think that? I know she was working with the Doctor on a performing enhancing drug, and they were to start production with it. Everything we have says she was happy with the arrangements. Do you have any evidence to the contrary?"

If you have any of the following codewords go to that section. Follow the list downwards and only go to the first section that you have a codeword in.

**Theft** - <u>452</u>

**Confess** - <u>930</u>

**Taunt** - <u>112</u>

**Grumble** - <u>446</u>

**Pads, Paddy, Silent Papers, Cold Blood, Murder, Hitman, Merto** - <u>415</u>

**Gutted** - <u>048</u>

Otherwise - <u>995</u>

## 302

Go to 199

## 303

The buzzer howls even louder this time and the number pad flashes before the numbers change from bright green to red. Looks like it's locked the door. More than that it will have set off an alarm. Time to get out of here. You run hard around the laboratory to the coastal path at 986

## 304

Go to 024

## 305

The magazine is open at a page discussing, in English, Patrick Davidson's company. You see it is a start-up and is rapidly growing but it also needs considerable backing as well as a large win to boost its financial position. There is discussion it will be announcing a major new drug breakthrough but there is little about the actual detail in the article. Enter code word **Tatler** in your code list.

Well, now we know what the deceased Doctor read on the loo, let's see what else we can find.

Do you

Examine the toilet (it still says that!) – <u>994</u>

Or

Examine the bed – <u>046</u>

Check the silk dressing gowns – <u>505</u>

Descend the stairs – <u>991</u>

Or leave the Lookout completely and head for the coastal path – <u>990</u>

# 306

You charge at the door and throw your shoulder at it but bounce back off it, having not moved it at all. Your shoulder is now very sore. Bad plan! Return to <u>464</u>

# 307

You splinter the wood along the edge of the drawer, but you have enough force to jimmy the drawer open and it springs out at you. Just as it flies open, a small dart fires out from the table leg but it glances the drawer and flies harmlessly away to the corner of the room. That was close!

Looking inside the drawer you see a sheet of paper and see something entitled The Code Store. In one column is a place and in the other a series of entries described as devices. You take a moment to study the list. **Make a note of this entry as you may need to refer to it for this list. Just remember to keep a note of where you are in the adventure.** The list is below.

## The Code Store

| *Location* | *Device* |
| --- | --- |
| Kitchen freezer | chart cupboard |
| Bathroom cabinet | computer lockout |
| Office wooden chair | boathouse locker |

So now you have something extra, what are you going to do

Try to put a code into the computer – 283

Read the papers – 500

Or just leave the desk alone and

Look at the small pile of books and the chair – 634

Check out the picture on the wall – 098

Examine the coat stand – 428

# 308

As you get close to the stools, you notice that one of them is smashed. It appears that there was a heated debate, or maybe even a fight. There are several pieces of paper on the floor, and you try to pick them up and place them on the nearby bench. You don't have all the pieces, but you can make out the words, "rejected for further trials". The letters DL are also recognisable.

Mean anything to you? Where now?

Do you

Examine the file – 572

Look in the refrigerator – 752

Check out the lab coats – 793

Or

If this is all too much you could return to the entrance hall – 212

# 309

This time the pad flashes red in a crazy fashion and you can hear an alarm going off. You look around you in a panic wondering if anyone is close and coming for you. Best not to wait around and besides you can't get into the Lookout anyway. You run to the coastal path to choose your next location at 990

# 310

You hold up your hands. "Look Mr Davidson, I'm no threat. I was framed, trust me. You understand. I just want to clear my name."

"I don't trust you, kid. You were holding the gun."

"But why would I kill my employer? I have it good here Mr Davidson," you tell him. "Somebody else must have wanted the Doctor dead. Do you know of anyone who would?"

"Well not me, kid. I needed the Doctor's drug to work. The one that enhances a person's physical performance. I have a lot of money tied up in all of this, it needs to work."

You can see the man is sweating and not happy with your presence. "So, who else would have a reason to kill my employer?" you ask.

"Well, I don't trust that journalist, Elsie. She was flirting like crazy with the Doctor, entranced him. But she has an agenda. I've done my research, kid, and she has written lots of anti-drug articles in the past. She's dead against manipulation of anyone's performance. She wrote that piece on the Olympics, lambasting the *dirty* athletes."

"So, she wouldn't want this drug to succeed. But would she know how to plant a gun on me?"

"Look, kid, journalists want a story, don't they? What better story than to frame you and stop what was happening." The man comes closer, seemingly more at home with you. "Let's go get a seat and talk properly, kid. I'll help you."

You nod and as you turn to walk out the door, Patrick shoves you against the wall and the man runs.

"Sorry, kid, I just can't afford to trust anyone."

As you get to your feet, he is long gone. You take a quick look around the canteen but there's no evidence here. Time to get going again.

Do you

Try to get into the cleaners' cupboard – 592

Examine the door belonging to Doctor Munro – 775

Try to enter the office of Kyla Mertens – 840

Or

Return to the hall – 805

# 311

The lawnmower is a filthy affair, and you wonder when it was last used. Maybe that's why this shed is open as it holds nothing of working interest. You realise that you could stand on the lawnmower and reach up to the shelves and maybe just grab those bottles. But it is dark up there.

As you stand on the lawnmower, you hear a crack, and you realise you have broken open a storage space under the seat. You find a small blowtorch there. This could be handy as the bottles are in the dark and maybe you could read the labels by the light of the blowtorch.

Do you

Fire up the blowtorch and climb on the lawnmower to look at the bottles – 866

Ignore the blowtorch and climb up to look at the bottles – 550

Or ignore the lawnmower and

Get the box on the shelf – 535

Examine the blanket on the floor – 699

Or leave the shed and

Check out the fountains area – 156

Take a look in the walled garden – 926

Make your way to the greenhouse – 745

Wander over to the gardening equipment sheds – 262

Or if you doubt the gardens will be of any use then take the coastal path at 211 but note that you have visited the gardens

# 312

The dressing gowns are made of silk and are simply immaculate. To the touch they feel like the best fabric you have ever handled, and the deep blue colour makes you feel like you are about to be enveloped in the sea. Having marvelled at their appearance you smell them both but only one has the scent of a man. The other has simply the smell of a recently cleaned garment.

Job done and a fascinating insight! So, what now? Do you

Examine the bed – 615

Check the alcove door – 586

Descend the stairs – 811

Or leave the Lookout completely and head for the coastal path – 988

# 313

You type in the code and realise that something is wrong. There is a whirring from the door and a claxon is sounding.

Go 314

# 314

With the claxon sounding and the door apparently locked you decide to search the room but find that all the drawers are locked and there is now the sound of gas escaping. A green gas pervades the room, and you cannot escape it, instead finding yourself succumbing and everything goes black.

The next thing you know is a jail cell and a lot of awkward questions to which you have no answers. You didn't discover anything that would help your case and you were also seen with the Doctor's body with a gun in your hand before being trapped while searching his room. They know you were looking for something and with the evidence stacked against you, the court case does not take long before your life sentence is pronounced.

It is several years when you receive a letter, thanking you for taking the blame and explaining how you were framed. Your eyes widen with interest as you see the signature at the bottom. The culprit is on their deathbed and maybe you can be free. If only you can get in touch with... Now that would be telling. Maybe next time you'll find out who did it!

Return to <u>001</u> and better luck next time!

# 315

The upper floor of the boathouse has a small corridor off of which are four doors. One of the doors states it is a chart room, another the toilet, a third the Rec Room and the last has no name on the door. The corridor has dim lighting produced by the emergency exit lights. There may be something of use up here.

Do you

Enter the toilet - <u>828</u>

Check out the chart room - <u>848</u>

Go to the Rec Room - <u>528</u>

Investigate the room with no name - <u>685</u>

Return to the lower floor - <u>370</u>

# 316

Taking your gun, you smack the butt of the weapon on the window. It reverberates off but you persist. Up here it would take a heck of a noise for people to notice, and you hit the window ten times before you see a chink in the pane. Carefully, you tap out the glass, before climbing inside the window. Enter the room at <u>824</u>

# 317

The sound is getting closer, like feet making the odd splash in the wet tunnel. Your gun is in your hand. Will it be too late to wait until you catch sight of what is approaching?

Do you

Fire the gun - <u>723</u>

Wait - <u>498</u>

# 318

You pick up the paper and in the light, you try to make out the writing. It is in cursive and difficult to understand but you soon get the flow of it. As best you can make out, it says

*Thanks for taking the rap, Peter. You're a nice lad if somewhat stupid. Still, you'll get out again after some twenty years or so!*

Your heart skips a beat, and you hear a crash. One of the bridges has collapsed and you see a figure with an axe running for the other one. You have a bit of a head start but not much. You pocket the note and make a run for it. Enter the word **Taunt** in your code list and go 260

# 319

You follow the wall and can hear the breathing beside you. It's heavy and extremely close. Your heart beats as you wonder what to do next. Maybe your gun if you have it? But there's no time as something pins your t-shirt to the wall causing you to struggle to break free.

How's your luck?

This good – 326

Maybe this good – 430

Or possibly this good – 780

# 320

What code will you enter?

2758 - <u>192</u>

3267 - <u>349</u>

9746 - <u>852</u>

4837 - <u>580</u>

Another code - <u>979</u>

# 321

You tell the detective about your threatening note from when someone tried to kill you at the fountains. The detective takes it away and returns an hour later with a smile on his face.

"We checked out your story about nearly being killed and the handwriting on the note. I believe you son, and the writing is that of Kyla Mertens. I have just arrested her for your attempted murder. However, there is still the question of Doctor Munro's murder. Do you have anything further?"

You shake your head.

If you have any of the following codewords go to that section. Follow the list downwards and only go to the first section that you have a codeword in.

**Grumble – 446**

**Pads, Paddy, Silent Papers, Cold Blood, Murder, Hitman, Merto – 415**

**Gutted – 048**

Otherwise, read on:

The detective still says you have enough evidence against you that you have to go to trial. It seems that the jury sees enough uncertainty for you are found not guilty. However, the papers do not see it that way, a man with a gun in his hand at a body. Your life becomes a hell, followed by the press, until you leave the country. It might seem unfair but at least you are not in jail. As for who actually killed the Doctor, you still don't know. Maybe try again at 001.

# 322

You grab the Radio and make a call on channel sixteen, asking the authorities to intercept you. It takes about ten minutes before you can rendezvous with a coastguard vessel, and they remove you to the mainland. It seems you need to prepare to defend yourself, but the cox of the coastguard vessel says that you may have been rather fortunate as they have rescued another person from the cruiser you escaped on. Now proceed to 519 and prepare to defend yourself.

# 323

You climb into the dinghy and push away with the oars. It's a struggle just to get out of the dock but you continue. As you start to make way you reach where the waves are breaking, and the dinghy is flung this way and that.

Do you have a lifejacket?

If so – 284

If not – 427

# 324

The cave is wet and slimy, but you see a hard surface beyond the water which has a few recliners. The whole area is lit up by ceiling lights. There is a fridge with a small selection of alcoholic beverages sitting on top of it. A bookcase is in the corner as well as a rail with several towels on it. But what makes you stare is the figure taking a drink at the fridge. It is Granma Munro, and she appears agitated. Enter codeword **Quiet Place** in your code word list.

There is not a lot here to look at but maybe Granma might have some helpful insights.

Do you

Engage Granma in conversation – <u>077</u>

Decide to leave her alone and retreat out of the cave

If you entered by torch light – <u>489</u>

Otherwise – <u>858</u>

## 325

Your t-shirt rips but you are clear and sprint up the steps to the upper deck. A knife flies past your ear as you run off the boat, but you don't look back and run for your life all the way to the coastal path. Once there you realise you are clear and fee to move on at <u>981</u>.

## 326

You struggle with the knife, but you can't free it. There's a blow to your head and then you don't know anymore. In the following days, the police blame you for the murder and the person who attacked you walks away scot-free from their dastardly deed with the Doctor. Of course, it's..., no you'll need to play again at <u>001</u>, but this time beware the dark.

# 327

"Do you know who framed me?"

Granma looks at you curiously. "Did they probe you? They tried that with me, but I fought them, I fought them hard. Poor Flavius didn't survive the probing. You be careful, they are not very gentle."

The woman appears to be crazy. Or is this a bluff?

Do you

Draw your gun (if you have one) and tell her to start talking – 627

Ask how she got here – 761

Or

Leave Granma in peace and retreat from the cave

If you entered by torch light – 489

Otherwise – 858

# 328

You tell the detective about your threatening note from when someone tried to kill you at the fountains. The detective takes it away and returns an hour later with a smile on his face.

"We checked out your story about nearly being killed and the handwriting on the note. I believe you son, and the writing is that of Elsie Gonzales. I have just arrested her for your attempted murder. However, you are still the prime suspect for the Doctor's death. Do you have any other evidence?"

If you have any of the following codewords go to that section. Follow the list downwards and only go to the first section that you have a codeword in.

**Grumble** – 583

**Pads, Paddy, Silent Papers, Cold Blood, Murder, Hitman, Merto** – 636

**Gutted** – 048

Otherwise read on:

The detective arrests you for the Doctor's murder saying that you were still seen with the gun over the body. All you have is a potential heated comment. At the trial you cut a lonely figure as it only takes the jury an hour to convict you. From your jail cell you wonder if you were right in your choice of killer. You'll never know. Maybe try again at 001.

# 329

The cruiser has two decks and as you clamber onboard the vessel, you are amazed at the luxury. You note the steps down to the lower deck and the two distinct sections to the upper deck. There is the main wheelhouse on top along with a rear section that contains several lockers. The boat, although large is definitely wobbling, and you reach out for a handhold.

Do you

Go to the lower deck via the stairs – 013

Check out the wheelhouse – 096

Look at the lockers at the aft of the upper deck – 601

Or

Jump onto the speedboat – 624

Or, if you haven't already,

Make for the main building – 370

Or

if you want to continue elsewhere take the coastal path at 981

# 330

Okay, so you have 12 digits, and you enter them one at a time. Add up all the digits, all of which should be single digits and then when you have the answer of that sum go to that entry number while keeping this entry open. Does the new entry make sense? If so, continue there (051). If not – 878

# 331

You hide out, fearing every sound in the cave and one day, a police officer walks through a secret passage in the cave, arresting you. Enter the codeword **Caught** in your list and try to defend yourself at 519

## 332

You can't move, your body won't support a swim right now. You close your eyes hoping the noise fades away. But it doesn't! You hear the policemen shouting at you and slowly try to raise your hands. Enter the codeword **Caught** in your list and get ready to make your defence at 519.

## 333

Go to 786

## 334

You tell the detective about the magazine article you read, that Patrick Davidson's company is a start-up in need of money.

"That's not evidence. It's a big jump to go from a magazine article to a conviction. You have nothing."

If you have any of the following codewords go to that section. Follow the list downwards and only go to the first section that you have a codeword in.

**Taunt** – 128

**Gutted** – 048

Otherwise – 995

## 335

There's a horrible buzzer that tells you that the code is wrong. Blimey, one more chance or you'll be locked out. What do you do? Try a different code

4837 - 713

9746 - 934

2758 - 512

Another code - 303


Or do you decide this is too risky and decide instead to

Hide in the undergrowth surrounding the facility and see what happens - 971

Walk around the facility and see what you can find - 739

Call this a bust and find the coastal path - 986


## 336

You think carefully about what evidence you have, weighing up what is the best thing to do. If you have the following codewords, go to the given section for further thoughts on what you have learnt. Remember to mark this section to come back to.

**Wheel** – <u>407</u>

**Shutdown** – <u>964</u>

**Bowl** – <u>993</u>

**Space Letter** – <u>242</u>

**Taunt** – <u>009</u>

When you are done considering what evidence you have, go to <u>850</u> and talk to the Detective Inspector.

# 337

You move the figure and place it in your desired spot. At first nothing happens but then you notice that the woman is crumbling. In a few seconds the entire figure has collapsed. You try to put your figure back but realise that the remaining three are all now stuck fast to the ground. How does this crazy game work? Frustrated you decide to move on.

Do you

Make for the tomb and shelter from the rain – <u>877</u>

Enter the temple – <u>273</u>

Check out the sacrificial slab – <u>742</u>

Or

Decide this area is no longer useful or too risky and continue along the coastal path at <u>996</u>

# 338

No one knows about this place except maybe the Doctor and Granma Munro. The Doctor is dead, and Grandma is nuts. Or is she? Sure, she's erratic but could a skilled interrogator find out about this place from her.

Possibly – 331

Maybe – 691

# 339

You quickly don your lifejacket and just in time, as the boat tips up and you are thrown out into the surf. You get caught by the undertow and you are dragged out before your lifejacket pulls you up to the surface. You fight hard and manage to swim to the boathouse. As you struggle back through the open doors of the boathouse, you gasp for breath. Hauling yourself back onto the side of the interior dock, you collapse and take a moment. You really should have been dead but for the lifejacket. Taking it off you believe you may be missing some things.

**Look at your inventory. From the top down, items 1, 2, 4 and 6 are missing if you have that many. The only exception is if the item is a lifejacket as you have it on.**

Well at least you are alive. What now?

Look at the lifejackets – 496

Take the stairs to the upper floor – 315

Check out the locker at the rear of the room – 584

Or

Head over to the marina – 909

Or if you want to continue elsewhere take the coastal path at 981

# 340

You check the balls on the pool table and find them to be normal game balls. A check of the pockets finds nothing and when you grab a cue, you find yourself shooting the two ball into the corner pocket. You need to snap out of this, you're trying to clear your name, not looking to become a hustler. Do something else quickly.

Look at the darts board – 163

Open the fridge – 559

Read the magazines – 531

Take hold of the scrap of paper – 790

Or

Enter the toilet – 828

Check out the chart room – 848

Investigate the room with no name – 685

Return to the lower floor – 370

# 341

You make your way to the edge of the vegetation and stare at the marina. You can see the large cruiser the Doctor uses and reckon it could outrun most vessels. Looking left and then right, you make a desperate charge across open ground towards the marina. But you are spotted by a police officer. He shouts for you to stop but you are committed. They won't stop you. You hear the shot ring out and you pitch forward as a bullet hits your chest. Your eyes grow dim and your breathing stutters and then fades away. Standing over you a smug officer believes he has killed the Doctor's murderer.

Alas you failed to achieve to clear your name or even escape. You can try again at <u>001</u>.

# 342

You ask Elsie, "How do we get out?", and she seems to misunderstand you muttering about escape.

"I guess it will be hard for you to prove your innocence but if you can find the right boat maybe this will help." Elsie hands you a key with a dolphin on the keyring. "It's for his cruiser, wherever he's moored it. He entertained me there and I snuck off with the key. I hope you can run to safety while I find out who did this." If you want to keep the key, you can enter it in your inventory as **Dolphin key**.

But does Elsie know another exit from the cave?

Do you

Draw your gun (if you have one) and tell her to start talking – 969

Leave the woman in peace and retreat from the cave by the water

If you entered by torch light – 441

Otherwise – 408

# 343

You punch in the code and the pad flashes green but nothing else happens and you are left with the pad again. You decide to leave the pad alone but enter the word **Baba** in your code list. Make your next choice at 037

# 344

You are thrown about here and there but the lifejacket keeps you afloat. The water is freezing but fortunately you are not that far from land, and you manage to reach a gravelly bay. Staggering up through the trees at the shores edge you find yourself at the perimeter path's junction for the boathouse. Well, you've had enough of that so decide where you go next at 981. But lose every item in your inventory other than the lifejacket, for they are now in the sea.

# 345

You launch an almighty kick at the desk which shakes it. But as you stand to admire your efforts, you hear a quiet, *psst!* and something hits you in the shoulder. Suddenly everything goes dark.

You wake up and the room looks the same, but you feel that time has passed. Suddenly you get nervous that you may have been here too long, and you need to get a move on. Without a thought you run out of the Lookout and make your way to the coastal path, keen to try and find clues in another location. Go to 990

# 346

Elsie bolts past you and you lift your arms up letting her go. As you watch her descend the stairs, you are amazed how she handles her heels and soon she has disappeared out into the rain.

You feel a little unsettled but look around the room. There are several canisters on the shelving, which must have looked like boxes in the dark. You open one and smell diesel. They are quite heavy, and you decide you can't simply carry them around. But you know where to come if you need them. Note the codeword **Fuel** in your code list.

That was eventful but what do you do next?

Check out the chart room – <u>618</u>

Go to the Rec Room – <u>234</u>

Investigate the room with no name – <u>521</u>

Return to the lower floor – <u>795</u>

# 347

Have you examined the hatch from the dining room side?

If so – <u>901</u>

If not – <u>706</u>

# 348

You step onto the slab and then lie prostrate on it to try and read the engraving in the middle. It is difficult and instead you trace it with your fingers. It takes a moment, but you manage it.

*Neptune says thanks for his lunch*

Well, that's a bit of a laugh from whoever restored this, after all that's not from anyone from the past. You chortle to yourself and then you hear ropes moving and the slab begins to tilt to the sea. You look across and someone is at the mechanism. You can't tell who and have little time to think about it as you descend off the slab and onto the rocks below.

They find your body over a week later when the sea gives you back. They say guilt drove you to it, but it was a murder. Problem is, you'll never know who. Next time let's not climb on board ancient killing devices! Try again at 001

# 349

You punch in the code and the pad turns red and a coarse noise like a bad input on a computer sounds. Nothing happens and you are left with the pad again.

Do you enter another code? Which one?

2758 - 774

3267 - 144

9746 - 343

4837 - 616

Another code - 078

Or do you leave the pad alone? If so, make your next choice at 037

# 350

You climb up but it's hard to see. As you stretch in the darkness, you knock over several bottles that fall to the ground. You start to smell fuel, maybe kerosene, diesel and petrol. Carefully you get down off the lawnmower and leave the shed, aware that a spark could ignite trouble. That was a lucky escape in many ways but maybe you shouldn't root around in the dark. But what next?

Leave the shed and

Check out the fountains area – 526

Take a look in the walled garden – 625

Make your way to the greenhouse – 722

Wander over to the gardening equipment sheds – 121

Or if you doubt the gardens will be of any use then take the coastal path at 770 but note that you have visited the gardens

# 351

You switch on the torch, and you are able to see somewhat better, but it is hardly perfect. You are still scrabbling about and can only see some ten feet ahead of you. But maybe you'll be lucky and find the Doctor's stash.

Try your luck

This lucky - 839

Or this fortunate - 552

Or is here your fate - 538

## 352

The letter is from Elsie Gonzales' newspaper editor advising that the staff are going to be on half wages and that the newspaper will close unless they can drive sales up significantly. The situation is dire, and you realise Elsie will be out of a job if things do not change. The editor is imploring his reporters for a story that will be a national success and drive paper sales.

This is quite a development, and you pocket the letter. Make a note in your code list of the code **Shutdown**.

There's nothing else in here so it's time to route back out of the tomb and instead

Enter the temple – 280

Check out the sacrificial slab – 246

Look at the gaming board – 426

Or

Decide this area is no longer useful or too risky and continue along the coastal path at 998

## 353

This is not a toy knife in the block but rather a very sharp meat cleaver. It could be used as a deadly weapon, for defence obviously in your case. The wooden handle is beautifully curved to your hand and what little you can see of the blade from pulling it out just a little, it could take a hand off.

Do you wish to take it?

If so go to 208

If not then choose one of the following

Check out the fridge freezer – 822

Have a look through the cupboards – 887

Examine the pots on the cooker – 129

Examine the hatch – 347

Return to the hall – 675

# 354

Stepping back, you ponder what to do. Above you, you can see the weathervane and it looks partially broken. Maybe you could break off a piece of metal with which to hit the window. However, it is windy up there and it would be a long fall down. The roof is rounded and wet, and no doubt slippery.

Do you

Go for it – 633

Choose another option at 004

## 355

The sound is getting closer, like feet making the odd splash in the wet tunnel. Your gun I sin your hand. Will it be too late to wait until you catch sight of what is approaching?

Do you

Fire the gun – 607

Wait – 469

## 356

How will you smash it? If you have a gun, you could

Shoot the window – 448

Break the window with the butt of the gun – 316

Or

Use your fists to break it – 145

Look for something else – 818

Or give up and climb back down the tower to 136 and choose another option.

# 357

You tell the detective about your threatening note from when someone tried to kill you at the fountains. The detective takes it away and returns an hour later with a smile on his face.

"We checked out your story about nearly being killed and the handwriting on the note. I believe you son, and the writing is that of Kyla Mertens. I have just arrested her for your attempted murder. Under pressure, she has also confessed to the murder of Doctor Munro, thanks to your additional evidence. You are a free man!"

He congratulates you and you step out into the fresh air once more. It feels good to be free and you wonder what else life has in store for you. Well done, super sleuth!

# 358

What the heck, you go for it and speed the boat out into the waters. At first it all goes swimmingly, but then you feel something hit the underside of the vessel and you are suddenly pitched overboard out into the cold sea.

Do you have a lifejacket?

Yes – 043

No – 870

## 359

You run upstairs but can hear footsteps following you. There's a yell and a knife hits the cockpit wall. You run as hard as you can for the coastal path, never looking back. Go to <u>981</u> and decide your next destination.

## 360

You tell the detective about the documents in your backpack relating to Daniel Lyles involvement and subsequent dropping from the drug tests the Doctor was conducting. The detective at first seems impressed but then frowns. "It is something but not exactly a clear-cut conviction. Have you anything else that could help?"

If you have any of the following codewords go to that section. Follow the list downwards and only go to the first section that you have a codeword in.

**Taunt** – <u>029</u>

**Grumble** – <u>583</u>

**Pads, Paddy, Silent Papers, Cold Blood, Murder, Hitman, Merto** – <u>636</u>

**Gutted** – <u>048</u>

Otherwise, read on:

The detective still says you have enough evidence against you that you have to go to trial. It seems that the jury sees enough uncertainty for you are found not guilty. However, the papers do not see it that way, a man with a gun in his hand at a body. Your life becomes a hell, followed by the press, until you leave the country. It might seem unfair but at least you are not in jail. As for who actually killed the Doctor, you still don't know. Maybe try again at 001.

# 361

The writing desk has several smaller drawers it as well as a small pad of paper in the middle of the desk which simply says *Don't touch, private my dear.* There are no locks on the drawers, but you can't see any handles with which to open them. Maybe you could force them open by shaking the desk. If you have a gun you could shoot them open. Or maybe you could hit the desk with the gun butt. Or you could kick the desk.

Do you

Shake the desk – 674

Kick the desk – 053

Hit the desk with a gun butt if you have one – 918

Shoot at the desk with your gun – 028

Or decide to leave well alone and

Examine the radio handset – <u>989</u>

Check out the photographs – <u>067</u>

Have a rifle through the drawers – <u>229</u>

Or

Climb up the spiral staircase – <u>824</u>

Descend the spiral staircase - <u>845</u>

Decide to leave the Lookout and make your way to the coastal path – <u>988</u>

# 362

"Hold it", you cry, "I didn't kill the Doctor!" Daniel stops momentarily but then shakes his head. He clearly doesn't believe you and is about to run again.

Do you

Tell him you know who the real killer is – <u>178</u>

Tell him you are scared too – <u>921</u>

If you have one, pull out your gun and threaten him with it for information – <u>646</u>

Let him go – <u>007</u>

# 363

You grab the cheese and throw it at the creature. At first it rears up and then sniffs the cheese. But it soon ignores it and begins to charge at you.

Do you have a gun? If so, use it – <u>261</u>

Otherwise – <u>960</u>

## 364

The wind lifts you off your feet and it blows you onto the balcony before knocking you off it, over the wall that surrounds it. A desperate hand of yours makes a grab for the ladder and you find yourself hanging momentarily before you lose grip and fall again. You reach out with both hands and manage to slow yourself down as you fall by contacting the ladder. A last gasp grab of the ivy takes most of the momentum out of your fall, and you hit the ground hard.

When you rise, something feels a little off inside, but you need to keep going. Make an entry in your code list of **Gutted**. Now return to the front of the Lookout at <u>151</u> and try another option. Note that you may no longer try and climb up the outside, due to the pain you are feeling.

## 365

When you were at the lookout, you saw a boat out on the sea. It's the opposite side to the boathouse and the authorities may not be out there. If you can get out to the boat you may be able to take it or stowaway on it. It's not an easy option but it could be your most viable.

If you want to use this option – <u>090</u>

If not, or you want to consider options then return to <u>1000</u>. You can return here if needed to follow this option.


# 366

You call the emergency number and an operator ask which service you require. Asking for the police, you wait a few seconds while you are connected.

'Police, what's your emergency?'

'Someone's been murdered. I've found the body.' You decide against telling them about the gun and your compromising situation but pass the details of where you are and the number of people on the island.

'Stay safe, sir, lock yourself in a room, if necessary, we will be there directly.'

'How long?' you ask.

'Given the weather, it could be hours, sir, so hide up, stay safe and out of sight.'

The authorities are coming but who knows when. You still need to solve this mystery and get some evidence to give to them when they do arrive, so hiding is not an option.


There's no time to hang about so you decide to explore elsewhere.

Do you (if you have not already done so):

Enter the sitting room – <u>763</u>

Enter the dining room – <u>576</u>

Enter the kitchen – <u>298</u>

Go upstairs – <u>119</u>

Leave by the front door – <u>384</u>

# 367

Okay, so clearly you are meant to move a piece. But which one and to where?

Do you

Move the snake – <u>663</u>

Move the eagle – <u>631</u>

Move the man – <u>732</u>

Move the woman – <u>754</u>

# 368

The table is missing its wine which you remember you were sent to fetch. Clearly, at some point tonight, the invited guests were going to dine, something the Doctor failed to tell you but then again you had brought significant provisions over these last few days. You are only the gofer after all.

There are six set places at the table, and you notice the name cards before each seat. The nearest seats show: Miss Elsie Gonzales, Doctor Flavius Monroe and Kyla Mertens. Clearly the Doctor was surrounding himself with his female guests. To check out the other settings you will need to go round the other side of the table which will bring you close to the curtains.

Do you want to examine the other side of the table – 140

Or do you decide enough is enough and then

Examine the hatch – 401

Take the door to the kitchen – 183

Check out what is causing the curtains to move – 251

## 369

The wind lifts you off your feet and it blows you onto the balcony before knocking you off it, over the wall that surrounds it. A desperate hand of yours makes a grab for the ladder and you find yourself hanging momentarily before you lose grip and fall again. You reach out with both hands and manage to slow yourself down as you fall by contacting the ladder. A last gasp grab of the ivy takes most of the momentum out of your fall, and you hit the ground hard.

When you rise, something feels a little off inside, but you need to keep going. Make an entry in your code list of **Gutted**. Now return to the front of the Lookout at 136 and try another option. Note that you may no longer try and climb up the outside, due to the pain you are feeling.

# 370

You slip in the side entrance of the boathouse and find yourself on the lower floor. Before you is a small dock holding a dinghy with oars. On the far wall are lifejackets and other maritime equipment. A set of stairs leads upstairs at the rear of the building and there is a locker across from them.

Do you

Examine the dinghy – 044

Look at the lifejackets – 496

Take the stairs to the upper floor – 315

Check out the locker at the rear of the room – 584

Decide there's nothing here for you and return outside – 692

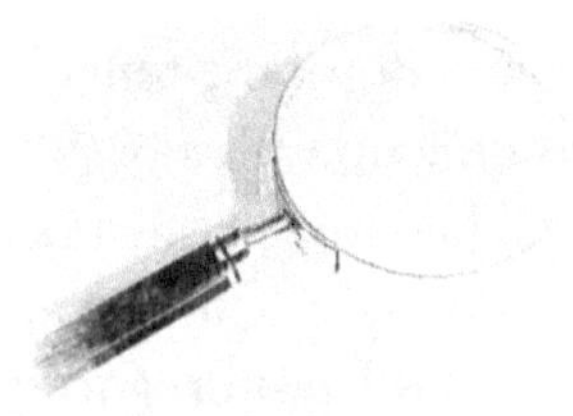

## 371

The lock on the door makes a whirring sound and you open it – go to 005

## 372

If you have codeword **Killer** then go to 748. If not read on.

You flick on the light and see Daniel Lyle, the athlete. He's wet through standing in trousers and a shirt but he's also looking very scared now that he's identified it's you.

Do you

Tell him not to panic, it wasn't you who shot the Doctor – 974

Ask him what he's doing here – 553

Draw your gun if you have one – 434

## 373

You shove your hand down the toilet bowl and poke around before coming up with a piece of wire with a piece of paper attached in a plastic pocket. You open the pocket and read a memo indicating that the Doctor is wishing to not sell his latest drug for profit and Patrick Davidson is furious. Maybe the Doctor found this in his pocket, who knows? Strange to flush it down the toilet. Note the codeword **Bowl** in your code list. And seriously, wash your hands afterwards!

Now that unhygienic investigation is over, do you

Read the magazine - 305

Or

Examine the bed - 046

Check the silk dressing gowns - 505

Descend the stairs - 991

Or leave the Lookout completely and head for the coastal path - 990


# 374

You hold your hands out in front of you and find the wall to guide you further into the tomb. As you blindly step in you can hear footsteps in the dark. Your breathing quickens as you know someone is in here with you.

Do you

Continue - 431

Retreat to another part of the ruins and

Enter the temple - 280

Check out the sacrificial slab - 246

Look at the gaming board - 426

Decide this area is no longer useful or too risky and continue along the coastal path at 998

# 375

Go to <u>002</u>

# 376

The number pad goes red, and you hear a horrible buzzer indicate you are wrong.

Do you try another number?

3267 - <u>309</u>

2758 - <u>856</u>

9746 - <u>032</u>

Another code – <u>294</u>

Or do you

Use the Doctor's swipe card on the reader if you have it – <u>134</u>

Try to climb the Ivy – <u>004</u>

 Or if this all seems to hard or unwise, you could simply keep on walking the coastal path to your next location at <u>990</u> but note that you have visited the Lookout

# 377

You make the connection, and you smile as the lights on the vessel come on. You don't waste a moment and go to the controls and start the engine. You know if you head west, you'll get to a foreign land. You cruise on through the night and only once do you see another vessel light once you have left the island area.

On landing ashore, you spend two weeks hiding out in a farmer's barn before making your way into town and finding a job mucking out pigs.

It takes five years before you have a steady job and income which lets you go to South America. Back home the police still look for you but quietly as they assume you died trying to escape. Still, you now have a different life. Is this a win? Maybe, maybe not, but you never found out who framed you. If you want to, start again at 001.

# 378

You punch in the code and the pad turns red and a coarse noise like a bad input on a computer sounds. Nothing happens and you are left with the pad again.

Do you enter another code? Which one?

2758 - <u>883</u>

3267 - <u>966</u>

9746 - <u>226</u>

4837 - <u>035</u>

Another code - <u>836</u>

Or do you leave the pad alone? If so, make your next choice at <u>816</u>

# 379

You swipe the card again but still you notice no difference. Enter the code **Sesame** in your code list. If you have the code **Baba** cross it out. What will you do now?

Enter a code on the pad (only if you have found one) – <u>491</u>

Or leave the item alone and

Check out the tin – <u>400</u>

Investigate the switch – <u>275</u>

Or if none of this inspires you, go back to the lagoon entrance and make another choice – <u>879</u>

# 380

You draw your weapon and shoot the lock, causing the padlock to shatter. You quickly open the locker but think you can hear someone nearby. You think about staying but choose to run, not wanting to be found. It was a bit daft to alert everyone to where you are. Desperately you flee the boathouse, and run to the coastal path at 981

# 381

You decide one swipe is enough. Enter the code **Baba** in your code list. If you have the code **Sesame**, cross it out. So, what next?

Enter a code on the pad (only if you have found one) (only if you have found one)  – 320

Or leave the item alone and

Check out the tin – 250

Investigate the switch – 003

Or if none of this inspires you, go back to the lagoon entrance and make another choice – 423

# 382

You switch off the beam of light and hunch down in the passageway. As you wait, holding your breath, you hear footsteps coming closer, making their way towards you. They are so very close.

Do you

Switch on the light – 147

Stay in the dark – 594

## 383

You fire a warning shot into the air and watch Patrick shudder and then run even harder. He's gone before you even know it. But that shot will possibly bring others and if the authorities have arrived then they will be here. You'll need to keep moving. You run to the coastal path at 770

## 384

Leaving the front door behind, you step out into some wild weather. The rain is beating down hard, and the wind is whipping its way around the comfortable house of Doctor Munro, and you don't want to venture too far. But the answers are not behind you, surely they are ahead.

As you brace yourself to depart, you see something in the garden glinting back the light from the house to you. What could it be? Maybe it is something the Doctor dropped but surely that would be strange. Maybe it's the killer lying in wait for you. Looking around, you try to see if the guests have followed a path away from the house, but you see all the evidence of such a move has been washed clean by the rain. Although the paths are gravel, many now have little puddles all over them and who knows who went where.

The house is surrounded by gardens of different types but all immediately accessible for they are of a manageable size for the daily gardener who also has the more substantial gardens to look after, also on the island. By the house is a private garden, a vegetable patch and also a patio space where the Doctor would sit on sunny days.

What will you do now? Do you

Pay a visit to the private garden where you saw the glint of light – 914

Examine the vegetable patch – 104

Take a look at the patio – 662

Or

Decide to head off on one of the paths – 297

# 385

You hear the door click shut behind you and a whirring sound makes you suspicious. You try the door behind you and find it locked. You are now trapped and need some way out. There's nothing to do except look around the room for help.

What will you look at?

Examine the desk with the computer – 220

Look at the small pile of books and the chair – 634

Check out the picture on the wall – 098

Examine the coat stand – 428

# 386

You tell the detective to check your belongings for the note from the Doctor to Patrick Davidson that you found in the toilet bowl. When the note is brought to the detective from your belongings, he gives it some careful attention before turning back to you.

"So, there was a change of plans and Mr Davidson didn't like it. But if he killed the Doctor then who would make the decision not to go ahead. Kyla Mertens told us she wanted the drug stopped from going on commercial sale so simply killing the Doctor may not have been enough Do you have anything else you can tell or show me."

You're still in trouble. What else do you have?

If you have the codeword **Taunt** – 128

If you have any of the following codewords go to that section. Follow the list downwards and only go to the first section that you have a codeword in.

**Grumble** – 446

**Pads, Paddy, Silent Papers, Cold Blood, Murder, Hitman, Merto** – 415

**Gutted** – 048

Otherwise – 995

# 387

You find yourself in the Doctor's bathroom with a toilet, sink, and a bath. Above the sink is a bathroom cabinet with a mirrored front but otherwise the bathroom is nothing special, although it is thankfully clean. Unless you want to check out the cabinet there's nothing here.

Do you

Examine the cabinet – 040

Return to the landing – 119

# 388

The copper vases are a striking feature in the hallway, and you realise that the Doctor had good taste. There is some soil inside the vases and the leafy plants seem to be doing well. In the third vase you notice a small piece of paper. It appears to be a speech but not in the Doctor's handwriting which you would recognise quite easily. There's truly little detail as the speech has been torn up at some point and this is a mere scrap. But someone knew what the Doctor was going to say.

Pocketing the piece of paper, you decide to move on.

Do you (if you have not already done so):

Enter the sitting room – <u>763</u>

Enter the dining room – <u>576</u>

Enter the kitchen – <u>298</u>

Go upstairs – <u>119</u>

Leave by the front door – <u>384</u>

# 389

At first glance it is a standard toilet with a wooden seat that no doubt doesn't give you a cold bottom. You force yourself to look behind it and only find a small spider trying to mind its own business. Glancing inside the bowl, you think you see something at the bottom of it, under the waterline.

Do you

Want to reach in and grab what's in the bowl (I know, I know) – <u>523</u>

Or are you done with all this toilet shenanigans and instead

Examine the bed – <u>615</u>

Check the silk dressing gowns – <u>312</u>

Descend the stairs – <u>811</u>

Or leave the Lookout completely and head for the coastal path – <u>988</u>

# **390**

You think about the best friend you could call in this situation. Janine Armstrong would be perfect, sensible but loyal. You dial her number and await her answer.

'Hello.'

'Is Janine there?' you ask.

'No, she's away this weekend. Can I help?' It's Janine's mother, not the most stable of women in the best of situations but she'll have to do. You tell her the details of what has happened and hear her breathing accelerate.

'Why did you kill him, Peter? Why? Police! I'm calling the police.' With that the telephone is put down and you are left holding the receiver. You try to wait and see if she picks up again but the tone on the line does not change. You replace the telephone earpiece wondering just what the woman will say to the police.

There's no time to hang about, you need to get on and find some evidence that clears you.

 Do you (if you have not already done so):

Enter the sitting room – 763

Enter the dining room – 576

Enter the kitchen – 298

Go upstairs – 119

Leave by the front door – 384

# 391

"Who's there?"

"Don't shoot me," says a voice and you recognise it as Elsie Gonzales. "Please switch on the light."

You flick on the light and see the newspaper reporter. She's soaked through, wearing a coat over her skirt and high heels. Her face seems to go into panic as she sees it's you.

Do you

Tell her not to panic, it wasn't you who shoot the Doctor – <u>152</u>

Ask her what she's doing here – <u>695</u>

Draw your gun if you have one – <u>835</u>

# 392

"Kyla Mertens," laughs the detective. "What on earth makes you think that? I know she was working with the Doctor on a performing enhancing drug, and they were to start production with it. Everything we have says she was happy with the arrangements. Do you have any evidence to the contrary?"

You think over your evidence, but you don't have anything that would incriminate Kyla Mertens, specifically.

If you have the codeword **Taunt** and wish to use that evidence – 173

If not and,

You have the codeword **Gutted** – 048

If you have neither – 048

## 393

Someone is there and you are taking no risks. It could be the murderer and you don't want to end up dead. You turn and run as hard as you can out to the hall and then straight through the door to the wind and rain outside. That may have been a lucky escape. Or you could have just been spooked by the wind. You'll never know but you are safe. Time to find more clues as to who framed you.

Go to 384

## 394

You think you may have something in the grass and your hand closes around some sort of gemstone. But then someone hits you from above and everything goes black.

Maybe there was a trial, maybe you were found guilty or innocent, maybe they caught someone else for the Doctor's murder. You'll never know because you were careless and now your life is over.

Thank goodness this is a gamebook and not real-life and you can reincarnate at 001 and try again. And this time, be careful. No, really, be careful!

# 395

You dive down to the object you see half-buried and find a small treasure box in the sandy residue at the bottom of the lagoon. You carefully haul it out and drag it onto the edge of the lagoon. As you take it from the water, and realise it is made from plastic. You flip a catch at the front and find a piece of paper inside and a photo.

*Congratulations, you believed the stories and you have found your treasure.*

You look at the photo and see it is of the Doctor's Mother with the words *my treasure*, written on it in pen.

What a waste of time! You climb to your feet ready to begin investigating again.

Do you

Dive back in and make for the potential passageway – 172

Or instead

Investigate "The Hollow" – 819

Climb up to the tree hut – 410

Decide you have had enough of the lagoon and make your move to the coastal path and your next destination – 549

# 396

The number pad goes red, and you hear a horrible buzzer indicate you are wrong.

Do you try another number?

3267 – 686

2758 – 006

9746 – 244

Another code – 651

Or do you

Use the Doctor's swipe card on the reader if you have it – 520

Try to climb the Ivy – 277

 Or if this all seems to hard or unwise, you could simply keep on walking the coastal path to your next location at 988 but note that you have visited the Lookout

## 397

You run as hard as you can, all the while watching the figure across from you with the axe. As you reach over halfway, they seem to panic and toss the axe over the cliff and run. You reach the far side of the bridge and double up, throwing up due to the crazy exertion you have just committed. When you recover, the figure is long gone, as is the axe. There's no way you are going back out to that hut, and you reckon you need to move quickly in case the mystery figure is still about. Flee the gardens now to the coastal path at 770

## 398

The vegetable garden has an array of crops growing from cauliflowers to lettuces and some have shrouds over them to protect them from the seasons. In the corner is a series of compost bins and there's a wheelbarrow against a far wall.

Do you

Examine the shrouds – 271

Open the compost bins – 080

Have a look at the wheelbarrow – 487

Or leave and

Enter the orchard – 447

Wander to the ornamental garden – 042

Or

Check out the fountains area – <u>156</u>

Make your way to the greenhouse – <u>745</u>

Wander over to the gardening equipment sheds – <u>262</u>

Or if you doubt the gardens will be of any use then take the coastal path at <u>211</u> but note that you have visited the gardens

# 399

You make the connection and suddenly a sharp pain rides through your body. You try to release your hand, but you can't and soon you black out never to wake again. Well, it was always a risk. You'll never know who set you up unless you return to <u>001</u> and give it another go!

# 400

You look at the tin and find it to be ornate and have a relief of cupcakes on the lid. Opening it, you find several cupcakes inside. Hungrily you eat, finding them to be delicious. However, that's enough stuffing your face. If you wish you can take them with you by entering **tin of cupcakes** in your inventory. But what next?

Do you

Look at the rubber cover – <u>816</u>

Investigate the switch – <u>275</u>

Or if none of this inspires you, go back to the lagoon entrance and make another choice – <u>879</u>

# 401

Have you examined the hatch from the kitchen side?

If so – <u>045</u>

If not – <u>259</u>

# 402

You take out your weapon and aim it at the lock. You shoot and must duck for cover as the bullet ricochets around the room. The noise is deafening and may have woken the dead. If anyone is near the boathouse they will surely be on their way here. You check the lock, but it remained intact.

You know you need to flee, lest someone else arrives but maybe that lock would break with a second shot?

Do you

Shoot again – <u>117</u>

Wait to see if anyone arrives – <u>730</u>

Scarper while you can all the way to the coastal path – <u>980</u>

# 403

"Flavius brought them here. Don't you see, before the aliens got him, he was set to get to the rocket and create a new mankind. Kyla was there to be the brains; her children would be clever. Elsie would have children who would be inquisitive and gorgeous. Patrick would bring enterprise to the offspring. And Daniel would produce strong children. And you, your children could drive everyone about."

You feel as if your talents are not really valued but is the woman just nuts. Or is she bluffing?

Do you

Draw your gun (if you have one) and tell her to start talking – 627

Ask how she got here – 761

Or

Leave Granma in peace and retreat from the cave

If you entered by torch light – 489

Otherwise – 858

# 404

You punch in the code and the pad flashes green but nothing else happens and you are left with the pad again. You decide to leave the pad alone but enter the word **Baba** in your code list. Make your next choice at 816

# 405

As you near the section you see that there is an open passageway in the rock, and you surface for another breath before diving back down and swimming through the gap in the rock. You swim for only a few yards before the rock above you disappears and you surface into a large cave at 324

# 406

How will you smash it? If you have a gun, you could

Shoot the window – 556

Break the window with the butt of the gun – 566

Or

Use your fists to break it – 950

Look for something else – 354

Or give up and climb back down the tower to 151 and choose another option.

## 407

You have Elsie's letter to the Doctor which explains her opposition to a drug the Doctor was working on. Having seen her brother put into a wheelchair by experimental drugs, Elsie states she would kill to prevent this type of experimentation. That's pretty good evidence, certainly a motive.

## 408

Do you

Swim for the half-buried object – 395

Or exit the water and

Investigate "The Hollow" – 819

Climb up to the tree hut – 410

Decide you have had enough of the lagoon and make your move to the coastal path and your next destination – 549

## 409

You tell the detective to check your belongings for the note from the Doctor to Patrick Davidson that you found in the toilet bowl. When the note is brought to the detective from your belongings, he gives it some careful attention before turning back to you.

"So, there was a change of plans and Mr Davidson didn't like it. But if he killed the Doctor then who would make the decision not to go ahead. Kyla Mertens told us she wanted the drug stopped from going on commercial sale so simply killing the Doctor may not have been enough Do you have anything else you can tell or show me."

You're still in trouble. What else do you have?

If you have any of the following codewords go to that section. Follow the list downwards and only go to the first section that you have a codeword in.

**Taunt** – 321

**Grumble** – 446

**Pads, Paddy, Silent Papers, Cold Blood, Murder, Hitman, Merto** – 415

**Gutted** – 048

Otherwise read on:

The detective arrests you for the Doctor's murder saying that you were still seen with the gun over the body. All you have is a potential heated comment. At the trial you cut a lonely figure as it only takes the jury an hour to convict you. From your jail cell you wonder if you were right in your choice of killer. You'll never know. Maybe try again at 001.

# 410

You make your way over to the tree hut and climb a wooden ladder up to the small balcony at the front of the house. Stepping inside, you see a single room but one with a small kitchenette, a double bed, and a small wardrobe. There is a television on the wall and a small wine collection on a table. There are also two relaxing chairs in the middle of the room.

Well, the doctor certainly knows how to live but is there anything worth looking at in here?

Do you

Look inside the wardrobe – 072

Examine the bed – 804

Rifle through the kitchenette – 768

Try out the chairs – 630

Or

Investigate "The Hollow" – 819

Dive into the lagoon and see if you can find the Doctor's secret stash – 924

Decide you have had enough of the lagoon and make your move to the coastal path and your next destination – 549

# 411

You panic and taking your gun, you simply shoot the old woman. This is a rather extreme and brutal measure and not very helpful as you are trying to solve a murder, not commit more. The woman slumps to the ground and you realise she's dead, but the shot made a heck of a noise and there may be people coming your way. You decide you need to get away from this mistake as soon as you can. You run to the coastal path at <u>990</u> and make your next choice there. But note **Cold Blood** in your code list.

# 412

You take out the gun and fire it quickly four times. Something in front of you is knocked back several feet but the noise of the gun reverberates around the room and probably the building. You are able to escape by the way you entered the building, leaving the creature for dead, but decide to strike out on foot for the coastal path before anyone arrives to find out the reason for the gunshots. Join the coastal path at <u>983</u>

# 413

You run as hard as you can, but the figure is mighty quick with the axe. Go <u>803</u>

# 414

You peer into the darkness but you can only hear someone coming. You hold your breath, eyes straining but as you finally catch the faint outline of a figure, you realise it is on top of you. Something hits you on top of the head.

In the following days, the police blame you for the murder and the person who attacked you walks away scot-free from there dastardly deed with the Doctor. Of course, it's..., no you'll need to play again at 001, but this time beware the dark

# 415

"We've found other bodies, Mr O'Malley. You've been busy!" You remember the blood you spilt. That's what they will see. "Take him away, officer!"

It seems your lot is sealed. Not enough evidence gathered to protect yourself. Try again at 001 and see if you can get more evidence next time. Oh, and don't kill anyone!

# 416

You shout into the darkness, and you hear your voice reverberate around the tomb. If someone is in there they will certainly know you are coming. You decide that without a torch it would be foolish to proceed.

If you have a torch and wish to try it – 658

If not,

Enter the temple – 273

Check out the sacrificial slab – 742

Look at the gaming board – 165

Or

Decide this area is no longer useful or too risky and continue along the coastal path at 996

# 417

You hear a horrible buzz come from the keypad indicating it has not accepted the code. Will you try again?

3267 – 176

4837 – 486

2758 – 567

9746 – 875

Or a different code – 108

Or

Return to the hall – 212

# 418

"Grandma Munro," says the detective stroking his moustache. "You're going to have to show me some evidence sunshine, she's just an old woman. How on earth do you believe it's her? What can you tell me?"

You think over your evidence, but you don't have anything that would incriminate Daniel Lyle, specifically.

If you have the codeword **Taunt** and wish to use that evidence - 116

If not and,

You have the codeword **Gutted** - 048

If you have neither - 048

# 419

The view out to sea is breath-taking and you scan the horizon for any boats or helicopters that might be coming to the island. You can see none and for a moment feel as if you can do this, time being on your side. Even the chill of your wet clothes is not enough to down your spirits.

Your heart skips a beat as you hear a crash. One of the bridges has collapsed and you see a figure with an axe running for the other one. You have a bit of a head start but not much. You pocket the note and make a run for it. Go 826

# 420

The ornamental garden has a bewildering array of plants, and you struggle to identify even a quarter of them. But that's not your purpose here and you look around the ground for anything unusual. There appears to be a small aperture in the ground beside a hazel tree. Just beyond it is a lever on a pipe running just above the ground. Maybe this could be something.

Do you

Turn the lever - 529

Or leave and

Enter the orchard - 560

Walk to the vegetable garden - 014

Or

Check out the fountains area - 526

Make your way to the greenhouse - 722

Wander over to the gardening equipment sheds - 121

Or if you doubt the gardens will be of any use then take the coastal path at 770 but note that you have visited the gardens

## 421

You grab the phials and throw them at the creature. At first it rears up and then sniffs the broken phials. But it soon ignores it and begins to charge at you.

Do you have a gun? If so, use it - 261

Otherwise - 960

## 422

The bottles fall and the fuel inside spills all over the floor. Luckily it misses you and luckier still, the blowtorch went out as it hit the ground. Carefully you pick yourself up and delicately extract yourself from the shed. That was close. But what next?

Leave the shed and

Check out the fountains area - 526

Take a look in the walled garden - 625

Make your way to the greenhouse - 722

Wander over to the gardening equipment sheds - 121

Or if you doubt the gardens will be of any use then take the coastal path at 770 but note that you have visited the gardens

## 423

The rain is pouring down as you arrive along the stony path to the lagoon, a large expanse of water separated from the sea by a thin stretch of land. It is difficult to see before your arrival as a perimeter of trees surround it and you are grateful for the small lights that are running around the water's edge, an idea of the Doctor's.

Looking around the lagoon, you realise you have only ever walked past it once when making an initial tour of the island and you now take a moment to look at it more thoroughly. You can see several features that may be worth exploring. There is a space called "The Hollow" which is basically a small open hut that has been sunk into the ground allowing you to sit and gaze at the lagoon from water level. There is also a tree hut which overlooks the lake although *hut* may be too simple a word for the construct. There is also the lagoon itself, and you know the rumours about the sunken treasure that lies within, a relic from an ancient pirate but also thought of as one of the Doctor's secret stashes for his most sensitive work.

Sheltering under a tree, you ponder your next move. Do you

Investigate "The Hollow" – 819

Climb up to the tree hut – 410

Dive into the lagoon and see if you can find the Doctor's secret stash – 924

Decide you have had enough of the lagoon and make your move to the coastal path and your next destination – 549

## 424

The magazines are a mess on the floor, but you see an article in one that tells of the terrific improvement made by Daniel Lyle on the athletics track, specifically how he seems to be lasting much better over long distances, having almost no drop off in pace. His much hailed improvement seems to be taking him places.

Interesting read but do you

Examine the pool table – 110

Look at the darts board – 248

Open the fridge – 075

Take hold of the scrap of paper – 270

Or

Enter the toilet – 655

Check out the chart room – 618

Investigate the room with no name – 521

Return to the lower floor – 795

## 425

The special projects door has a keypad on it which is currently green. It is looking for a 4-digit code and advises you have two attempts before an alarm will sound. It looks very similar to the keypad on the front door and has a swipe card reader on the side. Beyond the door, you can see only darkness through the glass.

Do you wish to open the door?

Use the Doctor's access card if you have it – <u>504</u>

Try a code (only if you have found one) – <u>904</u>

Try and break down the door – <u>751</u>

# 426

You approach a fascinating marble board with four characters on it. It sits on the ground, slightly pronounced with a lip on all four edges of the board. The board has chess type squares but has only three squares per side giving a total of nine squares. You can see four different figurines on the board.

In the middle of the board is a carving of a woman with a laurel wreath on her head. She wears a long flowing garment and is cast in white. She has a sad look on her face with tears falling from one eye.

Two of the other figures are in the middle of a side, one to the left of the woman as you look and one beyond her. The last figure is on a corner square.

The three figures are a snake with three heads, an eagle with its wings outstretched, and a man with a large broadsword holding it high above his head. He is wearing chainmail and is facing the woman. The snake has one head extended out to the woman and the eagle has a wing reaching for her.

Walking around the board you can see no crevices, or openings. Giving the eagle a gentle push, you find it can be easily lifted, as can the other pieces when you try them.

Do you

Try to figure out this mystery – 367

Shoot the pieces and board with your gun (if you have one) – 755

Decide this is a waste of time and

Make for the tomb and shelter from the rain – 033

Enter the temple – 280

Check out the sacrificial slab – 246

Or

Decide this area is no longer useful or too risky and continue along the coastal path at 998

# 427

The boat tips up and you are thrown out into the surf. You get caught by the undertow and you are dragged out. You have no extra buoyancy and cannot get to the surface. Despite your best efforts you don't find the surface of the water again.

It's three weeks before your body surfaces at an inlet on the mainland. The police had thought you escaped because the dinghy was never found but now, they know their killer has suffered natural justice. Who actually killed the Doctor? Well, you'll never know.

Next time, listen to the maritime authorities and take a lifejacket. You can try again at <u>001</u>

# 428

There is a lab coat on the stand and a pair of boots underneath which seem to be caked in mud. You search the coat pockets but only find a dirty tissue inside which kind of sticks to your fingers. The boots underneath deposit some of the mud as you pick them up, but you see they are simple work boots with a steel toe cap. Inside one of them is a newspaper cutting.

The cutting shows a picture of Daniel Lyle from a few years ago winning a sprint race and testifies to his future. However, the face of Daniel has a red cross over it.

There is nothing further of note here.

Do you

Examine the desk with the computer – <u>220</u>

Look at the small pile of books and the chair – <u>634</u>

Check out the picture on the wall – <u>098</u>

## 429

You fire a shot at the woman, but it glances past her. You run after her, but she is gone into the night. You realise the shot must have echoed around the tomb and would have been so noisy, it would have cut through the weather outside. You decide you need to move on before anyone comes.

You make for the coastal path at 998

## 430

Your t-shirt rips but you are clear and sprint up the steps to the upper deck. A knife flies past your ear as you run off the boat, but you don't look back and run for your life all the way to the coastal path. Once there you realise you are clear and fee to move on at 980.

## 431

You sit in the dark hearing the footsteps come right past you and you feel the sweat on your brow. You shake a little but control your nerves, remaining quiet as the footsteps pass by and go to the exit of the tomb. You wait several minutes until all is quiet again and you are sure the unknown intruder is clear of the tomb. It's too dark in here and you can't see anything. Who knows who is lurking in here? You decide to retreat to another part of the ruins and

Enter the temple – <u>280</u>

Check out the sacrificial slab – <u>246</u>

Look at the gaming board – <u>426</u>

Or

Decide this area is no longer useful or too risky and continue along the coastal path at <u>998</u>

## 432

Go to <u>417</u>

## 433

Is it a key with green tape?

If so – <u>536</u>

If not, the key does not fit, and you'll need to try something else at <u>277</u>

## 434

Daniel looks terrified. You have him trapped with a gun in a room with one door. He reminds you of a rabbit in the headlights, his eyes wide and unblinking. And then he bolts for the door.

Do you

Shoot – <u>186</u>

Let him go - <u>245</u>

# 435

You tell the detective about your threatening note from when someone tried to kill you at the fountains. The detective takes it away and returns an hour later with a smile on his face.

"We checked out your story about nearly being killed and the handwriting on the note. I believe you son, and the writing is that of Kyla Mertens. I have just arrested her for your attempted murder. However, there is still the question of Doctor Munro's murder. Do you have anything further?"

You shake your head.

If you have any of the following codewords go to that section. Follow the list downwards and only go to the first section that you have a codeword in.

**Grumble** – 446

**Pads, Paddy, Silent Papers, Cold Blood, Murder, Hitman, Merto** – 415

**Gutted** – 048

Otherwise, read on:

The detective arrests you for the Doctor's murder saying that you were still seen with the gun over the body. All you have is a potential heated comment. At the trial you cut a lonely figure as it only takes the jury an hour to convict you. From your jail cell you wonder if you were right in your choice of killer. You'll never know. Maybe try again at <u>001</u>.

## 436

You walk around the dock to the lifejackets and see an array of orange devices. Trying them on you find one that fits and if you want to take it with you, note **lifejacket** in your inventory. You also find a scrap of paper tucked inside one lifejacket. It looks like the Doctor's lifejacket and seems to be a company resume for Patrick Davidson's company. It gives a glowing report in the little you can read but there is red pen across it saying *CHECK* in capital letters.

That appears to be it for the lifejackets. Do you

Examine the dinghy – <u>060</u>

Take the stairs to the upper floor – <u>581</u>

Check out the locker at the rear of the room – <u>957</u>

Or

Head over to the marina – <u>465</u>

Or if you want to continue elsewhere take the coastal path at <u>980</u>

## 437

You tell the detective about the notelet you found where the Doctor told Elsie all about Grandma

Munro's problems. The detective seems intrigued and studies the note for a while before disappearing. As he returns, he has a smile on his face.

"Good news, Peter. Elsie was questioned about your attempted murder, and she tried to blame Grandma Munro. With you as her victim, she also tried to blame Grandma for the Doctor's death, but we can see what she has been planning. Grandma was to be her scapegoat. But we got her, Peter, thanks to you."

You step outside and smell the fresh air and know you will not be going to jail. It seems crazy but you've done it. No longer framed. Well done, top sleuth!

## 438

You grab the handset and, being an experienced operator, you press the handset down firmly.

"Mayday, mayday, mayday, this is the shore station at Munro Island. We have a distress situation concerning an attack on the owner of the island. Request assistance. I repeat, request, assistance. Medical and Police."

The reply is faint.

"....Island... Mayday acknowledged.... Weather improving.... Expect.... Delay.... 3 hours.... Longer...."

You try several more times but there is no further reply. Maybe the set is malfunctioning or something else is at play. Whatever has happened, you got your message out. Note the word **Coastguard** in your code list.

Now, do you

Check out the photographs – 184

Have a rifle through the drawers – 865

Look at the writing desk – 897

Or

Climb up the spiral staircase – 506

Descend the spiral staircase - 821

Decide to leave the Lookout and make your way to the coastal path – 990

# 439

The door which states it leads to the Doctor's office is locked but there is a keypad on the door and a swipe strip for a card. Otherwise, you are not sure how to get the door open.

Do you have the Doctor's access card and wish to use it? If so – 057

Otherwise, you can try the access code. However, you note that it has a warning underneath saying that entering the wrong code twice will set off an alarm which will bring the attention of the security services. If you have a code and wish to try it then

4837 – 287

9746 – 902

3267 – 135

2758 – 293

Another code – 115

If none of this excites you then do you

Enter the canteen – 071

Try to get into the cleaners' cupboard – 571

Try to enter the office of Kyla Mertens – 237

Or return to the hall – 212

# 440

You try to take shelter from the driving rain under a large plant with enormous leaves. There are a number of exotic plants on the island, and you wish you understood them better but at least this one is providing protection as good as a bus shelter.

You sit tight looking along the path and towards the laboratory, waiting to see if anything will happen. If nothing happens soon then you will need to move on to find other evidence to prove your innocence.

Then you hear the crunch of stones and in the driving rain you lose just how the person arrived at the front door of the laboratory. It looks like Patrick Davidson, the businessman, and he is punching in a code to the keypad. Pulling open the door, he enters and disappears inside.

The front door is closing slowly, and you might just make it before it closes. On the other hand, you might run into Patrick Davidson and that might not be a good idea. Would you rather search in private? Will you get a chance to search the laboratory at all if you don't take this chance?

Do you

Run for the closing door – 174

Ignore the door and sit tight – 008

# 441

You swim back out with your torch lighting up the water in front of you. Climbing back out of the lagoon you ponder your next move.

Investigate "The Hollow" – 819

Climb up to the tree hut – 410

Decide you have had enough of the lagoon and make your move to the coastal path and your next destination – 549

# 442

"Daniel Lyle," says the detective stroking his moustache. "You're going to have to show me some evidence sunshine, as he's a respected athlete. I know he was here for the launch of the new drug and maybe that would help with his sports but what evidence do you have that he was up to something more sinister. What can you tell me?"

If you have any of the following codewords go to that section. Follow the list downwards and only go to the first section that you have a codeword in.

**Tests** – 360

**Taunt** – 932

**Grumble** – 583

**Pads, Paddy, Silent Papers, Cold Blood, Murder, Hitman, Merto** – 636

**Gutted** – 048

Otherwise – 995

# 443

"Daniel Lyle," says the detective stroking his moustache. "You're going to have to show me some evidence sunshine, as he's a respected athlete. I know he was here for the launch of the new drug and maybe that would help with his sports but what evidence do you have that he was up to something more sinister. What can you tell me?"

You think over your evidence, but you don't have anything that would incriminate Daniel Lyle, specifically.

If you have the codeword **Taunt** and wish to use that evidence - 173

If not and,

You have the codeword **Gutted** - 048

If you have neither - 048

# 444

The small folly is wooden and just over a man high and only 6 feet wide. As you approach, you see a candle is alight inside it and that a small wooden chair is placed beside a writing table.

If you have a torch, you try it and find that it has run out of battery. You'll need to keep your eyes peeled.

Opening the door, you can see an amount of liquid spilled on the table and it is dripping onto the chair. It seems to have come from a small canister which is lying on its side, and which has also dropped its contents onto paper which is in the middle of the table. The rest of the folly is empty.


Do you

Pick up the paper to read – 480

Pick up the canister to examine – 056

Grab the candle to examine everything a lot closer – 782

Or leave the folly and choose to look elsewhere – 156


# 445

The cruiser has two decks and as you clamber onboard the vessel, you are amazed at the luxury. You note the steps down to the lower deck and the two distinct sections to the upper deck. There is the main wheelhouse on top along with a rear section that contains several lockers. The boat, although large is definitely wobbling, and you reach out for a handhold.

Do you

Go to the lower deck via the stairs – 543

Check out the wheelhouse – 861

Look at the lockers at the aft of the upper deck – 954

Or

Jump onto the speedboat – 869

Or, if you haven't already,

Make for the main building – <u>795</u>

Or if you want to continue elsewhere take the coastal path at <u>980</u>

## 446

"It seems we have your DNA on the Doctor's body, Mr O'Malley. Peter, they saw you there, a gun in your hand, your DNA's on the body and you have no other credible evidence implicating anyone else in the Doctor's death. Take him away, officer!"

It seems your lot is sealed. Not enough evidence gathered to protect yourself. Try again at <u>001</u> and see if you can get more evidence next time.

## 447

The orchard is abundant with fruit, and you know you would probably have been asked to come and help with the picking in the coming weeks. However, as much as it is abundant, it is also devoid of any life. There's not much to do here and you cannot see anything of use.

Do you

Try an apple – <u>687</u>

Try a pear – <u>537</u>

Leave and

Walk to the vegetable garden - <u>398</u>

Wander to the ornamental garden - <u>042</u>

Or

Check out the fountains area - <u>156</u>

Make your way to the greenhouse - <u>745</u>

Wander over to the gardening equipment sheds - <u>262</u>

Or if you doubt the gardens will be of any use then take the coastal path at <u>211</u> but note that you have visited the gardens

## 448

You draw your gun and fire a shot straight at the window. Even in the wind that shot must have been heard a mile off. The smashing of the window would not have helped either. You look around nervously. If they heard that and come for you, you will be trapped in the Lookout. You cannot take that risk. So much for stealth. You climb down the ladder and then drop down via the ivy until you are back on the ground. Time is of the essence if they are coming so you run to the coastal path at <u>988</u>

## 449

You tell the detective about the documents in your backpack relating to Daniel Lyles involvement and subsequent dropping from the drug tests the Doctor was conducting. The detective at first seems impressed but then frowns. "It is something but not exactly a clear-cut conviction. Have you anything else that could help?"

If you have any of the following codewords go to that section. Follow the list downwards and only go to the first section that you have a codeword in.

**Taunt** – 683

**Grumble** – 583

**Pads, Paddy, Silent Papers, Cold Blood, Murder, Hitman, Merto** – 636

**Gutted** – 048

Otherwise, read on:

The detective still says you have enough evidence against you that you have to go to trial. It seems that the jury sees enough uncertainty for you are found not guilty. However, the papers do not see it that way, a man with a gun in his hand at a body. Your life becomes a hell, followed by the press, until you leave the country. It might seem unfair but at least you are not in jail. As for who actually killed the Doctor, you still don't know. Maybe try again at 001.

# 450

The note reads,

"I don't know how much longer she can stay on the island as her madness grows daily. I don't wish to send her to some institution, but it is becoming dangerous. Who knows what she can do, Elsie?"

Note the code word **Notelet** in your list and return to the entry you came from.

# 451

You gleefully pick up the coin and lob it skilfully in beside the cherub. Did you make a wish?

If so – 532

If not - 737

# 452

You tell the detective about the note you found in the ruins that is in your backpack. He retrieves it and take a while studying it before returning to you.

"Now that is interesting, but it is also not proof. You still have a lot to answer for. Do you have anything to back up this solid piece of evidence?"

If you have any of the following codewords go to that section. Follow the list downwards and only go to the first section that you have a codeword in.

**Confess** - <u>767</u>

**Taunt** - <u>876</u>

**Grumble** - <u>446</u>

**Pads, Paddy, Silent Papers, Cold Blood, Murder, Hitman, Merto** - <u>415</u>

**Gutted** - <u>048</u>

Otherwise, read on:

The detective still says you have enough evidence against you that you have to go to trial. It seems that the jury sees enough uncertainty for you are found not guilty. However, the papers do not see it that way, a man with a gun in his hand at a body. Your life becomes a hell, followed by the press, until you leave the country. It might seem unfair but at least you are not in jail. As for who actually killed the Doctor, you still don't know. Maybe try again at <u>001</u>.

# 453

You take out your weapon and aim it at the lock. You shoot and must duck for cover as the bullet ricochets around the room. The noise is deafening and may have woken the dead. If anyone is near the boathouse they will surely be on their way here. You check the lock, but it remained intact.

You know you need to flee, lest someone else arrives but maybe that lock would break with a second shot?

Do you

Shoot again – 510

Wait to see if anyone arrives – 701

Scarper while you can all the way to the coastal path – 981

# 454

You climb up using the window ledge and haul yourself onto the roof. Lying flat, you crawl your way over the rounded surface to the weathervane. The wind is wild up here and you gulp knowing that you need to stand up to pull a piece of metal off the vane. Carefully you rise up and start to work at the metal, but you feel yourself being buffeted. The metal comes free in your hand just as a gust sweeps you off your feet.

How lucky are you?

This lucky – 886

Maybe this lucky - 195

What? This lucky - 369

# 455

"Elsie Gonzales? She was here to report on the big release of the new drug. I'm not seeing that one, sunshine. Have you got any evidence?"

If you have the following codeword **Taunt** – <u>116</u>

Otherwise – <u>995</u>

# 456

The Detective Inspector brushes his moustache as he enters the room and takes a seat opposite you. A recording machine is started and the man stares at you before giving a cough. His eyes are old and have seen everything, or so it seems to you. Can you bluff this man? Or will you tell the truth?

He says that everyone saw you beside the Doctor's body. He says at this time you are the prime suspect. However, he wants you to admit to it as things will be a lot quicker that way. Of course, they will be, but you are innocent!

The detective now sits back in the chair and asks you to explain what happened. Do you know? Who will you blame?

"I didn't murder the Doctor. In fact, it was..."

Who will you say killed the Doctor? Remember you'll need some evidence to help your cause.

Was it

# 457

You chase after the young woman, but she slips into the alcove. When you enter it, you find a wall of rock and she is gone. Carefully you trace your hands around the wall of rock, but you can find no secret exit. Time and again you shove and push, but the wall does not budge.

You return to the main cave and search the fridge finding a cheesecake but nothing else. There is nothing else to do here so you decide to leave.

If you entered by torch light – 441

Otherwise – 408

# 458

Go to 337

# 459

Do you have a surfer key on you? – 020

If not – 254

# 460

You take out the connecting wire you found and connect one end up to the connection you spotted with the missing wire. However, you cannot remember which terminal it should go to. There is a choice of three labelled, 526, JJ7 and U88.

This is a shot in the dark. What will you do?

Attach the wire to 526 – 124

Attach the wire to JJ7 – 399

Attach the wire to U88 – 377

Or decide this is a bad plan and instead surrender – 648

# 461

You run as hard as you can, all the while watching the figure across from you with the axe. As you reach over halfway, they seem to panic and toss the axe over the cliff and run. You reach the far side of the bridge and double up, throwing up due to the crazy exertion you have just committed. When you recover, the figure is long gone, as is the axe. There's no way you are going back out to that hut, and you reckon you need to move quickly in case the mystery figure is still about. Flee the gardens now to the coastal path at 770

# 462

You tell the detective about your threatening note from when someone tried to kill you at the fountains. The detective takes it away and returns an hour later with a smile on his face.

"We checked out your story about nearly being killed and the handwriting on the note. I believe you son, and the writing is that of Elsie Gonzales. I have just arrested her for your attempted murder."

If you have any of the following codewords go to that section. Follow the list downwards and only go to the first section that you have a codeword in.

**Grumble** - <u>583</u>

**Pads, Paddy, Silent Papers, Cold Blood, Murder, Hitman, Merto** - <u>636</u>

**Gutted** - <u>048</u>

Otherwise read on:

The detective arrests you for the Doctor's murder saying that you were still seen with the gun over the body. At the trial you cut a lonely figure as it only takes the jury an hour to convict you. From your jail cell you wonder if you were right in your choice of killer. You'll never know. Maybe try again at <u>001</u>.

# 463

You mention that there was a note in the folly which you accidentally burnt down. Of course, you don't know what it said. The detective looks at you incredulously.

If you have any of the following codewords go to that section. Follow the list downwards and only go to the first section that you have a codeword in.

**Grumble** - <u>446</u>

**Pads, Paddy, Silent Papers, Cold Blood, Murder, Hitman, Merto** - <u>415</u>

**Gutted** - <u>048</u>

Otherwise, read on:

The detective arrests you for the Doctor's murder saying that you were still seen with the gun over the body. All you have is a potential heated comment. At the trial you cut a lonely figure as it only takes the jury an hour to convict you. From your jail cell you wonder if you were right in your choice of killer. You'll never know. Maybe try again at 001.

# 464

The special projects door has a keypad on it which is currently green. It is looking for a 4-digit code and advises you have two attempts before an alarm will sound. It looks very similar to the keypad on the front door and has a swipe card reader on the side. Beyond the door, you can see only darkness through the glass.

Do you wish to open the door?

Use the Doctor's access card if you have it – 562

Try a code (only if you have found one) – 719

Try and break down the door – 306

# 465

Standing at the marina, you see the large cruiser with its two decks. You have never been on it, but you know that the Doctor enjoyed it thoroughly when he travelled abroad on it. The weather continues unabated, and you watch the pontoons wobble on the water. The speedboat beyond the cruiser seems to be bouncing and you wonder if it can handle the sea tonight.

Do you

Go onboard the cruiser - 445

Jump onto the speedboat - 869

Or, if you haven't already,

Make for the main building - 795

Or

if you want to continue elsewhere take the coastal path at 980

# 466

Did you come through the window? - 148

If not, you turn for the door and find that there is another keypad. As you try to use it, something rakes along your back, and you fall to the floor. You are now face to face with some red eyes. You think you can make out the image of a rat, but it is a large one and those claws felt like a lion's on your back. What is this?

You need to stand and fight, but what with?

Do you have

A gun - 412

Some cheese and phials - 799

Your fists - 781

# 467

Go to 199

# 468

You try to run upstairs but someone trips you and then a knife comes down on your top but fortunately it misses your skin. However, you are now pinned to the stairs by the knife, and you hear a laugh. You desperately try to pull your top clear.

How's your luck?

This good – 525

Maybe this good – 325

Or possibly this good – 598

# 469

You begin to sweat, even through your already soaked clothes as something approaches. As it nears you struggle to see it but it's an animal of some sort with padded feet and it is quick. Seeing you, it tears past, about the height of your knees. You pocket the gun and go to 166

# 470

You lower your gun and run from the temple. Getting a short distance away, you turn back and look at Kyla who is standing against the wind in her long coat. She shakes her head and then turns back, walking into the temple.

You decide to stay clear of the temple, but you can still search other parts of the ruins of you haven't already.

Do you

Make for the tomb and shelter from the rain – 877

Check out the sacrificial slab – 742

Look at the gaming board – 165

Or

Decide this area is no longer useful or too risky and continue along the coastal path at 996

# 471

You run as hard as you can, all the while watching the figure across from you with the axe. As you reach over halfway, they seem to panic and toss the axe over the cliff and run. You reach the far side of the bridge and double up, throwing up due to the crazy exertion you have just committed. When you recover, the figure is long gone, as is the axe. There's no way you are going back out to that hut, and you reckon you need to move quickly in case the mystery figure is still about. Flee the gardens now to the coastal path at 211

# 472

There's a horrible buzzer that tells you that the code is wrong. Blimey, one more chance or you'll be locked out. What do you do? Try a different code

4837 – 064

9746 – 203

3267 – 787

2758 – 107

Or do you decide this is too risky and decide instead to

Hide in the undergrowth surrounding the facility and see what happens – 440

Walk around the facility and see what you can find – 608

Call this a bust and find the coastal path – 983

# 473

You switch off the beam of light and hunch down in the passageway. As you wait, holding your breath, you hear footsteps coming closer, making their way towards you. They are so very close.

Do you

Switch on the light – 593

Stay in the dark – 179

# 474

You hold up your offering and approach Granma who looks at them and licks her lips. You sit down on a recliner, and she joins you on the one beside, and you let her tuck into the food.

"Thank you, young man, "she says, "you are very kind. Did they come for you though? That businessman, the one called Patrick is an alien. Did you see his eyes? He's not real, made of plastic. I told Flavius, he was to take that newsgirl, take her to the rocket and then they could escape to Mars and start a new life, make a new world. If he comes back, you could go too."

You stare at the old woman wondering if she's genuine, but she seems fully convinced of what she's saying. Have you missed something? You try to ask more pertinent questions but she's now just eating. Poor woman. Or is she?


Do you

Ask how she got here – 761

Draw your gun (if you have one) and tell her to start talking – 627

Or

Leave Granma in peace and retreat from the cave

If you entered by torch light – 489

Otherwise – 858

## 475

You decide one swipe is enough. Enter the code **Baba** in your code list. If you have the code **Sesame**, cross it out. So, what next?

Enter a code on the pad (only if you have found one) – 491

Or leave the item alone and

Check out the tin – 400

Investigate the switch – 275

Or if none of this inspires you, go back to the lagoon entrance and make another choice – 879

## 476

Go to 082

## 477

You are able to avoid some nasty rocks as you make your way out of the larger bay the island sits in. But the wind and rain, along with the waves, are buffeting your vessel and you find it tipping over from time to time. A particularly large wave hits you and the boat tips dangerously.

Does the god of speedboats shine on you?

Maybe – <u>488</u>

Possibly – <u>585</u>

# 478

You walk steadily forward towards the sound. The sound remains and if anything comes closer. You can see so little until you are hit on the head and fall to the ground, unconscious.

Really, you think yourself invincible. There's a killer out there. And guess what they have struck again. Start over at <u>001</u>.

# 479

You think it's all getting too much, and you can't just wait for the police to arrive. If you can get away, maybe you can escape to the mainland and beyond to start a new life in another country.

You open up the gate doors of the dock and see the wild sea outside. The waves are crashing in and now the door is open, the water really starts to splash inside the dock. The dinghy bounces about but you are an experienced sailor, albeit on larger vessels.

Do you want to take the boat out - <u>323</u>

Or is this a bad idea. Is so do you,

Look at the lifejackets - <u>436</u>

Take the stairs to the upper floor - <u>581</u>

Check out the locker at the rear of the room - <u>957</u>

Or

Head over to the marina - <u>465</u>

Or if you want to continue elsewhere take the coastal path at <u>980</u>

# 480

You pick up the papers on the table and find them to be a letter, dated today but the writing, made in pen, is slightly blurred due to the leaking liquid on the table which has contaminated the page. The writing is hard to make out and may be better in daylight.

Do you

Try to read it with the help of the candle - <u>735</u>

Read it anyway without any increased light - <u>922</u>

Or simply leave it and decide on a different option - <u>444</u>

# 481

You grab one of the phials and hurl it at the creature. At first it rears up and then sniffs the phial. But it soon ignores it and begins to charge at you.

Do you have a gun? If so, use it – 261

Otherwise – 960

# 482

What code will you enter?

4837 – 376

3267 – 070

2758 – 264

9746 – 653

Another code – 744

# 483

You quietly sneak over to the greenhouse and there seems to be no one outside. You open the greenhouse door and march in. There's no one here and you decide to hide in amongst the shrubbery in the building. It isn't long before the police arrive however, and they start to comb the greenhouse. You are trapped inside and there's no way out, so they soon corner you and address you. Get ready to make your defence at 519

## 484

Go to 965

## 485

You enter the cold water and suddenly find yourself beginning to freeze. Your breath is short and your head spins. As you take a moment you think you can hear someone along the shoreline. You're not fit to enter this water right away but to stay might be a risk.

Do you

Dive into the water and swim for the boat – 813

Stay put and hope the noises are nothing – 332

## 486

The keypad goes red, and a claxon begins to sound, deafening you. This is likely to bring lots of people and you decide to get as far away as possible from the building. You run out of the front door and make your way to the coastal path. Go there now at 986

# 487

You take the handle of the wheelbarrow, and it promptly falls off in your hands. You then see there is a giant hole in the middle of the barrow and clock it for the heap of junk it is.

Do you

Examine the shrouds – 271

Open the compost bins – 080

Or leave and

Enter the orchard – 447

Wander to the ornamental garden – 042

Or

Check out the fountains area – 156

Make your way to the greenhouse – 745

Wander over to the gardening equipment sheds – 262

Or if you doubt the gardens will be of any use then take the coastal path at 211 but note that you have visited the gardens

# 488

Well, it seems he hates you as the boat capsizes and you find yourself out in the maelstrom of the sea.

Do you have a lifejacket?

Yes – 043

No – 870

# 489

You swim back out with your torch lighting up the water in front of you. Climbing back out of the lagoon you ponder your next move.

Investigate "The Hollow" – 509

Climb up to the tree hut – 171

Decide you have had enough of the lagoon and make your move to the coastal path and your next destination – 503

# 490

You fire a warning shot into the air and watch Daniel shudder and then run even harder. He's gone before you even know it. But that shot will possibly bring others and if the authorities have arrived then they will be here. You'll need to keep moving. You run to the coastal path at 211

# 491

What code will you enter?

2758 – 947

3267 – 554

9746 – 404

4837 – 378

Another code – 292

# 492

"Hold it", you cry, "I didn't kill the Doctor!" Patrick stops momentarily but then shakes his head. He clearly doesn't believe you and is about to run again.

Do you

Tell him you know who the real killer is - 736

Tell him you are scared too - 743

If you have one, pull out your gun and threaten him with it for information - 127

Let him go - 920

# 493

You kneel down in the shadows of the garden and begin to feel around with your hands, but you can hear someone close by. There's heavy breathing and despite the wind and rain you swear you heard a crack of a twig.

Do You

Continue to search the grass - 394

Stand up and try to confront the unseen person - 978

Or flee the garden and

Examine the vegetable patch - 104

Take a look at the patio - 662

Or

Decide to head off on one of the main paths - 297

# 494

Slowly you enter the tunnel, and you can feel that it's as damp in here as it was outside. There is water running down the wall and up ahead you can see next to nothing. Gingerly, you edge forward. There's a flicker of something coming toward you, a blur of shadows. Your heart beats fast and you tense up. You can't see anything now, but you can hear something padding towards you.

If you have a gun, you can draw it now – <u>355</u>

If you want to run, you'll have to run all the way to the coastal path - <u>211</u>

Will you stand and face what is coming towards you – <u>589</u>

# 495

"Patrick Davidson," says the detective, stroking his moustache. "You're going to have to show me some evidence, sunshine, as he's a respected businessman. I know he was backing the Doctor's new drug. What can you tell me?"

If you have any of the following codewords go to that section. Follow the list downwards and only go to the first section that you have a codeword in.

**Tatler** – <u>938</u>

**Bowl** – <u>299</u>

**Taunt** – <u>649</u>

**Gutted** – <u>048</u>

Otherwise – <u>995</u>

# 496

You walk around the dock to the lifejackets and see an array of orange devices. Trying them on you find one that fits and if you want to take it with you, note **lifejacket** in your inventory. You also find a scrap of paper tucked inside one lifejacket. It looks like the Doctor's lifejacket and seems to be a company resume for Patrick Davidson's company. It gives a glowing report in the little you can read but there is red pen across it saying *CHECK* in capital letters.

That appears to be it for the lifejackets. Do you

Examine the dinghy – <u>044</u>

Take the stairs to the upper floor – <u>315</u>

Check out the locker at the rear of the room – <u>584</u>

Or

Head over to the marina – <u>909</u>

Or if you want to continue elsewhere take the coastal path at <u>981</u>

# 497

No one knows about this place except maybe the Doctor and Elsie, but then again, you took care of her. It is a rough two weeks, and you are barely getting by on water and the little food there is in the cave. You carefully come out at night after the fortnight and find the island mainly deserted except for the laboratory. The police must have come and gone, and you are able to sneak away from the island in the Doctor's cruiser.

You make for a foreign land and once ashore you manage to find some basic work and hide out in the country for a few years. One day on the television you see your face, described as the island murderer. Of course, you have no hair now and wear glasses. It seems you need to live in exile for the rest of your life.

Maybe this is a win, but you still don't know who set you up. Try to solve the mystery again at 001.

# 498

You begin to sweat, even through your already soaked clothes as something approaches. As it nears you struggle to see it but it's an animal of some sort with padded feet and it is quick. Seeing you, it tears past, about the height of your knees. You pocket the gun and go to 214

# 499

The gardens had some nifty hiding places, and you race into the island vegetation, determined to get their and hide. When you arrive at the edge of the vegetation that surrounds the gardens you realise the place is crawling with police. To hide will not be easy and you realise that the greenhouse is the least patrolled area. You could make a bid to hide there but it all looks so risky.

Do you

Make a run for the greenhouse - 639

Instead, route to the boathouse - 568

Go to the ruins to try and hide - 838

Or

If you checked the following codewords while making your initial decision, then you may follow their options

Codeword **Boat** - 090

Codeword **Quiet Place** - 224

Or give yourself up - 519

# 500

You pick up the papers from the computer desk and study them furiously. There are many numbers all pulled together in tables and you have no idea what they mean. Here and there the Doctor has circled a few. You see 3267, 8475 and 2232. You have no idea what they mean. Best to move on.

Do you

Try to put a code into the computer (only if you have found one)  - 283

Try to open the drawers - 219

Or do you leave the desk and computer alone and

Look at the small pile of books and the chair - 634

Check out the picture on the wall - 098

Examine the coat stand - 428

# 501

The apple is red and crispy, and you sink your teeth into it hungry as you are. Now you have finished off that tasty treat, what next? It's not like you have a murder or anything to solve while you stuff your face.

Do you

Try a pear - 847

Or leave and

Walk to the vegetable garden - 014

Wander to the ornamental garden - 420

Or

Check out the fountains area - 526

Make your way to the greenhouse - 722

Wander over to the gardening equipment sheds - 121

Or

if you doubt the gardens will be of any use then take the coastal path at 770 but note that you have visited the gardens

# 502

You have the note from the Doctor to Elsie regarding Granma Munro. It seems she may not be simply a little old woman but may in fact have other more deadly urges. And with this note you can prove the possibility.

# 503

You come to the path and see it running two ways. Remember you cannot go back the way you came so you must continue either clockwise or anti-clockwise depending on your previous route.

If you came from the gardens before the lagoon, you must now make a beeline for the laboratory – 797

If you came from the laboratory before the lagoon then you must head to the gardens – 689

# 504

You swipe the card along the reader, and you hear a click and some whirring. You try the handle, and the door opens easily. Go 854

# 505

The dressing gowns are made of silk and are simply immaculate. To the touch they feel like the best fabric you have ever handled, and the deep blue colour makes you feel like you are about to be enveloped in the sea. Having marvelled at their appearance you smell them both but only one has the scent of a man. The other has simply the smell of a recently cleaned garment.

Job done and a fascinating insight! So, what now? Do you

Examine the bed - 046

Check the alcove door - 952

Descend the stairs - 991

Or leave the Lookout completely and head for the coastal path - 990

# 506

You are in a bedroom, all be it a round one, and it is tastefully decorated with a plush carpet on the floor and a demur bedspread on a double bed that sits in the middle of the room. A metal spiral staircase descends from the room and soft lighting is still switched on. You see two silk dressing gowns hanging on pegs on the wall and there is a mirror for a person to groom themselves. A small alcove has a door in it, which causes the room to lose its perfect circle.

Do you

Examine the bed – <u>046</u>

Check the silk dressing gowns – <u>505</u>

Check the alcove door – <u>952</u>

Descend the stairs – <u>991</u>

Or leave the Lookout completely and head for the coastal path – <u>990</u>

# 507

You cautiously turn the lever but find it is a touch stiff. With a concerted effort you push the lever back and a jet of water flies up from the aperture hitting you in the face. So that's how they water this part of the garden. Now stop messing about and get on with your investigation.

Do you

Enter the orchard – <u>447</u>

Walk to the vegetable garden – <u>398</u>

Or

Check out the fountains area – <u>156</u>

Make your way to the greenhouse – <u>745</u>

Wander over to the gardening equipment sheds – <u>262</u>

Or if you doubt the gardens will be of any use then take the coastal path at <u>211</u> but note that you have visited the gardens

# 508

You keep the gun trained on Patrick and tell him to start talking about what's going on.

"It's just a special drug that means a person performs much better physically for much longer. That's what the Doctor was working on with his assistant. I mean that's why we're all here," he blurts out, almost hysterical. "I backed it, backed it all, put so much of the company into it, it has to work. I mean what's your beef with him, kid. Why did you kill the Doctor?"

"I didn't kill him," you say.

"But we saw you with the gun in your hand. I mean who else wants to stop the drug. And why did you, tell me why? You'll ruin me."

You lower your eyes, trying to think how to pose the next question. The man looks desperate. Then he runs at you, hands stretched before him, seizing you by the neck. You choke and panic before your hand seizes shut. There is a single gunshot and Patrick falls backwards, stumbling to the ground. You see a red patch on his shirt. Record the codeword **Pads** in your codeword list.

The gunshot could bring people running and the last thing you need is to be seen with the gun in your hand again, over what could be a dead body. You turn and flee from the building, heading for the coastal path before anyone else shows up. Go now to 983

# 509

You walk around the lagoon until you reach the Hollow. It sits in the ground, and you have to step down until you find yourself staring at eyelevel along the surface of the lagoon. The night may be dark and the rain pelting down causing the surface of the water to be constantly disturbed but the lights around the feature make the surface look almost eerie.

You search in the darkness of the feature and find three things. There is a rubber cover on a small electrical outlet, a tin lies in the corner, and there is a switch on the far wall of the Hollow.

Do you

Look at the rubber cover – 816

Check out the tin – 400

Investigate the switch – 275

Or if none of this inspires you, go back to the lagoon entrance and make another choice – 879

# 510

You lean back and fire your gun again. The bullet ricochets again and bounces off something before hitting you in the neck. You fall to the ground, unable to breathe properly with your punctured neck.

Ironically as you slip away to the blackness, the cupboard door swings open, but you don't see what's inside as you sink into oblivion.

Gunplay never ends well. But learn that lesson by returning to 001 and having another go.

# 511

"What's the deal with the drug? Why is it so important?"

Kyla comes closer and smiles at you. "It is a work of genius. It makes a human being maintain their top performance for longer; physically, mentally and, dare I say it, spiritually."

You have no idea what *spiritually* having a top performance means but you are aware she is getting very close now.

Do you

Step into her embrace, after all you need a friend – 783

Walk away from the ruins, she's a threat – 257

Draw your gun for a better answer – 025

# 512

The door clicks open, and you pull the handle, allowing yourself to step inside. Time to find some evidence. Go to 212

# 513

You think there is a door in the rock but as much as you push at the rock within the outline you can see, nothing moves. You dive down several times, but nothing changes. Maybe it's nothing. You climb out of the lagoon and decide you won't go back to the door unless you find some way to move that doorway.

Do you

Swim for the half-buried object - 395

Or exit the water and

Investigate "The Hollow" - 819

Climb up to the tree hut - 410

Decide you have had enough of the lagoon and make your move to the coastal path and your next destination - 549

# 514

Well, that's nice. Was a good wish? This is a murder investigation, not Cinderella. Come on, pick it up, sunshine, as all the best Inspectors say! Now investigate something worthwhile and stop clowning about.

Do you

Make your way to the folly - 444

Head for the tunnel - 605

Walk down to the final fountain and its walkway - 524

Or go back to the fountains area entrance - 156

# 515

In the dark you realise you don't know where you are going. It's just a lot of water after all. You don't have much to guide your path and by morning you are unsure where you are. A police launch picks you up in the sea off the mainland as you must have doubled back on yourself in your confusion. Oh, well, let's see if you can explain it all to the investigators. The proceed to 519

# 516

As you approach the curtains you begin to see them move. Someone is behind them. You can hear a breath that is deepening as you get closer. Is someone lying in wait for you? Will you be attacked? Or is there someone who might help behind the curtains?

Do you:

Open the curtains – 091

Leave the room immediately. If so, where do you go? If you have not entered these rooms before you may:

Enter the dining room – 576

Enter the kitchen – 298

Or

Go upstairs – 119

Leave by the front door – 384

## 517

You lower your weapon and let her approach. Kyla is an older and maybe she can sort this out for you. She has opened her long coat offering you shelter in it from the rain, and you gratefully step into her embrace in a moment of supreme trust. As she wraps you up you think about how good a judge of character you are. But when you find yourself struggling to breathe as she constricts your neck with her arm, you realise you made a bad judgement. The woman is deadly, and you slowly drift off to an eternal sleep.

Was she the killer? Maybe, or did she think you were the killer and had to defend herself. Either way, you need to get with what's happening. People are scared or they have a reason to kill. Let's not be so trusting next time! Start over at 001

## 518

The lounger and table are dimly lit by the house lights and are currently soaking wet from the rain. You see nothing on the table and lean over to see if anything is on the lounger. As you run your hands across it you feel an itching in the underside of it. You spin the lounger over and see the figures 2758 scrawled into the wood. What could that mean. There's nothing else on the lounger or table.

Do you

Examine the BBQ area – <u>827</u>

Or

Pay a visit to the private garden where you saw the glint of light – <u>914</u>

Take a look at the patio – <u>662</u>

Or

Decide to head off on one of the paths – <u>297</u>

# 519

You have been arrested and taken off island to a local police station where a stern looking Detective Inspector with a bushy moustache has you sitting behind a table with your hands cuffed to it. All the possessions you were carrying were recorded and taken from you before being bagged.

Do you have the codeword **Capernum**? If so, go to <u>266</u>

The detective's people are still combing the island, but he has decided to interview you so that you can give your side to what happened. He warns you that you are under caution, and also his chief suspect in the murder of Doctor Munro. Although he fails to see how you are not the murderer, he is willing to let you prove it otherwise to him.

Check your codewords and proceed to the next section that corresponds to the pair of codewords you have in your list.

**Playtime, Ferry Gone** - 665

**Playtime, Swim** - 336

**Tower, Collapsed** - 671

**Tower, Ferry Gone** - 561

**Grass, Collapsed** - 644

**Grass, Swim** - 666

# 520

You swipe the Doctor's access card, and the lock makes a whirring sound. Pushing the door, it opens freely. Enter at 845

# 521

The door of the room opens with a creak, and you see that there is no light on inside. As your eyes adjust to the darkness, you can make out a set of shelving at the rear of the room with a collection of things sitting on them, large, box-like. But your heart goes cold as you can also see a figure there. It's indistinct and not moving but has voluminous hair. Your hand feels the wall beside it, and you touch the light switch.

Our heart pounds as you wonder who this is in front of you. Maybe it's the killer. How should you play this?

Do you even want to play at all, or should you just cut and run? Or is there something important in this room that will prove your innocence?

Do you

Switch on the light – 955

Draw your gun if you have one – 778

Speak out into the darkness – 391

Run away back to the outside – 087

## 522

You advised the authorities you were in the boathouse and on a cruiser. Not surprisingly they are looking for such a vessel and you are picked up very quickly despite your attempts to stay incognito. And now make your way to 519 and prepare to defend yourself.

## 523

You shove your hand down the toilet bowl and poke around before coming up with a piece of connecting wire with two rusted inputs at either end. Maybe the Doctor found this in his pocket, who knows? Strange to flush it down the sink though as you know that connection is quite common in boat engines. If you want, you can pocket the **connecting wire by noting it**

**in your inventory.** And seriously, wash your hands afterwards!

Now that unhygienic investigation is over, do you

Read the magazine - <u>682</u>

Or

Examine the bed - <u>615</u>

Check the silk dressing gowns - <u>312</u>

Descend the stairs - <u>811</u>

Or leave the Lookout completely and head for the coastal path - <u>988</u>

# 524

The last fountain is quite a wonder. Although its base stands at the top of the cliffs, it has a rope bridge which leads from two points out to a lookout platform, a small hut held up high above the tempestuous sea below. You gaze at the hut wondering if it could have anything inside. It is then you notice the light.

The light is dim but there is something inside the hut. However, to get out to it you need to walk one of the two rope bridges. That will leave you pretty exposed as you need to come back on the rope bridges and if someone else were at the fountain, they could block you off. You ponder if it is worth the risk as you look at the fountain's jet of water swinging in an arc above the hut and down into the sea.

Do you

Walk out to the hut along the rope bridge – <u>235</u>

Decide it is too risky and retreat. If so, to where?

Make your way to the folly – <u>444</u>

Check out the coin throwing area – <u>704</u>

Head for the tunnel – <u>605</u>

Walk down to the final fountain and its walkway – <u>524</u>

Or

Take a look in the walled garden – <u>926</u>

Make your way to the greenhouse – <u>745</u>

Wander over to the gardening equipment sheds – <u>262</u>

Or

Decide to leave the Gardens by going to the coastal path – <u>211</u>

# 525

You struggle with the knife, but you can't free it. There's a blow to your head and then you don't know anymore. In the following days, the police blame you for the murder and the person who attacked you walks away scot-free from there dastardly deed with the Doctor. Of course, it's..., no you'll need to play again at <u>001</u>, but this time beware the dark.

# 526

The fountains area has got four descending fountains, leading down to the final water feature where the water is sent shooting through the air into the sea. The Doctor once told you that sea water was taken up to the top fountain by pump to then find its way through the various features back into the sea. But, as wonderful as the features are, there is not much to search.

Looking closely, you see a few potential areas to examine. There is a small folly beside the largest fountain, nearest to you. The second fountain has an area where you are able to throw coins into the fountain. There is a tunnel at the third fountain which you have never been in. And the last fountain has the walkway that the fountain shoots over before the water falls to the sea.

Do you

Make your way to the folly – 766

Check out the coin throwing area – 579

Head for the tunnel – 125

Walk down to the final fountain and its walkway – 676

Or take a look in the walled garden – 625

Make your way to the greenhouse – 722

Wander over to the gardening equipment sheds – 121

Or decide to leave the Gardens by going to the coastal path – 770

# 527

"Grandma Munro," says the detective stroking his moustache. "You're going to have to show me some evidence sunshine, she's just an old woman. How on earth do you believe it's her? What can you tell me?"

If you have any of the following codewords go to that section. Follow the list downwards and only go to the first section that you have a codeword in.

**Notelet** – 141

**Space letter** – 656

**Granferno** – 017

**Taunt** – 027

**Gutted** – 048

Otherwise – 995

# 528

You step inside the rec room and see a pool table in the middle with a darts board on the far wall. There's a fridge holding beers along the nearest wall as well as a sofa and some magazines scattered around. There's also a scrap of paper on the floor, under the pool table.

The room is decorated with a sports theme, and you know it as the Doctor's hangout when down at the boats, but you have never been in this room. After all, you are only staff! Or at least you were.

Do you

Examine the pool table – <u>340</u>

Look at the darts board – <u>163</u>

Open the fridge – <u>559</u>

Read the magazines – <u>531</u>

Take hold of the scrap of paper – <u>790</u>

Or

Enter the toilet – <u>828</u>

Check out the chart room – <u>848</u>

Investigate the room with no name – <u>685</u>

Return to the lower floor – <u>370</u>

# 529

You cautiously turn the lever but find it is a touch stiff. With a concerted effort you push the lever back and a jet of water flies up from the aperture hitting you in the face. So that's how they water this part of the garden. Now stop messing about and get on with your investigation.

Do you

Enter the orchard – <u>560</u>

Walk to the vegetable garden – <u>014</u>

Or

Check out the fountains area – <u>526</u>

Make your way to the greenhouse – <u>722</u>

Wander over to the gardening equipment sheds – <u>121</u>

Or if you doubt the gardens will be of any use then take the coastal path at <u>770</u> but note that you have visited the gardens

## 530

You turn and dive out the open window before running off in the dark as far away as possible. At first you hear something behind you but then it must have given up for there is nothing you can hear. Shaking and wet you arrive at the coastal path – <u>986</u>

## 531

The magazines are a mess on the floor, but you see an article in one that tells of the terrific improvement made by Daniel Lyle on the athletics track, specifically how he seems to be lasting much better over long distances, having almost no drop off in pace. His much hailed improvement seems to be taking him places.

Interesting read but do you

Examine the pool table – 340

Look at the darts board – 163

Open the fridge – 559

Take hold of the scrap of paper – 790

Or

Enter the toilet – 828

Check out the chart room – 848

Investigate the room with no name – 685

Return to the lower floor – 370

# 532

Well, that's nice. Was a good wish? This is a murder investigation, not Cinderella. Come on, pick it up, sunshine, as all the best Inspectors say! Now investigate something worthwhile and stop clowning about.

Do you

Make your way to the folly – 766

Head for the tunnel – 125

Walk down to the final fountain and its walkway – 676

Or go back to the fountains area entrance – 526

# 533

The telephone is an old-style candlestick device with an earpiece to be lifted up and a dialling circle at the bottom. Lifting the earpiece up, you can hear a dialling tone. There's been a murder and you really should report it. But you are the main suspect. Do you want to alert the authorities right away before you solve the mystery of who framed you? Outside you can hear the wind whipping around and the rain beginning. It was destined to be a wild night and the weather is living up to its billing. Maybe the authorities won't get here too soon.

Do you:

Place a call to the authorities – 366

Call a friend: - 390

Or do you instead replace the receiver and (if you have not already done so)

Enter the sitting room – 763

Enter the dining room – 576

Enter the kitchen – 298

Go upstairs – 119

Leave by the front door – 384

# 534

Go to 965

# 535

You reach up to the box on the shelf and pull it down. It appears to be an old wooden box, quite long and slender. There is a lock at the front of it and the box is shut tight. Do you have a key to try on the box? If so – 851

If not there's two choices

You could try and smash the box by throwing it onto the ground – 715

Or you could leave it alone and instead

Take a look at the lawnmower – 311

Examine the blanket on the floor – 699

Or leave the shed and

Check out the fountains area – 156

Take a look in the walled garden – 926

Make your way to the greenhouse – 745

Wander over to the gardening equipment sheds – 262

Or if you doubt the gardens will be of any use then take the coastal path at 211 but note that you have visited the gardens

# 536

The door opens easily, and you step inside at <u>824</u>

# 537

There's something not quite right about this pear which although golden is firm. As you bite through the flesh you see a small worm looking back at you and throw the pear to the ground. Interesting though that diversion was, can we get on?

Do you

Try an apple – <u>687</u>

Or leave and

Walk to the vegetable garden – <u>398</u>

Wander to the ornamental garden – <u>042</u>

Or

Check out the fountains area – <u>156</u>

Make your way to the greenhouse – <u>745</u>

Wander over to the gardening equipment sheds – <u>262</u>

Or if you doubt the gardens will be of any use then take the coastal path at <u>211</u> but note that you have visited the gardens

# 538

You are swimming near the middle of the lagoon and close to the bottom when you come across a small treasure box in the sandy residue at the bottom. You carefully haul it out and drag it onto the edge of the lagoon. As you take it from the water, you shine your torch on it and realise it is made from plastic. You flip a catch at the front and find a piece of paper inside and a photo.

*Congratulations, you believed the stories and you have found your treasure.*

You look at the photo and see it is of the Doctor's Mum with the words *my treasure*, written on it in pen.

What a waste of time! You get out of the lagoon and climb to your feet ready to begin investigating again.

Do you

Investigate "The Hollow" – 509

Climb up to the tree hut – 171

Decide you have had enough of the lagoon and make your move to the coastal path and your next destination – 503

# 539

You swim closer to the rocky side of the lagoon and see the passageway in front of you.

Do you have any of the following codes in your code list?

Code **Sesame** – 548

Code **Baba** – 747

Neither – 693

# 540

You swim around for a half hour, finding nothing but then come across the edge of the lagoon and a strange section of rock under the water.

Do you have any of the following codes in your code list?

Code **Sesame** – 169

Code **Baba** – 941

Neither – 812

# 541

The bookcase while being small is still fully loaded with books on a subject you find quite surprising. How to paint and draw seems to be the order of the day which are filed in alphabetical order. You take them out and shake them, but none have anything inside. This is not a side to the Doctor you had noticed, and you find the subject matter somewhat surprising.

You feel it's only safe to check out two items in this room before moving on.

Do you:

Check out the China hutch – <u>792</u>

Examine the drinks cabinet – <u>635</u>

Examine the curtains – <u>516</u>

Or

if you have already examined two items, or want to leave this room (and have not already visited these places),

Enter the dining room – <u>576</u>

Enter the kitchen – <u>298</u>

Go upstairs – <u>119</u>

Leave by the front door – <u>384</u>

# 542

With your life jacket on, you enter the cold water and find yourself floating while you await the initial shock of the water to subside. Slowly you begin to kick under the water and steadily make your way towards the boat. The waves are choppy, but you float over each rise, your head clear of the water and your breathing unaffected.

As you reach the boat you realise it is quiet and dark. It takes you three attempts, but you manage to grab the side of the vessel and haul yourself on board. Once there you can see why there's no interest in this boat. Maybe the coastguard has already looked at it or know it is abandoned. There is seemingly no power on the vessel and you go to the engine and look carefully over it. You have some experience from running the ferry boat and you believe that a wire is missing from a connection.

Do you have a **connecting wire** – 460

If not – 648


# 543

As you descend below the upper deck, everything becomes dark. You feel your way to the bottom of the circular stairs and can just about make the outline of a corridor out in the dark. Reaching out with your hands, you can feel a door behind you, there's open space before you and the walls also move away to one side.


As you stand there wondering what to do, you can hear scratching from the area ahead of you. You're not sure but it may be someone. If you have a gun you realise that you can't see anywhere, and you'll need both hands to move about, so you keep it tucked away.


Do you

Try the door behind you – 066

Walk directly ahead to investigate – 911

Follow the wall to the side and trace your way along there – 319

Or

Check out the wheelhouse – 861

Look at the lockers at the aft of the upper deck – 954

Or go back onto the pontoons and jump onto the speedboat – 869

Or, if you haven't already, make for the main building – 795

Or if you want to continue elsewhere take the coastal path at 980

# 544

You pull out your weapon and you peer into the darkness. You hear the whisper on the wind "Oh no, a gun." Something hits you on the head and you fall to the ground. A pair of shoes can be heard running from the room but by the time you recover your assailant is gone.

You feel a little unsettled but look around the room. There are several canisters on the shelving, which must have looked like boxes in the dark. You open one and smell diesel. They are quite heavy, and you decide you can't simply carry them around. But you know where to come if you need them. Note the codeword **Fuel** in your code list.

That was eventful but what do you do next?

Check out the chart room – **618**

Go to the Rec Room – **234**

Investigate the room with no name – **521**

Return to the lower floor – **795**

## 545

The letter you found in the folly, from Kyla Mertens about her current work. "... must be stopped. ........................... appropriate credit....................... make sure........sees no reward from the work."

That was all you could see. It's now in evidence and you didn't read all of it. Should you tell the police to read it? Will it help?

## 546

The Detective Inspector brushes his moustache as he enters the room and takes a seat opposite you. A recording machine is started and the man stares at you before giving a cough. His eyes are old and have seen everything, or so it seems to you. Can you bluff this man? Or will you tell the truth?

He says that everyone saw you beside the Doctor's body. He says at this time you are the prime suspect. However, he wants you to admit to it as things will be a lot quicker that way. Of course, they will be, but you are innocent!

The detective now sits back in the chair and asks you to explain what happened. Do you know? Who will you blame?

"I didn't murder the Doctor. In fact, it was…"

Who will you say killed the Doctor? Remember you'll need some evidence to help your cause.

Was it

Kyla Mertens – <u>278</u>

Patrick Davidson – <u>837</u>

Elsie Gonzales – <u>455</u>

Daniel Lyle – <u>949</u>

Grandma Munro – <u>418</u>

# 547

The door clicks open, and you pull the handle, allowing yourself to step inside. Time to find some evidence. Go to <u>805</u>

# 548

You think there is a door in the rock but as much as you push at the rock within the outline you can see, nothing moves. You dive down several times, but nothing changes. Maybe it's nothing. You climb out of the lagoon and decide you won't go back to the door unless you find some way to move that doorway.

Do you

Swim for the half-buried object – 923

Or exit the water and

Investigate "The Hollow" – 509

Climb up to the tree hut – 171

Decide you have had enough of the lagoon and make your move to the coastal path and your next destination – 503

# 549

You come to the path and see it running two ways. Remember you cannot go back the way you came so you must continue either clockwise or anti-clockwise depending on your previous route.

If you have visited six locations (including the house) go to 011

Or

If you came from the gardens before the lagoon, you must now make a beeline for the laboratory - <u>797</u>

If you came from the laboratory before the lagoon then you must head to the gardens - <u>689</u>

# 550

You climb up but it's hard to see. As you stretch in the darkness, you knock over several bottles that fall to the ground. You start to smell fuel, maybe kerosene, diesel and petrol. Carefully you get down off the lawnmower and leave the shed, aware that a spark could ignite trouble. That was a lucky escape in many ways but maybe you shouldn't root around in the dark. But what next?

Leave the shed and

Check out the fountains area - <u>156</u>

Take a look in the walled garden - <u>926</u>

Make your way to the greenhouse - <u>745</u>

Wander over to the gardening equipment sheds - <u>262</u>

Or if you doubt the gardens will be of any use then take the coastal path at <u>211</u> but note that you have visited the gardens

# 551

You enter a special projects area and can hear something moving. As you walk, you feel something breath on the side of your face and jump before you realise you are in a room of cages. You decide to stay quiet, rather than wake whatever are in the cages but there is a general murmuring starting.

Suddenly, something can be heard scurrying in the dark and there is a flurry of wings and squawking from the cages. The hairs on your neck rise and your hands begin to shake with fear. The door is just behind you. Should you flee? But maybe there's something else worth having in the special projects area, something which could help prove your innocence.

Do you flee – 466

Stand your ground – 412

# 552

You spend half an hour swimming around, diving up and down but to no avail. The rumours of the Doctor's treasure are ill-founded. You climb out of the lagoon and decide you won't go back in unless you find better lighting. So, what next?

Do you

Investigate "The Hollow" – <u>509</u>

Climb up to the tree hut – <u>171</u>

Decide you have had enough of the lagoon and make your move to the coastal path and your next destination – <u>503</u>

# 553

"What are you doing here, Daniel?"

"Peter, you killed him!" The man shrinks back, and you see he is in terror. He crumples to the ground, shaking. "Don't kill me!" he yells.

Do you

Protest your innocence – <u>974</u>

Go up to Daniel and wrap your arms around him – <u>777</u>

Decide this is all a bit too much and leave the boathouse – <u>925</u>

# 554

You punch in the code and the pad turns red and a coarse noise like a bad input on a computer sounds. Nothing happens and you are left with the pad again.

Do you enter another code? Which one?

2758 - 883

3267 - 966

9746 - 226

4837 - 035

Another code - 836

Or do you leave the pad alone? If so, make your next choice at 816

# 555

You pour one of the phials on the cheese and throw it at the creature. At first it rears up and then sniffs the cheese. But it soon ignores it and begins to charge at you.

Do you have a gun? If so, use it – 412

Otherwise – 781

# 556

You draw your gun and fire a shot straight at the window. Even in the wind that shot must have been heard a mile off. The smashing of the window would not have helped either. You look around nervously. If they heard that and come for you, you will be trapped in the Lookout. You cannot take that risk. So much for stealth. You climb down the ladder and then drop down via the ivy until you are back on the ground.

Time is of the essence if they are coming so you run to the coastal path at <u>990</u>

# 557

The lock on the door makes a whirring sound and you open it - go to <u>005</u>

# 558

The lawnmower is a filthy affair, and you wonder when it was last used. Maybe that's why this shed is open as it holds nothing of working interest. You realise that you could stand on the lawnmower and reach up to the shelves and maybe just grab those bottles. But it is dark up there.

As you stand on the lawnmower, you hear a crack, and you realise you have broken open a storage space under the seat. You find a small blowtorch there. This could be handy as the bottles are in the dark and maybe you could read the labels by the light of the blowtorch.

Do you

Fire up the blowtorch and climb on the lawnmower to look at the bottles – 036

Ignore the blowtorch and climb up to look at the bottles – 350

Or ignore the lawnmower and

Get the box on the shelf – 182

Examine the blanket on the floor – 267

Or leave the shed and

Check out the fountains area – 526

Take a look in the walled garden – 625

Make your way to the greenhouse – 722

Wander over to the gardening equipment sheds – 121

Or if you doubt the gardens will be of any use then take the coastal path at 770 but note that you have visited the gardens

# 559

The waft of cold air hits you as you open the fridge and look at the wide range of beer inside. Maybe you could take some time and sup a cold one. After all you have been under pressure.


Do you

Put your feet up and have a beer - 138

Or continue your search

Examine the pool table - 340

Look at the darts board - 163

Read the magazines - 531

Take hold of the scrap of paper - 790

Or

Enter the toilet - 828

Check out the chart room - 848

Investigate the room with no name - 685

Return to the lower floor - 370


# 560

The orchard is abundant with fruit, and you know you would probably have been asked to come and help with the picking in the coming weeks. However, as much as it is abundant, it is also devoid of any life.

There's not much to do here and you cannot see anything of use.

Do you

Try an apple – 501

Try a pear – 847

Leave and

Walk to the vegetable garden – 014

Wander to the ornamental garden – 420

Or

Check out the fountains area – 526

Make your way to the greenhouse – 722

Wander over to the gardening equipment sheds – 121

Or if you doubt the gardens will be of any use then take the coastal path at 770 but note that you have visited the gardens

# 561

You think carefully about what evidence you have, weighing up what is the best thing to do. If you have the following codewords, go to the given section for further thoughts on what you have learnt. Remember to mark this section to come back to.

**Tatler** – 841

**Wheel** – 407

**Notelet** – 502

**Space Letter** – 242

**Taunt** – 009

When you are done considering what evidence you have, go to **185** and talk to the Detective Inspector.

# 562

You swipe the card along the reader, and you hear a click and some whirring. You try the handle, and the door opens easily. Go <u>551</u>

# 563

You'll sort this out because you're the kind of guy who takes no nonsense. You reach forward and grab the curtain pulling it away. In the darkness you cannot make out the face of the person who is standing behind the curtain. However, you can make out the knife that is quickly descending and making a mess of your top. Your hands reach froward, grabbing your assailant but it's too late as you are wounded in the neck, and you start to gurgle.

The pain doesn't last long, and your last view is of a pair of shoes. You are too weak to even think about who they belong to, and you slip into unconsciousness ready to journey into the great beyond, albeit with a forced start.

Oh dear, you didn't last long. I suggest you start over, and this time take a bit more care when you see possible danger, after all, there is a murderer afoot.

**Return to <u>001</u> and start again. And this time, please be more careful.**

# 564

You reach the ruins and see the caves, realising that the Police are only at the temple area. You sneak around and make your way into the dark. Deep in the cave you sit down, your body tense and your mind racing. You hear the Police outside and try to remain as quiet as you can. As the time wears on and the police are still outside you begin to tire form your ordeal, eventually falling asleep.

You wake up with a flashlight in your face, and a gun pointed at you. Enter the codeword **Caught** into your list. Now go to <u>519</u> and explain why you shouldn't be charged with murder.

# 565

You run as hard as you can, all the while watching the figure across from you with the axe. As you reach over halfway, they seem to panic and toss the axe over the cliff and run. You reach the far side of the bridge and double up, throwing up due to the crazy exertion you have just committed. When you recover, the figure is long gone, as is the axe. There's no way you are going back out to that hut, and you reckon you need to move quickly in case the mystery figure is still about. Flee the gardens now to the coastal path at 211

## 566

Taking your gun, you smack the butt of the weapon on the window. It reverberates off but you persist. Up here it would take a heck of a noise for people to notice, and you hit the window ten times before you see a chink in the pane. Carefully, you tap out the glass, before climbing inside the window. Enter the room at 506

## 567

You enter the numbers, and you hear a click and some whirring. You try the handle, and the door opens easily. Go 854

## 568

You decide to make for the boathouse and push into the undergrowth knowing that you have to keep off the main paths. As soon as you get near the boathouse you realise this is a bad idea as there are a myriad of police and coastguard officers around the area. You realise this will be a kamikaze mission, but it might just work if you are really lucky. However, you still have time to think about another option.

Do you,

Continue for the boathouse – 341

Hide out in the gardens – 499

Go to the ruins to try and hide – 838

Or

If you checked the following codewords while making your initial decision, then you may follow their options

Codeword **Boat** – 090

Codeword **Quiet Place** – 224

Or give yourself up - 519

# 569

The cake on the table is half eaten and there is a note with it.

*Sir, I have left the extra mug as requested. Please advise when I can clear away fully. Kathy*

The only Kathy you know is the cleaner, but she left not long after the guests arrived when the last boat headed for the mainland. You look at the mug on the table and see it has lipstick still on it. As you are unaware of the Doctor ever wearing lipstick, you feel he must have been entertaining.

There's nothing else here, so what next? Do you

Examine the books around the wall - <u>943</u>

Look out the window - <u>657</u>

Proceed up the spiral staircase - <u>991</u>

Decide to leave the Lookout and make your way to the coastal path - <u>990</u>

# 570

You make your way hesitantly along stony paths until you see the splendid gardens of the island before you. The rain is tipping down and your shorts and t-shirt are becoming sodden. This garden is not a mere trifle such as those landscapes at the house but rather something more magnificent altogether. Despite the dark night, you can make out through some dim lighting four distinct areas of the gardens. First are the magnificent fountains, set in a cascade and making their way down to the sea. Across from them is the walled garden with its array of planted rows and wondrous trees from all round the world. There is also an enormous greenhouse which has lights currently burning bright inside. Finally, you can see the sheds where the gardening equipment is kept. Enter the code word **Grass** in your code list.

You need to see if there are any clues to the murder of the Doctor here, unlikely as it may seem so. Where will you investigate first? Do you

Check out the fountains area - 156

Take a look in the walled garden - 926

Make your way to the greenhouse - 745

Wander over to the gardening equipment sheds - 262

Or if you doubt the gardens will be of any use then take the coastal path at 211 but note that you have visited the gardens

# 571

The cleaners cupboard has a lock. You try the handle, but the door is locked and you'll need a key. But do you have any?

If you have a key to try, is it

An ornate key - 700

A key with green tape - 679

Another key - 168

Or do you give up on the cleaners cupboard and instead if you haven't already

Enter the canteen - 071

Examine the door belonging to Doctor Munro - 439

Try to enter the office of Kyla Mertens - 237

Or

Return to the hall - 212

# 572

You open the file and almost start as you realise this is a paper on a drug you heard the Doctor was working on. As you read through, you understand it makes a human perform at their top standard for a lot longer than they can do now. You also see that one of the test subjects is referred to as DL – could that be Daniel Lyle? There is also a lot of science that is beyond your comprehension, but one thing strikes you about the volume and that is you cannot find Kyla Mertens name anywhere on the paper. Usually, documents you have carried, have both the Doctor's and Miss Mertens' name on them, especially if they are about research. This seems odd. It also seems somewhat strange that the document is lying here, as it would normally be in the offices. You wonder what this means but not for too long.

What now?

Look in the refrigerator – 752

Check out the lab coats – 793

Wander over to the stools – 308

Or, if this is all too much, you could return to the entrance hall – 212

# 573

You enter the numbers, and you hear a click and some whirring. You try the handle, and the door opens easily. Go 551

## 574

You chase after the old woman, but she slips into the alcove. When you enter it, you find a wall of rock and she is gone. Carefully you trace your hands around the wall of rock, but you can find no secret exit. Time and again you shove and push, but the wall does not budge.

You return to the main cave and search the fridge finding a cheesecake but nothing else. There is nothing else to do here so you decide to leave.

If you entered by torch light – 489

Otherwise – 858

## 575

Do you have the gun, and do you want to use it? – 977

If you don't have a gun or don't want to use it – 217

## 576

The dining room is small but immaculately set with crystal wine glasses and porcelain plates. A rich red carpet is on the floor and there is a small chandelier hanging above the table. There is a hatch to the kitchen in one of the walls and several framed pictures on the others. The only window has its curtains drawn and you think you can see them moving. A light switch is beside the curtains close to where a door leads to the kitchen.

The room is small, but you still need to be quick. Part of you wonders if the curtains are being blown because the window beyond is open but you feel no draught. Will there be anything of note on the table? Is anything left at the hatch? Would it be safer to move through to the kitchen? Should you make sure no one is behind the curtain? Is that a sensible idea? It could be the murderer.

Do you,

Examine the table – 368

Examine the hatch – 401

Take the door to the kitchen – 183

Check out what is causing the curtains to move – 251

# 577

You remember the letter you found in the ruins from Kyla Mertens to the Doctor accusing him of stealing her work on a performance enhancing drug and which talked about a meeting.

This certainly shows motive and may help you. But is it enough to show she murdered the Doctor?

# 578

You switch on the beam and see a pair of legs. They are slender in their trousers, and you struggle to remember what the women were wearing when you were found with the gun in your hand, the same one you are holding now. Whoever it is runs.

Do you

Shout at them to stop – 143

Run after them – 591

# 579

The second fountain down the slope has a paved area by its side with a carving of a small child who is in the act of throwing money into the fountain. Emerging from the fountain is a small cherub with a face that beckons you. Beside it, you can see coins lying in the fountain. A sign indicates that the cherub will answer wishes for money, if you simply lob a few coins in. You don't have any on you but beside you a small coin has been dropped on the paved area.

Do you pick up the coin and throw it in? – 451

Ignore the fountain and instead

Make your way to the folly – 766

Head for the tunnel – 125

Walk down to the final fountain and its walkway – 676

Or go back to the fountains area entrance – 526

# 580

You punch in the code and the pad turns red and a coarse noise like a bad input on a computer sounds. Nothing happens and you are left with the pad again.

Do you enter another code? Which one?

2758 - 774

3267 - 144

9746 - 343

4837 - 616

Another code - 078

Or do you leave the pad alone? If so, make your next choice at 037

# 581

The upper floor of the boathouse has a small corridor off which are four doors. One of the doors states it is a chart room, another the toilet, a third the Rec Room and the last has no name on the door. The corridor has dim lighting produced by the emergency exit lights. There may be something of use up here.

Do you

Enter the toilet – 655

Check out the chart room – 618

Go to the Rec Room – 234

Investigate the room with no name – 521

Return to the lower floor – 795

## 582

Go to <u>002</u>

## 583

The detective disappears for a while before returning. "Your evidence is impressive, but your DNA is on the body, and you were holding a gun and seen by all. No jury will overlook that for someone who merely said she might kill."

It turns out the detective is right, and you are convicted at trial. As you contemplate your long jail term you ponder who the murderer was. Guess you won't know. Try again at <u>001</u>.

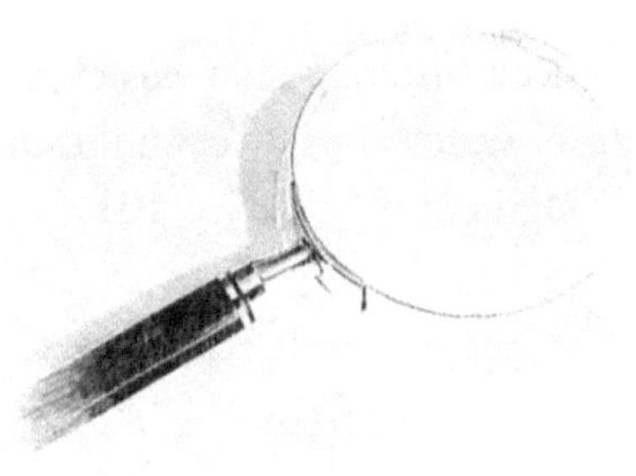

## 584

The locker is of the stand-up variety and has a padlock on it. The lock has four dials, and you recognise this as the Doctor's private locker, so you don't know the combination.

Do you

Want to try a code (only if you have found one) – <u>177</u>

Shoot the lock if you have a gun – <u>380</u>

Or

Examine the dinghy – <u>044</u>

Look at the lifejackets – <u>496</u>

Take the stairs to the upper floor – <u>315</u>

Or

Head over to the marina – <u>909</u>

Or if you want to continue elsewhere take the coastal path at <u>981</u>

# 585

The boat tips up but somehow it manages to come back down without tipping. That was close but you soon find calmer water as you reach the open sea and make for a foreign country. Go to **101**.

# 586

You approach the alcove door, and it opens easily. Inside you see a toilet in a rather cramped space. You guess the Doctor has functions like everyone else. On the floor is a magazine but there is little else here other than the toilet and a roll of toilet paper.

Do you

Read the magazine – 682

Examine the toilet (yes, it really does say that!) – 389

Or

Examine the bed – 615

Check the silk dressing gowns – 312

Descend the stairs – 811

Or leave the Lookout completely and head for the coastal path – 988

# 587

Go to 337

# 588

Stepping back inside the hut, you feel safer away from the wind and rain and that lunatic on the other side. Congratulating yourself as you see the bridge you would have been running across fall to the sea, you then watch the figure head to the other bridge. They are going to cut that one too.

Do you

Try to run across the last remaining bridge – 958

Stay where you are – 714

# 589

You begin to sweat, even through your already soaked clothes as something approaches. As it nears you struggle to see it but it's an animal of some sort with padded feet and it is quick. Seeing you, it tears past, about the height of your knees. Go 166

# 590

You take the candle in one hand, and pulling the paper close, you start to read.

"Dearest Flavius, they are coming for me. Last night they appeared in the sky, their ship spinning round and round before the beam caught me and lifted me up into the belly of the ship. There they probed me with wicked devices, taking samples of my DNA to create a hybrid creature on their planet. Flavius, you must run, for they will come for you next. They want us to be the key component in a race of super aliens. I cannot protect you, even though I am your mother. Run!"

You smile until you realise how close the candle is to the paper. A small section catches fire and the whole paper erupts in a blaze which causes you to yell out in pain and drop the flaming letter. It lands on the table which also catches fire, and you dive out of the door as the whole folly becomes ablaze.

Standing safely on the outside of the fire, you understand that while Granma is clearly mad, you have just lost the evidence in the inferno before you. Note **Granferno** in your code list.

With the fire ablaze, others may come, and you feel you need to get clear of the gardens and search elsewhere. You run to the coastal path, there to make your next choice at 770.

# 591

You run after the woman, but you slip on the wet floor and when you pick yourself up, she's away. By the time you reach the entrance, she is gone into the night. You return to the tomb and sweep the torch around finding a letter on the ground. Read it at 252

# 592

The cleaners cupboard has a lock. You try the handle, but the door is locked and you'll need a key. But do you have any?

If you have a key to try, is it

An ornate key – 750

A key with green tape – 710

Another key – 942

Or do you give up on the cleaners cupboard and instead if you haven't already

Enter the canteen – <u>083</u>

Examine the door belonging to Doctor Munro – <u>775</u>

Try to enter the office of Kyla Mertens – <u>840</u>

Or

Return to the hall – <u>805</u>

# 593

You switch on the beam and see a pair of legs. They are slender in their trousers, and you struggle to remember what the women were wearing when you were found with the gun in your hand, the same one you are holding now. Whoever it is runs.

Do you

Shout at them to stop – <u>143</u>

Run after them – <u>591</u>

Shoot at them – <u>703</u>

# 594

You sit in the dark hearing the footsteps come right past you and you feel the sweat on your brow. You shake a little but control your nerves, remaining quiet as the footsteps pass by and go to the exit of the tomb. You wait several minutes until all is quiet again and you are sure the unknown intruder is clear of the tomb. Then you switch your torch back on and sweep the passageway again. You find a document on the floor of the tomb, which looks like a letter. Read it at <u>352</u>

# 595

You tell the detective about the note from Kyla Mertens to her father, saying how Doctor Munro must be stopped and that she is entering a dark place.

"Now that is interesting, but it is also not proof. You still have a lot to answer for. Do you have anything to back up this evidence?"

If you have any of the following codewords go to that section. Follow the list downwards and only go to the first section that you have a codeword in.

**Taunt** – <u>201</u>

**Grumble** – <u>446</u>

**Pads, Paddy, Silent Papers, Cold Blood, Murder, Hitman, Merto** – <u>415</u>

**Gutted** – <u>048</u>

Otherwise, read on:

The detective arrests you for the Doctor's murder saying that you were still seen with the gun over the body. All you have is a potential heated comment. At the trial you cut a lonely figure as it only takes the jury an hour to convict you. From your jail cell you wonder if you were right in your choice of killer. You'll never know. Maybe try again at 001.

## 596

You take a chart off the wall you recognise well, removing the drawing pins and fold it up. Place it in your inventory as **local chart**. What will you do next?

Try to enter a code for the cupboard (only if you have found one) – 895

Shoot the cupboard open – 402

Or

Go to the Rec Room – 234

Investigate the room with no name – 521

Return to the lower floor – 795

## 597

The keypad goes red, and a claxon begins to sound, deafening you. This is likely to bring lots of people and you decide to get as far away as possible from the building. You run out of the front door and make your way to the coastal path. Go there now at 983

## 598

Go to 325

## 599

"Elsie Gonzales? She was here to report on the big release of the new drug. I'm not seeing that one, sunshine. Have you got any evidence?"

If you have any of the following codewords go to that section. Follow the list downwards and only go to the first section that you have a codeword in.

**Wheel** – 058

**Taunt** – 684

Otherwise – 995

## 600

You open the file and almost start as you realise this is a paper on a drug you heard the Doctor was working on. As you read through, you understand it makes a human perform at their top standard for a lot longer than they can do now. You also see that one of the test subjects is referred to as DL – could that be Daniel Lyle? There is also a lot of science that is beyond your comprehension, but one thing strikes you about the volume and that is you cannot find Kyla Mertens name anywhere on the paper. Usually, documents you have carried, have both the Doctor's and Miss Mertens' name on them, especially if they are about research. This seems odd. It also seems somewhat strange that the document is lying here, as it would normally be in the offices. You wonder what this means but not for too long.

What now?

Look in the refrigerator – 054

Check out the lab coats – 652

Wander over to the stools – 233

Or, if this is all too much you could return to the entrance hall – 805


# 601

The lockers are open and contain several fishing rods and other fishing items such as a scoop net and different tackle. You dig deep under this and find a memo from Kyla Mertens to the Doctor. It states that the drug is too powerful, and they need to backtrack and not release the item in a general fashion. Her language is aggressive, and you can hear the anger in her tone.

Other than this argument, there's nothing else of note here. But there's still a whole boat left to check out. Do you

Go to the lower deck via the stairs – 013

Check out the wheelhouse – 096

Or jump onto the speedboat – <u>624</u>

Or, if you haven't already,

Make for the main building – <u>370</u>

Or if you want to continue elsewhere take the coastal path at <u>981</u>

## 602

This coat is weighed down in one pocket and on searching, you find a camera, slim but very expensive. You switch it on and scan through the pictures on it, viewing them on the rear screen. There are a lot of pictures of the Doctor, including several of him in boxer shorts in a hotel bedroom. But there are also photos showing documents, but they are too small for you to read. The lab coat also has a heady smell of a rich perfume, quite intoxicating and you remember it from somewhere, although you cannot quite put your finger on where.

You can pocket the camera if you wish, make a note in your **inventory**. Then return to <u>793</u>

## 603

This coat is weighed down in one pocket and on searching, you find a camera, slim but very expensive. You switch it on and scan through the pictures on it, viewing them on the rear screen. There are a lot of pictures of the Doctor, including several of him in boxer shorts in a hotel bedroom. But there are also photos showing documents, but they are too small for you to read. The lab coat also has a heady smell of a rich perfume, quite intoxicating and you remember it from somewhere, although you cannot quite put your finger on where.

You can pocket the camera if you wish, make a note in your **inventory**. Then return to 652

# 604

You cannot believe what you are hearing and throw your hands up. "No way," you cry, eyes wide in disbelief. You see the anger in her eyes but cannot stop her simply shoving you and you fall backwards off the cliff. You don't know if they ever catch her as you don't last beyond the fall.

Maybe next time you should be a touch more subtle. Still, try again at 001, and this time, trust no one!

# 605

You make your way down to the third fountain which has a dolphin in a mid-air pose with gushing water coming from it. The rain pouring down makes you feel less impressed than you maybe should be but the thought of getting clear of the downpour for a moment in the tunnel is certainly appealing.

As you approach the fountain and see the entrance to the underground section, you think you see a shadow moving into the tunnel. Could this be one of the other guests? If there is someone in there, should you go in?

Maybe you have the gun and could question them under duress? Or maybe it's a trap?

Do you

Enter the tunnel – 494

Hold off in the rain and wait – 975

Or

Take a look in the walled garden – 926

Make your way to the greenhouse – 745

Wander over to the gardening equipment sheds – 262

Or if you doubt the gardens will be of any use then take the coastal path at 211 but note that you have visited the gardens

# 606

You take the handle of the wheelbarrow, and it promptly falls off in your hands. You then see there is a giant hole in the middle of the barrow and clock it for the heap of junk it is.

Do you

Examine the shrouds – 620

Open the compost bins – 872

Or leave and

Enter the orchard – 560

Wander to the ornamental garden – 420

Or

Check out the fountains area – <u>526</u>

Make your way to the greenhouse – <u>722</u>

Wander over to the gardening equipment sheds – <u>121</u>

Or if you doubt the gardens will be of any use then take the coastal path at <u>770</u> but note that you have visited the gardens

# 607

There's no time to wait and you fire the gun into the dark, momentarily lighting up the tunnel. But the sound reverberates around the enclosed space, and you have to cover your ears. But they ring and you almost miss the small creature with padded feet running past you.

There's nothing here but people will soon come at the sound of that gunshot. You shake your head and pocket the gun before running all the way to the coastal path, to move on and avoid any new arrivals. Join the path at <u>211</u>

# 608

You walk around the crisp concrete walls of the laboratory and try to look in the windows to see if there is anything that may assist you. At first, everything you see is locked down tight but towards the rear of the facility you notice that a window is broken. The glass has not fallen through but there are clear lines of cracking. You are not sure what is inside as it is so dark and there appears to be no lights on. Maybe this could be an opportunity to find more out by breaking in. Or maybe that will cement your guilt when the police arrive.

Do you

Wrap your t-shirt around your elbow and try to break the glass – 936

Continue your walk around the facility – 290

Forget all this and find the coastal path to somewhere else – 983

# 609

You run upstairs but can hear footsteps following you. There's a yell and a knife hits the cockpit wall. You run as hard as you can for the coastal path, never looking back. Go to 980 and decide your next destination.

# 610

Kyla gets close to you and reaches out a hand. You don't trust her and fire your gun. You're not the best at handling a firearm and you watch her tumble to the ground. After a few moments, she doesn't move. You get close and realise you have killed her.

Enter the codeword **Murder** in your code list. You do realise that you are meant to be investigating a murder, not committing one. The gunshot was loud, and you think others may now come so you decide to get out of here by running to the coastal path at 996

# 611

Go to 513

# 612

You pocket the letter. Note the word **Water** in your code list. Now leave the folly and

Check out the coin throwing area - 704

Head for the tunnel - 605

Walk down to the final fountain and its walkway - 524

Or go back to the fountains area entrance - 156

# 613

"Do you know who framed me?"

Elsie looks at you curiously. "How do I know you didn't do it? I know a lot about the others, I'm a journalist. But you still had the gun in your hand."

Elsie seems to be wondering about you, conflicted by her thoughts.

Do you

Draw your gun (if you have one) and tell her to start talking – 969

Ask how she got here – 342

Or leave Elsie in peace and retreat from the cave

If you entered by torch light – 441

Otherwise – 408

# 614

Your heart sinks as the keypad flashes and then the numbers turn red. A claxon begins sounding in the building. You feel the panic rising and glance up and down the hall. You need to get out of here quickly. It's time to move on to the coastal path. You flee the building and reach the path at 986

# 615

The bed has not been slept in, but you find some reading material under it. There is a newspaper, showing a story from what you think may be the financial section, judging by the suits in every photo, and a rather distressed picture of Patrick Davidson. The story is in Spanish, and you have no idea what it means. Otherwise, there is nothing of interest.

Do you

Check the silk dressing gowns - <u>312</u>

Check the alcove door - <u>586</u>

Descend the stairs - <u>811</u>

Or leave the Lookout completely and head for the coastal path - <u>988</u>

# 616

You punch in the numbers and the pad flashes red and a claxon sounds, deafening all around you. Someone might be on their way with all that noise, so you decide you need to run. Make your way to the coastal path at <u>549</u> and escape to another location.

# 617

You tell the detective about the note you found in the ruins that is in your backpack. He retrieves it and take a while studying it before returning to you.

"Now that is interesting, but it is also not proof. You still have a lot to answer for. Do you have anything to back up this solid piece of evidence?"

If you have any of the following codewords go to that section. Follow the list downwards and only go to the first section that you have a codeword in.

**Confess** - <u>130</u>

**Taunt** - <u>357</u>

**Scrap** - <u>239</u>

**Grumble** - <u>446</u>

**Pads, Paddy, Silent Papers, Cold Blood, Murder, Hitman, Merto** - <u>415</u>

**Gutted** - <u>048</u>

Otherwise, read on:

The detective still says you have enough evidence against you that you have to go to trial. It seems that the jury sees enough uncertainty for you are found not guilty. However, the papers do not see it that way, a man with a gun in his hand at a body. Your life becomes a hell, followed by the press, until you leave the country. It might seem unfair but at least you are not in jail. As for who actually killed the Doctor, you still don't know. Maybe try again at <u>001</u>.

# 618

The chart room is awash with charts of the nearby waters on the wall. Having sailed back and forwards across these waters you know that outside your well-travelled route the sea is treacherous and a chart to navigate would be essential. Most of the charts are however locked away in a filing cupboard which has long thin drawers. However, it has a code lock on it. If you want any charts beyond the local waters, then you will need to access the cupboard.

Do you

Take a local chart off the wall – _596_

Try to enter a code for the cupboard (only if you have found one) – _895_

Shoot the cupboard open – _402_

Or

Go to the Rec Room – _234_

Investigate the room with no name – _521_

Return to the lower floor – _795_

## 619

The cave is wet and slimy, but you see a hard surface beyond the water which has a few recliners. The whole area is lit up by ceiling lights. There is a fridge with a small selection of alcoholic beverages sitting on top of it. A bookcase is in the corner as well as a rail with several towels on it. You search the fridge finding a cheesecake but nothing else. There is nothing else to do here so you decide to leave.

If you entered by torch light – _441_

Otherwise – _408_

## 620

The shrouds look like cheap versions and a number of them are falling apart. You wonder just how invested in his vegetable garden the Doctor is. In the soil you discover a bottle labelled _Capernaum antidote._ If you have the codeword **Capernaum**, you drink the contents quickly. Enter the codeword **Cure** in your list. If you don't have this codeword you may pocket the bottle if you wish. Do you

Open the compost bins – 872

Have a look at the wheelbarrow – 606

Or leave and

Enter the orchard – 560

Wander to the ornamental garden – 420

Or

Check out the fountains area – 526

Make your way to the greenhouse – 722

Wander over to the gardening equipment sheds – 121

Or if you doubt the gardens will be of any use then take the coastal path at 770 but note that you have visited the gardens

# 621

Do you have code **Silent Papers** – 619

If not – 798

# 622

This lab coat seems heavily of cheese and has large gouges through the material. You see a name on it: Hugo. There was a Hugo who visited two weeks ago, and you took him across the water to the mainland to an ambulance as he had an injured arm. No one ever said what the issue had been, but the man was white as a sheet when you transported him across the water. But there's nothing in the pockets except a few crumbs of mouldy cheese. Return to 793

# 623

The lock on the door makes a whirring sound and you open it - go to 005

# 624

The speedboat bobs about despite being tied to the pontoon. It looks powerful but is also quite small. You note it needs fuel and also a set of keys to start it. Searching around it you find nothing.

The speedboat seems to hold no clues but there could be a different option here. Maybe you could flee the island and make a life for yourself elsewhere. It's a risky ploy because if you get caught you may look like a killer. It's also unlikely you will prove your innocence if you don't stay.

If you don't have the codeword **Fuel** and the **speedboat keys** or the **surfer logo keys,** then the option is not open to you. If this is the case, return to 909 and make a different decision to those already made, or, if this plan is not for you then return to 909 and choose another path.

If you have the codeword **Fuel,** and the **speedboat keys** or the **surfer logo keys**, and want to go for this then go to 961

# 625

The walled garden is a dark and foreboding. As you approach you can see there are three different sections: an orchard, a vegetable garden, and an ornamental garden. Each looks as dark as the other but maybe one holds something important.

Do you

Enter the orchard – 560

Walk to the vegetable garden – 014

Wander to the ornamental garden – 420

# 626

Your heart sinks as the keypad flashes and then the numbers turn red. A claxon begins sounding in the building. You feel the panic rising and glance up and down the hall. You need to get out of here quickly. It's time to move on to the coastal path. You flee the building and reach the path at 986

# 627

You draw your gun and Granma throws her arms up in the air, turns and runs towards the back of the cave where you see a small alcove. She's getting away and she has the jump on you, so you might not catch her before she disappears.

Do you

Fire your gun at her – 725

Run after Granma – 574

# 628

Go to 199

# 629

The Doctor's office is full of filing cabinets, and you quickly open up many of the drawers, but you are simply overwhelmed by the amount before you. Most of the papers are talking about a new drug that is being commissioned and how it helps humans achieve a peak level of performance for an elongated period of time. The word revolutionary is used many times. Much of the paperwork is however beyond you using technical terms about how the drug works and you find yourself panicking for time and not able to comprehend the science.

As you turn to his desk, you see a set of personal correspondence between the Doctor and Elsie the newspaper reporter. The letters are deeply romantic and there are even some photographs of Elsie waving on beaches in various items of swimwear. What interests you most is one particular letter where Elsie seems to be vehemently attacking the use of performance drugs.

"... I must implore you to stop your work on the drug for it can only bring trouble. My brother was forever affected by a performance enhancing drug that went wrong, causing him to be in a wheelchair for life. You know we are close, and I ask that you do this for me and not betray the feelings that I have for you. It would break my heart to be at opposition to you, but I will be if you do not desist from your research. We would kill to stop such experimentation as this..."

The attitude of Elsie is quite shocking, but it could be something to be aware of. In your code list write the word **wheel**.

You search but there is nothing else of interest in the office. Leaving the office and closing the door, where will you go now

Enter the canteen – 071

Try to get into the cleaners' cupboard – 571

Try to enter the office of Kyla Mertens – 237

Or

Return to the hall – 212

# 630

Well, it's a pair of chairs, fairly modern and designed for comfort. Stuffed under the cushioning of one is a magazine. It is open at a page that tells the tale of a UFO sighting, not far from the island and someone has circled a section. An elderly woman known only as *Norma* has reported the arrival of tall necked men who are here to conduct examinations of the people of earth.

What does the circling of the article mean? Who knows?

Do you

Look inside the wardrobe – <u>072</u>

Examine the bed – <u>804</u>

Rifle through the kitchenette – <u>768</u>

Or

Investigate "The Hollow" – <u>819</u>

Dive into the lagoon and see if you can find the Doctor's secret stash – <u>924</u>

Decide you have had enough of the lagoon and make your move to the coastal path and your next destination – <u>549</u>

# 631

Where do you move the eagle?

Beside the snake – <u>709</u>

Beside the man – <u>097</u>

On the other side of the woman – <u>291</u>

# 632

You tell the detective about your threatening note from when someone tried to kill you at the fountains. The detective takes it away and returns an hour later with a smile on his face.

"We checked out your story about nearly being killed and the handwriting on the note. I believe you son, and the writing is that of Elsie Gonzales. I have just arrested her for your attempted murder. However, you are still the prime suspect for the Doctor's death. Do you have any other evidence?"

If you have any of the following codewords go to that section. Follow the list downwards and only go to the first section that you have a codeword in.

**Notelet** - 437

**Grumble** - 583

**Pads, Paddy, Silent Papers, Cold Blood, Murder, Hitman, Merto** - 636

**Gutted** - 048

Otherwise read on:

The detective still says you have enough evidence against you that you have to go to trial. It seems that the jury sees enough uncertainty for you are found not guilty. However, the papers do not see it that way, a man with a gun in his hand at a body. Your life becomes a hell, followed by the press, until you leave the country. It might seem unfair but at least you are not in jail. As for who actually killed the Doctor, you still don't know. Maybe try again at 001.

# 633

You climb up using the window ledge and haul yourself onto the roof. Lying flat, you crawl your way over the rounded surface to the weathervane. The wind is wild up here and you gulp knowing that you need to stand up to pull a piece of metal off the vane. Carefully you rise up and start to work at the metal, but you feel yourself being buffeted. The metal comes free in your hand just as a gust sweeps you off your feet.

How lucky are you?

This lucky – 640

Maybe this lucky - 807

What? This lucky - 364

# 634

You pick up some of the books and a note falls from it to the floor. It reads "Really need to see about mother's medication. Maybe the diagnosis of insanity is correct. Further investigations required. You are about to return to note from the floor to the book when you see something scratched into the wooden easy chair's side. There's a number, 3267. Maybe that's important.

Otherwise, there's nothing unusual here. Do you

Examine the desk with the computer – 220

Check out the picture on the wall – 098

Examine the coat stand – 428

## 635

The drinks cabinet is a fine antique, and you reckon at an auction it would be worth a fortune. Of course, you cannot put a price on it, but you do recognise many of the drinks inside. There's also an A4 folder inside the cabinet and, pulling it out, you open it. You see several articles inside, cut from newspapers and see the name, Elsie Gonzales. It seems the Doctor was quite taken with her for alongside the articles are a few photographs of the newspaper reporter, taken candidly from across the street. She clearly had no idea she was being photographed.

The articles do not relate to the Doctor or his work, mentioning places far off and in vastly different lines of work from Dr Munro.

You feel it's only safe to check out two items in this room before moving on.


Do you

Check out the China hutch – 792

Look at the bookcase – 541

Examine the curtains – 516

Or if you have already examined two items, or want to leave this room (and have not already visited these places),

Enter the dining room – 576

Enter the kitchen – 298

Go upstairs – 119

Leave by the front door – 384

# 636

The detective disappears for a while before returning. "Nice story, Peter, but you have been busy. The Doctor wasn't your only victim. We match weapons and bullets, sunshine. You're going down for a long time."

And you do! Who killed the Doctor? You'll never know. Try again at 001.

# 637

You remember the letter you found in the folly and ask the detective to fetch it from your bag. Now in the full light he reads it to you. It is a letter stating that

Doctor Munro has been taking the credit for Kyla's work.

"He must be stopped. And if I cannot get the appropriate credit then I shall make sure he sees no reward from the work."

"Wow," says the detective, "that helps you a lot, but do you have anything more.

If you have any of the following codewords go to that section. Follow the list downwards and only go to the first section that you have a codeword in.

**Scrap** – 288

**Taunt** – 201

**Grumble** – 583

**Pads, Paddy, Silent Papers, Cold Blood, Murder, Hitman, Merto** – 636

**Gutted** – 048


Otherwise read on:


The detective still says you have enough evidence against you that you have to go to trial. It seems that the jury sees enough uncertainty for you are found not guilty. However, the papers do not see it that way, a man with a gun in his hand at a body. Your life becomes a hell, followed by the press, until you leave the country. It might seem unfair but at least you are not in jail. As for who actually killed the Doctor, you still don't know. Maybe try again at 001.

# 638

You turn the speedboat around and put the throttle down. Then you feel the strong arms of an athlete pulling you off the wheel. He smacks you with a punch to the jaw and you tumble off the speedboat. The water throws you this way and that but eventually you succumb to the waves and descend to the depths of the sea.

It's 3 weeks before your body surfaces and it's found on a coastal beach. By then you are seen as the killer of Dr Munroe but at least you're too cold to feel the stigma or serve time for your crime.

Maybe escaping was not a good plan. You can ty again at 001.

# 639

Do you have the codewords **Killer** or **Hitman** – 081
Otherwise – 483

# 640

You really are not lucky! The wind lifts you off your feet and right off the roof past the balcony and into a glorious three story fall to the ground. The way down is quite exhilarating, but the abrupt stop is not so pleasant. Wo knows if they cleared your name, and what does it matter to a dead man? Try again at 001

# 641

"I guess we are all involved in some way or other. Patrick's the money but I think there's other issues there. Kyla's his assistant so no surprise she's here. The Doctor doted on his mother, and she's nuts and can't be left alone. And it looks like poor Daniel may be here to be shut up. He was the guinea pig after all. And as for me, I'm just a journalist looking a good story."

Do you

Draw your gun (if you have one) and tell her to start talking – 969

Ask how she got here – 342

Or

Leave Elsie in peace and retreat from the cave

If you entered by torch light – 441

Otherwise – 408

# 642

The letter between Elsie and the Doctor about her wheelchair-bound brother is brought from your belongings and the detective peruses it. "Wow, this is great. Says she would kill. That should help your defence. She's certainly a possibility. But have you anything else?"

Do you have the codeword **Taunt** – <u>935</u>

If not, and you have any of the following codewords go to that section. Follow the list downwards and only go to the first section that you have a codeword in.

**Grumble** – <u>583</u>

**Pads, Paddy, Silent Papers, Cold Blood, Murder, Hitman, Merto** – <u>636</u>

**Gutted** – <u>048</u>

Otherwise read on:

The detective arrests you for the Doctor's murder saying that you were still seen with the gun over the body. All you have is a potential heated comment. At the trial you cut a lonely figure as it only takes the jury an hour to convict you. From your jail cell you wonder if you were right in your choice of killer. You'll never know. Maybe try again at <u>001</u>.

# 643

Your heart sinks as the keypad flashes and then the numbers turn red. A claxon begins sounding in the building. You feel the panic rising and glance up and down the hall. You need to get out of here quickly. It's time to move on to the coastal path. You flee the building and reach the path at <u>986</u>

## 644

You think carefully about what evidence you have, weighing up what is the best thing to do. If you have the following codewords, go to the given section for further thoughts on what you have learnt. Remember to mark this section to come back to.

**Tatler** - 841

**Theft** - 577

**Confess** - 841

**Bowl** - 993

**Taunt** - 009

**Tests** - 131

**Blaze** - 944

**Water** - 545

**Inferno** - 150

**Scrap** - 223

When you are done considering what evidence you have, go to 546 and talk to the Detective Inspector.

## 645

You keep the gun trained on Kyla and tell her to start talking about what's going on.

"It's just a special drug that means a person performs much better physically for much longer. That's what the Doctor was working on with me. I mean that's why they're all here," she blurts out, almost hysterical. "But it's too powerful, we can't release it. But what was your problem with it, Peter. Why did you kill the Doctor?"

"I didn't kill him," you say.

"But we saw you with the gun in your hand. I mean who else wants to kill the Doctor. And why did you, tell me why?"

You lower your eyes, trying to think how to pose the next question. The woman looks desperate. Then she runs at you, hands stretched before her, seizing you by the neck. You choke and panic before your hand seizes shut. There is a single gunshot and Kyla falls backwards, stumbling to the ground. You see a red patch on her shirt. Record the codeword **Merto**

The gunshot could bring people running and the last thing you need is to be seen with the gun in your hand again, over what could be a dead body. You turn and flee from the building, heading for the coastal path before anyone else shows up. Go now to <u>986</u>

# 646

You draw your gun. "I want to know everything." You see the panic in Daniel's eyes. He turns and begins to run. You can't hope to catch him.

Do you

Fire a warning shot – <u>490</u>

Shoot at Daniel – <u>247</u>

Let him go – <u>007</u>

# 647

Drawing your gun, you fire several shots into the desk, splintering the wood. Standing to admire your work, you hear a quiet, *psst!* and something hits you in the shoulder. Suddenly everything goes dark.

You wake up and the room looks the same, but you feel that your hands have been tied. Someone has tied you up and your weapon is gone. You rage in frustration, but you can do nothing until the police eventually arrive and take you into custody. Did you get all the evidence you needed to exonerate yourself? Now go to the 519 to discover your destiny

# 648

This is pointless and you make your way to the rear of the boat, waving your arms and calling for help. It takes some six hours before you are spotted, and a coastguard vessel picks you up. You hand yourself over and must now prepare your defence. Note the codeword **Caught** in your list and make your best plea at 519.

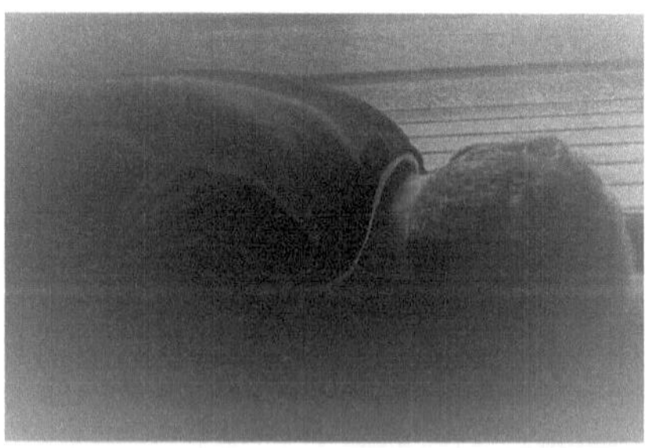

# 649

You tell the detective about the note you received at the fountains when someone tried to kill you. You say it's from Patrick Davidson and the detective disappears for a few hours before returning.

"Well, Peter, it seems that your story checks out, Patrick Davidson did try to kill you. It's his handwriting and we are looking to charge him with your attempted murder.

If you have any of the following codewords go to that section. Follow the list downwards and only go to the first section that you have a codeword in.

**Grumble** – 446

**Pads, Paddy, Silent Papers, Cold Blood, Murder, Hitman, Merto** – 415

**Gutted** – 048

Otherwise read on:

The detective still says you have enough evidence against you that you have to go to trial. It seems that the jury sees enough uncertainty for you are found not guilty. However, the papers do not see it that way, a man with a gun in his hand at a body. Your life becomes a hell, followed by the press, until you leave the country. It might seem unfair but at least you are not in jail. As for who actually killed the Doctor, you still don't know. Maybe try again at 001.

# **650**

Well, it's a pair of chairs, fairly modern and designed for comfort. Stuffed under the cushioning of one is a magazine. It is open at a page that tells the tale of a UFO sighting, not far from the island and someone has circled a section. An elderly woman known only as *Norma* has reported the arrival of tall necked men who are here to conduct examinations of the people of earth.

What does the circling of the article mean? Who knows?


Do you

Look inside the wardrobe - <u>896</u>

Examine the bed - <u>789</u>

Rifle through the kitchenette - <u>159</u>

Or


Investigate "The Hollow" - <u>509</u>

Dive into the lagoon and see if you can find the Doctor's secret stash - <u>810</u>

Decide you have had enough of the lagoon and make your move to the coastal path and your next destination - <u>503</u>

# 651

This time the pad flashes red in a crazy fashion and you can hear an alarm going off. You look around you in a panic wondering if anyone is close and coming for you. Best not to wait around and besides you can't get into the Lookout anyway. You run to the coastal path to choose your next location at 988

# 652

There are three lab coats, and each is hanging from its own hook. The one on the left is clearly being weighed down by something in its pocket but the others seem to be rather dirty. In fact, the first one seems torn.

Are these worth bothering with?

Do you

Examine the torn lab coat – 784

Look at the untorn dirty lab coat – 946

Check out the weighted down lab coat – 603

Or if these lab coats are too dull to bother with

Examine the file – 600

Look in the refrigerator – 054

Wander over to the stools – 233

Or

If this is all too much you could return to the entrance hall – 805

# 653

There is a whirring sound from the lock, and you gently push the door open. Step inside at <u>821</u>

# 654

"Hello there," you say climbing out of the water.

"Get back, get back. You're a murderer. You killed the Doctor."

You can see the fear in her eyes, and she seems genuinely concerned about your presence. How should you play this?

Do you

Pull your gun (if you have one) and tell her to start explaining how you were framed - <u>969</u>

Offer the woman some food if you have any in your inventory - <u>016</u>

Ask her if she knows who framed you - <u>613</u>

Ask if she knows anything about why everyone was here - <u>641</u>

# 655

You enter a tiny room with a toilet before you. The lid is up and there is a small cleaning brush in a stand beside the bowl. On the wall is a toilet roll. It is indeed a toilet. On the bright side, it is a clean one! If you feel the need, by all means use it, but then let's get on.

Do you

Check out the chart room – **618**

Go to the Rec Room – **234**

Investigate the room with no name – **521**

Return to the lower floor – **795**

# 656

You tell the Detective about the note you found in the gardens but haven't read. He retrieves it from your belongings and reads it to you.

"Dearest Flavius, they are coming for me. Last night they appeared in the sky, their ship spinning round and round before the beam caught me and lifted me up into the belly of the ship. There they probed me with wicked devices, taking samples of my DNA to create a hybrid creature on their planet. Flavius, you must run, for they will come for you next. They want us to be the key component in a race of super aliens. I cannot protect you, even though I am your mother. Run!"

The detective looks at you and just laughs. This defence is not going well for you.

If you have any of the following codewords go to that section. Follow the list downwards and only go to the first section that you have a codeword in.

**Taunt** – 027

**Grumble** – 446

**Pads, Paddy, Silent Papers, Cold Blood, Murder, Hitman, Merto** – 415

**Gutted** – 048

Otherwise – 995

# 657

From the window, you look out onto a rough sea which is a mass of dark shades, constantly changing. But then you see a boat out there, a motor cruiser of some sort from the shapes you can make out, the vessel being lit up by its own lights.

But that's it, except for the rain. Note the code **Boat** in your code list

So, what next? Do you

Examine the books around the wall – 943

Check out the table with its cup and cake – 569

Proceed up the spiral staircase – 991

Decide to leave the Lookout and make your way to the coastal path – 990

# 658

You take your torch out and switch it on. The beam of light penetrates the darkness but there are still plenty of dark areas either side of the beam. Yet you can see a passageway heading down into the ground and you feel a chill from the walls. The air is certainly colder down here. As you walk deeper into the tomb, you hear a sound up ahead, like footsteps. You freeze instantly.

Do you have a gun and wish to draw it – 863

Do you wish to switch off the torch and wait in the dark for the owner of the footsteps – 190

Do you want to keep on searching – 997

Or

Decide this is a bad idea and instead

Enter the temple – 273

Check out the sacrificial slab – 742

Look at the gaming board – 165

Or

Decide this area is no longer useful or too risky and continue along the coastal path at 996

# 659

You take out the cheese and pour the liquid from the two phials quickly over it and then throw the cheese at the creature. You see it rear up, and then it begins to eat the cheese before collapsing. You decide to let sleeping rats lie and return to the hall, glad to be alive. Go to 805

# 660

Go to 082

# 661

You tell the detective about your threatening note from when someone tried to kill you at the fountains. The detective takes it away and returns an hour later with a smile on his face.

"We checked out your story about nearly being killed and the handwriting on the note. I believe you son, and the writing is that of Elsie Gonzales. I have just arrested her for your attempted murder, but she blamed Kyla Mertens. On further questioning they both fell apart. They were in it together, Kyla because she had her work taken by the Doctor, and Elsie to get a news story. Congratulations, Peter, you are a free man!"

You step outside and smell the fresh air and know you will not be going to jail. It seems crazy but you've done it. No longer framed. Well done, top sleuth!

# 662

The patio is made from wood and brick and is holding up well to the battering it is receiving. There is a wooden lounger without its cover and a small table. There is also a BBQ area in the darkness of the patio, but you cannot see what lies within it today. There may be ashes for the Doctor was prone to a BBQ.

Do you

Check out the lounger and table – <u>518</u>

Examine the BBQ area – <u>827</u>

# 663

Where do you move the snake?

Beside the eagle – 199

Beside the man – 628

On the other side of the woman – 467

# 664

You scratch your head looking at the complicated series of pulleys and ropes but one thing you can tell, is that everything has been replaced in the last year or so and this device may work. You can't think why it is in working order, but it is a work of art.

Do you

Climb onto the slab and read the engraving – 348

Leave the slab alone and

Make for the tomb and shelter from the rain – 033

Enter the temple – 280

Look at the gaming board – 426

Or

Decide this area is no longer useful or too risky and continue along the coastal path at 998

# 665

You think carefully about what evidence you have, weighing up what is the best thing to do. If you have the following codewords, go to the given section for further thoughts on what you have learnt. Remember to mark this section to come back to.

**Wheel** – 407

**Notelet** – 502

**Bowl** – 993

**Shutdown** – 964

**Space Letter** – 242

**Taunt** – 009

When you are done considering what evidence you have, go to 086 and talk to the Detective Inspector.

# 666

You think carefully about what evidence you have, weighing up what is the best thing to do. If you have the following codewords, go to the given section for further thoughts on what you have learnt. Remember to mark this section to come back to.

**Tests** - <u>131</u>

**Blaze** – <u>944</u>

**Water** – <u>545</u>

**Inferno** - <u>150</u>

**Scrap** – <u>223</u>

**Taunt** – <u>009</u>

**Bowl** – <u>993</u>

**Taunt** – <u>009</u>

When you are done considering what evidence you have, go to <u>170</u> and talk to the Detective Inspector.

# 667

It's probably nothing. You continue to hunt through the ashes and then something pops out in front of you. You jump up but then see a rat. You shoo it away and note that it was standing on a piece of burnt paper.

You take the paper up to the house and by a dim light you read a piece of paper which indicates that Dr Munro had borrowed significant amounts of money from Patrick Davidson. How was he going to pay that back?

You note that evidence and ponder your next move

Check out the lounger and table – <u>518</u>

Or

Pay a visit to the private garden where you saw the glint of light – 914

Take a look at the patio – 662

Or

Decide to head off on one of the paths – 297

# 668

The radio handset appears to be functional, and you set it to channel 16. You hear some banal chatter from the Coastguard and another vessel, but you know the set to be working.

Do you

Contact the Coastguard to tell them of the situation – 438

Or

Switch off the set and let sleeping dogs lie, and instead

Check out the photographs – 184

Have a rifle through the drawers – 865

Look at the writing desk – 897

Or

Climb up the spiral staircase – 506

Descend the spiral staircase - 821

Decide to leave the Lookout and make your way to the coastal path – 990

# 669

You take out the cheese and pour the liquid from the two phials quickly over it and then throw the cheese at the creature. You see it rear up, and then it begins to eat the cheese before collapsing. You decide to let sleeping rats lie and return to the hall, glad to be alive. Go to 212

# 670

Did you come through the window? – 530

If not, you turn for the door and find that there is another keypad. As you try to use it, something rakes along your back, and you fall to the floor. You are now face to face with some red eyes. You think you can make out the image of a rat, but it is a large one and those claws felt like a lion's on your back. What is this?

You need to stand and fight, but what with?

Do you have

A gun – 261

Some cheese and phials – 788

Your fists – 960

# 671

You think carefully about what evidence you have, weighing up what is the best thing to do. If you have the following codewords, go to the given section for further thoughts on what you have learnt. Remember to mark this section to come back to.

**Space Letter** – 242

**Taunt** – 009

**Wheel** – 407

**Tatler** – 841

**Theft** – 577

**Confess** – 841

When you are done considering what evidence you have, go to 456 and talk to the Detective Inspector.

# 672

What code will you enter?

4837 – 396

3267 – 796

2758 – 711

9746 – 268

Another code – 888

## 673

You take the gun out and turn it around offering the handle to the woman. She looks at it in a crazy fashion before grabbing it from you and holding it up to her face.

"This is no ray gun. Idiot, you are an idiot. How are we meant to defend the world with people like you around?" Without warning, she turns the gun around and shoots you. You can hear her striding off down the stairs as you lie there desperately trying to call for help but finding your breath becoming so very short and your voice failing.

Who knows who killed the Doctor? Not you, since you gave a loaded gun to a mad woman. Still, you won't be going to jail! You can try again at 001

## 674

You grab the desk with both hands and begin to shake it violently, trying to open the drawers. As you shake them, you hear a quiet, *psst!* and something hits you in the shoulder. Suddenly everything goes dark.

You wake up and the room looks the same, but you feel that time has passed. Suddenly you get nervous that you may have been here too long, and you need to get a move on. Without a thought you run out of the Lookout and make your way to the coastal path, keen to try and find clues in another location. Go to 988

# 675

You are in the hallway of the house, decorated with numerous paintings, most of famous scientists. There is a set of stairs and a door to the outside of the house. There are also three other doors which you know lead to the kitchen, the dining room and the sitting room. In the hallway, you see a telephone and a small table with a diary on it.

Do you: (if you have not already):

Examine items in the hallway - 050

Enter the sitting room - 763

Enter the dining room - 576

Enter the kitchen - 298

Go up the stairs - 119

Leave by the front door - 384

# 676

The last fountain is quite a wonder. Although its base stands at the top of the cliffs, it has a rope bridge which leads from two points out to a lookout platform, a small hut held up high above the tempestuous sea below. You gaze at the hut wondering if it could have anything inside. It is then you notice the light inside.

The light is dim but there is something inside the hut. However, to get out to it you need to walk one of the two rope bridges. That will leave you exposed as you need to come back on the rope bridges and if someone else were at the fountain, they could block you off. You ponder if it is worth the risk as you look at the fountain's jet of water swinging in an arc above the hut and down into the sea.

Do you

Walk out to the hut along the rope bridge – 801

Decide it is too risky and retreat. If so, to where?

Make your way to the folly – 766

Check out the coin throwing area – 579

Head for the tunnel – 125

Walk down to the final fountain and its walkway – 676

Or

Take a look in the walled garden – 625

Make your way to the greenhouse – 722

Wander over to the gardening equipment sheds – 121

Or

Decide to leave the Gardens by going to the coastal path – 770

# 677

Do you have a surfer key on you? – 049

If not – 727

# 678

The door to the laboratory is unlocked and you open it quietly and peer into the room beyond. There are all sorts of devices sitting on the bench on the far wall, most of which you don't recognise. There is also a large collection of glassware including bottles, jars, petri dishes and stirrers. You also see some Bunsen burners but beyond this collection are other items you never covered in school chemistry.

You can see a file with notes hanging out on the worksurface at the rear of the room. There's also a refrigerator close by the door as well as a number of lab coats hanging on a set of hooks on the wall. A number of stools have also been knocked over at the far bench.

Do you

Examine the file – 572

Look in the refrigerator – 752

Check out the lab coats – 793

Wander over to the stools – 308

Or

If this is all too much you could return to the entrance hall – 212

# 679

You put the key into the lock and the door unlocks and you open it. The cupboard is small and has an array of cleaning products and mops inside. However, there is also a diary on a shelf. You look inside the diary and find it to be a mundane tome mainly about the cleaning lady's rather disastrous love life. But one entry interests you from only two days before.

"Entered the Doctors office to see him occupied on the phone. I went to leave but he held up his hand and I simply stood there. I did not mean to eavesdrop, but I heard the Doctor almost shout down the phone at someone called Daniel that he was under no circumstances getting the drug. I tried to look the other way until the Doctor put down the phone and then asked me to empty his bin. He said he wished everyone was as reliable as me which made me feel pretty good."

There's nothing else of note in the cupboard so you close the door and lock it again before deciding your next course of action.

If you haven't already

Enter the canteen – 071

Examine the door belonging to Doctor Munro – 439

Try to enter the office of Kyla Mertens – 237

Or

Return to the hall – 212

# 680

How fast can you run?

This fast – 397

Maybe this quick – 461

Surely not this quick – 893

# 681

Go to 228

# 682

The magazine is open at a page discussing, in English, Patrick Davidson's company. You see it is a start-up and is rapidly growing but it also needs considerable backing as well as a large win to boost its financial position. There is discussion it will be announcing a major new drug breakthrough but there is little about the actual detail in the article. Enter code word **Tatler** in your code list.

Well, now we know what the deceased Doctor read on the loo, let's see what else we can find.

Do you

Examine the toilet (it still says that!) – <u>389</u>

Or

Examine the bed – <u>615</u>

Check the silk dressing gowns – <u>312</u>

Descend the stairs – <u>811</u>

Or leave the Lookout completely and head for the coastal path – <u>988</u>

# 683

You tell the detective about your threatening note from when someone tried to kill you at the fountains. The detective takes it away and returns an hour later with a smile on his face.

"We checked out your story about nearly being killed and the handwriting on the note. I believe you son, and the writing is that of Kyla Mertens. I have just arrested her for your attempted murder. However, you are still the prime suspect for the Doctor's death. Do you have any other evidence?"

If you have any of the following codewords go to that section. Follow the list downwards and only go to the first section that you have a codeword in.

**Grumble** – 583

**Pads, Paddy, Silent Papers, Cold Blood, Murder, Hitman, Merto** – 636

**Gutted** – 048

Otherwise read on:

The detective still says you have enough evidence against you that you must go to trial. It seems that the jury sees enough uncertainty for you are found not guilty. However, the papers do not see it that way, a man with a gun in his hand at a body. Your life becomes a hell, followed by the press, until you leave the country. It might seem unfair but at least you are not in jail. As for who actually killed the Doctor, you still don't know. Maybe try again at 001.

# 684

You tell the detective about your threatening note from when someone tried to kill you at the fountains. The detective takes it away and returns an hour later with a smile on his face.

"We checked out your story about nearly being killed and the handwriting on the note. I believe you son, and the writing is that of Elsie Gonzales. I have just arrested her for your attempted murder, but she blamed Kyla Mertens. On further questioning, Kyla says she has nothing to do with it all."

If not, and you have any of the following codewords go to that section. Follow the list downwards and only go to the first section that you have a codeword in.

**Grumble** - 583

**Pads, Paddy, Silent Papers, Cold Blood, Murder, Hitman, Merto** - 636

**Gutted** - 048

Otherwise read on:

You are set free, but Elsie is taken to court where she is found guilty of your attempted murder but not of the Doctor. The press hound you, believing it was you and your life becomes a hell, forcing you to leave the country. But at least you are not in a jail cell. There are worse outcomes. Try again at 001.

# 685

The door of the room opens with a creak, and you see that there is no light on inside. As your eyes adjust to the darkness, you can make out a set of shelving at the rear of the room with a collection of things sitting on them, large, box-like. But your heart goes cold as you can also see a figure there. It's indistinct and not moving but has voluminous hair. Your hand feels the wall beside it, and you touch the light switch.

Our heart pounds as you wonder who this is in front of you. Maybe it's the killer. How should you play this? Do you even want to play at all, or should you just cut and run? Or is there something important in this room that will prove your innocence?

Do you

Switch on the light – 372

Draw your gun if you have one – 544

Speak out into the darkness – 919

Run away back to the outside – 925

# 686

This time the pad flashes red in a crazy fashion and you can hear an alarm going off. You look around you in a panic wondering if anyone is close and coming for you. Best not to wait around and besides you can't get into the Lookout anyway. You run to the coastal path to choose your next location at 988

# 687

The apple is red and crispy, and you sink your teeth into it hungry as you are. Now you have finished off that tasty treat, what next? It's not like you have a murder or anything to solve while you stuff your face.

Do you

Try a pear – 537

Or leave and

Walk to the vegetable garden – <u>398</u>

Wander to the ornamental garden – <u>042</u>

Or

Check out the fountains area – <u>156</u>

Make your way to the greenhouse – <u>745</u>

Wander over to the gardening equipment sheds – <u>262</u>

Or if you doubt the gardens will be of any use then take the coastal path at <u>211</u> but note that you have visited the gardens

## 688

Where do you move the man?

Beside the Eagle – <u>458</u>

Beside the man – <u>587</u>

On the other side of the woman – <u>940</u>

## 689

You make your way hesitantly along stony paths until you see the splendid gardens of the island before you. The rain is tipping down and your shorts and t-shirt are becoming sodden. This garden is not a mere trifle such as those landscapes at the house but rather something more magnificent altogether. Despite the dark night, you can make out through some dim lighting four distinct areas of the gardens. First are the magnificent fountains, set in a cascade and making their way down to the sea. Across from them is the walled garden with its array of planted rows and wondrous trees from all round the world. There is also an enormous greenhouse which has lights currently burning bright inside. Finally, you can see the sheds where the gardening equipment is kept.

You need to see if there are any clues to the murder of the Doctor here, unlikely as it may seem so. Where will you investigate first?

Do you

Check out the fountains area – 526

Take a look in the walled garden – 625

Make your way to the greenhouse – 722

Wander over to the gardening equipment sheds – 121

Or if you doubt the gardens will be of any use then take the coastal path at 770 but note that you have visited the gardens

# 690

You tell the detective about the notelet you found where the Doctor told Elsie all about Grandma Munro's problems. The detective seems intrigued and studies the note for a while before disappearing. As he returns, he has a smile on his face.

"Well Peter, that certainly helps your case but is there anything else we should know?"

You can't think of anything and hope you have done enough.

If you have any of the following codewords go to that section. Follow the list downwards and only go to the first section that you have a codeword in.

**Grumble** – 583

**Pads, Paddy, Silent Papers, Cold Blood, Murder, Hitman, Merto** – 636

**Gutted** – 048

Otherwise read on:

The detective still says you have enough evidence against you that you have to go to trial. It seems that the jury sees enough uncertainty for you are found not guilty. However, the papers do not see it that way, a man with a gun in his hand at a body. Your life becomes a hell, followed by the press, until you leave the country. It might seem unfair but at least you are not in jail. As for who actually killed the Doctor, you still don't know. Maybe try again at 001.


# 691


It is a rough two weeks, and you are barely getting by on water and the little food there is in the cave. You carefully come out at night after the fortnight and find the island mainly deserted except for the laboratory. Granma must have been too mad for the authorities. The police must have come and gone, and you are able to sneak away from the island in the Doctor's cruiser.

You make for a foreign land and once ashore you manage to find some basic work and hide out in the country for a few years. One day on the television you see your face, described as the island murderer. Of course, you have no hair now and wear glasses. It seems you need to live in exile for the rest of your life.

Maybe this is a win, but you still don't know who set you up. Try to solve the mystery again at <u>001</u>.

# 692

The boathouse lies ahead of you at the end of the coastal path. Beyond it you see the path going on into the trees. The rain is beating down and the wind howls showing you a rough sea before you. The white of the wave tops come and go and despite the rain, the sound of crashing waves can be heard.

The boathouse has a small marina attached to it, with a large cruiser and a speedboat docked there. The main building is in darkness, much as you left it earlier that day, but you note that the ferry boat you usually pilot is gone, having made a return to the other side earlier that day for workers to get home.

The building has two levels, the lower level a covered dock and the upper level containing rooms for charting and refreshment. It all looks a lot less friendly than usual, given the darkness and the situation.

Do you

Make for the main building – 370

Head over to the marina – 909

Or if you want to continue elsewhere take the coastal path at 981


# 693

Go to 548


# 694

You lower your gun and run from the temple. Getting a short distance away, you turn back and look at Kyla who is standing against the wind in her long coat. She shakes her head and then turns back, walking into the temple.

You decide to stay clear of the temple, but you can still search other parts of the ruins of you haven't already.

Do you

Make for the tomb and shelter from the rain – 033

Check out the sacrificial slab – 246

Look at the gaming board – 426

Or

Decide this area is no longer useful or too risky and continue along the coastal path at 998

# 695

"What are you doing here, Elsie?"

"Peter, you killed him!" The woman shrinks back, and you see she is in terror. She crumples to the ground, shaking. "Don't kill me!" she shrieks.

Do you

Protest your innocence – 152

Go up to Elsie and wrap your arms around her – 126

Decide this is all a bit too much and leave the boathouse – 087

# 696

You grab the cheese and throw it at the creature. At first it rears up and then sniffs the cheese. But it soon ignores it and begins to charge at you.

Do you have a gun? If so, use it – 412

Otherwise – 781

# 697

When you switched the underwater lights on at the hollow you were enchanted by how the water lit up from underneath. Now that you are below the surface, you see the real advantage of the lighting. Although there is the blurriness that looking through any volume of water will bring, you can see quite clearly as you swim around.

The lagoon has a sandy bottom, and you can see an object half-buried towards the middle of the lagoon. However, as you swim around you also see that one of the rocky sides of the feature has what appears to be an entrance to somewhere. Well, it's certainly an outline of a passageway at this distance, but who knows when you get close.

Do you

Swim towards the passageway – 172

Dive down to the half-buried item – 395

Or decide you have seen enough and exit the lagoon. In which case do you

Investigate "The Hollow" – 819

Climb up to the tree hut – 410

Decide you have had enough of the lagoon and make your move to the coastal path and your next destination – 549

# 698

You see the door close and huddle up tight under your large leafy plant. After an hour nothing else has happened and you wonder how long before the police get here. You decide you need to keep moving and on to other locations in search of evidence to clear your name. Go to 986

# 699

You kneel down and look at the blanket on the floor. There is the smell of a woman's perfume on it, and you think it may be that worn by Elsie Gonzales. Turning the blanket over, you find a note underneath which simply says

*The shed, four o'clock. We'll get a half hour. The Doctor*

Well, I think we can see what's going on there. There's nothing else unusual about the blanket or the ground around it so what now?

Do you

Take a look at the lawnmower – 311

Get the box on the shelf – 535

Or leave the shed and

Check out the fountains area – 156

Take a look in the walled garden – 926

Make your way to the greenhouse – 745

Wander over to the gardening equipment sheds – 262

Or if you doubt the gardens will be of any use then take the coastal path at 211 but note that you have visited the gardens

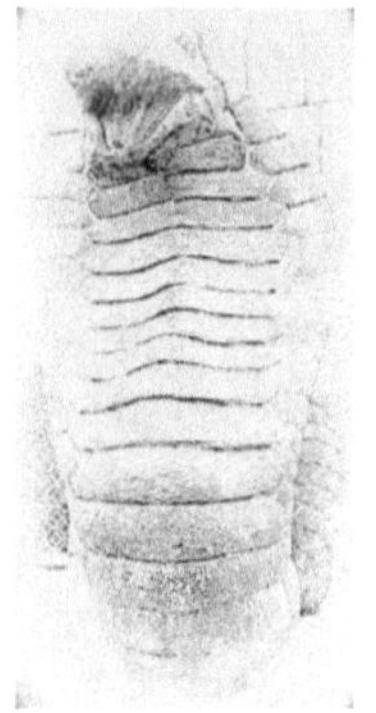

# 700

You try the key in the lock but that's not working. Do you have another key? If not then you'll need to go elsewhere.

If you have another key, is it

A key with green tape - <u>679</u>

Another key – <u>168</u>

If not then do you, if you haven't already

Enter the canteen – <u>071</u>

Examine the door belonging to Doctor Munro – <u>439</u>

Try to enter the office of Kyla Mertens – <u>237</u>

Or

Return to the hall – <u>212</u>

# 701

Maybe no one heard the shot. You wait in silence, desperately hoping no one has but then you hear footsteps outside. You wait to see a head peer in but it's just an arm with a hand that's holding a gun. You raise your own gun but too late and you fall to the ground, finally knowing how the Doctor truly felt.

Gunplay never ends well. But learn that lesson by returning to 001 and having another go.

# 702

"Patrick Davidson," says the detective stroking his moustache. "You're going to have to show me some evidence sunshine, as he's a respected businessman. I know he was backing the Doctor's new drug. What can you tell me?"

If you have any of the following codewords go to that section. Follow the list downwards and only go to the first section that you have a codeword in.

**Tatler** – 334

**Taunt** – 128

**Gutted** – 048

Otherwise – 995

# 703

You fire a shot at the woman, and she pitches to the ground. You expect she will struggle as you arrive, but it seems you hit her in the head. The woman is dead and as you turn her over you realise it is Kyla Mertens. More than that, the shot echoed around the tomb and must have been so noisy outside it would have cut through the weather. Enter the code word **Scientist Down** in your code list. You decide you need to move on lest you are found with another dead body.

You make for the coastal path at 996

# 704

The second fountain down the slope has a paved area by its side with a carving of a small child who is in the act of throwing money into the fountain. Emerging from the fountain is a small cherub with a face that beckons you. Beside it, you can see coins lying in the fountain. A sign indicates that the cherub will answer wishes for money, if you simply lob a few coins in. You don't have any on you but beside you a small coin has been dropped on the paved area.

Do you pick up the coin and throw it in? - 785

Ignore the fountain and instead

Make your way to the folly – 444

Head for the tunnel – 605

Walk down to the final fountain and its walkway – 524

Or go back to the fountains area entrance – 156

## 705

Slowly you enter the tunnel, and you can feel that it's as damp in here as it was outside. There is water running down the wall and up ahead you can see next to nothing. Gingerly, you edge forward. There's a flicker of something coming toward you, a blur of shadows. Your heart beats fast and you tense up. You can't see anything now, but you can hear something padding towards you.

If you have a gun, you can draw it now – 317

If you want to run, you'll have to run all the way to the coastal path - 770

Will you stand and face what is coming towards you – 225

## 706

The hatch has a sliding lock, and you pull it back allowing the hatch to open. However, you see a complimentary door on the other side, which is locked closed, possibly from the other side. After all that's how these food hatches work. You are about to close the hatch up again when you notice a small key at the side of the opening. It has not markings except for a small piece of green tape on it.

Pocket it if you want and make a note of it in your inventory as **green tape key.**

What now?

Check out the fridge freezer – <u>822</u>

Have a look through the cupboards – <u>887</u>

Examine the pots on the cooker – <u>129</u>

Look at the knife block – <u>353</u>

Return to the hall – <u>675</u>

# 707

The cake on the table is half eaten and there is a note with it.

*Sir, I have left the extra mug as requested. Please advise when I can clear away fully. Kathy*

The only Kathy you know is the cleaner, but she left not long after the guests arrived when the last boat headed for the mainland. You look at the mug on the table and see it has lipstick still on it. As you are unaware of the Doctor ever wearing lipstick, you feel he must have been entertaining.

There's nothing else here, so what next? Do you

Examine the books around the wall – <u>757</u>

Look out the window – <u>092</u>

Proceed up the spiral staircase – <u>811</u>

Decide to leave the Lookout and make your way to the coastal path – <u>988</u>

## 708

Go to 337



## 709

Go to 199

## 710

You put the key into the lock and the door unlocks and you open it. The cupboard is small and has an array of cleaning products and mops inside. However, there is also a diary on a shelf. You look inside the diary and find it to be a mundane tome mainly about the cleaning lady's rather disastrous love life. But one entry interests you from only two days before.

"Entered the Doctors office to see him occupied on the phone. I went to leave but he held up his hand and I simply stood there. I did not mean to eavesdrop, but I heard the Doctor almost shout down the phone at someone called Daniel that he was under no circumstances getting the drug. I tried to look the other way until the Doctor put down the phone and then asked me to empty his bin. He said he wished everyone was as reliable as me which made me feel pretty good."

There's nothing else of note in the cupboard so you close the door and lock it again before deciding your next course of action.

If you haven't already

Enter the canteen – 083

Examine the door belonging to Doctor Munro – 775

Try to enter the office of Kyla Mertens – 840

Or

Return to the hall – 805

# 711

The number pad goes red, and you hear a horrible buzzer indicate you are wrong.

Do you try another number?

4837 – 210

3267 – 686

9746 – 244

Another code – 651

Or do you

Use the Doctor's swipe card on the reader if you have it – 520

Try to climb the Ivy – 277

Or if this all seems to hard or unwise, you could simply keep on walking the coastal path to your next location at 988 but note that you have visited the Lookout

# 712

You draw your weapon and shoot the lock, causing the padlock to shatter. You quickly open the locker but think you can hear someone nearby. You think about staying but choose to run, not wanting to be found. It was a bit daft to alert everyone to where you are. Desperately you flee the boathouse, and run to the coastal path at 980

# 713

The buzzer howls even louder this time and the number pad flashes before the numbers change from bright green to red. Looks like it's locked the door. More than that it will have set off an alarm. Time to get out of here. You run hard around the laboratory to the coastal path at 986

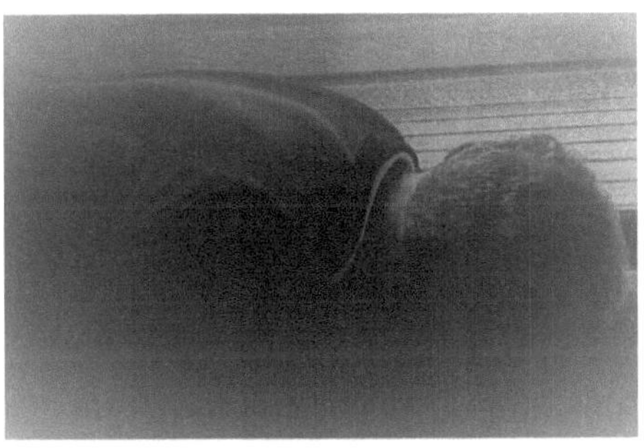

# 714

You hold your position as the figure runs to the other bridge and then begins their work with the axe. Soon that bridge falls to the sea. But you are safe if a little trapped. You have a fretful night until the morning comes, and you see police officers by the fountain. It takes most of the day for a specialist team to rescue you and you are then placed under arrest. Do you have much evidence? Will you be able to defend yourself because they clearly think you committed the murder of Doctor Munro? Go to 519

# 715

You pick up the box and hurl it at the ground in front of you. There's an almighty crack of gunfire and a shot ricochets briefly around the shed. Fortunately, it doesn't hit you, but that noise was so loud, you panic and decide to get out of the gardens quickly. You flee to the coastal path at 211

# 716

You hold your hands out in front of you and find the wall to guide you further into the tomb. As you blindly step in you can hear footsteps in the dark. Your breathing quickens as you know someone is in here with you.

Do you

Continue – <u>023</u>

Retreat to another part of the ruins and

Enter the temple – <u>273</u>

Check out the sacrificial slab – <u>742</u>

Look at the gaming board – <u>165</u>

Or

Decide this area is no longer useful or too risky and continue along the coastal path at <u>996</u>

# 717

"Elsie Gonzales? She was here to report on the big release of the new drug. I'm not seeing that one, sunshine. Have you got any evidence?"

If you have any of the following codewords go to that section. Follow the list downwards and only go to the first section that you have a codeword in.

**Wheel** – <u>729</u>

**Taunt** – <u>328</u>

Otherwise – <u>995</u>

# 718

The letter between Elsie and the Doctor about her wheelchair-bound brother is brought from your belongings and the detective peruses it. "Wow, this is great. Says she would kill. That should help your defence. She's certainly a possibility. But have you anything else?"

Do you have the codeword **Taunt** - 933

If not, and you have any of the following codewords go to that section. Follow the list downwards and only go to the first section that you have a codeword in.

**Grumble** - 583

**Pads, Paddy, Silent Papers, Cold Blood, Murder, Hitman, Merto** - 636

**Gutted** - 048

Otherwise read on:

The detective still says you have enough evidence against you that you have to go to trial. It seems that the jury sees enough uncertainty for you are found not guilty. However, the papers do not see it that way, a man with a gun in his hand at a body. Your life becomes a hell, followed by the press, until you leave the country. It might seem unfair but at least you are not in jail. As for who actually killed the Doctor, you still don't know. Maybe try again at 001.

# 719

What code will you try?

3267 - 142

4837 - 484

2758 - 573

9746 - 534

Or a different code - 965

# 720

In the dark you realise you don't know where you are going. It's just a lot of water after all. You don't have much to guide your path and by morning you are unsure where you are. A police launch picks you up in the sea off the mainland as you must have doubled back on yourself in your confusion. Oh, well, let's see if you can explain it all to the investigators. Proceed to 011

# 721

Where do you move the eagle?

Beside the snake - 034

Beside the man - 708

On the other side of the woman - 885

# 722

If you have codeword **Pads** go to 982

The greenhouse is lit up from inside and is a stunning piece of architecture, with many details on the outer structure. However, it is inside you want to investigate, and you are glad to step out of the driving rain. As you drip onto the floor, you note the number of leaves on the ground and the warmth of the building. This puts you at ease and you stroll through the paths examining the plants growing within. As you turn a corner, you almost freeze, for there in front of you is a shaking man on the ground, hugging his knees tight to him. It is Patrick Davidson, and he has heard you and turns quickly, rising to his feet. You see the shock on his face, and he goes to run.

Do you

Tell him to wait and that it was not you who killed the Doctor - 492

Tell him you know who the real killer is - 736

Tell him you are scared too - 743

If you have one, pull out your gun and threaten him with it for information - 127

Let him go - 920

# 723

There's no time to wait and you fire the gun into the dark, momentarily lighting up the tunnel. But the sound reverberates around the enclosed space, and you have to cover your ears. But they ring and you almost miss the small creature with padded feet running past you.

There's nothing here but people will soon come at the sound of that gunshot. You shake your head and pocket the gun before running all the way to the coastal path, to move on and avoid any new arrivals. Join the path at 770

# 724

Looking at the ruins you see there are masses of Police in the area, particularly at the temple area, where you killed Kyla. This won't work, and you'll need to try something else.

Make a run for the boathouse – 568

Hide out in the gardens – 499

Or

If you checked the following codewords while making your initial decision, then you may follow their options

Codeword **Boat** – 090

Codeword **Quiet Place** – 224

Or if these don't seem like good options, you can always surrender yourself – 519

## 725

You draw your gun and fire at the old woman who tumbles to the ground. Blimey, that was a bit over the top! You run up to her but find a pool of blood beside her. She's not breathing. Oh dear, you've killed her. Enter **Granocide** in your code list.

You decide to beat a hasty retreat from the lagoon and make for the coastal path at <u>503</u> to find other places to investigate

## 726

You make for the mainland, your hand on the wheel and Daniel watching you from the aft of the boat. He seems scared but you fight through the waves before arriving at a small beach alcove which Daniel points out. As you get closer to the land you can see flashing lights. The police are there in abundance.

Do you

Take the boat in and hand yourself over - <u>862</u>

Turn the boat around – <u>638</u>

# 727

"I'm sorry, I really want to help you but have no key for the boat."

"Okay," says Elsie "but I'm not staying here with you. Be careful. There are people here who truly didn't like the Doctor. I loved him despite his manufacture of drugs. Why he wanted people to use drugs to become better, I really don't know. But I saw past that evil, and I was getting close to him. But there are others who don't feel that way. Take care, Peter."

With that, she steps forward and kisses you on the forehead before slipping past you. As you watch her descend the stairs, you are amazed how she handles her heels and soon she has disappeared out into the rain.

You feel a little unsettled but look around the room. There are several canisters on the shelving, which must have looked like boxes in the dark. You open one and smell diesel. They are quite heavy, and you decide you can't simply carry them around. But you know where to come if you need them. Note the codeword **Fuel** in your code list.

That was eventful but what do you do next?

Check out the chart room – <u>618</u>

Go to the Rec Room – <u>234</u>

Investigate the room with no name – <u>521</u>

Return to the lower floor – <u>795</u>

# 728

You scramble to your feet and don't look back. You need to get away from the house, so you'd better pick one of the main paths to another part of the island and don't slow down. Go to <u>297</u>

# 729

The letter between Elsie and the Doctor about her wheelchair-bound brother is brought from your belongings and the detective peruses it. "Wow, this is great. Says she would kill. That should help your defence. She's certainly a possibility. But have you anything else?"

If you have any of the following codewords go to that section. Follow the list downwards and only go to the first section that you have a codeword in.

**Taunt** – <u>632</u>

**Notelet** – <u>690</u>

**Grumble** – <u>583</u>

**Pads, Paddy, Silent Papers, Cold Blood, Murder, Hitman, Merto** – <u>636</u>

**Gutted** – <u>048</u>

Otherwise read on:

The detective arrests you for the Doctor's murder saying that you were still seen with the gun over the body. All you have is a potential heated comment. At the trial you cut a lonely figure as it only takes the jury an hour to convict you. From your jail cell you wonder if you were right in your choice of killer. You'll never know. Maybe try again at <u>001</u>.

# 730

Maybe no one heard the shot. You wait in silence, desperately hoping no one has but then you hear footsteps outside. You wait to see a head peer in but it's just and arm with a hand that's holding a gun. You raise your own gun but too late and you fall to the ground, finally knowing how the Doctor truly felt.

Gunplay never ends well. But learn that lesson by returning to <u>001</u> and having another go.

# 731

You put the key in the lock and twist it opening the box. Inside you find a gun and realise it is fully loaded. You can pocket it if you want by **noting the gun in your inventory.** What now?

Do you

Take a look at the lawnmower – 311

Examine the blanket on the floor – 699

Or leave the shed and

Check out the fountains area – 156

Take a look in the walled garden – 926

Make your way to the greenhouse – 745

Wander over to the gardening equipment sheds – 262

Or if you doubt the gardens will be of any use then take the coastal path at 211 but note that you have visited the gardens

# 732

Where do you move the man?

Beside the Eagle – 302

Beside the snake – 953

On the other side of the woman – 215

# 733

The Doctor's neat suit has been covered in blood and as you rifle through his clothing you find that the blood gets onto your own. You berate yourself for being so stupid but feel less aggrieved when you pull a ripped piece of paper from the Doctor's pocket. Scanning it, you realise it is the beginning of his speech for the evening and you read with interest.

It tells you that the Doctor has indeed made a discovery with a drug he is working on that enhances sporting performance. The enhancement is so significant, he believes the increase it causes in metabolism will allow an athlete to perform at their highest level for ten times longer than previous. It is also virtually undetectable.

You place the note in your pocket, knowing that having touched it, the piece of paper would be a risk to you if found and you'll need to jettison it somewhere safe.

You search the rest of the Doctor's clothing but find nothing of interest. He has clearly been shot and is dead. A few of the bottles behind him have smashed and you believe several shots may have been fired.

Write the word **grumble** in your code list.

Do you (if you have not already):

Examine the cellar – 263

Leave the cellar – 675

# 734

Is the key an ornate key – 241

If not, the key does not fit the lock. Go back to 182 and make another choice

# 735

You take the candle in one hand and, pulling the paper close, you start to read. It appears that Kyla Mertens has written a letter to a friend showing total disgust for her employer. Doctor Munro appears to be hijacking all of Kyla's work and passing it off as his own, to such a point that it seems that she is getting no credit for what she has done at all. Her anger is obvious and at one point, she says

"he must be stopped. And if I cannot get the appropriate credit then I shall make sure he sees no reward from the work."

Wow, that's a threat if ever you heard one. You smile smugly until you realise how close the candle is to the paper. A small section catches fire and the whole paper erupts in a blaze which causes you to yell out in pain and drop the flaming letter. It lands on the table which also catches fire, and you dive out of the door as the whole folly becomes ablaze.

Standing safely on the outside of the fire, you understand that while Kyla has a motive, you have just lost the evidence in the inferno before you. Note **Inferno** in your code list.

With the fire ablaze, others may come, and you feel you need to get clear of the gardens and search elsewhere. You run to the coastal path, there to make your next choice at 211.

# 736

"Patrick, just stop, I know who the real killer is." Patrick holds up but keeps a distance from you.

"Maybe you do, maybe you don't but just keep away from me, alright. When they come from the mainland, you can tell them, and they can sort it all out. Until then I am staying clear of everyone. You understand. It's the safest way."

With that Patrick looks to run away.

Tell him you are scared too – 743

If you have one, pull out your gun and threaten him with it for information – 127

Let him go – 920

# 737

So, you threw a coin in a fountain. Were you expecting much to happen because nothing does? This is a murder investigation, not Cinderella. Come on, pick it up, sunshine, as all the best Inspectors say! Now investigate something worthwhile and stop clowning about.

Do you

Make your way to the folly – 766

Head for the tunnel – 125

Walk down to the final fountain and its walkway – 676

Or go back to the fountains area entrance – 526

# 738

You grab the radio microphone and clicking it you transmit a Mayday call explaining that someone has been killed on the island. The coastguard responds asking for your position. You tell them you are on the island, and they tell you to stay put as vessels are already on their way. They tell you to stay hidden and safe as the police will be there very shortly.

Is this a good thing? Will you have time to solve the mystery before they arrive? Have you just hastened your arrest? Enter the codeword **Late Rescue** into your codeword list.

If you have the code word **Fuel** – 300

If not, then that appears to be it in the wheelhouse, so

Do you

Go to the lower deck via the stairs – 013

Look at the lockers at the aft of the upper deck – 601

Or

Jump onto the speedboat – 624

Or, if you haven't already,

Make for the main building – 370

Or

if you want to continue elsewhere take the coastal path at 981

# 739

You walk around the crisp concrete walls of the laboratory and try to look in the windows to see if there is anything that may assist you. At first, everything you see is locked down tight but towards the rear of the facility you notice that a window is broken. The glass has not fallen through but there are clear lines of cracking. You are not sure what is inside as it is so dark and there appears to be no lights on. Maybe this could be an opportunity to find more out by breaking in. Or maybe that will cement your guilt when the police arrive.

Do you

Wrap your t-shirt around your elbow and try to break the glass – 814

Continue your walk around the facility – 881

Forget all this and find the coastal path to somewhere else – 986

# 740

I don't know where you got that code from but it's a dud and a claxon goes off and you hear some whirring around the door. You race over and try to open the door again, but it won't move.

Go 314

# 741

You hold your ground unable to see but the noise in the passage seems to be coming closer. There is some heavy breathing. Suddenly it all seems so close, and you feel your heart thumping.

Do you

Run back upstairs – 962

Stay and face whatever's coming – 414

# 742

The sacrificial slab is a large wooden block with a slab inset and appears to have been restored. The slab, a square piece of marble, framed by wood, has several ropes running from it to a lever several metres away. Half of the slab hangs out over the sea, and you think you might understand how this works. In the old days, the poor victim would be sacrificed by the slab being tipped and the person would be deposited into the sea below. It seems somewhat brutal but surely a replica.

From your position beside the slab, you can see writing in the middle of it, but it is very finely engraved, probably from wear. The mechanism across from you looks fascinating.

Do you

Examine the mechanism – 970

Climb onto the slab and read the engraving – 218

Leave the slab alone and

Make for the tomb and shelter from the rain – 877

Enter the temple – 273

Look at the gaming board – 165

Or

Decide this area is no longer useful or too risky and continue along the coastal path at 996

# 743

"Look Patrick, I'm scared too. Someone has framed me and I'm just running frightened like you. You understand. I'm of no age, I had no gripe against the Doctor."

"Neither did I. I backed his wonder drug; I got my board behind it, and we funded his experiments. And it was all good, all going well until he decides to make it patent free. That's not his choice, he can't just do that. I just needed to talk him around on that point. Anyway, if you didn't do it, good luck. If you did, go and rot!"

With that Patrick turns away again.

Do you

If you have one, pull out your gun and threaten him with it for information – 127

Let him go – 920

# 744

The number pad goes red, and you hear a horrible buzzer indicate you are wrong.

Do you try another number?

4837 - <u>279</u>

3267 - <u>309</u>

2758 - <u>856</u>

9746 - <u>032</u>

Or do you

Use the Doctor's swipe card on the reader if you have it - <u>134</u>

Try to climb the Ivy - <u>004</u>

 Or if this all seems to hard or unwise, you could simply keep on walking the coastal path to your next location at <u>990</u> but note that you have visited the Lookout

# 745

The greenhouse is lit up from inside and is a stunning piece of architecture, with many details on the outer structure. However, it is inside you want to investigate, and you are glad to step out of the driving rain. As you drip onto the floor, you note the number of leaves on the ground and the warmth of the building. This puts you at ease and you stroll through the paths examining the plants growing within. As you turn a corner, you almost freeze, for there in front of you is a shaking man on the ground, hugging his knees tight to him. It is Daniel Lyle, and he has heard you and turns quickly, rising to his feet. You see the shock on his face, and he goes to run.

Do you

Tell him to wait and that it was not you who killed the Doctor – <u>362</u>

Tell him you know who the real killer is – <u>178</u>

Tell him you are scared too – <u>921</u>

If you have one, pull out your gun and threaten him with it for information – <u>646</u>

Let him go – <u>007</u>

# 746

"Elsie Gonzales? She was here to report on the big release of the new drug. I'm not seeing that one, sunshine. Have you got any evidence?"

If you have the following codeword **Taunt** – <u>932</u>

Otherwise – <u>995</u>

# 747

As you near the section you see that there is an open passageway in the rock, and you surface for another breath before diving back down and swimming through the gap in the rock. You swim for only a few yards before the rock ceiling above you disappears and you surface in a large cave at 324

# 748

There's no one here. It must have been shadows or your mind. You feel a little unsettled but look around the room. There are several canisters on the shelving, which must have looked like boxes in the dark. You open one and smell diesel. They are quite heavy, and you decide you can't simply carry them around. But you know where to come if you need them. Note the codeword **Fuel** in your code list.

That was eventful but what do you do next?

Check out the chart room – 848

Go to the Rec Room – 528

Investigate the room with no name – 685

Return to the lower floor – 370

# 749

You swipe the card again but still you notice no difference. Enter the code **Sesame** in your code list. If you have the code **Baba** cross it out. What will you do now?

Enter a code on the pad (only if you have found one) - <u>320</u>

Or leave the item alone and

Check out the tin - <u>250</u>

Investigate the switch - <u>003</u>

Or if none of this inspires you, go back to the lagoon entrance and make another choice - <u>423</u>

# 750

You try the key in the lock but that's not working. Do you have another key? If not then you'll need to go elsewhere.

If you have another key, is it

A key with green tape – <u>710</u>

Another key – <u>942</u>

If not then do you, if you haven't already

Enter the canteen – <u>083</u>

Examine the door belonging to Doctor Munro – <u>775</u>

Try to enter the office of Kyla Mertens – <u>840</u>

Or

Return to the hall – <u>805</u>

# 751

You charge at the door and throw your shoulder at it but bounce back off it, having not moved it at all. Your shoulder is now very sore. Bad plan! Return to <u>425</u>

# 752

Inside the refrigerator you see a left-over chicken sandwich and two small phials marked rat deterrent. Otherwise, the appliance is empty and smells a little of stale cheese. You can take any of these items with you, and if you wish to do so, mark them in your **inventory**. There's nothing further in the refrigerator and you ponder what to do next.

Do you, if you haven't already,

Examine the file – <u>572</u>

Check out the lab coats – <u>793</u>

Wander over to the stools – <u>308</u>

Or

If this is all too much you could return to the entrance hall – <u>212</u>

# 753

You set out on the path to the laboratory, dancing amid the puddles that have formed on the stone path. Your shorts are wet through, and your top is beginning to drip but with the humid heat of the night you don't feel cold. As you walk along the dark path, you can hear your feet crunch the stones and hope no one is close. You really need to get inside and take some shelter. You climb up the path and down into a dell where you see the splendid laboratory before you.

You are not quite sure what the Doctor does in here and you have heard various tales about what lies in the depths of the laboratory. However, you have never been inside for there are various keypads that need to be accessed. Usually, you just drop any deliveries by the door.

The path swings down to a glass door which is the entrance to the lab facilities. There is low level lighting in operation, and you can see corridors that disappear into darkness inside. Enter the codeword **Playtime** into your code list.

There appears to be no one around and you approach the front door. It is locked and won't open. On the side of the door is a keypad with the usual single digits, 1 to 9 lit up in fluorescent green.

What will you do?

Do you have a code and wish to try the keypad – 907

Hide in the undergrowth surrounding the facility and see what happens – 440

Walk around the facility and see what you can find – 608

Call this a bust and find the coastal path – 983

# 754

Where do you move the woman?

Beside the Snake – 082

Beside the man – 660

Beside the Eagle – 476

## 755

You draw your gun and shot at the pieces causing pieces to fly off them. None of them seem to fall over and now when you try to lift them, they seem stuck fast. More than that, the noise from firing the gun caused a loud retort and echo and will surely bring people this way. You decide you need to move on quick and high tail it to the coastal path at 998

## 756

You take the key and start to fiddle with the lock. Suddenly, a dart flies out from a crevice between the drawers and the table leg. Whatever hits you works quickly, and you suddenly pass out.

The next thing you know is a jail cell and a lot of awkward questions to which you have no answers. You didn't discover anything that would help your case and you were also seen with the Doctor's body with a gun in your hand before being trapped while searching his room. They know you were looking for something and with the evidence stacked against you, the court case does not take long before your life sentence is pronounced.

It is several years when you receive a letter, thanking you for taking the blame and explaining how you were framed. Your eyes widen with interest as you see the signature at the bottom. The culprit is on their deathbed and maybe you can be free. If only you can get in touch with... Now that would be telling. Maybe next time you'll find out who did it!

Return to <u>001</u> and better luck next time!

# 757

The number of books amaze you and you see that most of the books appear to be scientific books, mainly about how the body functions. Most are of far too high a level for your understanding, but you see that one particular section of books seems to be jutting out more than others. You grab a book from this section and see a book with a Spanish title. When you open it, a photograph falls out of Elsie Gonzales. The black and white image is signed *Elsie, all my love* and it seems to be heavily creased as if it has been looked at a lot.

What now? Do you

Check out the table with its cup and cake - <u>707</u>

Look out the window - <u>092</u>

Proceed up the spiral staircase - <u>811</u>

Decide to leave the Lookout and make your way to the coastal path - <u>988</u>

# 758

You turn to leave the hut and see a figure at the far end of one of the rope bridges. The figure wears a coat with a hood, and you struggle to work out who it is, but you can see the large axe they are holding. You gasp in horror as you step out onto the bridge, for the figure is now chopping at the rope bridge support strands with the axe.

Do you

Run as hard as you can across this rope bridge - <u>803</u>

Step back inside the hut and remain there as it is safe – <u>588</u>

Turn around and run for the other rope bridge - <u>680</u>

# 759

You arrive via the stony coastal path at the ruins and see lightening race across the sky and light up the abandoned stone structures before you. The Doctor has always told you to stay clear of the ruins as they are unsafe, and you have obeyed him in that. But now you think there may be something he was keeping you from in here. Is this area part of the puzzle of the guests and what was passing between the Doctor and them? It's time to find out. Enter code word **Collapsed** in your code list.

There are four main areas in the ruins: the temple, the tomb, the sacrificial slab at the cliff, and the gaming board. The tomb leads underground but the other areas are open to the pouring rain. There is no light other than that which the lightening brings, and you will need to watch your footing. In truth, this place is scaring you, as you could be being watched so easily without ever seeing your foe.

Do you

Make for the tomb and shelter from the rain – 877

Enter the temple – 273

Check out the sacrificial slab – 742

Look at the gaming board – 165

Or

Decide this area is no longer useful or too risky and continue along the coastal path at 996

## 760

There's a horrible buzzer that tells you that the code is wrong. Blimey, one more chance or you'll be locked out. What do you do? Try a different code

4837 – <u>713</u>

9746 – <u>934</u>

3267 – <u>303</u>

2758 – <u>512</u>

Or do you decide this is too risky and decide instead to

Hide in the undergrowth surrounding the facility and see what happens – <u>971</u>

Walk around the facility and see what you can find – <u>739</u>

Call this a bust and find the coastal path – <u>986</u>

# 761

You ask the old woman how she got into the cave as you cannot believe she swam but she doesn't seem to understand. "How do we leave?" you ask trying to ask the question in a different way. Granma stops eating and reaches inside her skirt pocket. Taking out a key, she hands it to you.

The key has a dolphin keyring attached and you stand and begin to search the cave for a lock to put the key into. However, you can see nothing. You try to ask her where the lock is, but she is almost catatonic. If you want to keep the key, you can enter it in your inventory as **Dolphin key**.

But does Granma know another exit?

Do you

Draw your gun (if you have one) and tell her to start talking – 627

Leave the woman in peace and retreat from the cave

If you entered by torch light – 489

Otherwise – 858

# 762

You get a smug feeling as you motor past some rescue vessels making their way to the island. They call you on the radio and you spin some a story about cruising past on your way north. It seems to work, and it is the following morning as your eyes get tiered that you realise you are clear of any police or rescuers.

Your eyes struggle to stay open having been at the wheel all night but you make your way down into the hull of the vessel looking for sustenance. As you enter the main passageway on the lower deck, something hits you on the head. You hear a laugh and feel your hands being tied up, along with your feet.


About ten minutes later you are taken up on the main deck and unceremoniously tossed overboard. It appears someone had joined you on the cruiser. And now they are making their escape as you sink beneath the waves. Maybe next time you'll try to solve the mystery, not simply become a fugitive. Try again at 001


# 763

The sitting room is immaculate, ready for guests who will not be requiring it any longer. There is a suite in a floral pattern and a China hutch at the rear wall. The curtains are drawn, and a small bookcase stands beside them. There's also an antique drinks cabinet which is half open. Nothing looks out of the ordinary, but you might manage a look at a few items if you want to before you feel it would be time to keep moving.

Do you

Check out the China hutch – <u>792</u>

Examine the drinks cabinet – <u>635</u>

Look at the bookcase – <u>541</u>

Examine the curtains – <u>516</u>

Ignore this room and instead (if you have not already done so):

Enter the dining room – <u>576</u>

Enter the kitchen – <u>298</u>

Go upstairs – <u>119</u>

Leave by the front door – <u>384</u>

# 764

You type the code into the computer, and you hear some whirring sounds from the door, before a claxon sounds. A computer-generated voice speaks to you from the computer.

"You have activated the failsafe for your office lockdown. Please leave immediately and then contact your MacTavish Secure Door rep to allow for system reset. If you do not leave within twenty seconds you will be trapped until security forces arrive. The door will remain locked once the twenty seconds are over."

You have been warned. Do you

Leave immediately – <u>916</u>

Decide to remain because there is more to find out in this room – <u>314</u>

# 765

You enter the numbers, and you hear a click and some whirring. You try the handle, and the door opens easily. Go <u>551</u>

# 766

The small folly is wooden and just over a man high and only 6 feet wide. As you approach, you see a candle is alight inside it and that a small wooden chair is placed beside a writing table.

If you have a torch, you try it and find that it has run out of battery. You'll need to keep your eyes peeled.

Opening the door, you can see an amount of liquid spilled on the table and it is dripping onto the chair. It seems to have come from a small canister which is lying on its side, and which has also dropped its contents onto paper which is in the middle of the table. The rest of the folly is empty.

Do you

Pick up the paper to read - <u>286</u>

Pick up the canister to examine - <u>063</u>

Grab the candle to examine everything a lot closer – <u>041</u>

Or leave the folly and choose to look elsewhere - <u>526</u>

# 767

You tell the detective of your conversation with Kyla in the ruins and of how she admitted to feeling the drug was her work stolen by the Doctor.

"That's all well and good son, but it's still hearsay. Have you anything else?"

If you have any of the following codewords go to that section. Follow the list downwards and only go to the first section that you have a codeword in.

**Taunt** - <u>661</u>

**Grumble** - <u>446</u>

**Pads, Paddy, Silent Papers, Cold Blood, Murder, Hitman, Merto** - <u>415</u>

**Gutted** - <u>048</u>

Otherwise, read on:

The detective still says you have enough evidence against you that you have to go to trial. It seems that the jury sees enough uncertainty for you are found not guilty. However, the papers do not see it that way, a man with a gun in his hand at a body. Your life becomes a hell, followed by the press, until you leave the country. It might seem unfair but at least you are not in jail. As for who actually killed the Doctor, you still don't know. Maybe try again at <u>001</u>.

# 768

The kitchenette has all the best of equipment including a coffee maker and a small grill. It also has a fridge and inside you find some sandwiches in a plastic tub. You open it and try one – salmon, your favourite. But here's no time to eat now. You can take the sandwiches with you by entering **Sandwiches** in your inventory. But time to get on.

Do you

Look inside the wardrobe – <u>072</u>

Examine the bed – <u>804</u>

Try out the chairs – <u>630</u>

Or

Investigate "The Hollow" – <u>819</u>

Dive into the lagoon and see if you can find the Doctor's secret stash – <u>924</u>

Decide you have had enough of the lagoon and make your move to the coastal path and your next destination – <u>549</u>

# 769

Oh dear, that hasn't worked. You have one try left. Do you wish to try again? If so

4837 – 243

9746 – 371

3267 – 880

2758 – 255

Another code – 132

Or if you have the Doctor's access card you could try that – 557

If none of this excites you then do you

Enter the canteen – 083

Try to get into the cleaners' cupboard – 592

Try to enter the office of Kyla Mertens – 840

Or return to the hall – 805

# 770

You find the coastal path at the end of the gardens and realise you can walk one of two ways; take the right-hand path to the lagoon or take the left to the ruins. Choose wisely for you won't be coming back this way.

If you have visited six locations (including the house) go to 011

Do you

Go right to the lagoon – <u>423</u>
Go left to the ruins – <u>937</u>


# 771

You grab one of the phials and hurl it at the creature. At first it rears up and then sniffs the phial. But it soon ignores it and begins to charge at you.

Do you have a gun? If so, use it – <u>412</u>

Otherwise – <u>781</u>


# 772

Go to <u>111</u>


# 773

You tell the detective to check your belongings for the note from the Doctor to Patrick Davidson that you found in the toilet bowl. When the note is brought to the detective from your belongings, he gives it some careful attention before turning back to you.

"So, there was a change of plans and Mr Davidson didn't like it. But if he killed the Doctor then who would make the decision not to go ahead. Kyla Mertens told us she wanted the drug stopped from going on commercial sale so simply killing the Doctor may not have been enough Do you have anything else you can tell or show me."

You're still in trouble. What else do you have?

If you have any of the following codewords go to that section. Follow the list downwards and only go to the first section that you have a codeword in.

**Taunt** – 892

**Grumble** – 446

**Pads, Paddy, Silent Papers, Cold Blood, Murder, Hitman, Merto** – 415

**Gutted** – 048

Otherwise read on:

The detective still says you have enough evidence against you that you have to go to trial. It seems that the jury sees enough uncertainty for you are found not guilty. However, the papers do not see it that way, a man with a gun in his hand at a body. Your life becomes a hell, followed by the press, until you leave the country. It might seem unfair but at least you are not in jail. As for who actually killed the Doctor, you still don't know. Maybe try again at 001.

## 774

You punch in the numbers and the pad flashes red and a claxon sounds, deafening all around you. Someone might be on their way with all that noise, so you decide you need to run. Make your way to the coastal path at _549_ and escape to another location.

## 775

The door which states it leads to the Doctor's office is locked but there is a keypad on the door and a swipe strip for a card. Otherwise, you are not sure how to get the door open.

Do you have the Doctor's access card and wish to use it? If so – _557_

Otherwise, you can try the access code. However, you note that it has a warning underneath saying that entering the wrong code twice will set off an alarm which will bring the attention of the security services. If you have a code (only if you have found one)  and wish to try it then

4837 – <u>089</u>

9746 – <u>623</u>

3267 – <u>039</u>

2758 – <u>249</u>

Another code – <u>769</u>

If none of this excites you then do you

Enter the canteen – <u>083</u>

Try to get into the cleaners' cupboard – <u>592</u>

Try to enter the office of Kyla Mertens – <u>840</u>

Or

Return to the hall – <u>805</u>

# 776

Do you have codeword **Cold Blood** – <u>149</u>

If not – <u>338</u>

# 777

You gently approach Daniel, careful not to scare him. Slowly you wrap your hands around him, but he suddenly lashes out catching you on the chin, causing you to fall to the ground. He reaches towards you and grabs the top item on your inventory list off you. **Cross it off your list now.** His eyes are wild as he runs away from you, leaving you nursing a sore chin.

He's gone and that's that. Time to get on with things.

You feel a little unsettled but look around the room. There are several canisters on the shelving, which must have looked like boxes in the dark. You open one and smell diesel. They are quite heavy, and you decide you can't simply carry them around. But you know where to come of you need them. Note the codeword **Fuel** in your code list.

That was eventful but what do you do next?

Check out the chart room – 848

Go to the Rec Room – 528

Investigate the room with no name – 685

Return to the lower floor – 370

# 778

You pull out your weapon and you peer into the darkness. You hear the whisper on the wind "Oh no, a gun." Something hits you on the head and you fall to the ground. A pair of shoes can be heard running from the room but by the time you recover your assailant is gone.

You feel a little unsettled but look around the room. There are several canisters on the shelving, which must have looked like boxes in the dark. You open one and smell diesel. They are quite heavy, and you decide you can't simply carry them around. But you know where to come if you need them. Note the codeword **Fuel** in your code list.

That was eventful but what do you do next?

Check out the chart room – <u>618</u>

Go to the Rec Room – <u>234</u>

Investigate the room with no name – <u>521</u>

Return to the lower floor – <u>795</u>

the room with no name – <u>521</u>

Return to the lower floor – <u>795</u>

# 779

Go to <u>002</u>

# 780

Go to <u>430</u>

# 781

You throw up your hands as the creature attacks, but it is no use. When the police arrive, they find their main suspect has died while trying to pilfer the laboratory. Few attend your burial, and your name is sullied forever not that you ever find out. Next time remember these places have protected doors for a reason. That's if you dare try again at <u>001</u>.

# 782

You take the candle and bend down to the table with it bringing it close to the paper. Suddenly flames erupt and you drop the candle from the shock causing the chair to catch fire as well. You dive out of the door as the whole folly becomes ablaze.

Standing safely on the outside of the fire, you realise, others may come, and you feel you need to get clear of the gardens and search elsewhere. Note the code word **Blaze** in your codeword list. You run to the coastal path, there to make your next choice at 211.

# 783

Kyla is an older and maybe she can sort this out for you. She has opened her long coat offering you shelter in it from the rain, and you gratefully step into her embrace in a moment of supreme trust. As she wraps you up you think about how good a judge of character you are. But when you find yourself struggling to breathe as she constricts your neck with her arm, you realise you made a bad judgement. The woman is deadly, and you slowly drift off to an eternal sleep.

Was she the killer? Maybe, or did she think you were the killer and had to defend herself. Either way, you need to get with what's happening. People are scared or they have a reason to kill. Let's not be so trusting next time! Start over at 001

# 784

This lab coat seems heavily of cheese and has large gouges through the material. You see a name on it: Hugo. There was a Hugo who visited two weeks ago, and you took him across the water to the mainland to an ambulance as he had an injured arm. No one ever said what the issue had been, but the man was white as a sheet when you transported him across the water. But there's nothing in the pockets except a few crumbs of mouldy cheese. Return to 652

# 785

You gleefully pick up the coin and lob it skilfully in beside the cherub. Did you make a wish?

If so – 514

If not - 976

# 786

You enter the room and struggle to see anything. There's a smell of something in the air and you wonder what it is until a hand closes over your mouth. You pass out almost immediately.

You wake up and your eyes are stunned by bright light. The lights are on in Kyla Mertens' office, and you don't know how long you have been unconscious. There's an alarm going off in the building as well and you suddenly panic. It's time to get away quick.

You run as fast as you can down the stairs to the hall and out to the path that leads to the coastal circuit and your next choice at 986

# 787

The buzzer howls even louder this time and the number pad flashes before the numbers change from bright green to red. Looks like it's locked the door. More than that it will have set off an alarm. Time to get out of here. You run hard around the laboratory to the coastal path at 983

# 788

What will you do with the items?

Use the cheese with one phial - 167

Use the cheese with two phials - 669

Use the cheese on its own - 363

Use both phials - 421

Use only one phial - 481

# 789

The bed has soft and silky sheets but looks undisturbed. It's large enough for two people and you lie down on it, feeling like you could sleep forever. But then you find yourself about to doze and you sit back up, abruptly, a pain in your back. You were lying on a rubber torch. If you want to take it by adding **torch** to your inventory. You look under the bed but there's nothing on the floor. Guess it's just a bed.

Do you

Look inside the wardrobe - <u>896</u>

Rifle through the kitchenette - <u>159</u>

Try out the chairs - <u>650</u>

Or

Investigate "The Hollow" – 509

Dive into the lagoon and see if you can find the Doctor's secret stash – 810

Decide you have had enough of the lagoon and make your move to the coastal path and your next destination – 503

# 790

The scrap of paper is heavily crumpled but unravelling it you see a message.

*E, meet me at the lookout, love F*

You are beginning to think that the Doctor may not be so good at secret messages. Maybe that was important information. But it's time to move on.

Do you

Examine the pool table – 340

Look at the darts board – 163

Open the fridge – 559

Read the magazines – 531

Or

Enter the toilet – 828

Check out the chart room – 848

Investigate the room with no name – 685

Return to the lower floor – 370

# 791

You gasp at the opulence of the Doctor's bedroom, which has fine teak furniture and a four-poster bed. There are several drawers and wardrobes, and a large mirror in the room. The bed is fully made and looks like it has not been slept in recently. The plush red carpet looks gaudy but must have cost a fortune.

Do you

Examine the bed – <u>269</u>

Check out the drawers and wardrobes – <u>010</u>

Return to the landing – <u>119</u>

# 792

The China hutch has two levels and at the top is a range of plates that may be valuable. You don't know as a plate is a plate to you, but they certainly look expensive. Beneath the top layer in closed drawers underneath, you find a coffee set, complete with plates and saucers. It's certainly a fine-looking item but there's nothing of use here. However, your foot kicks something beneath the hutch. You reach down and find a crowbar. Take it if you wish and make a note of the **crowbar** in your inventory.

You feel it's only safe to check out two items in this room before moving on.

Do you:

Examine the drinks cabinet - <u>635</u>

Look at the bookcase - <u>541</u>

Examine the curtains - <u>516</u>

Or if you have already examined two items, or want to leave this room (and have not already visited these places),

Enter the dining room - <u>576</u>

Enter the kitchen - <u>298</u>

Go upstairs - <u>119</u>

Leave by the front door - <u>384</u>

# 793

There are three lab coats, and each is hanging from its own hook. The one on the left is clearly being weighed down by something in its pocket but the others seem to be rather dirty. In fact, the first one seems torn.

Are these worth bothering with?

Do you

Examine the torn lab coat - <u>622</u>

Look at the untorn dirty lab coat - <u>891</u>

Check out the weighted down lab coat - <u>602</u>

Or if these lab coats are too dull to bother with

Examine the file – <u>572</u>

Look in the refrigerator – <u>752</u>

Wander over to the stools – <u>308</u>

Or

If this is all too much you could return to the entrance hall – <u>212</u>

# 794

As soon as you go to pull open the curtains a knife plunges through them and stabs you in the heart. You fall to your knees and desperately cling to the curtains, but it is no use. You fall to the floor and the only view you see of your attacker is their shoes. However, you are slipping away, off to the journey into the great beyond and your mind cannot decipher whose shoes they are.

Oh dear, you didn't last long. I suggest you start over, and this time take a bit more care when you see possible danger, after all, there is a murderer afoot.

**Return to <u>001</u> and start again. And this time, please be more careful.**

# 795

You slip in the side entrance of the boathouse and find yourself on the lower floor. Before you is a small dock holding a dinghy with oars. On the far wall are lifejackets and other maritime equipment. A set of stairs leads upstairs at the rear of the building and there is a locker across from them.

Do you

Examine the dinghy – 060

Look at the lifejackets – 436

Take the stairs to the upper floor – 581

Check out the locker at the rear of the room – 957

Decide there's nothing here for you and return outside – 191

# 796

The number pad goes red, and you hear a horrible buzzer indicate you are wrong.

Do you try another number?

4837 – 210

2758 – 006

9746 – 244

Another code – 651

Or do you

Use the Doctor's swipe card on the reader if you have it – 520

Try to climb the Ivy – 277

Or if this all seems to hard or unwise, you could simply keep on walking the coastal path to your next location at 988 but note that you have visited the Lookout

# 797

You set out on the path to the laboratory, dancing amid the puddles that have formed on the stone path. Your shorts are wet through, and your top is beginning to drip but with the humid heat of the night you don't feel cold. As you walk along the dark path, you can hear your feet crunch the stones and hope no one is close. You really need to get inside and take some shelter. You climb up the path and down into a dell where you see the splendid laboratory before you.

You are not quite sure what the Doctor does in here and you have heard various tales about what lies in the depths of the laboratory. However, you have never been inside for there are various keypads that need to be accessed. Usually, you just drop any deliveries by the door.

The path swings down to a glass door which is the entrance to the lab facilities. There is low level lighting in operation, and you can see corridors that disappear into darkness inside.

There appears to be no one around and you approach the front door. It is locked shut and won't open. On the side of the door is a keypad with the usual single digits, 1 to 9 lit up in fluorescent green.

What will you do?

Do you have a code and wish to try the keypad (only if you have found one)  – 236

Hide in the undergrowth surrounding the facility and see what happens – 971

Walk around the facility and see what you can find – 739

Call this a bust and find the coastal path – 986


# 798

The cave is wet and slimy, but you see a hard surface beyond the water which has a few recliners. The whole area is lit up by ceiling lights. There is a fridge with a small selection of alcoholic beverages sitting on top of it. A bookcase is in the corner as well as a rail with several towels on it. But what makes you stare is the figure taking a drink at the fridge. It is Elsie Gonzales, and she appears agitated. Enter codeword **Quiet Place** in your code word list.

There is not a lot here to look at but maybe Elsie might have some helpful insights.

Do you

Engage Elsie in conversation – 654

Decide to leave her alone and retreat out of the cave

If you entered by torch light – 441

Otherwise – 408

# 799

What will you do with the items?

Use the cheese with one phial – <u>555</u>

Use the cheese with two phials – <u>659</u>

Use the cheese on its own – <u>696</u>

Use both phials – <u>102</u>

Use only one phial – <u>771</u>

# 800

You pocket the letter. Note the word **Spaceletter** in your code list. Now leave the folly and

Check out the coin throwing area – <u>579</u>

Head for the tunnel – <u>125</u>

Walk down to the final fountain and its walkway – <u>676</u>

Or go back to the fountains area entrance – <u>526</u>

# 801

You cautiously step out onto the rope bridge nearest to you which is swinging in the wind. You don't trust it and place two hands on the ropes at either side and slowly make your way over to the hut. When you reach it you step inside but find the platform it is standing on to be moving in the wind as well and you stomach goes queasy.

The hut is very basic with a bench and a table but also with lots of room for a crowd to stand. The wind howls outside and you shiver as you bend down to the table. There is a sheet of paper on the table with some rather swirly handwriting.

Do you

Decide there's nothing here and return via the rope bridge – 758

Examine the paper closely - 161

Look out to sea and check if there is anyone coming to the island, maybe the authorities – 849

# 802

The keypad goes red, and a claxon begins to sound, deafening you. This is likely to bring lots of people and you decide to get as far away as possible from the building. You run out of the front door and make your way to the coastal path. Go there now at 983

# 803

You run across the rope bridge towards the figure but as you are halfway, one of the support strands comes loose and the bridge twists throwing you to one side.

Your legs fall through the gap, and you throw out a hand clinging to the single cord you see above you. With a great effort, you swing up your other hand and grab the cord. Maybe you can do this and get to safety.

But then you see that the figure is still chopping with the axe. Another support strand is undone, and the bridge now falls down and you drop into the wild sea beneath you.

They find your washed-up body four days later and there are questions about whether you did kill the Doctor. But you are not party to any of this. What's the point of being innocent if you are dead?

Next time remember there's a killer out there and beware any corners you can't back out of. Try again at 001

# 804

The bed has soft and silky sheets but looks undisturbed. It's large enough for two people and you lie down on it, feeling like you could sleep forever. But then you find yourself about to doze and you sit back up, abruptly, a pain in your back. You were lying on a rubber torch. If you want to take it by adding **torch** to your inventory. You look under the bed but there's nothing on the floor. Guess it's just a bed.

Do you

Look inside the wardrobe - <u>072</u>

Rifle through the kitchenette - <u>768</u>

Try out the chairs - <u>630</u>

Or

Investigate "The Hollow" - <u>819</u>

Dive into the lagoon and see if you can find the Doctor's secret stash - <u>924</u>

Decide you have had enough of the lagoon and make your move to the coastal path and your next destination - <u>549</u>

# 805

The entrance hall of the laboratory is clean and efficient with some chairs and a table with magazines. But there is no reception desk, and you wonder if they get many visitors. From the hall, there are three doors indicating the following: Offices, laboratory, special projects.

Do you

Try the door labelled "Offices" - <u>146</u>

See if you can enter the laboratory - <u>992</u>

Head off to the special projects - <u>464</u>

Or

maybe you could check out the magazines - <u>984</u>

Or

Leave the building and head to the coastal path to try another location - <u>983</u>

# 806

You stand and watch for a while in the rain, but nothing emerges from the tunnel, and nothing else enters. Did your mind play a trick on you? Are you actually alone? What will you do now?

Enter the tunnel - <u>705</u>

Or

Make your way to the folly - <u>766</u>

Check out the coin throwing area - <u>579</u>

Walk down to the final fountain and its walkway - <u>676</u>

Or

Take a look in the walled garden - <u>625</u>

Make your way to the greenhouse - <u>722</u>

Wander over to the gardening equipment sheds - <u>121</u>

Or if you doubt the gardens will be of any use then take the coastal path at <u>770</u> but note that you have visited the gardens

# 807

The wind takes the feet from under you, but you fall heavily onto the roof before sliding off and landing clumsily on the balcony. It takes you several minutes to recover but you are in one piece, a little bruised but nothing broken. When you rise, you manage to smash the window with the piece of metal from the weathervane and gratefully step into the room beyond, delighted you are still in one piece. Go <u>506</u>

# 808

As you near the section you see that there is an open passageway in the rock, and you surface for another breath before diving back down and swimming through the gap in the rock. You swim for only a few yards before the rock ceiling above you disappears and you surface in a large cave at 621

# 809

You take a shot at Patrick and watch him fall to the ground. Hopefully you've tagged him so he can't escape. You approach and there seems to be quite a bit of blood. Getting nearer, you check his breathing and realise he isn't. Well, if you weren't a murderer before, you are now. You'd better get moving and also start thinking how to explain this away. Note the codeword **Hitman** in your code list. Run hard to the coastal path at 770 and try to live with your guilt.

# 810

You psyche yourself up to dive into the lagoon but find it pleasantly warm as you step into it.

Do you have the codeword **Beam** on your code list – 903

If not, as soon as you dive under the water you struggle to see anything. It would be blurry without googles but in the dark water you can see nothing. If only you had some light.

Do you have a rubber torch – <u>351</u>

If not, this is just madness as you can see nothing in a large lagoon such as this. You get out and reassess your options.

Do you

Investigate "The Hollow" – <u>509</u>

Climb up to the tree hut – <u>171</u>

Decide you have had enough of the lagoon and make your move to the coastal path and your next destination – <u>503</u>

# 811

The middle floor of the Lookout features a small kitchenette and a simple two person dining area. There's a radio handset on the round shelf that runs completely around the room. A number of photographs are here as well as a set of drawers and a writing desk. The spiral staircase runs both up and down to the other floors of the building. The overall feeling is of a simple man's abode, but it is clean and tidy.

Do you

Examine the radio handset - <u>989</u>

Check out the photographs - <u>067</u>

Have a rifle through the drawers - <u>229</u>

Look at the writing desk - <u>361</u>

Or

Climb up the spiral staircase - <u>824</u>

Descend the spiral staircase - <u>845</u>

Decide to leave the Lookout and make your way to the coastal path - <u>988</u>


# 812

You think there is a door in the rock but as much as you push at the rock within the outline you can see, nothing moves. You dive down several times, but nothing changes. Maybe it's nothing. You climb out of the lagoon and decide you won't go back in unless you find better lighting.

Do you

Investigate "The Hollow" - <u>819</u>

Climb up to the tree hut - <u>410</u>

Decide you have had enough of the lagoon and make your move to the coastal path and your next destination - <u>549</u>

# 813

You panic and dive into the water and try to swim but your body seizes, and you find your brain struggles to focus. You find yourself sinking and then you are dragged out under the water. You never surface and they find your body some three weeks later, the island murderer finally discovered. You can try again at <u>001</u>, and let's get some evidence this time.

# 814

You take off your t-shirt ignoring the cold and wrap it around your elbow. Clenching your teeth tight you drive your elbow at the glass, right where the crack lines emanate from. The glass cracks further with a small circle shattering inside. You hit the window again and more glass falls inside, causing a tinkling sound as it hits the floor.

You think you can hear something inside, a scurrying of some sort but you are not sure if it is in the room beyond the window or from further inside the facility. You raise you elbow and smash the glass again and there is now a hand sized hole which will allow you to operate the window handle on the inside. But there's that scurrying sound and this time it's accompanied by a howl. It's like a coyote call but much hoarser. What on earth belongs to that hideous cry? You wonder if you should go inside.

Do you

Open the window and climb inside the room – <u>854</u>

Decide against this and either

Go back to the front and hide in the undergrowth to await developments – <u>971</u>

Forget all this and find the coastal path to somewhere else – <u>986</u>

# 815

Kyla is an older and maybe she can sort this out for you. She has opened her long coat offering you shelter in it from the rain, and you gratefully step into her embrace in a moment of supreme trust. As she wraps you up you think about how good a judge of character you are. But when you find yourself struggling to breathe as she constricts your neck with her arm, you realise you made a bad judgement. The woman is deadly, and you slowly drift off to an eternal sleep.

Was she the killer? Maybe, or did she think you were the killer and had to defend herself. Either way, you need to get with what's happening. People are scared or they have a reason to kill. Let's not be so trusting next time! Start over at <u>001</u>

# 816

You take hold of the rubber cover, and it flips up easily, revealing a number keypad and a swipe card reader. Looking about you, you cannot see anything the pad could activate but it's obviously important. It also warns that a double failure of a code entry will result in an alarm going off and authorities being advised. Sounds serious. Should you activate it? Do you know how? What will it do?

Do you

Swipe the card reader with the Doctor's access card, if you have it – 118

Enter a code on the pad (only if you have found one) – 491

Or leave the item alone and

Check out the tin – 400

Investigate the switch – 275

Or if none of this inspires you, go back to the lagoon entrance and make another choice – 879

# 817

You open the heavy door and give a cursory look inside, seeing a desk with a computer on it and large piles of printed paper here and there. There's a small pile of books on a low wooden table which is on the right-hand side of a chair made from wood which seems to be quite flexible. On the wall is a picture of a gathering of people. There's also a coat stand with a single white laboratory coat on it and pair of boots underneath. You hold the door with one hand, as it is spring loaded and trying to close, whilst you look around.

Do you

Enter fully, letting the door close – 385

Or forget this room and

Enter the bedroom – 791

Enter the third room – 387

Return to the hall – 675

# 818

Stepping back, you ponder what to do. Above you, you can see the weathervane and it looks partially broken. Maybe you could break off a piece of metal with which to hit the window. However, it is windy up there and it would be a long fall down. The roof is rounded and wet, and no doubt slippery.

Do you

Go for it – 454

Choose another option at 277

# 819

You walk around the lagoon until you reach the Hollow. It sits in the ground, and you have to step down until you find yourself staring at eyelevel along the surface of the lagoon. The night may be dark and the rain pelting down causing the surface of the water to be constantly disturbed but the lights around the feature make the surface look almost eerie.

You search in the darkness of the feature and find three things. There is a rubber cover on a small electrical outlet, a tin lies in the corner, and there is a switch on the far wall of the Hollow.

Do you

Look at the rubber cover – 037

Check out the tin – 250

Investigate the switch – 003

Or if none of this inspires you, go back to the lagoon entrance and make another choice – 423

# 820

Okay, so clearly you are meant to move a piece. But which one and to where?

Do you

Move the snake – 289

Move the eagle – 721

Move the man – 688

Move the woman – 256

## 821

The ground floor of the Lookout tower has a library of books built along the circular wall. Close to the edge of the far section of the wall a metallic, spiral staircase climbs up through the ceiling. In the middle of the room is a reading chair with a lamp and a small table where the remnants of a cake and a cup of something linger. Otherwise, there is one window which breaks the smothering of the wall by the books.

This looks like the abode of a studious man, and you might learn something about the Doctor's interests and pleasures. Do you

Examine the books around the wall – 943

Check out the table with its cup and cake – 569

Look out the window – 657

Proceed up the spiral staircase – 991

## 822

As you open the door of the fridge freezer you feel the cold chill of the air inside. There is a large number of foodstuffs in there, including cheese, milk, lettuce and cold meats and if you were planning a picnic, it would be a perfect place to start. You open the freezer section and note that one of the labels on the drawers has been turned around and has black pen written on it. There is a number code 4837. Maybe this is important, or maybe it's the access code for the car stereo. Who knows? Note it down if you want.

So, unless you are ready to prepare a picnic, what next?

Have a look through the cupboards - 887

Examine the pots on the cooker - 129

Examine the hatch - 347

Look at the knife block - 353

Return to the hall - 675

# 823

"Hey, it's okay, I'm innocent. I was knocked out and then the gun planted on me. Maybe you could help find out who killed the Doctor. See who framed me. Please, I really need some assistance."

Kyla steps forward a little nervous, but with an outstretched hand. You take it and she pulls you close before driving her knee up into your groin. You fall to the floor and hear her running off.

When you recover, albeit a little sore, she is long gone. So much for friendship!

Do you

Try to get into the cleaners' cupboard - 571

Examine the door belonging to Doctor Munro - 439

Try to enter the office of Kyla Mertens - 237

Or return to the hall - 212

# 824

You are in a bedroom, all be it a round one, and it is tastefully decorated with a plush carpet on the floor and a demur bedspread on a double bed that sits in the middle of the room. A metal spiral staircase descends from the room and soft lighting is still switched on. You see two silk dressing gowns hanging on pegs on the wall and there is a mirror for a person to groom themselves. A small alcove has a door in it, which causes the room to lose its perfect circle.

Do you

Examine the bed – 615

Check the silk dressing gowns – 312

Check the alcove door – 586

Descend the stairs – 811

Or leave the Lookout completely and head for the coastal path – 988

# 825

You turn around but don't even see your attacker as something strikes you across the face. There in the pouring rain and driving wind you breathe your last as the person who framed you, dispatches you.

Maybe there was a trial, maybe you were found guilty or innocent, maybe they caught someone else for the Doctor's murder. You'll never know because you were careless and now your life is over.

Thank goodness this is a gamebook and not real-life and you can reincarnate at <u>001</u> and try again. And this time, less of the heroics. That Belgium detective never tried any fisty-cuffs!

## 826

How fast can you run?

This fast – <u>917</u>

Maybe this quick – <u>565</u>

Surely not this quick – <u>106</u>

## 827

The BBQ area is dark, and you have to kneel down at the bottom of it where you find ashes. But you hear something close by. There's a scraping sound, audible despite the wind and rain, and you begin to tense up. Is someone close?

Do you

Continue your search – <u>667</u>

Stand up and investigate – <u>575</u>

Leave immediately heading for the main paths, after all it's not safe round here – <u>297</u>

## 828

You enter a tiny room with a toilet before you. The lid is up and there is a small cleaning brush in a stand beside the bowl. On the wall is a toilet roll. It is indeed a toilet. On the bright side, it is a clean one! If you feel the need, by all means use it, but then let's get on.

Do you

Check out the chart room – 848

Go to the Rec Room – 528

Investigate the room with no name – 685

Return to the lower floor – 370

## 829

There's a horrible buzzer that tells you that the code is wrong. Blimey, one more chance or you'll be locked out. What do you do? Try a different code

4837 - <u>064</u>

3267 - <u>203</u>

2758 - <u>107</u>

Another code - <u>787</u>

Or do you decide this is too risky and decide instead to

Hide in the undergrowth surrounding the facility and see what happens - <u>440</u>

Walk around the facility and see what you can find - <u>608</u>

Call this a bust and find the coastal path - <u>983</u>

# 830

You turn the boat to the open seas and into the eye of the storm. The journey is rough with a number of jaw-dropping moments as the speedboat drops off large waves and water flows across the deck behind you. Daniel watches you closely the whole time, never taking his eyes off you.

It's two days later when you come across a lonely island and Daniel suggests it's a good place to stop for a rest. You beach the boat and under a moonlit sky you both drift off to sleep. Later that night you hear the sound of an engine, and your eyes fly open. Looking at the bay where you beached the boat, you see the vessel riding out into the light surf, Daniel on board.

Sprinting across the sands, you wave frantically at him. He ignores you completely, turning the speedboat out to sea and disappearing. The days after involve you hunting for water which does not seem available except for sea water. You thirst and then hallucinate before you drift into unconsciousness.

Three weeks later a police boat finds your body on the island beach, confident they have finally found the Doctor's killer. You are unable to tell them different.

Unsurprisingly, Daniel was still suspicious of you. Still, try again at <u>001</u>, and this time, trust no one!

# 831

You grab the handset and, being an experienced operator, you press the handset down firmly.

"Mayday, mayday, mayday, this is the shore station at Munro Island. We have a distress situation concerning an attack on the owner of the island. Request assistance. I repeat, request, assistance. Medical and Police."

The reply is faint.

"....Island... Mayday acknowledged.... Weather unsuitable.... Expect.... Delay.... 6 hours.... Longer...."

You try several more times but there is no further reply. Maybe the set is malfunctioning or something else is at play. Whatever has happened, you got your message out. Note the word **Coastguard** in your code list.

Now, do you

Check out the photographs – 067

Have a rifle through the drawers – 229

Look at the writing desk – 361

Or

Climb up the spiral staircase – 824

Descend the spiral staircase - 845

Decide to leave the Lookout and make your way to the coastal path – 988

# 832

"I didn't kill him, someone else did and framed me. I'm the victim here." You stare at Kyla, hoping she can read your sincere face. You have so little evidence to offer.

Kyla smiles at you. "Poor thing. Someone has played us both. And you are so young. Come to me. You must be cold. We can hide away in the tomb over there. It's sheltered."

Kyla steps towards you and you wonder just what this woman is to you.

Do you

Step into her embrace, after all you need a friend – <u>783</u>

Run away from the ruins, she's a threat – <u>928</u>

Draw your gun for a better answer – <u>025</u>

# 833

You switch off the Automatic Identification system in a bid to evade the authorities. But you are unsure if being incognito in the water will be enough.

Do you have the codeword **Late Rescue**? If so go to <u>522</u>

If not **762**

# 834

You yell at the woman to stop but she's away and by the time you reach the entrance she is gone into the night. You return to the tomb and sweep the torch around finding a letter on the ground. Read it at <u>352</u>

# 835

Elsie looks terrified. You have her trapped with a gun in a room with one door. She reminds you of a rabbit in the headlights, her eyes wide and unblinking. And then she bolts for the door.

Do you

Shoot – 258

Let her go - 346

# 836

You punch in the numbers and the pad flashes red and a claxon sounds, deafening all around you. Someone might be on their way with all that noise, so you decide you need to run. Make your way to the coastal path at 503 and escape to another location.

# 837

"Patrick Davidson," says the detective, stroking his moustache. "You're going to have to show me some evidence, sunshine, as he's a respected businessman. I know he was backing the Doctor's new drug. What can you tell me?"

If you have any of the following codewords go to that section. Follow the list downwards and only go to the first section that you have a codeword in.

**Tatler** – <u>209</u>

**Bowl** - <u>409</u>

**Taunt** – <u>915</u>

**Gutted** – <u>048</u>

Otherwise – <u>995</u>

# 838

You work your way slowly through the off-path vegetation towards the ruins and come eventually to the edge of the greenery.

Do you have the following codewords?

**Scientist down** – <u>114</u>

**Murder** – <u>724</u>

If not – <u>564</u>

# 839

You swim around for a half hour, finding nothing but then come across the edge of the lagoon and a strange section of rock under the water.

Do you have any of the following codes in your code list?

Code **Sesame** – <u>681</u>

Code **Baba** – <u>405</u>

Neither – <u>228</u>

# 840

The door to Kyla Mertens' office appears to be open but there are no lights on in the office. You hesitate at the door and think you can hear someone inside the office. Maybe this is not such a good idea.

Do you

Continue inside – 024

Stand and wait – 276

Or if you haven't already

Enter the canteen – 083

Try to get into the cleaners' cupboard – 592

Examine the door belonging to Doctor Munro – 775

Or

Return to the hall – 805

# 841

"Some people would say you did me a favour. You know he was stealing my work. Trumped up little Doctor. He was the face to the world, but it was my work. Do you understand? And then you killed him."

The words still haunt you, Kyla convinced that you were the killer but letting you know she was glad the Doctor was dead. Does that eliminate her as a suspect, or was it a bluff? If you tell the police what you heard will it sound like you are wriggling out from your guilt or will they simply believe you. You will need to choose wisely when is the right time to use these words.

# 842

You lower your weapon and let her approach. Kyla is an older and maybe she can sort this out for you. She has opened her long coat offering you shelter in it from the rain, and you gratefully step into her embrace in a moment of supreme trust. As she wraps you up you think about how good a judge of character you are. But when you find yourself struggling to breathe as she constricts your neck with her arm, you realise you made a bad judgement. The woman is deadly, and you slowly drift off to an eternal sleep.

Was she the killer? Maybe, or did she think you were the killer and had to defend herself. Either way, you need to get with what's happening. People are scared or they have a reason to kill. Let's not be so trusting next time! Start over at 001

# 843

You see the body of the woman you killed, and it makes you shudder, but you steel yourself. No one knows about this place except maybe the Doctor and the woman you killed. It is a rough two weeks, and you are barely getting by on water and the little food there is in the cave. You carefully come out at night after the fortnight and find the island mainly deserted except for the laboratory. The police must have come and gone, and you are able to sneak away from the island in the Doctor's cruiser.

You make for a foreign land and once ashore you manage to find some basic work and hide out in the country for a few years. One day on the television you see your face, described as the island murderer. Of course, you have no hair now and wear glasses. It seems you need to live in exile for the rest of your life.

Maybe this is a win, but you still don't know who set you up. Try to solve the mystery again at <u>001</u>.

# 844

The door behind you swings open easily and you quietly sneak inside. There is almost complete darkness inside and you gently feel around before your hand finds a note on the floor. You open it and try to read it but cannot. You'll need to get out to some light to read it. The next time you are above this deck, read the note at <u>846</u> before returning to the section you had reached.

You can still hear movement in the passage you came from.

Do you

Stay here and wait – <u>188</u>

Run back upstairs – <u>359</u>

Walk directly ahead in the passage to investigate – <u>478</u>

Follow the wall to the side and trace your way along there – <u>882</u>

# 845

The ground floor of the Lookout tower has a library of books built along the circular wall. Close to the edge of the far section of the wall a metallic, spiral staircase climbs up through the ceiling. In the middle of the room is a reading chair with a lamp and a small table where the remnants of a cake and a cup of something linger. Otherwise, there is one window which breaks the smothering of the wall by the books.

This looks like the abode of a studious man, and you might learn something about the Doctor's interests and pleasures.

Do you

Examine the books around the wall – <u>757</u>

Check out the table with its cup and cake – <u>707</u>

Look out the window – <u>092</u>

Proceed up the spiral staircase – <u>811</u>

# 846

The note reads,

"I told him as his research assistant that the drug is too powerful and not suitable for public distribution, but he will not listen. I need to take decisive action, father. I shall mail this note to you and pray for me as I enter a dark place."

Note the code word **Scrap** in your list and return to the entry you came from.

# 847

There's something not quite right about this pear which although golden is firm. As you bite through the flesh you see a small worm looking back at you and throw the pear to the ground. Interesting though that diversion was, can we get on?

Do you

Try an apple – <u>501</u>

Or leave and

Walk to the vegetable garden – <u>014</u>

Wander to the ornamental garden – <u>420</u>

Or check out the fountains area – <u>526</u>

Make your way to the greenhouse – <u>722</u>

Wander over to the gardening equipment sheds – <u>121</u>

Or if you doubt the gardens will be of any use then take the coastal path at <u>770</u> but note that you have visited the gardens

# 848

The chart room is awash with charts of the nearby waters on the wall. Having sailed back and forwards across these waters you know that outside your well-travelled route the sea is treacherous and a chart to navigate would be essential. Most of the charts are however locked away in a filing cupboard which has long thin drawers. However, it has a code lock on it. If you want any charts beyond the local waters, then you will need to access the cupboard.

Do you

Take a local chart off the wall – <u>153</u>

Try to enter a code for the cupboard (only if you have found one)  – <u>972</u>

Shoot the cupboard open – <u>453</u>

Or

Go to the Rec Room – <u>528</u>

Investigate the room with no name – <u>685</u>

Return to the lower floor – <u>370</u>

## 849

The view out to sea is breath-taking and you scan the horizon for any boats or helicopters that might be coming to the island. You can see none and for a moment feel as if you can do this, time being on your side. Even the chill of your wet clothes is not enough to down your spirits.

Your heart skips a beat as you hear a crash. One of the bridges has collapsed and you see a figure with an axe running for the other one. You have a bit of a head start but not much. You pocket the note and make a run for it. Go <u>958</u>

## 850

The Detective Inspector brushes his moustache as he enters the room and takes a seat opposite you. A recording machine is started and the man stares at you before giving a cough. His eyes are old and have seen everything, or so it seems to you. Can you bluff this man? Or will you tell the truth?

He says that everyone saw you beside the Doctor's body. He says at this time you are the prime suspect. However, he wants you to admit to it as things will be a lot quicker that way. Of course, they will be, but you are innocent!

The detective now sits back in the chair and asks you to explain what happened. Do you know? Who will you blame?

"I didn't murder the Doctor. In fact, it was…"

Who will you say killed the Doctor? Remember you'll need some evidence to help your cause.


Was it

Kyla Mertens – 392

Patrick Davidson – 296

Elsie Gonzales – 884

Daniel Lyle – 443

Grandma Munro – 527


# 851

Is the key an ornate key – 731

If not, the key does not fit the lock. Go back to 535 and make another choice

## 852

You punch in the code and the pad flashes green but nothing else happens and you are left with the pad again. You decide to leave the pad alone but enter the word **Baba** in your code list. Make your next choice at 037

## 853

The door clicks open, and you pull the handle, allowing yourself to step inside. Time to find some evidence. Go to 212

## 854

You enter the special projects area and can hear something moving. As you walk, you feel something breath on the side of your face and you jump, before realising you are in a room of cages. You decide to stay quiet, rather than wake whatever are in the cages but there is a general murmuring starting.

Suddenly, something can be heard scurrying in the dark and there is a flurry of wings and squawking from the cages. The hairs on your neck rise and your hands begin to shake with fear. The door is just behind you. Should you flee? But maybe there's something else worth having in the special projects area, something which could help prove your innocence.

Do you flee - <u>670</u>

Stand your ground - <u>261</u>

# 855

The keypad goes red, and a claxon begins to sound, deafening you. This is likely to bring lots of people and you decide to get as far away as possible from the building. You run out of the front door and make your way to the coastal path. Go there now at <u>983</u>

# 856

This time the pad flashes red in a crazy fashion and you can hear an alarm going off. You look around you in a panic wondering if anyone is close and coming for you. Best not to wait around and besides you can't get into the Lookout anyway. You run to the coastal path to choose your next location at <u>990</u>

# 857

You turn to leave the hut and see a figure at the far end of one of the rope bridges. The figure wears a coat with a hood, and you struggle to work out who it is, but you can see the large axe they are holding. You gasp in horror as you step out onto the bridge, for the figure is now chopping at the rope bridge support strands with the axe.

Do you

Run as hard as you can across this rope bridge – 931

Step back inside the hut and remain there as it is safe – 074

Turn around and run for the other rope bridge – 260

# 858

Do you

Swim for the half-buried object – 923

Or exit the water and

Investigate "The Hollow" – 509

Climb up to the tree hut – 171

Decide you have had enough of the lagoon and make your move to the coastal path and your next destination – 503

# 859

Go to 417

# 860

You decide to silence Kyla by knocking her out and rush forward to the frightened woman and grab her by the throat. Surprisingly, she's quick and steps to one side before kneeing you right where it hurts, and you double over.

When you manage to get back up to your feet, Kyla is long gone. So much for that.

Do you

Try to get into the cleaners' cupboard – 571

Examine the door belonging to Doctor Munro – 439

Try to enter the office of Kyla Mertens – 237

Or

Return to the hall – 212

# 861

The wheelhouse contains charts of the local area and is looking quite messy. Maybe someone has been planning a trip, but you also notice that a few coffee cups lie about unwashed. You find several paper clippings on the floor. One talks about dementia in elderly people while another is commentary from a national paper written by Elsie Gonzales, lambasting today's overreliance on drugs.

There is a radio onboard, but you cannot start it as it seems to require the power to be switched on, and you don't have a key that seems to fit the ignition.

That appears to be it in the wheelhouse, so

Do you

Go to the lower deck via the stairs – 543

Look at the lockers at the aft of the upper deck – 954

Or

Jump onto the speedboat – 869

Or, if you haven't already,

Make for the main building – 795

Or

if you want to continue elsewhere take the coastal path at 980

# 862

You slowly come into the beach and ground the speedboat. You are met by the police who take Daniel and you to the station to make statements.

You have trusted yourself to the law and will have to take your chances with an investigation by their finest. Go to 519 and see how it all works out for you.

# 863

You pull your gun out with your other hand and sweep the torch back and forth. But you see nothing. And there's those footsteps again.

Do you wish to switch off the torch and wait in the dark for the owner of the footsteps - 473

Do you want to keep on searching - 997

Or

Decide this is a bad idea and instead

Enter the temple - 273

Check out the sacrificial slab - 742

Look at the gaming board - 165

Or

Decide this area is no longer useful or too risky and continue along the coastal path at 996

# 864

You tell the detective about your threatening note from when someone tried to kill you at the fountains. The detective takes it away and returns an hour later with a smile on his face.

"We checked out your story about nearly being killed and the handwriting on the note. I believe you son, and the writing is that of Kyla Mertens. I have just arrested her for your attempted murder. However, there is still the question of Doctor Munro's murder. Do you have anything further?"

You shake your head.

If you have any of the following codewords go to that section. Follow the list downwards and only go to the first section that you have a codeword in.

**Grumble** – 446

**Pads, Paddy, Silent Papers, Cold Blood, Murder, Hitman, Merto** – 415

**Gutted** – 048


Otherwise, read on:

The detective still says you have enough evidence against you that you have to go to trial. It seems that the jury sees enough uncertainty for you are found not guilty. However, the papers do not see it that way, a man with a gun in his hand at a body. Your life becomes a hell, followed by the press, until you leave the country. It might seem unfair but at least you are not in jail. As for who actually killed the Doctor, you still don't know. Maybe try again at 001.


# 865

You examine the set of drawers beginning at the top, finding a selection of socks and pants. There is also a set of keys hidden away and you wonder what they could be for. They are silver, modern and have a surfer logo attached to them. You may enter **surfer logo keys** in your inventory if you wish to. They do seem very familiar.

The remaining drawers have sweaters and trousers and other daywear but there is little else of note.

Let's move on.

Do you

Examine the radio handset – 668

Check out the photographs – 184

Look at the writing desk – 897

Or

Climb up the spiral staircase – 506

Descend the spiral staircase - 821

Decide to leave the Lookout and make your way to the coastal path – 990

# 866

Well, this is enterprising! You fire up the blowtorch and then climb onto the lawnmower, reaching up to the higher shelves and try to read the bottles. As you stretch you see the words petrol, kerosene, and diesel on the bottles. But you also feel yourself tipping and grab the shelf in your hand. It comes away and you fall to the ground, the bottles coming down with you.

Are you a lucky person? Try your luck

Here - 155

Or here - 973

# 867

You enter the canteen and pull out the gun. The figure turns around and it's Patrick Davidson but he's shaking as he sees your weapon.

"Don't do it, kid, whatever it is you want don't do it. Lower the gun and we'll talk."

You see the fear in his eyes, and you may have him on the rack. On the other hand, maybe some trust might gain some rewards.

Do you

Lower the gun - 310

Keep the gun pointing at Patrick - 508

# 868

Is it a key with green tape?

If so - 047

If not, the key does not fit, and you'll need to try something else at 004

# 869

The speedboat bobs about despite being tied to the pontoon. It looks powerful but is also quite small. You note it needs fuel and also a set of keys to start it. Searching around it you find nothing.

The speedboat seems to hold no clues but there could be a different option here. Maybe you could flee the island and make a life for yourself elsewhere. It's a risky ploy because if you get caught you may look like a killer. It's also unlikely you will prove your innocence if you don't stay.

If you don't have the codeword **Fuel** and the **speedboat keys** or the **surfer logo keys,** then the option is not open to you. If this is the case, return to <u>465</u> and make a different decision to those already made.

If this plan is not for you then return to <u>465</u> and choose another path.


If you have the codeword **Fuel,** and the **speedboat keys** or the **surfer logo keys**, and want to go for this then go to <u>967</u>

# 870

Glug, glug, glug. Oh dear, you don't make it, drowning in the bay. Tough luck but then you were basically on the run and life was not going to be great. Try for a better life by returning to <u>001</u>.

# 871

Do you have the **foreign charts**?

If so – 905

If not – 515

# 872

You open the top of the nearest compost bin and recoil. It stinks! Regardless, you tip it out and start poking through it. You find some paperwork form Elsie Gonzales. It appears to be a letter from her boss stating that the paper is not selling well. It's not directed to Elsie in particular but rather a general employee message.

After further searching you find nothing else and decide to continue elsewhere.

Do you

Examine the shrouds – 620

Have a look at the wheelbarrow – 606

Or leave and

Enter the orchard – 560

Wander to the ornamental garden – 420

Or

Check out the fountains area – 526

Make your way to the greenhouse – 722

Wander over to the gardening equipment sheds – 121

Or

If you doubt the gardens will be of any use then take the coastal path at <u>770</u> but note that you have visited the gardens

## 873

Taking your weapon, you turn it round and begin to beat the desk with the butt. Blow after blow rains in until you hear a quiet, *psst!* and something hits you in the shoulder. Suddenly everything goes dark.

You wake up and the room looks the same, but you feel that time has passed. Suddenly you get nervous that you may have been here too long, and you need to get a move on. Without a thought you run out of the Lookout and make your way to the coastal path, keen to try and find clues in another location. Go to <u>990</u>

## 874

You tell the detective about the note from Kyla Mertens to her father, saying how Doctor Munro must be stopped and that she is entering a dark place.

"Now that is interesting, but it is also not proof. You still have a lot to answer for. Do you have anything to back up this evidence?"

If you have any of the following codewords go to that section. Follow the list downwards and only go to the first section that you have a codeword in.

**Taunt** – 864

**Grumble** – 446

**Pads, Paddy, Silent Papers, Cold Blood, Murder, Hitman, Merto** – 415

**Gutted** – 048

Otherwise, read on:

The detective arrests you for the Doctor's murder saying that you were still seen with the gun over the body. All you have is a potential heated comment. At the trial you cut a lonely figure as it only takes the jury an hour to convict you. From your jail cell you wonder if you were right in your choice of killer. You'll never know. Maybe try again at 001.

# 875

The keypad goes red, and a claxon begins to sound, deafening you. This is likely to bring lots of people and you decide to get as far away as possible from the building. You run out of the front door and make your way to the coastal path. Go there now at 986

# 876

You tell the detective about your threatening note from when someone tried to kill you at the fountains. The detective takes it away and returns an hour later with a smile on his face.

"We checked out your story about nearly being killed and the handwriting on the note. I believe you son, and the writing is that of Elsie Gonzales. I have just arrested her for your attempted murder."

If you have any of the following codewords go to that section. Follow the list downwards and only go to the first section that you have a codeword in.

**Grumble** - 446

**Pads, Paddy, Silent Papers, Cold Blood, Murder, Hitman, Merto** - 415

**Gutted** - 048

Otherwise, read on:

The detective still says you have enough evidence against you that you have to go to trial. It seems that the jury sees enough uncertainty for you are found not guilty. However, the papers do not see it that way, a man with a gun in his hand at a body. Your life becomes a hell, followed by the press, until you leave the country. It might seem unfair but at least you are not in jail. As for who actually killed the Doctor, you still don't know. Maybe try again at 001.

## 877

The tomb entrance may be in darkness but there is an even darker shade through the hole that leads to the interior. You trip over a stone as you run down to the entrance, highlighting just how dark it is. Reaching the entrance, you step inside the tomb and stop almost immediately once you are clear of the wind and rain. You can see nothing. Reaching out with your hands, you find a wall and realise it goes on into the darkness.

This is precarious to say the least. But maybe there's something inside the tomb.

Do you

Have a torch – <u>658</u>

Shout into the darkness to see if anyone is there – <u>416</u>

Proceed into the darkness anyway – <u>716</u>

Decide this is a bad idea and instead

Enter the temple – <u>273</u>

Check out the sacrificial slab – <u>742</u>

Look at the gaming board – <u>165</u>

Or

Decide this area is no longer useful or too risky and continue along the coastal path at <u>996</u>

# 878

Oops. A claxon has gone off and is deafening you. Green gas is flooding the room. But you don't panic. The green gas has sent you off to sleep long before you can manage a scream.

The next thing you know is a jail cell and a lot of awkward questions to which you have no answers. You didn't discover anything that would help your case and you were also seen by the Doctor's body with a gun in your hand before being trapped while searching his room. They know you were looking for something and with the evidence stacked against you, the court case does not take long before your life sentence is pronounced.

It is several years when you receive a letter, thanking you for taking the blame and explaining how you were framed. Your eyes widen with interest as you see the signature at the bottom. The culprit is on their deathbed and maybe you can be free. If only you can get in touch with... Now that would be telling. Maybe next time you'll find out who did it!

Return to <u>001</u> and better luck next time!

# 879

The rain is pouring down as you arrive along the stony path to the lagoon, a large expanse of water separated from the sea by a thin stretch of land. It is difficult to see before your arrival as a perimeter of trees surround it and you are grateful for the small lights that are running around the water's edge, an idea of the Doctor's.

Looking around the lagoon, you realise you have only ever walked past it once when making an initial tour of the island and you now take a moment to look at it more thoroughly. You can see several features that may be worth exploring. There is a space called "The Hollow" which is basically a small open hut that has been sunk into the ground allowing you to sit and gaze at the lagoon from water level. There is also a tree hut which overlooks the lake although *hut* may be too simple a word for the construct. There is also the lagoon itself, and you know the rumours about the sunken treasure that lies within, a relic from an ancient pirate but also thought of as one of the Doctor's secret stashes for his most sensitive work. Enter the code word **Swim** in your code list.

Sheltering under a tree, you ponder your next move. Do you

Investigate "The Hollow" – <u>509</u>

Climb up to the tree hut – <u>171</u>

Dive into the lagoon and see if you can find the Doctor's secret stash – <u>810</u>

Decide you have had enough of the lagoon and make your move to the coastal path and your next destination – <u>503</u>

## 880

Your heart sinks as the keypad flashes and then the numbers turn red. A claxon begins sounding in the building. You feel the panic rising and glance up and down the hall. You need to get out of here quickly. It's time to move on to the coastal path. You flee the building and reach the path at <u>983</u>

## 881

You quickly scout round the rest of the laboratory, but it is locked up tight. Looks like your options are limited and that rain is getting heavier if anything.

Do you

Go back to the window and try and break it – 814

Go back to the front and hide in the undergrowth to await developments – 971

Forget all this and find the coastal path to somewhere else – 986

# 882

You follow the wall and can hear the breathing beside you. It's heavy and extremely close. Your heart beats as you wonder what to do next. Maybe your gun if you have it? But there's no time as something pins your t-shirt to the wall causing you to struggle to break free.

How's your luck?

This good – 525

Maybe this good – 325

Or possibly this good – 598

# 883

You punch in the numbers and the pad flashes red and a claxon sounds, deafening all around you. Someone might be on their way with all that noise, so you decide you need to run. Make your way to the coastal path at 503 and escape to another location.

# 884

"Elsie Gonzales? She was here to report on the big release of the new drug. I'm not seeing that one, sunshine. Have you got any evidence?"

If you have any of the following codewords go to that section. Follow the list downwards and only go to the first section that you have a codeword in.

**Shutdown** - 065

**Wheel** - 642

**Taunt** - 462

Otherwise - 995

# 885

Go to 337

# 886

You really are not lucky! The wind lifts you off your feet and right off the roof past the balcony and into a glorious three story fall to the ground. The way down is quite exhilarating, but the abrupt stop is not so pleasant. Wo knows if they cleared your name, and what does it matter to a dead man? Try again at 001

# 887

You begin to pull out drawers and find a large amount of crockery and utensils inside, but nothing appears to be unusual. The Doctor clearly doesn't keep any written material in here but maybe there are some useful items. You can take any number of the following and easily carry it with you: A spoon, a fork, packet of sweeteners or a small whisk. Note them in your inventory.

What now?

Check out the fridge freezer – 822

Examine the pots on the cooker – 129

Examine the hatch – 347

Look at the knife block – 353

Return to the hall – 675

# 888

The number pad goes red, and you hear a horrible buzzer indicate you are wrong.

Do you try another number?

4837 – 210

3267 – 686

2758 – 006

9746 – 244

Or do you

Use the Doctor's swipe card on the reader if you have it – 520

Try to climb the Ivy – 277

 Or if this all seems to hard or unwise, you could simply keep on walking the coastal path to your next location at 988 but note that you have visited the Lookout

# 889

You pull your gun out with your other hand and sweep the torch back and forth. But you see nothing. And there's those footsteps again.

Do you wish to switch off the torch and wait in the dark for the owner of the footsteps – 382

Do you want to keep on searching –999

Or

Decide this is a bad idea and instead

Enter the temple – 280

Check out the sacrificial slab – 246

Look at the gaming board – 426

Or

Decide this area is no longer useful or too risky and continue along the coastal path at 998

## 890

There's a horrible buzzer that tells you that the code is wrong. Blimey, one more chance or you'll be locked out. What do you do? Try a different code

4837 – 713

3267 – 934

2758 – 512

Another code – 303

Or do you decide this is too risky and decide instead to

Hide in the undergrowth surrounding the facility and see what happens – 971

Walk around the facility and see what you can find – 739

Call this a bust and find the coastal path – 986


## 891

This lab coat is pristine and reminds you of someone. It must be Kyla Mertens' coat as you never see her in a lab coat that is not immaculate. It certainly would fit her. You search the pockets and find a note inside. It reads simply "edam plus liquids". Otherwise, there's nothing unusual about the lab coat. Return to 793

# 892

You tell the detective about your threatening note from when someone tried to kill you at the fountains. The detective takes it away and returns an hour later with a smile on his face.

"We checked out your story about nearly being killed and the handwriting on the note. I believe you son, and the writing is that of Patrick Davidson. I have just arrested him for your attempted murder. More than that I am arresting him for the murder of Doctor Munro, and you are free to go, Peter. Well done on solving this case because frankly, it had me down the wrong path."

You walk outside and smell the fresh air knowing that your life can go back to where it was before all this trouble. Congratulations, super sleuth!

# 893

You run as hard as you can, but the figure is mighty quick with the axe. Go 803

# 894

You turn the boat to the open seas and into the eye of the storm. The journey is rough with a number of jaw-dropping moments as the speedboat drops off large waves and water flows across the deck behind you. But

Elsie holds you close her head on your neck and you feel she is not just a running mate but that she may want to be more.

It's two days later when you come across a lonely island and Elsie suggests you hide out for a while. You beach the boat and together under a moonlit sky you both drift off to sleep. Later that night you hear the sound of an engine, and your eyes fly open. Looking at the bay where you beached the boat, you see the vessel riding out into the light surf, Elsie on board.

Sprinting across the sands you wave frantically at her. She blows you a kiss and shouts a 'thank you' before turning the speedboat out to sea and disappearing. The days after involve you hunting for water which does not seem available except for the sea water. You thirst and then hallucinate before you drift into unconsciousness.

Three weeks later a police boat finds your body on the island beach, confident they have finally found the Doctor's killer. You are unable to tell them different.

That's a big leap of faith that went wrong for you. Still, try again at 001, and this time, trust no one!

# 895

You look at the tumble lock on the cupboard and realise you need to enter 4 single numbers to unlock it. Do you have a code to try (only if you have found one) ? If so, take the first number and multiply it by the second, then multiply the result by the third number.

Now add the fourth number to the total. Go to the section number that is the same as your result. If it doesn't start **Yippee**, then you have the wrong code.

If you can't get the code to work, do you

Take a local chart off the wall – 596

Shoot the cupboard open – 402

Or

Go to the Rec Room – 234

Investigate the room with no name – 521

Return to the lower floor – 795


# 896

The wardrobe has a jacket hanging inside and you search it thoroughly before finding an envelope inside. Opening it, you find correspondence to Doctor Munro from a mental health specialist regarding his mother. It seems she has some delusions about her current life and there is a recommendation that she be taken into care. There is a large *NO* written in red pen across the letter.

The wardrobe contains nothing else so what now?

Examine the bed – 789

Rifle through the kitchenette – 159

Try out the chairs – 650

Or

Investigate "The Hollow" – <u>509</u>

Dive into the lagoon and see if you can find the Doctor's secret stash – <u>810</u>

Decide you have had enough of the lagoon and make your move to the coastal path and your next destination – <u>503</u>

# 897

The writing desk has several smaller drawers it as well as a small pad of paper in the middle of the desk which simply says *Don't touch, private my dear.* There are no locks on the drawers, but you can't see any handles with which to open them. Maybe you could force them open by shaking the desk. If you have a gun you could shoot them open. Or maybe you could hit the desk with the gun butt. Or you could kick the desk.

Do you

Shake the desk – <u>205</u>

Kick the desk – <u>345</u>

Hit the desk with a gun butt if you have one – <u>873</u>

Shoot at the desk with your gun – <u>647</u>

Or decide to leave well alone and

Examine the radio handset – <u>668</u>

Check out the photographs – <u>184</u>

Have a rifle through the drawers – <u>865</u>

Or

Climb up the spiral staircase – <u>506</u>

Descend the spiral staircase - <u>821</u>

Decide to leave the Lookout and make your way to the coastal path – <u>990</u>

# 898

You promise Elsie and she plants a kiss on your lips before taking you in the car across country. She stops briefly at a service station and while she uses the toilets, you tell a worker there to call the police. Shortly after, you are both arrested. Let's hope your story is good. Go to <u>519</u>.

# 899

Go to <u>313</u>

# 900

The light switch is just beyond the curtains, and you stroll over confidently believing there to be a wind disturbing the curtains. As you reach the switch, you hear a sound from behind and turn quickly to see the curtain bulging. With how dark it is you cannot be sure if it's the wind of maybe that's a human figure pushing at the curtain. The different shades of the material in this dim scene are so hard to read. As you freeze to the spot, you see what could be a knife point pressing against the curtain, and up above that a bulge that could be a person.

Do you

Turn again for the light switch – 160

Flee the room around the far side of the table – 393

Reach for the curtain and try to pull it away – 563

# 901

The hatch functions exactly as it does from the dining room side. There's nothing different looking in from this side.

What now?

Check out the fridge freezer – 822

Have a look through the cupboards – 887

Examine the pots on the cooker – 129

Look at the knife block – 353

Return to the hall – 675

# 902

The lock on the door makes a whirring sound and you open it – go to 629

# 903

When you switched the underwater lights on at the hollow you were enchanted by how the water lit up from underneath. Now that you are below the surface, you see the real advantage of the lighting. Although there is the blurriness that looking through any volume of water will bring, you can see quite clearly as you swim around.

The lagoon has a sandy bottom, and you can see an object half-buried towards the middle of the lagoon. However, as you swim around you also see that one of the rocky sides of the feature has what appears to be an entrance to somewhere. Well, it's certainly an outline of a passageway at this distance, but who knows when you get close.

Do you

Swim towards the passageway – 539

Dive down to the half-buried item – 923

Or decide you have seen enough and exit the lagoon. In which case do you

Investigate "The Hollow" – 509

Climb up to the tree hut – 171

Decide you have had enough of the lagoon and make your move to the coastal path and your next destination – 503

# 904

What code will you try?

3267 - <u>432</u>

4837 - <u>859</u>

2758 - <u>206</u>

9746 - <u>052</u>

Or a different code - <u>417</u>

# 905

You pull out the charts you found in the main building and motor off into the night, reaching the coast of a foreign country by dawn. At first you hide out but soon find a local farmer who lets you tend his sheep for some pay and food and lodgings. Over the next two years you earn enough to start again and have a comfortable life.

One day in a café you see a newspaper article which states that you are the killer of a prominent researcher back in your home country. Whoever was responsible has got away but at least you have been able to start again, albeit away from any loved ones or friends you know.

This may not be a win but it's not a loss either. Maybe it's a draw. If you want to do better, head back to <u>001</u> and start again. At the moment you certainly cannot call yourself a super sleuth!

# 906

"No, I need to stay here and clear my name."

"Okay," says Elsie "but be careful. There are people here who truly didn't like the Doctor. I loved him despite his manufacture of drugs. Why he wanted people to use drugs to become better, I really don't know. But I saw past that evil, and I was getting close to him. But there are others who don't feel that way. Take care, Peter."

With that, she steps forward and kisses you on the forehead before slipping past you. As you watch her descend the stairs, you are amazed how she handles her heels and soon she has disappeared out into the rain.

You feel a little unsettled but look around the room. There are several canisters on the shelving, which must have looked like boxes in the dark. You open one and smell diesel. They are quite heavy, and you decide you can't simply carry them around. But you know where to come if you need them. Note the codeword **Fuel** in your code list.

That was eventful but what do you do next?

Check out the chart room – **618**

Go to the Rec Room – **234**

Investigate the room with no name – **521**

Return to the lower floor – **795**

# 907

So, you have a code. As you go to type in the numbers you realise that there is a sign underneath stating that only 2 attempts are allowed before a lockout ensues for an hour and an alert is sent. Crikey, you'd better get this right.

What code do you enter?

4837 - 285

9746 - 829

3267 - 908

2758 - 547

Another code - 472

Or do you decide this is too risky and decide instead to

Hide in the undergrowth surrounding the facility and see what happens - 440

Walk around the facility and see what you can find - 608

Call this a bust and find the coastal path - 983

# 908

There's a horrible buzzer that tells you that the code is wrong. Blimey, one more chance or you'll be locked out. What do you do? Try a different code

4837 – 064

9746 – 203

2758 – 107

Another code – 787

Or do you decide this is too risky and decide instead to

Hide in the undergrowth surrounding the facility and see what happens – 440

Walk around the facility and see what you can find – 608

Call this a bust and find the coastal path – 983

# 909

Standing at the marina, you see the large cruiser with its two decks. You have never been on it, but you know that the Doctor enjoyed it thoroughly when he travelled abroad on it. The weather continues unabated, and you watch the pontoons wobble on the water. The speedboat beyond the cruiser seems to be bouncing and you wonder if it can handle the sea tonight.

Do you

Go onboard the cruiser – 329

Jump onto the speedboat – 624

Or, if you haven't already,

Make for the main building – 370

Or

if you want to continue elsewhere take the coastal path at 981

# 910

"Kyla Mertens," laughs the detective. "What on earth makes you think that? I know she was working with the Doctor on a performing enhancing drug, and they were to start production with it. Everything we have says she was happy with the arrangements. Do you have any evidence to the contrary?"

If you have any of the following codewords go to that section. Follow the list downwards and only go to the first section that you have a codeword in.

**Water** - 637

**Scrap** - 595

**Taunt** - 435

**Inferno** - 281

**Blaze** - 463

**Grumble** - 583

**Pads, Paddy, Silent Papers, Cold Blood, Murder, Hitman, Merto** - 636

**Gutted** - 048

Otherwise - 995

# 911

You walk steadily forward towards the sound. The sound remains and if anything comes closer. You can see so little until you are hit in the head and fall to the ground, unconscious.

Really, you think yourself invincible. There's a killer out there. And guess what they have struck again. Start over at 001.

# 912

You tell the detective about the note you received at the fountains when someone tried to kill you. You say it's from Patrick Davidson and the detective disappears for a few hours before returning.

"Well, Peter, it seems that your story checks out, that someone did try to kill you. And it is Patrick Davidson. We are looking to charge him with your attempted murder. However, we still see you as the number one suspect."

If you have any of the following codewords go to that section. Follow the list downwards and only go to the first section that you have a codeword in.

**Grumble - 446**

**Pads, Paddy, Silent Papers, Cold Blood, Murder, Hitman, Merto - 415**

**Gutted - 048**

Otherwise read on:

The detective still says you have enough evidence against you that you have to go to trial. It seems that the jury sees enough uncertainty for you are found not guilty. However, the papers do not see it that way, a man with a gun in his hand at a body. Your life becomes a hell, followed by the press, until you leave the country. It might seem unfair but at least you are not in jail. As for who actually killed the Doctor, you still don't know. Maybe try again at 001.

# 913

You are swimming near the middle of the lagoon and close to the bottom when you come across a small treasure box in the sandy residue at the bottom. You carefully haul it out and drag it onto the edge of the lagoon. As you take it from the water, you shine your torch on it and realise it is made from plastic. You flip a catch at the front and find a piece of paper inside and a photo.

*Congratulations, you believed the stories and you have found your treasure.*

You look at the photo and see it is of the Doctor's Mum with the words *my treasure*, written on it in pen.

What a waste of time! You get out of the lagoon and climb to your feet ready to begin investigating again.

Do you

Investigate "The Hollow" – 819

Climb up to the tree hut – 410

Decide you have had enough of the lagoon and make your move to the coastal path and your next destination – 549

# 914

You swallow hard and make you way along the short path that leads to private garden. It is encompassed by a hedge and is barely ten metres square. The grass is neatly cut and as you enter you can't manage to see what was causing the glint. Maybe if you knelt down in this poor light, you might be able to feel around the grass and find what was there. Otherwise, this private garden is holding little of interest other than the hedgerow that encompasses it and which is taking a battering in the wind. Is there something in there?

Do you

Feel around on the grass – 493

Examine the hedgerow – 194

Or do you decide the private garden can look after itself and instead

Examine the vegetable patch – 104

Take a look at the patio – 662

Or

Decide to head off on one of the main paths – 297

# 915

You tell the detective about the note you received at the fountains when someone tried to kill you. You say it's from Patrick Davidson and the detective disappears for a few hours before returning.

"Well, Peter, it seems that your story checks out, that someone did try to kill you. Unfortunately, it's Elsie Gonzales' handwriting. We are looking to charge her with your attempted murder.

If you have any of the following codewords go to that section. Follow the list downwards and only go to the first section that you have a codeword in.

**Grumble** – 446

**Pads, Paddy, Silent Papers, Cold Blood, Murder, Hitman, Merto** – 415

**Gutted** – 048

Otherwise read on:

The detective arrests you for the Doctor's murder saying that you were still seen with the gun over the body. All you have is a potential heated comment. At the trial you cut a lonely figure as it only takes the jury an hour to convict you. From your jail cell you wonder if you were right in your choice of killer. You'll never know. Maybe try again at 001.

# 916

You flee the office, but the claxon is still sounding. You run down the stairs and out of the front door, scared that you may bring attention to yourself and possibly the presence of the killer. Run now to the outside of the house – 384

# 917

You run as hard as you can, but the figure is mighty quick with the axe. Go 931

# 918

Taking your weapon, you turn it round and begin to beat the desk with the butt. Blow after blow rains in until you hear a quiet, *psst!* and something hits you in the shoulder. Suddenly everything goes dark.

You wake up and the room looks the same, but you feel that time has passed. Suddenly you get nervous that you may have been here too long, and you need to get a move on. Without a thought you run out of the Lookout and make your way to the coastal path, keen to try and find clues in another location. Go to 988

# 919

"Who's there?"

"Don't shoot me," says a voice and you recognise it as Daniel Lyle. "Please switch on the light."

You flick on the light and see Daniel Lyle, the athlete. He's wet through standing in trousers and a shirt but he's also looking very scared now that he's identified it's you.

Do you

Tell him not to panic, it wasn't you who shot the Doctor – 974

Ask him what he's doing here – 553

Draw your gun if you have one – 434

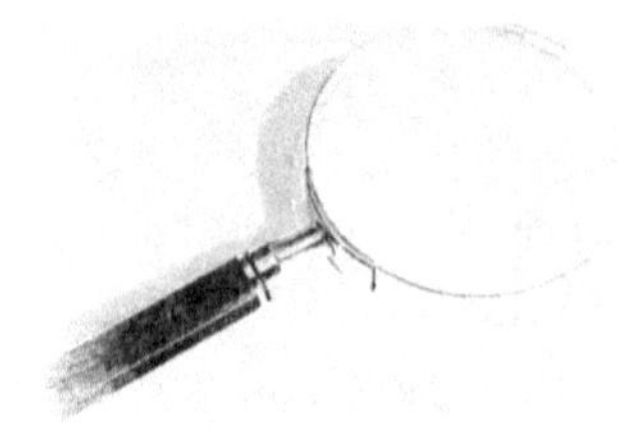

# 920

You watch in silence as Patrick sprints away from you and out of the building. He's an athlete and you'll never catch him. You search the rest of the building but there's nothing of note.

Do you

Check out the fountains area – 526

Take a look in the walled garden – 625

Wander over to the gardening equipment sheds – 121

Or if you doubt the gardens will be of any use then take the coastal path at 770 but note that you have visited the gardens

# 921

"Look Daniel, I'm scared too. Someone has framed me and I'm just running frightened like you. You understand. I'm of no age, I had no gripe against the Doctor."

"Neither did I. He used me to test his drug, did you know that? He tested it on me, and it gave me increased performance, it really did. And now when he's ready to reveal it, he's using a different test subject. I'm just a lab rat that got dumped. And more than that he tells me now when he's ready to reveal it. I could have been famous, the top athlete. It's not easy to stay at the top. You ever tried it. Anyway, if you didn't do it, good luck. If you did, go and rot!"

With that Daniel turns away again.

Do you

If you have one, pull out your gun and threaten him with it for information – 646

Let him go – 007

# 922

You peer at the paper and realise it is a letter written by Kyla Mertens. However, it is very hard to make out. It is definitely about the current work being undertaken but you can make out so little of it that you are struggling to catch the mood of the letter. One section reads,

"... must be stopped. .......................... appropriate credit.....................make sure........sees no reward from the work."

It's just so hard to read, maybe some light would help.

Do you

Try to use the candle to read the letter – <u>735</u>

Pocket the letter – <u>612</u>

# 923

You dive down to the object you see half-buried and find a small treasure box in the sandy residue at the bottom of the lagoon. You carefully haul it out and drag it onto the edge of the lagoon. As you take it from the water, you realise it is made from plastic. You flip a catch at the front and find a piece of paper inside and a photo.

*Congratulations, you believed the stories and you have found your treasure.*

You look at the photo and see it is of the Doctor's Mother with the words *my treasure*, written on it in pen.

What a waste of time! You climb to your feet ready to begin investigating again.

Do you

Dive back in and make for the potential passageway – <u>539</u>

Or instead

Investigate "The Hollow" – <u>509</u>

Climb up to the tree hut – <u>171</u>

Decide you have had enough of the lagoon and make your move to the coastal path and your next destination – <u>503</u>

# 924

You psyche yourself up to dive into the lagoon but find it pleasantly warm as you step into it.

Do you have the codeword **Beam** on your code list – <u>697</u>

If not, as soon as you dive under the water you struggle to see anything. It would be blurry without googles but in the dark water you can see nothing. If only you had some light.

Do you have a rubber torch – <u>956</u>

If not, this is just madness as you can see nothing in a large lagoon such as this. You get out and reassess your options.

Do you

Investigate "The Hollow" – <u>819</u>

Climb up to the tree hut – <u>410</u>

Decide you have had enough of the lagoon and make your move to the coastal path and your next destination – <u>549</u>

# 925

You turn to run away, and someone throws something at you. It hits the wall, but you don't stop until you reach the coastal path at <u>980</u>. Go there and choose your next destination quickly.

# 926

The walled garden is a dark and foreboding. As you approach you can see there are three different sections: an orchard, a vegetable garden, and an ornamental garden. Each looks as dark as the other but maybe one holds something important.

Do you

Enter the orchard – <u>447</u>

Walk to the vegetable garden – <u>398</u>

Wander to the ornamental garden – <u>042</u>

# 927

You delve down with your hands into the sticky soil and almost immediately find a package wrapped up in an A4 plastic folder. You make your way to the house whereby in the glare of a nearby light you study what's in front of you.

This is quite a find. The folder contains a document which indicates that Kyla Mertens has not been happy with the respect given to her by Dr Munro. Specifically, she believes he is taking credit for her work where it is not merited. The tone is quite furious, but you cannot tell if this is a draft or if this is the sent letter. There's also a note that Kyla believes that the drug they are working on should be available to all and not simply used for commercial gain.

You might not know everything but that seems like some serious motive. Did Kyla Mertens, do it? She always seemed so lovely, if a little focused.

Anyway, you pocket what may be evidence and decide to continue to look for more.

Do you

Pay a visit to the private garden where you saw the glint of light – <u>914</u>

Take a look at the patio – <u>662</u>

Or

Decide to head off on one of the paths – <u>297</u>

## 928

There is no way you are going to trust this woman and she's now coming very close. You believe there's no point in engaging any further and simply turn and run away to the coastal path. She seems to be staying at the ruins and you catch your breath before walking to your next destination at 998

## 929

What key do you have? Is it

A key with green tape - 779

An ornate key - 582

A surfer logo key – 375

A dolphin key – 123

If you have any other key you try it, and it does not fit. Return to 096 and make a different decision.

# 930

You tell the detective of your conversation with Kyla in the ruins and of how she admitted to feeling the drug was her work stolen by the Doctor.

"That's all well and good son, but it's still hearsay. Have you anything else?"

If you have any of the following codewords go to that section. Follow the list downwards and only go to the first section that you have a codeword in.

**Taunt** – 661

**Grumble** – 446

**Pads, Paddy, Silent Papers, Cold Blood, Murder, Hitman, Merto** – 415

**Gutted** – 048


Otherwise, read on:

The detective still says you have enough evidence against you that you have to go to trial. It seems that the jury sees enough for you are to be found guilty. As you sit in your jail cell, you wonder if Kyla really did kill the Doctor. You'll never know. Maybe try again at 001.


# 931

You run across the rope bridge towards the figure but as you are halfway, one of the support strands comes loose and the bridge twists throwing you to one side. Your legs fall through the gap, and you throw out a hand clinging to the single cord you see above you. With a great effort, you swing up your other hand and grab the cord. Maybe you can do this and get to safety.

But then you see that the figure is still chopping with the axe. Another support strand is undone, and the bridge now falls down and you drop into the wild sea beneath you.

They find your washed-up body four days later and there are questions about whether you did kill the Doctor. But you are not party to any of this. What's the point of being innocent if you are dead?

Next time remember there's a killer out there and beware any corners you can't back out of. Try again at 797

# 932

You tell the detective about your threatening note from when someone tried to kill you at the fountains. The detective takes it away and returns an hour later with a smile on his face.

"We checked out your story about nearly being killed and the handwriting on the note. I believe you son, and the writing is that of Patrick Davidson. I have just arrested him for your attempted murder. However, you are still the prime suspect for the Doctor's death. Do you have any other evidence?"

If you have any of the following codewords go to that section. Follow the list downwards and only go to the first section that you have a codeword in.

**Grumble** - 583

**Pads, Paddy, Silent Papers, Cold Blood, Murder, Hitman, Merto** - 636

**Gutted** - 048

Otherwise read on:

The detective arrests you for the Doctor's murder saying that you were still seen with the gun over the body. All you have is a potential heated comment. At the trial you cut a lonely figure as it only takes the jury an hour to convict you. From your jail cell you wonder if you were right in your choice of killer. You'll never know. Maybe try again at 001.

# 933

You tell the detective about your threatening note from when someone tried to kill you at the fountains. The detective takes it away and returns an hour later with a smile on his face.

"We checked out your story about nearly being killed and the handwriting on the note. I believe you son, and the writing is that of Elsie Gonzales. I have just arrested her for the murder of the Doctor and your attempted murder. Let's hope we don't find any other bodies."

You are free! Congratulations, you found the killer and she's getting her just desserts. Enjoy your freedom and try and find a normal job with nicer people. WELL DONE, YOU HERO!

# 934

The buzzer howls even louder this time and the number pad flashes before the numbers change from bright green to red. Looks like it's locked the door. More than that it will have set off an alarm. Time to get out of here. You run hard around the laboratory to the coastal path at <u>986</u>

# 935

You tell the detective about your threatening note from when someone tried to kill you at the fountains. The detective takes it away and returns an hour later with a smile on his face.

"We checked out your story about nearly being killed and the handwriting on the note. I believe you son, and the writing is that of Elsie Gonzales. I have just arrested her for your attempted murder."

If you have any of the following codewords go to that section. Follow the list downwards and only go to the first section that you have a codeword in.

**Grumble** – <u>583</u>

**Pads, Paddy, Silent Papers, Cold Blood, Murder, Hitman, Merto** – <u>636</u>

**Gutted** – <u>048</u>


Otherwise read on:

The detective still says you have enough evidence against you that you have to go to trial. It seems that the jury sees enough uncertainty for you are found not guilty. However, the papers do not see it that way, a man with a gun in his hand at a body. Your life becomes a hell, followed by the press, until you leave the country. It might seem unfair but at least you are not in jail. As for who actually killed the Doctor, you still don't know. Maybe try again at <u>001</u>.


# 936

You take off your t-shirt ignoring the cold and wrap it around your elbow. Clenching your teeth tight you drive your elbow at the glass, right where the crack lines emanate from. The glass cracks further with a small circle shattering inside. You hit the window again and more glass falls inside, causing a tinkling sound as it hits the floor.

You think you can hear something inside, a scurrying of some sort but you are not sure if it is in the room beyond the window or from further inside the facility. You raise you elbow and smash the glass again and there is now a hand sized hole which will allow you to operate the window handle on the inside. But there's that scurrying sound and this time it's accompanied by a howl. It's like a coyote call but much hoarser. What on earth belongs to that hideous cry? You wonder if you should go inside.

Do you

Open the window and climb inside the room – 551

Decide against this and either

Go back to the front and hide in the undergrowth to await developments – 440

Forget all this and find the coastal path to somewhere else – 983

# 937

You arrive via the stony coastal path at the ruins and see lightening race across the sky and light up the abandoned stone structures before you. The Doctor has always told you to stay clear of the ruins as they are unsafe, and you have obeyed him in that. But now you think there may be something he was keeping you from in here. Is this area part of the puzzle of the guests and what was passing between the Doctor and them? It's time to find out.

There are four main areas in the ruins: the temple, the tomb, the sacrificial slab at the cliff, and the gaming board. The tomb leads underground but the other areas are open to the pouring rain. There is no light other than that which the lightening brings, and you will need to watch your footing. If you have a torch you decide not to use it as it will attract attention out here in the open. In truth, this place is scaring you, as you could be being watched so easily without ever seeing your foe.

Do you

Make for the tomb and shelter from the rain – 033

Enter the temple – 280

Check out the sacrificial slab – 246

Look at the gaming board – 426

Or

Decide this area is no longer useful or too risky and continue along the coastal path at 998

# 938

You tell the detective about the magazine article you read, that Patrick Davidson's company is a start-up in need of money.

"That's not evidence. It's a big jump to go from a magazine article to a conviction. You have nothing."

If you have any of the following codewords go to that section. Follow the list downwards and only go to the first section that you have a codeword in.

**Bowl** – 773

**Taunt** – 912

**Grumble** – 446

**Pads, Paddy, Silent Papers, Cold Blood, Murder, Hitman, Merto** – 415

**Gutted** – 048

Otherwise read on:

The detective arrests you for the Doctor's murder saying that you were still seen with the gun over the body. All you have is a potential heated comment. At the trial you cut a lonely figure as it only takes the jury an hour to convict you. From your jail cell you wonder if you were right in your choice of killer. You'll never know. Maybe try again at 001.

# 939

With no other evidence, you go to trial where your lawyer argues that you were an unwitting fool who was set up by Elsie Gonzales. It seems that the jury saw enough uncertainty for you are found not guilty.

However, the papers do not see it that way, possibly because one of their own is implicated. Your life becomes a hell, followed by the press, until you leave the country. It might seem unfair but at least you are not in jail. As for who actually killed the Doctor, you still don't know. Maybe try again at <u>001</u>.

# 940

You pick up the man and move him to the other side of the woman like you would jump a piece in checkers. As you let the male figurine, rest on his new space, you see a small drawer pop out from the edge of the board. Inside you find a key with a large dolphin on a key chain. You try to close the drawer, but it won't budge and when you now try to move the pieces, they seem to be stuck fast. How unusual. Still, you have a new key so note it in your inventory as **Dolphin key**. There seems to be nothing else you can do here so

Do you

Make for the tomb and shelter from the rain – <u>877</u>

Enter the temple – <u>273</u>

Check out the sacrificial slab – <u>742</u>

Or

Decide this area is no longer useful or too risky and continue along the coastal path at <u>996</u>

## 941

As you near the section you see that there is an open passageway in the rock, and you surface for another breath before diving back down and swimming through the gap in the rock. You swim for only a few yards before the rock above you disappears and you surface into a large cave at 621

## 942

You try the key in the lock but that's not working. Do you have another key? If not then you'll need to go elsewhere.

If you have another key, is it

A key with green tape – <u>710</u>

An ornate key – <u>750</u>

If not then do you, if you haven't already

Enter the canteen – <u>083</u>

Examine the door belonging to Doctor Munro – <u>775</u>

Try to enter the office of Kyla Mertens – <u>840</u>

Or return to the hall – <u>805</u>

# 943

The number of books amaze you and you see that most of the books appear to be scientific books, mainly ab0ut how the body functions. Most are of far too high a level for your understanding, but you see that one particular section of books seems to be jutting out more than others. You grab a book from this section and see a book with a Spanish title. When you open it, a photograph falls out of Elsie Gonzales. The black and white image is signed *Elsie, all my love* and it seems to be heavily creased as if it has been looked at a lot.

What now?

Do you

Check out the table with its cup and cake – <u>569</u>

Look out the window – <u>657</u>

Proceed up the spiral staircase – <u>991</u>

Decide to leave the Lookout and make your way to the coastal path – <u>990</u>

# 944

There was that letter in the folly. However, you set it ablaze. It might have been important and maybe you could tell the Police to look through the burned down folly for evidence. Seems a weak line, but if you are desperate.

# 945

What code will you try? Add the single digits of the code up and then go to that numbered section. If it starts with **Padlock opened**, continue with that section. If not, then return here.

If you cannot open the padlock and want to give up, then choose another option.

Examine the dinghy – 060

Look at the lifejackets – 436

Take the stairs to the upper floor – 581

Or

Head over to the marina – 465

Or if you want to continue elsewhere take the coastal path at 980

# 946

This lab coat is pristine and reminds you of someone. It must be Kyla Mertens' coat as you never see her in a lab coat that is not immaculate. It certainly would fit her. You search the pockets and find a note inside. It reads simply "edam plus liquids". Otherwise, there's nothing unusual about the lab coat. Return to 652

# 947

You punch in the code and the pad turns red and a coarse noise like a bad input on a computer sounds. Nothing happens and you are left with the pad again.

Do you enter another code? Which one?

2758 - 883

3267 - 966

9746 - 226

4837 - 035

Another code - 836

Or do you leave the pad alone? If so, make your next choice at 816

# 948

You wait, holding your breath, your ear cocked to the office. But now there's nothing, no sound and no observed movement.

Do you

Enter – <u>333</u>

Decide against it and if you haven't already

Enter the canteen – <u>071</u>

Try to get into the cleaners' cupboard – <u>571</u>

Examine the door belonging to Doctor Munro – <u>439</u>

Or

Return to the hall – <u>212</u>

# 949

"Daniel Lyle," says the detective stroking his moustache. "You're going to have to show me some evidence sunshine, as he's a respected athlete. I know he was here for the launch of the new drug and maybe that would help with his sports but what evidence do you have that he was up to something more sinister. What can you tell me?"

If you have any of the following codewords go to that section. Follow the list downwards and only go to the first section that you have a codeword in.

**Tests** - 449

**Taunt** - 116

**Grumble** - 583

**Pads, Paddy, Silent Papers, Cold Blood, Murder, Hitman, Merto** - 636

**Gutted** - 048

Otherwise - 995

# 950

You pummel the glass with your fists, but it doesn't want to budge. Time and again but to no avail you try, only giving yourselves sore hands in the process. You'll need to try something different back at 406

# 951

You are able to avoid some nasty rocks as you make your way out of the larger bay the island sits in. But the wind and rain, along with the waves, are buffeting your vessel and you find it tipping over from time to time. A particularly large wave hits you and the boat tips dangerously.

Does the god of speedboats shine on you?

Maybe – 120

Possibly – 231

## 952

Do you have the code word Granocide? Is so, go to 031

You approach the alcove door, and it opens easily. A woman is sitting on the toilet and as her wild face looks up, you realise it is the Doctor's mother, Grandma Munro. She stands suddenly, and you realise she was simply sitting there, rather than using the toilet.

"Do you have it? Do you have the gun?" The woman is reaching out towards you now and looks like she will frisk you for whatever it is she wants.

Do you

Take out a gun, if you have one, and offer it to her – 673

If you have a gun, take it out and shoot her – 411

Hold your hands up and tell her you have no gun – 180

## 953

Go to 199

# 954

The lockers are open and contain several fishing rods and other fishing items such as a scoop net and different tackle. You dig deep under this and find a doctor's report on formal paper. What it is doing here you have no idea, but it looks genuine. When you read it, you discover that Grandma Munro is not quite with it and is in an advanced form of dementia. It seems she is prone to fanciful ideas and schemes.

Other than this rather sad news there's nothing else of note here. But there's still a whole boat left to check out. Do you

Go to the lower deck via the stairs – 543

Check out the wheelhouse – 861

Or

Jump onto the speedboat – 869

Or, if you haven't already,

Make for the main building – 795

Or

if you want to continue elsewhere take the coastal path at 980

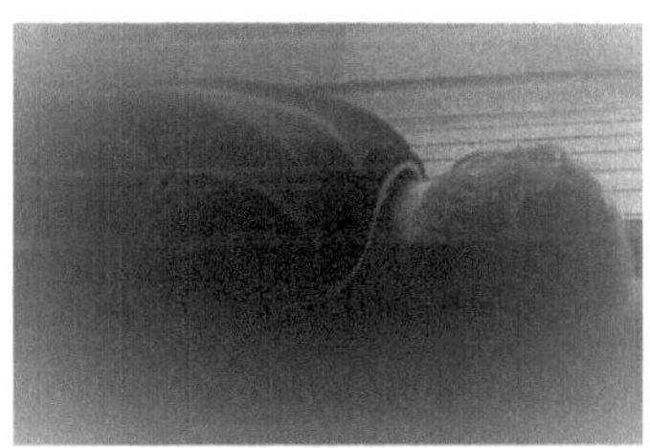

# 955

You flick on the light and see Elsie Gonzales, the newspaper reporter. She's soaked through, wearing a coat over her skirt and high heels. Her face seems to go into panic as she sees it's you.

Do you

Tell her not to panic, it wasn't you who shoot the Doctor – 152

Ask her what she's doing here – 695

Draw your gun if you have one – 835

# 956

You switch on the torch, and you are able to see somewhat better, but it is hardly perfect. You are still scrabbling about and can only see some ten feet ahead of you. But maybe you'll be lucky and find the Doctor's stash.

Try your luck

This lucky - 540

Or this fortunate - 227

Or is here your fate - 913

## 957

The locker is of the stand-up variety and has a padlock on it. The lock has four dials, and you recognise this as the Doctor's private locker, so you don't know the combination.

Do you

Want to try a code (only if you have found one)  – 945

Shoot the lock if you have a gun – 712

Or

Examine the dinghy – 060

Look at the lifejackets – 436

Take the stairs to the upper floor – 581

Or

Head over to the marina – 465

Or if you want to continue elsewhere take the coastal path at 980

## 958

How fast can you run?

This fast – 413

Maybe this quick – 461

Surely not this quick – 893

# 959

You draw your gun and fire at the young woman who tumbles to the ground. Blimey, that was a bit over the top! You run up to her but find a pool of blood beside her. She's not breathing. Oh dear, you've killed her. Enter **Iberian** in your code list.

You decide to beat a hasty retreat from the lagoon and make for the coastal path at 549 to find other places to investigate

# 960

You throw up your hands as the creature attacks, but it is no use. When the police arrive, they find their main suspect has died while trying to pilfer the laboratory. Few attend your burial, and your name is sullied forever not that you ever find out. Next time remember these places have protective doors for a reason. That's if you dare try again at 001.

# 961

You get the fuel from the main building and fill up the speedboat before starting the ignition with your keys. You look out to the sea which seems wild, and you know that locally there are some dangerous parts to avoid outside of your normal ferry route. As you recall they were on the local charts.

Do you have a local chart?

If so – <u>951</u>

If not and you still want to try this – <u>154</u>

Otherwise call it quits and return to the marina for another plan – <u>909</u>

# 962

You try to run upstairs but someone trips you and then a knife comes down on your top but fortunately it misses your skin. However, you are now pinned to the stairs by the knife, and you hear a laugh. You desperately try to pull your top clear.

How's your luck?

This good – <u>326</u>

Maybe this good – <u>430</u>

Or possibly this good – <u>780</u>

# 963

You swipe the reader with the Doctor's access card. You look around but cannot see anything different. Do you want to swipe it again?

If so – <u>749</u>

If not – <u>381</u>

# 964

You have the letter from Elsie Gonzales' newspaper editor advising that the staff are going to be on half wages and that the newspaper will close unless they can drive sales up significantly. The situation is dire, and Elsie will be out of a job if things do not change. The editor was imploring his reporters for a story that will be a national success and drive paper sales. Could Elsie have murdered to create the story and framed you in the process?  It certainly seems a strong motive if your career is on the line.

# 965

You hear a horrible buzz come from the keypad indicating it has not accepted the code. Will you try again?

3267 – 076

4837 – 855

2758 – 765

9746 – 802

Or a different code – 597

Or

Return to the hall – 805

# 966

You punch in the numbers and the pad flashes red and a claxon sounds, deafening all around you. Someone might be on their way with all that noise, so you decide you need to run. Make your way to the coastal path at 503 and escape to another location.

# 967

You get the fuel from the main building and fill up the speedboat before starting the ignition with your keys. You look out to the sea which seems wild, and you know that locally there are some dangerous parts to avoid outside of your normal ferry route. As you recall they were on the local charts.

Do you have a local chart?

If so – 477

If not and you still want to try this – 358

Otherwise call it quits and return to the marina for another plan – 465

# 968

You peer at the paper, unsure who has written it. Some of the language seems fanciful, mentioning a spaceship.

Do you

Try to use the candle to read the letter – 590

Pocket the letter – 800

# 969

You draw your gun and Elsie throws her arms up in the air, turns and runs towards the back of the cave where you see a small alcove. She's getting away and she has the jump on you, so you might not catch her before she disappears.

Do you

Fire your gun at her – 959

Run after Elsie – 457

# 970

You scratch your head looking at the complicated series of pulleys and ropes but one thing you can tell, is that everything has been replaced in the last year or so and this device may work. You can't think why it is in working order, but it is a work of art.

Do you

Climb onto the slab and read the engraving – 218

Leave the slab alone and

Make for the tomb and shelter from the rain – 877

Enter the temple – 273

Look at the gaming board – 165

Or

Decide this area is no longer useful or too risky and continue along the coastal path at 996

# 971

You try to take shelter from the driving rain under a large plant with enormous leaves. There are a number of exotic plants on the island, and you wish you understood them better but at least this one is providing protection as good as a bus shelter.

You sit tight looking along the path and towards the laboratory, waiting to see if anything will happen. If nothing happens soon then you will need to move on to find other evidence to prove your innocence.

Then you hear the crunch of stones and in the driving rain you lose just how the person arrived at the front door of the laboratory. It looks like Kyla Mertens, the scientist, and she is punching in a code to the keypad. Pulling open the door, she enters and disappears inside.

The front door is closing slowly, and you might just make it before it closes. On the other hand, you might run into Kyla Mertens and that might not be a good idea. Would you rather search in private? Will you get a chance to search the laboratory at all if you don't take this chance?

Do you

Run for the closing door – 232

Ignore the door and sit tight – 698

# 972

You look at the tumble lock on the cupboard and realise you need to enter 4 single numbers to unlock it. Do you have a code to try (only if you have found one)? If so, take the first number and multiply it by the second, then multiply the result by the third number. Now add the fourth number to the total. And now add 10. Go to the section number that is the same as your result. If it doesn't start **By golly**, then you have the wrong code.

If you can't get the code to work, do you

Take a local chart off the wall – 153

Shoot the cupboard open – 453

Or

Go to the Rec Room – 528

Investigate the room with no name – 685

Return to the lower floor – 370

## 973

The bottles fall and the fuel inside spills all over the floor. Luckily it misses you and luckier still, the blowtorch went out as it hit the ground. Carefully you pick yourself up and delicately extract yourself from the shed. That was close. But what next?

Leave the shed and

Check out the fountains area – 156

Take a look in the walled garden – 926

Make your way to the greenhouse – 745

Wander over to the gardening equipment sheds – 262

Or if you doubt the gardens will be of any use then take the coastal path at 211 but note that you have visited the gardens

## 974

"It wasn't me," you say holding your hands up to Daniel. "Someone has framed me."

Daniel looks at you quizzically. "That may or may not be so. But you are the pilot of the ferry, aren't you? You could help me escape. We could get away on one of the boats if you're not the killer. Maybe you could clear your name once we get away."

Do you

Wish to run away with Daniel on a boat – 459

Tell him no, you want to stay and clear your name – 158

# 975

You stand and watch for a while in the rain, but nothing emerges from the tunnel, and nothing else enters. Did your mind play a trick on you? Are you actually alone? What will you do now?

Enter the tunnel – 494

Or

Make your way to the folly – 444

Check out the coin throwing area – 704

Walk down to the final fountain and its walkway – 524

Or

Take a look in the walled garden – 926

Make your way to the greenhouse – 745

Wander over to the gardening equipment sheds – 262

Or if you doubt the gardens will be of any use then take the coastal path at 211 but note that you have visited the gardens

# 976

So, you threw a coin in a fountain. Were you expecting much to happen because nothing does? This is a murder investigation, not Cinderella. Come on, pick it up, sunshine, as all the best Inspectors say! Now investigate something worthwhile and stop clowning about.

Do you

Make your way to the folly – <u>444</u>

Head for the tunnel – <u>605</u>

Walk down to the final fountain and its walkway – <u>524</u>

Or go back to the fountains area entrance – <u>156</u>

## 977

You stand up and look all around you. With the rain, it's hard to hear but something suddenly moves to your right, directly towards you. You fire the gun and watch as a rat explodes. But that was loud. You'd better get out of here. Run to one of the main paths and decide which at <u>297</u>.

## 978

Do you have the gun with you?

Yes – <u>015</u>

No – <u>194</u>

## 979

You punch in the code and the pad turns red and a coarse noise like a bad input on a computer sounds. Nothing happens and you are left with the pad again.

Do you enter another code? Which one?

2758 - <u>774</u>

3267 - <u>144</u>

9746 - <u>343</u>

4837 - <u>616</u>

Another code - <u>078</u>

Or do you leave the pad alone? If so, make your next choice at <u>037</u>

# 980

The coastal path runs two ways, but you have to make your way to a new location you have not seen before.

Do you

Route clockwise for the Lookout – <u>151</u>

Make your way anticlockwise to the Laboratory – <u>797</u>

# 981

The coastal path runs two ways, but you have to make your way to a new location you have not seen before.

If you have visited six locations (including the house) go to <u>011</u>

Otherwise

Do you

Route clockwise for the Lookout – 151

Make your way anticlockwise to the Laboratory – 797

# 982

The greenhouse is lit up from inside and is a stunning piece of architecture, with many details on the outer structure. However, it is inside you want to investigate, and you are glad to step out of the driving rain. As you drip onto the floor, you note the number of leaves on the ground and the warmth of the building. This puts you at ease and you stroll through the paths examining the plants growing within. Well, it's certainly a fine collection of plants and flowers but you need to get on.

Do you

Check out the fountains area – 526

Take a look in the walled garden – 625

Wander over to the gardening equipment sheds – 121

Or if you doubt the gardens will be of any use then take the coastal path at 770 but note that you have visited the gardens

# 983

You walk to the rear of the laboratory and find the main path from the house now joins onto a circular route with two options. You know this path well as you have walked most of the island. But you need to either take a left to the lagoon or a right to the boathouse.

Do you

Take the path to the lagoon – 879

Take the path to the boathouse – 191

# 984

Well, the magazines let you know there's a royal scandal afoot, Liverpool drew a match some three months ago and also how to go mackerel fishing off the Isle of Skye. While this is all fascinating stuff, it's not really helping is it. Go back to 805 and let's start investigating properly.

# 985

Well, the magazines let you know there's a royal scandal afoot, Liverpool drew a match some three months ago and also how to go mackerel fishing off the Isle of Skye. While this is all fascinating stuff, it's not really helping is it. Go back to 212 and let's start investigating properly.

# 986

You walk to the rear of the laboratory and find the main from the house now joins onto a circular path with two options. You know this path well as you have walked most of the island. But you need to either take a left to the lagoon or a right to the boathouse.

If you have visited six locations (including the house) go to <u>011</u>

Otherwise, do you

Take the path to the lagoon – <u>423</u>

Take the path to the boathouse – <u>692</u>

# 987

You look around the canteen but despite opening drawings and cupboards all you see are some plates and mugs. There is no evidence here, so time to move on.

Do you

Try to get into the cleaners' cupboard – <u>571</u>

Examine the door belonging to Doctor Munro – <u>439</u>

Try to enter the office of Kyla Mertens – <u>237</u>

Or

Return to the hall – <u>212</u>

# 988

The circular path which runs around the island lies before you, allowing you to go to the Ruins at 759, or to the Boathouse at 191. Choose now and remember it cannot be a place you have visited already.

# 989

The radio handset appears to be functional, and you set it to channel 16. You hear some banal chatter from the Coastguard and another vessel, but you know the set to be working.

Do you

Contact the Coastguard to tell them of the situation – 831

Or

Switch off the set and let sleeping dogs lie, and instead

Check out the photographs – 067

Have a rifle through the drawers – 229

Look at the writing desk – 361

Or

Climb up the spiral staircase – 824

Descend the spiral staircase - 845

Decide to leave the Lookout and make your way to the coastal path – 988

# 990

If you have visited six locations (including the house) go to 011

Or if not

The circular path which runs around the island lies before you, allowing you to go to the Ruins at 937, or to the Boathouse at 692. Choose now and remember it cannot be a place you have visited already.

# 991

The middle floor of the Lookout features a small kitchenette and a simple two person dining area. There's a radio handset on the round shelf that runs completely around the room. A number of photographs are here as well as a set of drawers and a writing desk. The spiral staircase runs both up and down to the other floors of the building. The overall feeling is of a simple man's abode, but it is clean and tidy.

Do you

Examine the radio handset – 668

Check out the photographs – 184

Have a rifle through the drawers – 865

Look at the writing desk – 897

Or

Climb up the spiral staircase – <u>506</u>

Descend the spiral staircase - <u>821</u>

Decide to leave the Lookout and make your way to the coastal path – <u>990</u>

# 992

The door to the laboratory is unlocked and you open it quietly and peer into the room beyond. There are all sorts of devices sitting on the bench on the far wall, most of which you don't recognise. There is also a large collection of glassware including bottles, jars, petri dishes and stirrers. You also see some Bunsen burners but beyond this collection are other items you never covered in school chemistry.

You can see a file with notes hanging out on the worksurface at the rear of the room. There's also a refrigerator close by the door as well as a number of lab coats hanging on a set of hooks on the wall. A number of stools have also been knocked over at the far bench.

Do you

Examine the file – <u>600</u>

Look in the refrigerator – <u>054</u>

Check out the lab coats – <u>652</u>

Wander over to the stools – <u>233</u>

Or

If this is all too much you could return to the entrance hall – <u>805</u>

# 993

You have the memo indicating that the Doctor is not wishing to sell his latest drug for profit making Patrick Davidson furious. Could this be the reason Patrick Davidson killed the Doctor? It's certainly strong evidence of motive.

# 994

At first glance it is a standard toilet with a wooden seat that no doubt doesn't give you a cold bottom. You force yourself to look behind it and only find a small spider trying to mind its own business. Glancing inside the bowl, you think you see something at the bottom of it, under the waterline.

Do you

Want to reach in and grab what's in the bowl (I know, I know) – <u>373</u>

Or are you done with all this toilet shenanigans and instead

Examine the bed – <u>046</u>

Check the silk dressing gowns – <u>505</u>

Descend the stairs – <u>991</u>

Or leave the Lookout completely and head for the coastal path – <u>990</u>

# 995

"Sorry," says the Detective Inspector, "you have nothing, and they saw you there with the gun with the Doctor's body. You're going down, sunshine!"

The years ahead look bleak, prison for life. But you can try again at <u>001</u>, and next time get more evidence!

# 996

The coastal path runs in two directions, but you have decided not to retrace your steps in case anyone is following you.

If you came from the gardens, route now to the Lookout at <u>151</u>

However, if you were previously in the Lookout, go to the Gardens at <u>689</u>

# 997

You assume it's nothing and continue to sweep along the passageway with your torch. On the floor you see a document and bend down to pick it up. You feel a thud on the back of your head, and everything turns to dark. When you wake up, your torch is gone and everywhere is black. Delete **torch** from your inventory. You struggle along the tomb walls and find the exit, but you are now shaking with fear. Is your attacker still about? Was it the killer, leaving you still to take the fall for the Doctor's death? Are you being watched?

You decide to get away from the ruins and find somewhere safer. You run to the coastal path at 996 and make your next decision from there

# 998

The coastal path runs in two directions, but you have decided not to retrace your steps in case anyone is following you.

If you have visited six locations (including the house) go to 011

Otherwise,

If you came from the Gardens, route now to the Lookout at 151

However, if you were previously in the Lookout, go to the Gardens at 689

# 999

You assume it's nothing and continue to sweep along the passageway with your torch. On the floor you see a document and bend down to pick it up. You feel a thud on the back of your head, and everything turns to dark. When you wake up, your torch is gone and everywhere is black. Delete **torch** from your inventory. You struggle along the tomb walls and find the exit, but you are now shaking with fear. Is your attacker still about? Was it the killer, leaving you still to take the fall for the Doctor's death? Are you being watched?

You decide to get away from the ruins and find somewhere safer. You run to the coastal path at 998 and make your next decision from there

# 1000

Okay, so you're going to make a run for it. It won't be easy, and you'll need to get off the island. Or will you? Maybe there's some options on the island too. Think over what you have seen on your travels.

Do you have any of the following codewords. If so, you may examine these options. You can also return here if you do not like them.

Codeword **Boat** – 365

Codeword **Quiet Place** – 222

If you don't have these codewords, you ponder how to get off the island and believe it will need to be via the boathouse. There are several boats there but whether you can steal one and make a run for it is doubtful. Or maybe you could hide in the gardens, or maybe the ruins? One thing you know is that you cannot shoot your way out of this one. There are too many voices on the wind. It sounds like a massive search party. And you can hear dogs bark too. You need to get moving.

If you are not following any advice from the above codewords, do you

Make a run for the boathouse – <u>568</u>

Hide out in the gardens – <u>499</u>

Go to the ruins to try and hide – <u>838</u>

Or if these don't seem like good options, you can always surrender yourself – <u>519</u>

Framed

# Fugitive Sheet

INVENTORY:

# Codewords

- o   Baba
- o   Beam
- o   Blaze
- o   Boat
- o   Bowl
- o   Capernaum
- o   Caught
- o   Coastguard
- o   Cold Blood
- o   Collapsed
- o   Confess
- o   Cure
- o   Ferry Gone
- o   Fuel
- o   Granferno
- o   Granocide
- o   Grass
- o   Grumble
- o   Gutted
- o   Hitman
- o   Iberian
- o   Killer
- o   Inferno

- o   Last Sprint
- o   Late Rescue
- o   Merto
- o   Murder
- o   Notelet
- o   Paddy
- o   Pads
- o   Playtime
- o   Quiet Place
- o   Scientist Down
- o   Scrap
- o   Sesame
- o   Shutdown
- o   Silent Papers
- o   Space Letter
- o   Swim
- o   Tatler
- o   Taunt
- o   Tests
- o   Theft
- o   Tower
- o   Water
- o   Wheel

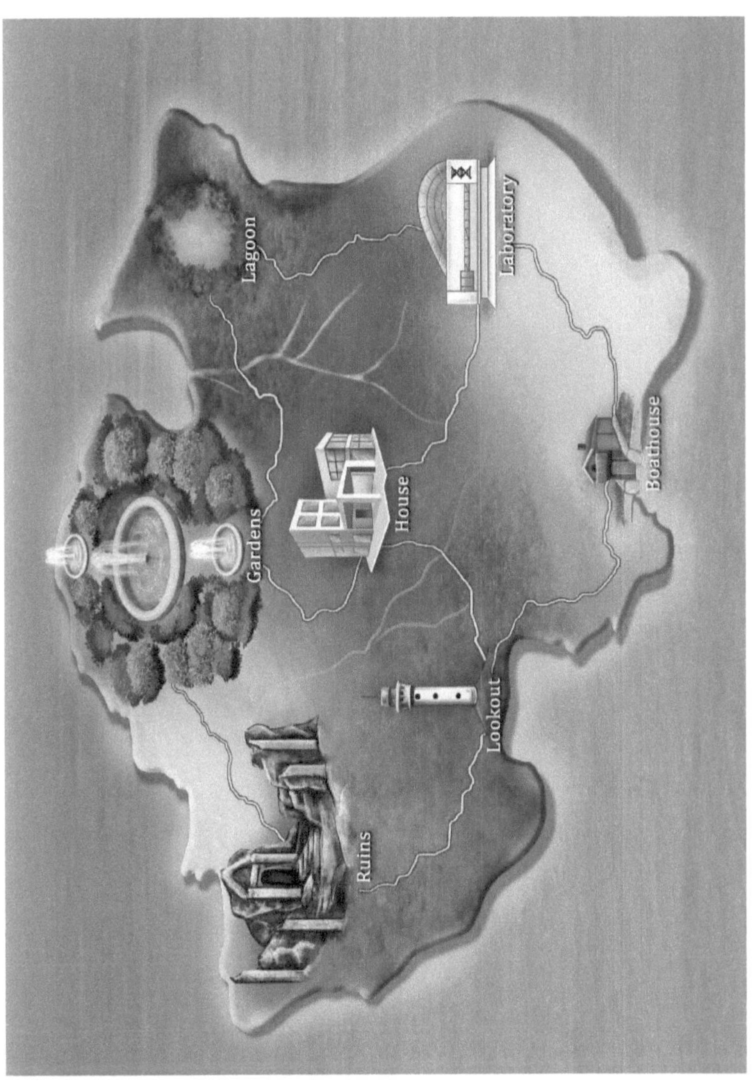

Lagoon
Laboratory
Boathouse
Gardens
House
Lookout
Ruins

Framed

# The Author

Framed

GR Jordan is a self-published author who finally decided at forty
that in order to have an enjoyable lifestyle, his creative beast
within would have to be unleashed. His books mirror that
conflict in life where acts of decency contend with self-
promotion, goodness stares in horror at evil and kindness blind-
side us when we at our worst. Corrupting our world with his
parade of wondrous and horrific characters, he highlights
everyday tensions with fresh eyes whilst taking his methodical,
intelligent mainstays on a roller-coaster ride of dilemmas, all the
while suffering the banter of their provocative sidekicks.

A graduate of Loughborough University where he masqueraded
as a chemical engineer but ultimately played American football,
Gary had worked at changing the shape of cereal flakes and
pulled a pallet truck for a living. Watching vegetables freeze at -
40'C was another career highlight and he was also one of the
Scottish Highlands "blind" air traffic controllers. These days he
has graduated to answering a telephone to people in trouble
before telephoning other people to sort it out.

Having flirted with most places in the UK, he is now based in
the Isle of Lewis in Scotland where his free time is spent
between raising a young family with his wife, writing, figuring
out how to work a loom and caring for a small flock of chickens.
Luckily his writing is influenced by his varied work and life
experience as the chickens have not been the poetical inspiration
he had hoped for!

# A Small Request

I loved writing this adventure and I hope you enjoyed playing it. If you did please give me a large pat on the back by going to your favourite online or high street bookstore and leaving a review. Outside of delivering a freshly ground cup of coffee, this is the best way to say thanks to the author. And if you want, feel free to tell me all about your Unravel Your Destiny experience at gary@grjordan.com.

Look out for further Unravel Your Destiny adventures coming soon.

Framed

# Notes

Feel free to make any notes you require on the following pages.

# Notes

# Notes

# Notes